THE *Backcountry* BRIDES

COLLECTION

8 Eighteenth-Century Women Seek Love on Colonial America's Frontier

THE *Backcountry* BRIDES
COLLECTION

Shannon McNear, Carrie Fancett Pagels,
Angela K. Couch, Debra E. Marvin,
Gabrielle Meyer, Jennifer Hudson Taylor,
Pegg Thomas, Denise Weimer

BARBOUR BOOKS
An Imprint of Barbour Publishing, Inc.

Print ISBN 978-1-68322-622-2

eBook Editions:
Adobe Digital Edition (.epub) 978-1-68322-624-6
Kindle and MobiPocket Edition (.prc) 978-1-68322-623-9

Published by Barbour Books, an imprint of Barbour Publishing, Inc., 1810 Barbour Drive, Uhrichsville, Ohio 44683, www.barbourbooks.com

Our mission is to inspire the world with the life-changing message of the Bible.

 Member of the
Evangelical Christian
Publishers Association

Printed in Canada.

Contents

Shenandoah Hearts

by Carrie Fancett Pagels

Dedication

To Jeffrey D. and Clark J. Pagels
and to my Shenandoah ancestors

Acknowledgments

Thank you Jesus, God, and Holy Spirit for making my writing ministry possible!
I'm grateful for my son and husband for understanding and letting me
use some of my limited energy for what God has called me to do.
Thank you to my amazing critique partner, Kathleen Maher.
Appreciation to Andrea Stephens for being my Beta reader!
A group hug to my Pagels Pals team.

I've had this dream of a colonial collection of backwoods/backcountry brides for
a long time—ever since I started the *Colonial American Christian Fiction* blog
many years ago. What an absolute delight to have that dream become a reality;
thanks to the amazing authors who have come in on this collection! So happy
to have both longtime *Colonial Quills* blog members Shannon McNear,
Jennifer Hudson Taylor, and Debra E. Marvin, as well as newer members
Pegg Thomas, Gabrielle Meyer, Angela Couch, and Denise Weimer.

Thank you to my agent, Joyce Hart, for her assistance
and to Becky Germany for helping us achieve this vision!

I "borrowed" a lot of names in this story. My orthopedic doctor, who keeps me
mobile, makes an appearance as fort surgeon. My cousin Scott Davis got a twist
on his name, which is used for the wagon master. Real-life Lieutenant Colonel
Matthew Ruckman's name is used for a militia member, and his son's name for
his fictional son in this story. Neighbor Donna Lilly's namesake gives my
hero some advice. And there are more! Thank you all!

Author's Note

Eighteenth-century Virginia residents were happy to welcome settlers to their backcountry, even if they didn't share in the Commonwealth's mandated Anglican religion. Newcomers put a physical barrier between the primarily coastal residents and the Native Americans and French who dwelt farther inland. At the time of this story (and until the Civil War), Virginia also included West Virginia and other wide swaths of land farther west. When reference is made to the characters in my story going on a mission to check on the Foyles in the far-western reaches of Virginia, that mission was to what is now West Virginia. Although the Foyles were a real family and an actual expedition was made to their home, this event is fictionalized in my story. According to Norman L. Baker's book *French & Indian War: In Frederick County, Virginia*, the attack on the Foyle family was even noted on maps of the day.

Long rifles, rather than muskets, were in use in the backcountry during this time frame by Germans and other immigrant people whose gunsmiths brought this technology with them.

My Roush ancestors lived in the Shenandoah Valley during this time frame. One of my ancestors was born in Fort Holman. Our *Colonial Quills* authors, Susan Craft, Carla Olson Gade, Elaine Marie Cooper, Kathleen L. Maher, Pat Iacuzzi, Lynne Squire, Kelly Long, and Dina Sleiman, participated with me in a Christmas serial story set at the fictional "Fort Providence" in the Shenandoah Valley. You may enjoy stopping by www.ColonialQuills.com and looking for our anthology and reading that before reading my novella.

Prologue

Philadelphia
1753

"Ladysmith, you have a gentleman caller—maybe two." The voice of her employer, Jacob Owens, held a slight tease. Heart lurching against her chest, Magdalene dropped the large silver spoon she'd been engraving. She covered it with a polishing cloth and rose from her workbench in the back of the Owens' store. Her hands shook as she rose, and she fumbled to place them in the heavy work pockets which hung over her apron from a band tied around her waist. She parted the heavy brocade curtains that separated her work nook from the front and stepped through, inhaling the scent of peppermint and cinnamon.

She met Jacob's inquisitive gaze and tried to assume an innocent face. For surely, she shouldn't have been daydreaming and engraving "Magdalene and Jacob" on the large spoon, even if she had paid for the piece from her earnings.

"Your brother is here." He lifted his chin over his shoulder. "Up front picking a treat from the candy."

"And the other person?" She frowned. There was no gentleman caller in her life, save for this handsome Welshman, her employer. And even then, he'd never declared any intentions toward her.

"That wagon master, Davis, is waiting for you on the walkway."

How embarrassing. Mama and Papa had demanded her answer last night about whether she'd relocate with them to the Shenandoah Valley in Virginia or not. Magdalene had begged for one more day to make her decision, hoping that Jacob would finally profess his feelings toward her. "I will speak with him and be right back."

He frowned. "Mr. Davis isn't known for making social calls during the day."

No, he wasn't. Scott Williams Davis, their three-surname wagon master, was a tight-lipped man who kept to himself. "I'm sure this won't take long."

She removed her heavy apron and set it aside then exited the room, Jacob holding back the curtain for her and casting a skeptical glance her way. What should she tell the wagon master? Her entire family was headed for the Shenandoah Valley in Virginia. Already three of her seven brothers had established a large cabin for them and had completed all the fences and brought in some livestock. Mother and Father had already begun packing their belongings. The remaining four brothers were assisting, and all were excited to go.

11

"How much candy should I let Michi have?" Jacob smiled. He knew how much her youngest brother loved treats.

"Only a couple of the sweets from the jar this time, *ja*?" She grinned back at him, and stifled the longing to reach out and squeeze his hand with affection. She'd been trained as a silversmith by her grandfather in Germany, but it was Jacob who'd brought out the artistry in her work. Jacob who'd helped her see how much people enjoyed her creations. And Jacob who had convinced Papa that he'd only have her work in his shop on days when Mama wasn't feeling so poorly.

Jacob gave her a salute and she laughed. His older brother, an officer in the military, had visited recently. Surely Colonel Dafydd Owens wasn't putting ideas of army service into Jacob's head, was he? The only thing Jacob had mentioned about his brother was his complaint that Dafydd addressed him by their father's Welsh version of his name, *Jago*.

As she passed Michi, Magdalene leaned in and kissed the top of his reddish-brown hair. He smelled of grass, sweat, and sugar. "How is Mama, little brother?"

"Fine."

So he wasn't at Owens' Shoppe for Mama. "Anything wrong?"

"*Nein.* I just brought Mr. Davis to you."

"Oh?" Why was the wagon master pushing her so hard to make a decision that he'd disturb her at work?

When Magda exited his shop, she took a bit of Jacob's heart with her. He stood for a moment, staring through the wavy glass that he was fortunate to have in his store-front. This lull in activity, right after lunchtime, was a welcome time during which he'd normally be reconciling his ledgers. Would he now have to reconcile himself with losing her?

Footfalls behind him announced that Michi was wandering the store, something Magda had been firm that he mustn't do. The lad pushed aside the curtains to the back.

"Michi?"

"Hmm?" The boy entered Magda's workroom.

"You belong out front, remember?"

"Just looking."

The door opened and Mrs. Lilly entered, swinging her empty basket from one arm and adjusting her panniers with the other as she gracefully made her way to the display of teacups on the far wall.

"Good day, Mrs. Lilly."

"Good day, Mr. Owens." She inclined her head to the row of china cups and saucers she'd been admiring the previous day. "I'm going to make my choice."

Something clanged onto the floor in the back. "Excuse me for a moment." Jacob hurried toward Magda's workspace.

By the time he got there, Michi was standing, hands clasped behind his back and rocking side to side.

"What fell?"

"Nothing." Michi's lips pulled in tight.

"All right, but come on out of there." Drawing in a deep breath, Jacob gently touched the boy's thin shoulder and directed him out of the room.

This child, more than any of the Sehler brothers, reminded Jacob of his oldest brother, Llywellyn, whose mind was ever inquisitive. Even now, Llywellyn searched the Shenandoah Valley for the right spot to mine and to build a large forge. Between Llywellyn's constant pleas for Jacob to join him and Dafydd's warnings of a militia buildup needed in that region, Jacob was torn. Should he continue to run this prosperous store, or was it time to move on? Magda was doing so well with her designs. And if it wasn't for the emotional reserve she'd always shown him, he'd have asked to court her long ago.

Michi took two steps forward and pointed outside. "Look! I think Mr. Davis is finally proposing to her!"

What? Heat seared Jacob's chest.

Mrs. Lilly turned to watch too.

Was Davis the reason for Magda's reticence toward Jacob? Was it, as little Michi had been insisting all along, that Magda wasn't interested in Jacob as a suitor—that she had another intended suitor who was approved by their parents? Now, right outside his business, the wagon master, who had to be twice Magda's age, pressed his tricornered cap to his chest, leaning in earnestly to speak with Magda.

She didn't reply. *Thank God.*

Michi pushed past Jacob and went out to join the two. He whispered something in his sister's ear. She glanced toward the building and, spotting Jacob, stared for a moment, longing on her face. Yet she was apparently about to commit herself to this much older man. Granted, Davis was well-off and attractive to the ladies, but Magda had never spoken of him, other than very recently. And even then, it was only in relation to the plans her family had to go with this man at the lead, to the Shenandoah Valley.

Magda slowly redirected her attention to Davis and then nodded.

Jacob's gut clenched.

Mrs. Lilly sighed. "That was not a very gentlemanly way of making a proposal of marriage, was it?"

"I couldn't agree more, ma'am."

Outside, the little scene continued to unfold as Michi threw his arms around his sister, kissed her, and then jumped up and down. Davis smiled and wrapped his arms around brother and sister for a moment. That was the oddest sort of proposal Jacob could imagine. But since he himself had made none at all, what did he really know? And since he couldn't hear him, perhaps Davis had waxed eloquent and made all manner of pretty speeches to the woman Jacob cared for so deeply.

One thing was for sure and for certain. Life would never be the same once Magda left Philadelphia.

"Sometimes, young man, you have to fight for what you want." Mrs. Lilly's clipped words caught Jacob's attention and he turned to face her. But her gaze was so fixed on Jacob it didn't seem she was referring to Mr. Davis.

"Ma'am?"

"I have eyes in my head, Mr. Owens. Certainly you do too." She smiled and nodded at Magda as she reentered the shop. "That is all I shall say about the matter. I believe the rest is up to you."

Chapter 1

Shenandoah Valley, Virginia
Late January, 1754

Rolling blue hills rose up in the distance, the sight of them still thrilling to Magdalene after all these months. Papa slowed the horses and Magdalene clutched the rifle on her lap. The first day they spied the Blue Ridge Mountains from their wagon train, Mr. Davis had bid them stop and set up camp. What a glorious feast for the eyes. They were almost to their destination. And that's when she'd finally humbled herself and said her apologies to Jacob and given him her thanks.

Who'd have thought that her employer and friend could have rescued her from so much misfortune over the course of their journey? The first time was Jacob's own fault, though. Magdalene had been in the back of her family's wagon, searching for a big kettle to put over the fire, when she'd heard Jacob's distinctively lyrical Welsh-accented voice. She'd been so startled he was there that she'd fallen backwards—right into his arms. He'd held her there for what seemed like the longest time, looking down at her like she was a long-lost treasure. Then Michi had come looking for her, and the kettle, and had yelled at the poor man. Her cheeks heated with the memory of Papa hastening back to check on them as if they were doing something improper.

She cast a glance at her father as he flicked the reins and urged the horses on to the market.

"We'll get all the goods we need, *liebling*, for a good feast, ja?"

"Ja. It'll be wonderfully good—especially if Widow Martin has the dried apples she promised us at church." The Sehlers' little German Lutheran church was no building as such. They met in a clockwise fashion in the cabins built in a circle in their settlement, the second one out from Fort Holman. The residents in Mrs. Martin's community, closest to the fort, sometimes joined them, Jacob included.

"Ja." His lips twitched.

Tomorrow, Jacob was coming to visit, with his officer brother accompanying him. Papa said there was something important to announce. *Was this to finally be the day?*

"The boys are taking turns roasting the pig and your *mutter* feels well enough to bake."

"Mama does seem happier here." And more energetic.

"Ja. The hills remind her of the Old Country."

Did it also remind her of all the wars there? Magdalene shivered and drew her wool blanket farther up on her lap.

The wheels creaked over the frozen earth, and soon they were to the next settlement, populated by another twenty German and English families. This village too had set up their homes to face in, but formed a square, with their market taking place in the center the first Wednesday of the month.

Some of the cabins were wide and low while others stood two stories and yet others were only a single room deep.

A flash of red near a far cabin caught Magdalene's eye. "Soldiers, Papa."

"Ja, they like to know what is going on in each settlement."

The redcoats were a reminder of the threats the settlers faced on the frontier. Her heartbeat sped up as she considered what could happen to them if they were attacked.

"Making an offer of marriage now is ludicrous." Dafydd paced the wooden floor of their quarters. A thin beam of sunlight pierced the keeping room's single window.

"Should you wait any longer?" Not when tensions with the French and the Indians were likely to resurface in the spring, as Jacob had been repeatedly told by Dafydd himself, scouts, and army personnel. "Things are at a lull, finally."

"Do you believe this quiet will persist?" His brother laughed. "Have you any idea the distress Charity shall feel if I am killed?"

"This is why you have not yet proposed marriage to Widow Martin?" Jacob sat down on one of the upholstered chairs he'd brought with him from Philadelphia.

"Do you think she'd like to be twice a widow, Jago? Dafydd's harsh tone held a bitterness Jacob had never heard before.

"You're God now?" Daffyd was sounding like their father, and even using Jacob's Welsh name as Father did. "You know this?"

Dafydd rubbed his arms and continued pacing, his boots thumping on the wide planks of the wooden floor and then hushing as he crossed the carpet to the fireplace. He lifted a log from the woodpile and set it atop the others in the fireplace, the bottom logs blazing red into coals.

"I don't want to chance it." Dafydd turned and scowled. "I believe someone else recently spoke those words."

"I was tired." And they were speaking in generalities. "It's different for you. You know Mrs. Martin cares for you and she is without a protector." Whereas Magda and he had not had any private moments together since they'd arrived. She was constantly surrounded by her brothers. If only he'd used their quiet times at work in Philadelphia to tell her how he felt. Even so, her youngest brother never lost an opportunity to conjecture why Magda would prefer a German husband rather than a Welshman. That being the case, why did she and her family encourage the wagon master's friendship? Davis was a fellow Welshman. And wouldn't little Michi be surprised to know that Jacob was a quarter German and named for his maternal grandfather? Mother had gotten her way with Jacob's name, but Father had prevailed with the rest, giving them Welsh names.

"You're almost thirty years yourself, with no room to be lecturing me about marrying."

Twenty-eight wasn't thirty years, but Jacob wouldn't belabor the point. If Mother hadn't died so young, would he and Dafydd have married earlier? "Maybe our sisters had the right of it—marrying young and beginning their families."

"Agreed. I'm going to speak with Charity today. But first I shall practice my speech."

Jacob chuckled. "We're too much alike in this way. You're overthinking. Just speak from your heart."

Dafydd's mouth opened, but then he clamped his lips tightly together and went to the oak desk by the window and sat down. He dipped his quill pen into the inkwell and commenced writing what was sure to be an eloquent and masterful speech.

Papa secured the wagon and helped Magdalene down. Their breath made puffs swirl around them in the chill air. He patted her shoulder. "I'm going to get Mr. Davis and I will be right back."

She couldn't help grinning. Mr. Davis had been pining over Mrs. Martin for months. A widower himself, it was surprising the man had been married before. He was so quiet and reserved, how had Mr. Davis gotten the words out for a proposal? If rumors were to be believed, his wife's father had chosen him over her other suitors because he thought Davis, an expert marksman, could protect her better. If such were the means of qualifying for marriage, then Jacob surely would be her top choice, for he'd proven to be a crack shot with the militia.

A gust of icy wind assailed her as she approached the widow's door. Magdalene tugged her wool cloak tighter around her shoulders. Before she could knock, the door opened.

"I heard the wagon. A welcome sound." The tiny woman gestured for Magdalene to enter.

The scent of cinnamon and apples filled the square room, which was dominated by the fireplace. A heavy iron trivet propped on the hearth held a bubbling apple pie.

"Come in. Have a seat." Mrs. Martin pointed to a wingback chair upholstered in a dark green and blue brocade.

"That is just like one I saw in Mr. Owens' shop in Philadelphia."

"One and the same." The older woman smiled and adjusted the creamy lace fichu at her bodice. "He gave it to me—from his own cabin mind you—when he saw that my rocking chair had broken."

That was Jacob. Kind and considerate. How many times had his father, the previous proprietor of the shop, fussed at Jacob that he shouldn't charge people less just because they were widowed or poor? And Jacob always set aside lightly damaged, but still-good merchandise, to distribute to those in need.

The widow's brow furrowed as she glanced out the window. "I thought Mr. Davis would have arrived by now."

"My father should be here soon."

"Is he bringing Mr. Davis?"

"He is."

Mrs. Martin looked as skittish as a young colt. "Might I ask a favor?" Her peridot eyes widened.

Magdalene stiffened. The last favor she'd done, for one of her brothers, had resulted in Papa almost putting a switch to Michi's behind for the prank he'd pulled with her unwitting assistance. "What is it?"

"Could you possibly take something over to Jacob Owens and his brother for me?"

"Are they here today?" Jacob had been gone so often with his suttler duties, supplying the forts, and his brother off with the army, that she'd not expected to see them. Hope rose and her heart began beating faster.

"Yes, I saw them earlier and promised them cornbread."

"If only I could have mine turn out like yours does."

"It's the corn I mix into the mush."

"Food is the way to a man's heart, that is what Mama says." Not that Magdalene's cooking was anything special.

Mrs. Martin's cheeks pinked up. "Oh, I'm not trying to sweeten either Owens man up. Heavens, they are both a decade or more younger than myself."

"I did not mean that. I was just commenting."

The woman sank into the other upholstered chair. "I hope Colonel Owens doesn't think I've meant anything by my gifts of food."

"He is a military officer and I'm sure grateful for any cooking you do for him."

Mrs. Martin pulled at her lacy-edged fichu again. "What I really wish is for Mr. Davis to finally speak plain with me."

"That is why Papa is bringing him."

"Can you leave us alone for a little bit?" Her cheeks were rosy and her eyes wide. "Can you make an excuse?"

"I will manage it." Magdalene looked toward the table and saw the golden square of bread. "I will take the cornbread to the Owens brothers and say it is for Jacob since he'd fussed over it at our last dinner when you were there."

"Yes, that would be good."

Magdalene was happy to oblige Mrs. Martin. Her calling on Jacob and Dafydd wouldn't seem so bold if she were bringing a gift at the behest of Mrs. Martin.

"I will send your father over to help Matthew Ruckman with the new gun rack he is building."

Magdalene cringed. They'd never had the need of rifles over the door in Philadelphia.

The rap at the door caused Jacob to cease polishing his long rifle. He set it on the table and answered the door.

Magda stood there holding a plate, a towel beneath it. He inhaled the scent of fresh cornbread. The rosy color of her cape complimented the wind-induced blush in her cheeks. Rooted to the spot, he drank the sight of her in. She was so beautiful. So sweet. So kind.

"May I enter?" She chuckled, as though she might have read his thoughts.

"Certainly!" He waved her inside. A gust of chill wind accompanied her before he closed and barred the door.

She removed her hood, revealing a mass of reddish-gold hair. Had she left her tresses unbraided deliberately? He stifled the desire to reach out and lift a stray lock that would likely feel as silky as it looked. He swallowed hard.

"Widow Martin sent this for you, Jacob." Magda cocked her head at him, a glimmer of humor in her eyes.

His brother clomped heavily across the wood floor, like an oaf instead of the officer he was. He stretched out his hands. "Miss Sehler, I believe that is for me."

Jacob gave a short laugh. "It is for me, but I will share."

Dafydd's tawny brows knit together. "Mrs. Martin sent that for Jacob? Are you sure you understood her?"

"My hearing is perfectly fine." Magda glanced around the room. "Where should I set the cornbread?"

"That small table by the fire." Dafydd's voice had assumed the snobbish British tone he used with underlings.

"I shall take it." Jacob stepped closer and reached for the plate. This near, he could see how Magda's dark eyelashes formed tiny star-like tips around her blue eyes. The warmth of the plate between them was nothing like the heat which seared his heart. He took the cornbread, his fingers brushing her gloved hands.

"Thank you."

Jacob set the plate down on the side table. "May I take your cloak?"

She chewed her lower lip. "Yes, thank you, but I can only stay a bit. Papa and I are visiting Mrs. Martin."

Jacob assisted her out of her cloak, enjoying the close proximity. He leaned in toward her back and inhaled the soft floral scent that wafted from her neck. He likely smelled of smoke, leather, and the salted ham that he and Dafydd had consumed for their meager breakfast.

Magda removed her gloves, a gift from him the previous winter, and handed them to him. He set them atop the pegged shelf which held the coats.

"Do come sit down, Miss Sehler." Dafydd waved toward one of the chairs. "Get us some tea, will you, Jacob?"

Jacob grimaced, grateful his back was turned to the two. He wasn't his brother's servant and didn't appreciate being treated as one.

After pouring tea and adding honey to Miss Sehler's cup, Jacob set the floral-trimmed china cup and saucer before her on the low table.

"Thank you." She looked up at him, her smile inviting.

"At your service, ma'am." He bowed and she laughed.

"Where's mine, Jago?" His brother barked his order.

Jacob scowled.

Magda sat erect as any noblewoman. "This may be an auspicious day for Mrs. Martin."

"Why's that?" Dafydd sipped his tea.

"I believe Mr. Davis is about to finally propose."

Dafydd's tea spewed past his lips and he set his cup, jangling hard, into its saucer on the table. "What?"

Joy and relief surged through Jacob. But he couldn't, and wouldn't, display his glee before his brother. That would be like rubbing salt into the wounds of someone who suffered, and the Bible warned against such behavior. Still, in his heart he could rejoice.

"Is that so?" Jacob set his tea down too, the contents sloshing onto the plate beneath it. "Mr. Davis is to wed Mrs. Martin?" *And not Magda?*

Relief coursed through him and he drew in a deep restorative breath, the black tea's scent a comfort. *But poor Dafydd.*

His brother shot up. "But she is mine!"

Jacob stood, positioning himself between his brother and Magda. He attempted a laugh, which emerged as a short cough. "What my brother means is that Charity Martin has so well supplied him with excellent victuals that he fears Mr. Davis will put a stop to that."

He turned toward his brother, who was staring out the window. If Jacob knew anything, it was that Dafydd most feared losing face in front of people. He reached out and squeezed his brother's red-coated shoulders. "Am I not right, brother?"

"Aye, you've got the right of it." Dafydd's hushed voice, his words, were almost believable.

"But we have Miss Sehler here to help us out."

Jacob turned to see her shocked expression.

But she recovered quickly. "Ja, we will cook for you all day tomorrow, in fact, so don't be disheartened, Colonel Owens."

Disheartened was far from how Jacob felt.

"Oh, I'm not." Dafydd met his gaze. "Just concerned about our upcoming journey to the far-western regions of the Commonwealth."

The army's mission was to affirm the veracity of the reports that the Foyle family had indeed been slaughtered the previous year as reported.

"And the militia shall accompany us." Dafydd looked pointedly at Jacob. "Just in case."

Leave it to Dafydd to squash Jacob's joy.

Chapter 2

The scent of roasted pork filled the Sehlers' yard, and with the wind lifting, likely the whole settlement, inviting friends to join them later. Magdalene crossed to the barn to feed her dog. This was supposed to be a day of celebration, but the pup didn't know that Jacob's brother had ruined the day for her. Clovis's long curly tail wagged in anticipation of the treat she had hidden in her pocket. She bent and rubbed the top of his silky head and handed him the big beef bone to gnaw on. They'd adopted the black-and-tan shepherding dog from a family friend, Guillame Richelieu. Formerly a French aristocrat, and for a time a French soldier in New France, Guy had left the army and become a scout—some said a spy. He should be back any day now from meeting with Colonel Christy in Philadelphia.

Michi lumbered across the yard, arms stacked high with firewood. "Clovis has earned his treat, and I hope I do too." Guy had named the dog for a French king, and Clovis had well earned his name, making the sheep in the field his obedient subjects.

"Ja, *bruder*, you may have a *Springerle* now, maybe two." Magda tamped down a grin. At the rate Michi was growing, it was all she and Mama could do to keep him from being hungry all the time.

He stopped walking. "Did you make them?"

Magdalene scowled at him as Clovis slumped down at her feet. "You saw Mama prepare them a few weeks ago." Time enough for them to become tender.

"Oh ja, that is right." He continued walking toward the house.

Bruders.

"I guess I can eat them then," Michi called over his shoulder.

Why was it she could repair intricate silver pieces and yet she couldn't get her baking to turn out right? Maybe her brothers were right—maybe it was her failed pastries and strudels that kept her from marrying. Or was it that she had eyes for no one but her employer, the man who'd honed her skills as a craftswoman? Or as a lady smith, which he enjoyed calling her in private.

Would Jacob return from the scouting mission to locate the Foyles? Or rather, their remains? Would he and the others be attacked? Would Indians attack them while they slept as they had reportedly done to the Foyles? Magdalene shivered as another gust of wind ruffled her heavy shawl. A nip of icy snow portended a coming storm. Maybe the colonel wouldn't take the men further west.

Clovis got up and pranced off toward the barn, more like a pony than a canine, and Magdalene followed across the yard, the wind slowing but pushing her skirts up around her ankles.

Just outside the barn, Papa, Franz, and Norbert had set up their sausage-stuffing operation. "Good morning, Magda, *meine kleine Tochter.*"

"I'm no more a little daughter, Papa." She kissed his cheek.

The scents of onion, garlic, and a multitude of pungent spices permeated the air. Norbert smiled at her in that way of his that she'd missed when they'd been apart—a grin that suggested he always had a secret, even if he didn't. Franz, who always kept busy and didn't even wear a cloak this chilly day, continued chopping pork slabs into small pieces.

Papa set his cleaver down on the block. "I will keep calling you my little daughter even when your hair is white like mine is getting."

"Or until you have a little girl of your own." Norbert winked at her. "I think Guy is due back soon. Maybe you can get him to settle here."

Franz laughed but kept chopping. Sweat soaked the front of his linsey-woolsey shirt, the one she'd sewn for him for Christmas. "If our *Schwester* threatens Guillame that he won't get to see Clovis anymore unless he marries her, that could secure *Ein Heiratsantrag.*"

Scowling at him, Magda moved closer and pinched his arm. "That pup is important to him, but not enough to make a proposal of marriage when he is already married."

Papa ceased stuffing sausage mixture into the casing. Norbert looked up from chopping meat into tiny pieces. The two exchanged a guilty look.

Magdalene cocked her head at them. "I've seen the miniature portrait he carries of his beautiful redheaded wife and his child. So don't be talking foolish when the poor man does return."

The three Sehler men's lips quirked. They weren't normally at a loss for a retort.

"So you did not know?" Magda sighed as another puff of mountain air swirled around her. "Men."

Franz finally stopped hacking at the meat. "He is widowed, Schwester. And childless."

"What?" Guy had lost his wife and child?

Papa raised a sausage-smeared hand. "Speak no more of this. We have much work to do."

"Yes, Papa." She cast a sideways glance at Norbert, and his tight features revealed he wished to say much more.

"The newly engaged couple should enjoy their feast." Papa's pronouncement meant that she must not dwell on Guy's loss. Not now.

"Yes, Papa."

"I'm sure a number of our neighbors will attend also." Norbert smirked.

Her brother knew how she and Mama didn't do well with unexpected guests. Had he invited more? If so, that meant more cooking, baking, and cleaning, plus she required a bath and had to tame her thick hair into something manageable. She'd wanted to do something special since Jacob was coming, but now she might only have time for a braid. Maybe she'd have Mama help her. And what about her clothes? She needed to air her best shift, her new gown, her best petticoat, and lace sleeves. But there was no time to wash anything but her fichu to give it time to dry. She didn't want to get into an argument with Norbert right now by asking if he was just aggravating her by implying more guests were coming.

Franz transferred the chopped pork from the board to a large bowl and frowned at her. "You'd best get busy."

"You look beautiful." Mama patted Magdalene's shoulder, tears in her eyes. If only those tears were from happiness instead of the pain that was etched in her features.

"Thank you. But you've done too much to help me, Mama." Magdalene fluffed the goose-down pillow on her parents' bed. "Lie back down and I will come get you when our guests arrive."

As she descended to the dining area, Magda's brothers' voices carried up the stairs.

"Ja."

"Nein!"

"Ja!"

Something crashed to the floor. Grabbing her skirts and pulling them out of the way, Magda quickly made it to the first floor of the cabin, where she saw an upturned tray and broken pastries littering the floorboards between nine-year-old Michi and fourteen-year-old Christof.

Was ist das? What were they doing?

To her horror, the cabin door opened and Jacob and his brother Dafydd entered, Papa ushering them in as Clovis shot past them. The dog greedily devoured the meat-and-cheese-stuffed tarts that Mama and she had so painstakingly assembled that afternoon.

"Nein, Clovis, nein!" Magdalene's shouts and her brothers' efforts to corral the dog were to no avail as her father helped the Owens brothers remove their cloaks.

Finally, Dafydd whistled and Clovis listened, stopping long enough to lick his greasy muzzle. *Naughty pup.*

Jacob took several long-legged strides to join her. Tonight he wore buff-colored wool breeches instead of his more recent attire of buckskins, and a navy coat, which he used to wear in Philadelphia. The familiarity of his shop attire made her smile despite Clovis's mischief. Jacob leaned in close enough that she could inhale his bayberry scent. "Well, they do look rather tasty."

"Even squashed and half-consumed?" She poked his chest.

He pulled back and laughed.

She chuckled too. "We have more, so you will have to see for yourself what enticed that pup."

Patting his flat stomach, Jacob nodded. "Let me help you bring them out."

He followed her to the back, his jaw dropping when he saw the number of platters. "Are you feeding the army?"

"No, but Mrs. Martin and Mr. Davis are coming."

"Ah, I hear they are to be congratulated."

"Yes." If only she and Jacob were the ones to be congratulated.

"My brother is quite put out still."

So maybe there was more to Dafydd's distress the previous day. "Does he care for Mrs. Martin?"

A muscle in Jacob's jaw jumped. Dafydd would be upset if Jacob shared his secret admiration for the widow and his plans for her, now destroyed. "I'd best not say."

A knowing gleam shone in Magda's intense cornflower-blue eyes. "You don't have to. But it is first come, first served, for marriages out here. Like eating at our table, with all my bruders grabbing the food."

Was that a nudge from her? Now that Davis was out of the running, that put Jacob back on track. "I think I understand."

"Could you help me carry the sausages and the potatoes out to the tables?"

Soon the pair had the two large parallel tables, each flanked by benches, loaded down with potatoes, ham slices, gravy bowls, platters of corn muffins, and green beans. Meanwhile, the scent of apple pies beckoned a return trip to the back.

Mr. Davis was assisting Mrs. Martin with her cloak as Johan Rousch and his eldest, a son, arrived. Johan carried an armful of tanned hides, and the child held a basket covered with a towel.

Magda's father led them in. "*Danke*, Johan, these are beautiful." He took the hides and laid them across a nearby chair, the flickering firelight dancing on the smooth leather.

"Your boys helped. You should thank them too." The tall golden-haired man grinned at Norbert, who was nearly his height.

Mr. Sehler turned and nodded at his sons. "Ja, *gute Arbeite*."

Good work indeed, from the look of the leather. Such would have brought a pretty penny in Philadelphia. If trouble continued to heat up on the Virginia frontier, if war came with the French and the Indians, then Rousch may well need to help supply the militia with his leather goods.

"Suzanne is unable to attend. Baby Noela has. . ." Johan made a motion over his stomach. "She has gut problem." He removed his cloak, and Franz took it and hung it on a peg.

Magda's brother Franz, the quiet one, bowed slightly toward the tanner. "We're sorry. But happy you brought your boy."

Rousch's blond son handed the basket to Norbert. "For the table, sir."

"I am sir now?" Norbert feigned mock offense. "Am I so old?"

The child's eyes widened. Franz ruffled his hair and pulled him in for a quick hug. "Danke, and ignore my bruder. He is a pest."

Rousch jerked a thumb toward the door. "We have brought another guest instead."

His son crossed his arms and nodded. "He doesn't cry as much as the baby."

"My wife's bruder has returned." Lines of concern bunched around Rousch's blue eyes. "He's gone to the barn looking for his *Hund*."

Magdalene looked up from where she was placing a crock of butter near the end of the table. Mr. Sehler and Franz shot glances full of meaning at the woman he hoped to court. His gut squeezed tight and it wasn't from hunger. The dark-haired Frenchman, Suzanne Richelieu Rousch's older brother, of aristocratic upbringing, was too handsome for his own good—even with that scar across his face and heading into his midthirties in years.

The door opened and Guillame Richelieu took two steps into the room, his black leather boots polished to a sheen, and knelt down. The dog bounded toward him, pushing past all the Sehler sons, now assembled in the room, past the widow and the wagon master, and into the Frenchman's open arms. From the corner of his eye, Jacob caught Magda staring at him, not at Richelieu.

A creaking on the stairs caught his attention, and Jacob turned. He quickly made his way to Mrs. Sehler's side and assisted her the rest of the way down. The frail woman's features were contracted with pain. "Let me help you."

Her faded blue eyes must have once looked like Magda's. She had a sweetness about her even in her frailty. "You're a good boy."

At twenty-eight, he was no boy. Did she think him good enough for her daughter? "Magda, have your brothers pull that special chair over for your mother."

Norbert and Franz pulled the padded and upholstered chair to the end of the table. Jacob lifted Magda's mother and carried her to her spot. She couldn't weigh more than six or seven stone. If such could happen to Magda, could he face the results? Yes, it would be worth it to have Magdalene by his side even if for the rest of their lives he would need to care for her in this manner. He looked up and caught the tender gaze of Mr. Sehler. Did he know what Jacob was thinking?

Mr. Sehler moved in. "Hannelore." He kissed his wife's forehead as she reached her hand up to hold his. "I'm sorry, my sweet, but this old papa is getting a little slower."

"Nein, *mein liebling*."

"Thank you, Jacob." Mr. Sehler drew in a deep sigh before motioning for their guests to join the table.

As all began to position themselves on the benches, Magda and Richelieu remained standing, Magda's back to Jacob. The scout ran a slim hand through his dark hair, his features serious. Magda took a step toward him, the dog nestling on his feet. Although Jacob could see the man's lips move, he couldn't hear him. Had he mouthed "My great love?" When Richelieu embraced Magda, Jacob ducked his chin. He couldn't just leave. For one thing, his brother and he had come together, and for another, it would be insufferably rude. He couldn't storm off in a huff, although he'd love to do just that.

"Please sit, Jacob." Mrs. Sehler pointed to a spot to her right where there was enough space for several more.

"Yes ma'am." But he hesitated. He struggled to push the irritation from his features.

When Magda and Richelieu approached the table, both the scout and Jacob extended their hand to the beautiful young woman to assist her onto the bench. It was now or never. Jacob must assert himself. "Why don't you step in first, Monsieur Richelieu, and I shall assist Miss Sehler."

Both gave him a skeptical glance, but Richelieu complied and slid in first. Jacob clasped Magda's hand, unwilling to release it. They stood there, the guests at both tables laughing and chatting, until Mr. Sehler cleared his throat and stood.

Magda leaned against Jacob and clasped his forearm. "Jacob, it would be best if you sat next to Guillame, so please be seated. I will need to be able to get up and help serve."

Jacob bent, his lips so close to her cheek that he felt the heat from her face and inhaled the scent of a soft rose perfume. "And I shall assist you." How he longed to add "my love," but he would have to wait for that privilege.

Later, they went for a long walk, trailed by Norbert.

Jacob wasn't sure where to begin, but he had to start somewhere. "For years, we have worked together, Magda. I feel I know you well."

"Tonight, in the kitchen, it felt so natural to be working beside you." She exhaled a sigh. "I've missed that—our time together."

"I have too. I hadn't realized how much so until we came out here into different settlements."

"Yes. I miss those days together in Philadelphia."

Soon they were laughing over some of their memories. An owl hooted and then flew, its wide wings flying almost soundlessly over them and to a nearby copse of woods.

Jacob waved toward the sky, lit by the almost full moon and dotted with hundreds of stars. "It is beautiful out here, isn't it?"

"Yes. No owls in Philadelphia and no blue mountains."

"No." But safer there. If only he'd spoken more freely with Magda there. "I hope we can spend more time together when I return."

"I would like that." She smiled up at him. "I'm very glad for our friendship."

But his feelings had grown. "I care for you deeply."

She stopped walking and he paused and took her hand in his. "Could I hope you might consider more than friendship?"

Norbert moved to join them. "No hand-holding unless you have asked Papa to court her."

Magda dropped his hand. "When you return. Then let us speak of this again."

Chapter 3

Y ou will wear a path into the floor if you keep that pacing up." Mama's gentle voice stopped Magdalene midstep in front of the window.

Two long weeks and the scouting group hadn't returned from the western edge of Virginia. Where was Jacob now? Was he cold? Hungry?

Mama patted the chair beside her. "Sit down and finish that hunting shirt you are making for Jacob."

"He is a much better stitcher than I am."

"He is a fine tailor, that is for certain. Not a single stitch has broken in the banyan he made for your papa three years past." Mama's blue eyes met hers. "Do you think Jacob has time for sewing now?"

"Nein." Neither did she.

"You've worked hard all afternoon."

Mama was right. With all the washing, scrubbing, rinsing, and hanging of clothes, Magdalene wasn't sure she had enough strength in her hands to manage any stitching tonight, but she did want to finish the blue linen shirt for Jacob's return. She lowered herself into the chair beside her mother.

Soon the two settled into companionable silence as each ran a needle and thread through the men's garments. Before too long, Magda had completed a double stitch of one seam. Mama stopped working and tried to rearrange her blanket on her lap, but it was stuck beneath her hip. Magdalene set aside her sewing and rose to help. With a gentle tug, she freed the soft wool covering. "Better?"

"Ja, danke." Mama patted Magdalene's cheek. Mama's eyebrows tugged together and her lips twitched as if she wished to say more, but she didn't.

Straightening, Magdalene tilted her head back to stretch. Hanging overhead was a tiny white star that Michi and Jacob had hung from the wooden ceiling. Her brother had promised that when the scouting party returned, he and Jacob would retrieve the star and let her read what they'd written on it. Michi initially had taken delight in tormenting Magdalene with his and Jacob's "secret," but in the past few days, he'd stopped his harassment. She pointed up to the star. "What do you think it says, Mama?"

A laugh so vibrant that it recalled the energetic, often laughing and joking mother of her youth, bubbled forth. "Why, I imagine it says the same as your beautiful tablespoon has engraved on it."

Magdalene felt her eyes widen as she bent her head forward and gaped at her mother. "You know?"

"It is beautiful, Magdalene. I had no idea what talent you have with silver." Mama cocked her head at her. "Why did you not tell us or show us your work before we left? I would have made that trip to the shop to see such beauty, even if no one could know that my daughter had crafted it."

What could Magda say? If she'd shown off her work, if she'd encouraged Mama to come to the shop to see it, would she and Papa have insisted Magdalene find a way to stay in Philadelphia?

Mama *tsk-tsk*ed. "You and that Jacob are just alike in keeping your feelings too. . ." She made a circular motion with her fist over her heart. "Too close. I think you will have to work on being more honest with one another."

"We are." Magda heard a slight creak behind her, but when she turned she saw nothing.

"Not about your feelings. You're both afraid of something."

What was Magda afraid of? Half of her family had been indentured when they'd arrived in the colonies. Only by the grace of God had the rest of them been able to find employment and remain together. The Owenses had been Magdalene's employers, had trained her. She wasn't of their same social station in life, and she understood it well in Philadelphia. Yet out here in the valley, by these blue mountains, those differences in status seemed to disappear. She'd not speak of past family servitude and upset her mother over something Magda was just now realizing was no longer relevant. But one fear she had Magdalene could admit to. "I'm afraid the men won't return."

"With all these prayers going up, I have to put my faith in God." Again, a creak sounded.

Michi popped up from behind the table. "Franz says he only puts his trust in his rifle."

"Michi!" Both Mama and Magdalene called his name.

Laughing, the boy sprang across the room. When he got to his mother, she set her stitching aside. He sank to his knees, his face suddenly somber, and lay his head on his mother's lap. She stroked his cheek and tugged gently at the leather tie that held his queue of tawny hair back from his face. "When are they going to come back, Mama?"

Her brother's trembling voice caused tears to form in Magdalene's eyes. She covered her mouth, lest her sobs escape. She turned and headed to the kitchen to make tea and put together a little plate of pumpkin biscuits for them, praying for the men as she worked. When all was ready, she placed three mugs and the plate beside the Bible at the table. She and her mother would show Michi God's promises in the Book.

Hopefully, she'd be encouraged as much as her brother needed to be. Any number of things could happen to the men en route.

"I am with you always."

And God was with Jacob too. She had to trust.

Jacob screamed and lurched upward on his cot, throwing his blanket aside as the images of charred remains shattered his peaceful sleep.

"Shh! It's all right, Jacob." Franz's surprisingly gentle voice calmed him.

Jacob's blanket was handed back to him and he rearranged it, although how he'd return to sleep, he didn't know. Even now, the stench of the Foyles' place of death seemed present. But the odor was only from the close proximity of many men in the tent, all of whom could use a bath, himself included.

What kind of man was Jacob, if he couldn't cope with the scene he'd witnessed? How would he handle himself if their party came under attack?

"Back to sleep!" Dafydd's command was laughable. As if by merely being an officer he could order them to slumber.

"Only one more day," Norbert whispered.

Then they'd be home. Home? How had Jacob come to think of the Shenandoah Valley as his home? *Dear Lord, give me peace in this situation, help me. Bring me sleep.* He lay there a while longer before darkness claimed him again.

The next day passed in a blur, excitement building as they neared the settlements. At each stop, Palatinate and English and Scotch settlers offered provisions for the men and their horses. Now they were almost to their own communities.

"Each of us has dropped at least a stone's weight while we have been gone." Franz patted his still-ample midsection and hastily consumed their last cold ham biscuit.

Dafydd exchanged a glance with Jacob before tipping his flask to his lips. His brother likely kept up his own weight by his consumption of brandy that he had until lately kept hidden in his saddlebag. Dafydd had seen more than his share of blood and carnage, far more than Jacob had. Jacob would not judge him harshly, but he was concerned with the frequency that Dafydd had been imbibing on this outing. And all along the way, the whispers of war increased. It was said that young Lieutenant Washington even now was forted in Pennsylvania, possibly under attack.

"We did our bit." Dafydd wiped his mouth. "We have sent our report."

"Yes. And thankfully, we have come back safely."

They might be safe, but a darkness had settled over all of them since they'd discovered the site of the massacre. Even Norbert had run out of jokes to tell them, and Franz had stopped singing songs over the campfire. But now, mounted and en route to their homes, the men began to speak again. Franz and Norbert were teasing each other about something.

Jacob wanted only to be clean, free from the feeling of filth in his body and soul. He nudged his gelding closer to Dafydd's. "Just so you know, I'm not using your dirty bathwater."

His brother arched a dark eyebrow. "I'd have to be deaf, dumb, and blind not to know exactly where you shall be going upon our return."

"I intend to marry her." Father would have apoplexy when he learned that Jacob had proposed to a shopgirl.

"Then I shall grant your request." Dafydd's dry tone held a tease. "You may have the first bathwater." He urged his horse forward, heading up their group as the pass narrowed ahead.

One by one, the men formed a queue. Dafydd had warned them on the way out to Virginia's western frontier, that in such circumstances they should remain deathly quiet. One never knew what was on the other side of a narrow pass. Heart hammering in his chest, his breath shallow, Jacob gently squeezed his legs against his horse's sides, and soon they were second in line.

Suddenly, Dafydd shouted.

"Thank God you found William and Shadrach when you did!" Magdalene wrung out another wet rag and pressed it against Shadrach Clark's forehead. She and Jacob had scarcely had a moment together since the men returned with the two wounded men—and the news that they were now heading toward war. Just thinking of it sent a chill skittering down her back.

"Actually, Shad found William and got him back to our trail." Jacob gently stroked her brow, pushing her hair back from her eyes. "But what a shock finding them dressed in war paint and bloody, leaning over their horses."

"I can only imagine!" Magdalene pressed the cloth against Shad's forehead and the scout groaned.

Thank God they hadn't all returned in such a state. And she was glad she hadn't heard the terrible details of what they had seen on the far frontier. While Michi stayed with the men to hear about their exploits, Mama and Magdalene had immediately begun tending Shadrach. Colonel Christy's sixteen-year-old son, William, had been left at the Rousches. Their niece, Sarah, would fuss over her long-time friend and help him recover.

"Luckily, my brother recognized them almost immediately." Jacob bent and pressed a quick kiss to her head.

"Good thing no one is here to see you do that." She leaned away and looked up at him. She touched Jacob's sleeve. "I'm glad you are in one piece."

His eyes lowered to half-mast. "I'm not."

"What?"

He leaned in again, his breath fanning across her cheek. "My heart is torn in half."

She pulled back. "What do you mean?"

"I left half of it here with you, Magda." Jacob moved closer again, so close she could see the golden flecks in his eyes reflect from the Betty lamps which lit the room.

She swallowed. Was he going to kiss her? She waited, and closed her eyes. But nothing happened. Magdalene opened one eye to peek up at Jacob, who was staring past her at Shadrach. She opened her other eye as Jacob straightened. She turned to see Shad, his eyes wide.

"Is this what passes for doctoring around here?" The scout scowled and glanced between the two of them.

Jacob laughed. "I can tell there's nothing wrong with your mouth, Shad."

"Or my noggin either." He shifted beneath the bedcovers. "I know two lovebirds when I see them."

"How's your head?" Magdalene reached to touch the blood-soaked bandage, but the man waved her away.

"As I said, nothing wrong with my ability to see, think, and reason." Shad attempted to move upward onto his elbows, groaned, and lay back down. "Oh, my. . ."

"You need to rest."

Jacob moved to the other side of the bed and whispered in her patient's ear.

She stood, intent on bringing Shad a nice chamomile tea with honey.

"How about I do a little doctoring duty for a while and you get some rest, Magda?" Jacob's sweet offer was too welcome to refuse. Even Shad nodded in agreement.

"All right." But she hesitated. Part of her wondered if the two men were up to something and the other part of her didn't want to leave Jacob.

"What is it?" Jacob's voice was hushed.

"I don't want to be away from you." Maybe it was the fatigue, but tears pricked her eyes.

Jacob rounded the bed and took her in his arms, pulling her close. What a blessed relief to know he was there, that he cared, that he could help. "Soon we won't ever be apart again."

What could he mean? Was he proposing? After she pulled free, she looked up at him, but he said nothing, only grinned. *Impossible man.*

Michi burst into the room, holding the star from the ceiling aloft. "May I show it to Schwester now, Jacob?"

Jacob arched an eyebrow. "I thought you were listening to the men's tales of our adventure."

Her brother's face paled. "Nein. I heard enough."

Magdalene wrapped an arm around him, but Michi pulled away and waved the star. "Look what it says."

"Jacob and Magda." Pure joy coursed through her like the rush of the Shenandoah River.

Chapter 4

L ambs skittered across the verdant fields, mama lambs bleating for their off-spring to come feed. Clovis paced the perimeter of the pasture as though he, like Magdalene's brother Christof, was tasked with inspecting the fence. Michi, meanwhile, chased some of the lambs around.

Christof squared his shoulders. "Checking the fences is boring."

"But necessary." She pointed toward the emerald-green pastures, but the youth didn't move.

Beside her, at the outdoor table beside the barn, Guy looked up from mending a harness.

She sighed. "Doesn't seem right, that it should be so pretty out here."

Christof's countenance hardened. "Feels like we're just waiting."

A gentle breeze carried a hint of wildflowers. How dare it be so beautiful when their very world could soon be torn apart?

"Oui, je suis d'accord." Guillame stretched out his fingers.

She arched an eyebrow at the scout. Her understanding of French wasn't good.

"I agree. And I'm just giving my hands a rest." He gave her a grin that quickly slipped from his face as he narrowed his eyes and raised a hand to his brow.

A chill chased around the back of her neck. "What is it?"

Guy touched the hatchet sheathed at his waist before quickly hoisting his rifle beneath his arm. "Go ring the bell!" He ran toward Michi, into the fields, waving and pointing to the far tree line.

Magdalene lifted her skirts and hastened to the front of the barn, where she rang the bell over and over again and then ran to the house. By the time she'd gone in, retrieved her rifle, and returned outside, half of her brothers had headed from tilling the fields over to where Michi now waved his arms overhead.

Guy held something, or someone, in his arms. A woman, with long, waving red hair that dragged almost to the ground, struggled and shifted before finally wrapping her arms around the Frenchman's neck.

From the corner of her eye, Magdalene spotted someone on horseback approaching from the east. It was Jacob, atop his gelding. He urged his horse to a gallop. When he neared her, he slowed his mount to a walk. "Magda, are you all right?"

"Yes."

Franz patted the black gelding's hindquarter. "What's going on, Jacob?"

"Indians were spotted nearby."

"Where?" Franz's face grew flushed.

"My brother's regiment spotted them about five miles south of here."

Norbert patted his rifle. "So close?"

Jacob's gaze fixed on Magdalene's face, sending warmth coursing through her despite the frightening news. "Dafydd sent word and warned our settlement. I came to check on you immediately."

"I'm all right, but Guillame has someone." Magdalene pointed toward the field.

Jacob frowned. "A woman? Do you know who it is?"

"No." Magdalene shook her head as did her brothers.

"Let me go help." Jacob dug his heels into his horse's sides and they were off.

"I'm going out too." Franz grasped his rifle and chased after Jacob.

In the distance, now outside the sheep fence, Guy stopped as Clovis barked and circled him and the woman before running toward the woods. Jacob dismounted and quickly raised his gun to his shoulder, as Guy also turned to face the woods. All around her, her brothers muttered and shifted their rifles back to their shoulders, but Magdalene hesitated. After what seemed hours with no activity from the tree line, Jacob handed his gun to Franz. Jacob went to Guy and helped lift the woman, now standing on her own, up onto the horse.

"What's going on?" Mama's voice carried from behind. Magadalene turned to spy Mama standing in the cabin's doorway.

The scent of roasting smoked ham carried from the interior as Papa too stepped outside. He coughed.

"You should go back inside, Gustav," Mama urged him.

Both of her parents were ailing with ague and didn't need to be outside.

Soon, Jacob rode back in the courtyard, a red-haired woman clutched in his arms. Even with her face smeared with soot, her features were pretty, her green eyes wide as she stared at them. Attired in a deerskin dress that had seen better times, she appeared like a wild Indian. She trembled from her wild mane of hair down to her moccasin-covered feet. The stranger's eyes fixed on Magdalene, shame flickering across her features as tears began to make trails through the dirt that covered her face.

"All she has been saying is. . ." Jacob shook his head

"Guillame." The woman's almost guttural voice startled Magdalene.

"Is that because he told her his name?" Why did Magdalene's words sound angry to her own ears?

Jacob shook his head. "No."

Magdalene shifted uneasily under the weight of jealousy. Her sweetheart's features tugged into an expression of compassion. She knew this man well. She shouldn't be jealous. He was likely thinking the same thing she was: that this woman, likely held captive by the Indians, would be facing a tough challenge. He nodded toward Magdalene, as if reading her thoughts, and she gave him a slight nod back.

"Let me help." Norbert stepped forward and held out his arms. He took the woman and set her on her feet. She leaned against him. Norbert inclined his head away, his nose wrinkling. She must smell pretty bad for him to do that.

Guy raced into the yard, followed by Clovis, who was barking. The Frenchman shouldered in on Norbert and wrapped an arm around the young woman.

"Guillame?" She touched the scout's face, stroking his jawline.

"*Oui.*" He pulled slightly back, his dark eyes narrowed as he tilted his head one way, and then another. "*Mais qui es-tu?*"

Norbert scowled. "Do you know her, Richelieu?"

"No."

She mumbled something.

Guillame's shoulders stiffened.

Jacob dismounted and handed the reins to Christof, who led the horse off to a nearby trough.

Franz joined the group around the woman. "Do you even know her?"

"No." Richelieu bent and uttered some more Shawnee words to the woman. She nodded and the scout's ruddy face paled. "She says she is to be my wife."

-⟨divider⟩-

Magda and her mother took the former captive's hands and led her toward the house—presumably to where she'd be bathed. Jacob had never inhaled such a foul odor. It was even worse than the streets of Philadelphia in summer.

The men in the courtyard headed back to their tasks in the fields and barns.

Jacob moved as close as he dared without getting another whiff of the unwashed woman. "Guillame, why does she say she is to be your wife?"

Richelieu's wife, reportedly a beauty with hair as red as this woman's, was said to have died the previous autumn—a fact Magdalene had seemed surprised to learn the day Guillame had returned.

The Frenchman exhaled loudly, sending puffs of foggy breaths into the air. "She is a *présent*—a gift."

Jacob flinched. "What do you mean?"

"The chief of a tribe friendly to me in my journeys sent her. He heard of my wife's death."

"He did not tell you she was coming?"

"No."

"And you do not know her?"

The Frenchman shook his head. He whistled, but his dog, the one Magda had adopted, was now nowhere to be seen.

Richelieu pointed to Jacob's gelding. "Mind if I borrow him?"

Before Jacob could respond, the scout had untied the horse and slipped onto his back, and the animal and rider were off at a trot across the newly green fields. Richelieu headed straight back to the tree line.

Magda's father joined him, gesturing to the scout. "Where's he going?"

Jacob fisted his hands. "I don't know. I can only hope he is making a safe decision." If Richelieu ran across Dafydd and his troops making their way forward, would they fire upon him? And if Richelieu was correct, and there were friendly natives in the woods, would the army shoot them too?

"What did he say about that girl?" Mr. Sehler coughed. "Did I hear him say she is to be his wife?"

"He doesn't even know her, sir."

Mr. Sehler lowered himself onto a bench but said nothing.

"How could Richelieu marry her?"

Mr. Sehler prepared and then lit his long-stemmed ceramic pipe. He glanced toward the house. "Tell me if you see my wife coming. She doesn't want me smoking with this cough."

"Perhaps with good reason, sir."

"Does all in life require reason?" Mr. Sehler inhaled on his pipe stem then exhaled several puffs of smoke. He raised a hand to his eyes and appeared to be scanning his land, which covered many acres, perhaps close to a hundred. All the land flowed out from the small settlement like spokes in a wheel, each owner having a cabin situated near the center and their land spreading outward. He removed his pipe. "Maybe it is not reasonable, but some people trust God when He calls them into a quick union with their spouse."

Hadn't Magda said her parents were married after less than a month of courtship? "Yes sir."

"Others seem to think they must wait until the sun, moon, and stars are all in perfect alignment." Mr. Sehler's blue gaze was direct, yet a smile tugged at his lips.

"Like me, is that what you mean?"

"Ja. For such an intelligent young man, you seem to have difficulty seeing what's right in front of your face."

"What do you mean?"

"My Tochter could have stayed with you in Philadelphia and been safe, if only you'd asked her."

"What?" Jacob shook his head and scratched the side of his neck. "No. Michi told me Magda did not care for me. Not in that way."

"Michi?" Mr. Sehler frowned.

"Yes sir."

"And you listened to him. Why?"

"Why, he. . ." Jacob was sputtering. "He and Magda are so close—I thought he knew."

"Ja, they are close." Mr. Sehler cupped his hands together at his waist. "Like that they are."

"Yes."

"Which is why a smart young man like you should have known the boy did not want to lose his Schwester!"

Thoroughly chastened, Jacob's cheeks heated. What could he say? Magda's father stuck his pipe back in his mouth, but then removed it when he had a coughing fit. Jacob patted the man's broad back until he finally stopped coughing.

"Just so you know, now I'm not so certain I'd grant my permission. Not if a boy of only nine years could dupe you so easily."

Grant permission? To marry his daughter? "But sir. . ." He'd not yet asked. And with the reported Indian uprising, now wasn't the time.

"But she loves you, that much I know." Mr. Sehler arched his salt-and-pepper brows. "I'm not a boy, but I do love her as much as Michi does and more. But unlike my son, I'm not so selfish as to try to spoil her chances at marriage."

Mama scrubbed the dirt from the young woman's back. *"Wie alt denkst du sie?"* She'd lapsed back into her native German. *"Zwanzig Sommer?"*

The young woman raised her head.

"How old are you?" Magdalene spoke slowly. She thought her to be closer to her own age than Mama thought, but she translated the words. "Twenty summers?"

"Yes. Twenty summers have passed." The voice crackled and sounded more childlike than her Shawnee words.

So she was nineteen or twenty. And she believed herself promised to Guillame. He had told Magdalene privately that he may have to marry her to save face and keep peace with allies. To refuse a gift from a chief would be a grave insult. But what about this young woman, already taken from her home? What about her family? What about her own wishes?

When the stranger flinched, Mama ceased scrubbing. "What is this?"

Magdalene bent closer. Although well healed, narrow and broader scars crisscrossed the woman's back. She sucked in a breath and met Mama's frightened gaze. What had those savages done to her?

Mama stared down. "This is what Guillame was speaking of—what they do to their captives?"

"Yes, to see if they are strong enough to survive." Could Magdalene survive such abuse? "Running the gauntlet."

Their guest looked up. "I live. Mama, Papa die. Brothers die. Sisters die. Only I live."

Lord have mercy. Tears pricked Magdalene's eyes. This young woman had no family.

Mama rolled her lips together, tears rolling down her cheeks. "I'm so sorry."

Feeling sorry wasn't going to help the girl right now though. "Let me take a turn washing her up."

Magdalene dipped the pitcher into the warm bath water and poured it. Their guest dipped her chin against her chest. Magdalene gently washed the young woman's back, the knotted skin a deep rose against the ivory of her flesh. She set the rag aside, filled the pitcher again, and poured the scented water over the young woman's tangled mass of hair.

"What is your name, child?" Mama patted their guest's arm.

A frown puckered the girl's forehead. "Not wish to say Shawnee name."

Magdalene didn't blame her. And she'd make sure that they didn't force an unwanted marriage upon the young woman. *Lord guide us, help us.*

"What of your first name? The name your parents gave you?" Mama cocked her head, her words soothing.

"Reg. . ." The young woman struggled to form the word. "Regina."

"Regina?"

A smile tugged at the young woman's lips. "Yes." Then the smile blossomed. She was beautiful with that captivating smile.

Mama smiled back at her. "We're glad you're safe now, Regina."

"Safe?" The word, stated with disbelief was followed by a choked sob.

Did she not believe them; did she doubt that she was safe? Or did Regina know something they did not?

Chapter 5

J acob's entire month of April was filled with militia drills and gathering supplies and delivering them to the forts on Virginia's frontier. In two villages farther out from their settlements, a raiding Shawnee party had taken the towns'
smoked meats and had abducted three women. Dafydd reported that the natives
blamed the militia from that community for killing some of their unattended women
and children and were exacting retribution. Before he'd left with the army again,
Dafydd had warned Jacob to make sure his men, his militia, understood the folly of
such brutal behavior.

Tywyll's ears twitched this way and that, and he snorted as Jacob directed
him onto the path toward his cabin. The gelding hadn't liked being hitched up to
the wagon on the last supply run, when one of the team had gone lame. But out
here, one had to do what one had to do. Soon, Jacob spotted the familiar lines
of the Ruckmans' laundry hung to dry in the breeze. Young Mrs. Ruckman kept
busy with her houseful of boys, with only her mother to help her with household
duties—much like the Sehler family. Did Magda resent having to, day in and day
out, perform all the duties needed to keep her family fed and in clean clothes?
If so, she didn't seem to show it. How would Mrs. Sehler manage once Magda
married him?

Ahead, his cabin beckoned. Weary to the bone, even his arm felt heavy as he
waved at the two oldest Ruckman boys playing a game of chase on the green. The
two gangly youths ran to his side. He offered them a coin to take care of Tywyll, and
soon the two were off. Jacob ambled toward his cabin. *Unlocked.* But since the Ruckman boys hadn't warned him of an intruder, he opened the door to find ore samples
and iron tools strewn across the table, evidence that his eldest brother, Llywellyn,
had finally arrived for a visit. What Jacob needed was a hot bath, a clean change of
clothes, a bit of supper, and a lie down. At least his brother had a kettle of water and
a fire going.

Tonight wasn't the time to be discussing the iron mine and forge that Llywellyn
and he had invested in. Jacob removed his thick leather wallet stuffed with payments
and set it on the table. This was for his wedding. It wasn't for additional funds for the
forge, even if that's what he and Llywellyn would both like to eventually be doing.

He wanted to show Mr. Sehler that he could provide for his daughter.

"Llywellyn?" Jacob called out as he looked first in what served as Dafydd's room and then in his own. Other than a satchel of clothes, there was no evidence of his oldest brother.

Someone banged on the door. Jacob hurried to open it. A gaunt Llywellyn stood before him, almost unrecognizable. It had only been two years since Jacob had seen him last, but he looked to have aged ten. "Brother!"

Llywellyn's embrace was just as strong as ever, thankfully. The two men pulled back and looked at one another. "Jago, you're getting a few white strands in that dark hair of yours."

"Ha! Look in a silvered mirror yourself and see how many you find!" Jacob jabbed playfully at his brother's too-lean midsection. Father would be shocked to see Llywellyn in this state.

"Aye, true it is that I've aged too much since last we met." Llywellyn gave him a gentle shove back. "But I can still wrestle you to the ground in a flash, so don't be forgetting that!"

Jacob raised both hands in surrender. "Let's have peace here."

"Indeed." Llywellyn rubbed at his scruff of a gray-brown beard.

"Let me put together some victuals for us and get caught up."

"Oh, no need. Mrs. Davis has been so kind as to offer us a repast at her home."

"That is very kind, but I wonder how she'll feel if my head ends up in her plate of mashed turnips?" Jacob stretched and yawned.

A twinkle lit his brother's hazel eyes. "Aren't you going to ask me why I'm here?"

"I've sent all manner of messages to you since I arrived."

Llywellyn jabbed a finger toward Jacob. "I've come bearing a gift."

"For me?" Jacob crossed his arms over his chest. "It's not my birthday, nor is it Christmas."

"Ah, but it is one of the finest examples from the new forge, Jago."

Magdalene waited patiently for Jacob to arrive, as he'd promised her at church meeting at the Ruckmans' home the previous Sunday. He'd finally returned from supplying the forts. And Magdalene had even gotten a chance to speak with his older brother, Llywellyn, who'd always been kind to her at the shop. The eldest of the Owens siblings had only stayed a few days before leaving again for the frontier of Virginia.

"He is here!" Michi came running from the path that led to the next settlement. "Jacob's coming!"

Ever since Jacob began having little secrets with Michi, her youngest brother seemed to have formed an attachment to him. Or maybe it was the treats Jacob always brought back for Michi and Mama when he returned from supplying the forts.

Before long, Franz had taken Jacob's horse and Michi had run off with Clovis to the fields. And Jacob was striding right toward Magdalene. She opened her arms to let him hug her, and he kissed her cheek soundly before pulling away from her and gazing down at her. "It's so good to see you, my sweet."

Her cheeks heated. Each of the few times she'd seen him in the past month, he'd had a new loving nickname for her.

"I'm glad your family could spare you for an afternoon." Jacob tucked her arm up beneath his as they strode out across the courtyard, toward the field.

"Since Regina arrived, my load has been lightened."

"That is good."

Regina had shared that she'd been taken captive when she was almost twelve. "Her English language skills are coming back completely."

Jacob leaned in. "What will Guillame do about Regina choosing your brother to be her mate?"

Magdalene shrugged. "Guy is going to tell the chief, if and when he sees him again, that Regina chose Franz, not him, to be her husband."

"And the chief will accept that?"

"He is hoping so. It is the tribe's custom for the woman to select her mate."

Jacob nodded. "And you say Guillame will cease scouting then?"

They strode on toward the fields, filled with crops. "He only did it for a season. He says he will go to Charleston, now that he is reconnected with his sister and her family."

"Suzanne and Johan will surely miss him." A shadow crossed over Jacob's face. Was he already missing Llywellyn after their brief reunion?

"Yes, but they have family amongst the Huguenots in South Carolina." She squeezed his arm.

"It's so far away."

"Like you would have been from me, had you remained in Philadelphia." How awful that would have been.

Jacob released her arm from his and turned, clasping both her hands as he faced her and leaned in. "I could not have stayed in Philadelphia. When the wagon master came for you and Michi said Davis was to marry you—"

Magdalene tugged against his hands. "Marry me?"

He arched an eyebrow at her. "Are you repeating what Michi told me, or are you asking me to marry you? Has Regina been giving you instruction?"

Her cheeks heated and she averted her gaze, but he laughed, a deep, low laugh. Magdalene frowned at him. "Mr. Davis came to demand if I was going to come with the group or not, because he wanted everything settled."

43

"And why had you waited to make your decision?" Yearning filled his voice. She swallowed. "Jacob, I kept hoping. . ."

"Michi the mischief maker. Had he not told me so many mistruths, we might be—"

Leaning her head against his chest, she inhaled the scent of damp wool and leather, the hint of forest, and a scent uniquely his. But no metallic residue, as she'd always smelled in her backroom where she'd smithed. "We might be running the shop together?"

He pulled her closer. "I was actually thinking more of whether we might now be expecting our first child."

A thrill rushed through her and she looked up into his warm brown eyes as he lowered his head and pressed his lips to hers. Heat coursed down to her booted toes as he pulled her closer yet. Her first kiss. So many years of waiting. Yet God had planned for this moment, she could feel it, just as certain as she knew Jacob loved her as much as she loved him.

From behind them, someone began clapping. Jacob broke the kiss and looked past her as more clapping commenced. Magdalene whirled around to spy her brothers clapping, laughing, and finally elbowing one another. It was a good thing Jacob's mastery of German was rudimentary, or he'd be able to understand all the teasing words they sent their way. But it was Reverend Hite whose unexpected presence seized her attention.

The German Lutheran pastor strode toward them, determination etched in his features. "No wonder your father asked me to come over, Fräulein Sehler."

Papa joined the reverend. "Ja. A wedding is needed for sure."

"Two weeks hence, I shall return."

"That should be sufficient time, Pastor Hite."

The clanging bell woke Magdalene from a sound sleep. Were the wedding bells finally chiming for her and Jacob? For ten long days, she and Mama and Regina had not only gotten the chores done, but had sewed wedding clothing and packed things up for her new home at Jacob's cabin. Now, in this sleepy haze, Magdalena stood in the cornfields, dressed in her best gown, a blue brocade gown edged with lace and an ecru satin petticoat beneath. But her feet were bare. No shoes, much less ones ornamented with shiny brass buckles. Regina stood in a white deerskin dress beside her. Again, the bell clanged, more urgently.

"Awake!" Regina pulled the covers from them. "Get up!"

The freed young woman scrambled from the bed and threw back the curtains. Magdalene sat up. In the far distance, a spot of light glowed.

"Fire!" Regina's guttural childlike cry brought back remembrances of when she'd first arrived.

Heavy footfalls descended the stairways. Sounds carried from downstairs when rifles rattled as they were pulled from their brackets on the wall.

Magdalene and Regina quickly flew to Mama's room, Papa exiting as they arrived. "Help her, girls, help Mama."

"Ja."

They'd been warned just the night before, and they should have listened. Jacob's brother Dafydd had arrived with one of his men and told them to go to the fort. Jacob was out making the rounds to all the militia, but the men in the village had hesitated. With the crops in the fields, who could force themselves to leave?

Would they die because of their recalcitrance? Would Magdalene be brutalized like Regina had been—but fail to pass through the gauntlet safely? *Lord, have mercy.*

"Shoes." Regina pushed a pair of leather shoes onto Mama's swollen feet. If they were detained at the new fort, she'd not be able to wear her customary cloth shoes for long. "Get yours, Magda."

"I will get our bag too."

"Mine and Papa's is right there." Mama pointed to a wooden crate, their family Bible on top.

Magdalene lifted the crate's cover and pushed the Bible inside before covering it again. Mama knew where their treasure lay: in God's Word.

Mere hours later, the three women huddled in the back of the wagon as it approached the fort from the eastern intersecting road, if a hard-packed trail rutted by wagons could be called such. The path to the fort ran northward. As they approached their turn, they were afforded a view of streams of settlers on foot, horseback, and in carts flowing into Fort Holman. Verdant fields mocked Magdalene and her family as they continued on toward the structure. Although its wooden posts pointed up to a blue sky holding the promise of spring, everything else seemed dark and foreboding.

Magdalene shivered beneath the thin wool blanket covering the three of them. Mama patted her leg. "We are all accounted for, mein liebling. Do not worry."

Regina touched Magdalene's shoulder. "Let's pray."

Regina's urging surprised Magdalene. "I have been teaching Regina those old prayers you taught us, Mama."

"In *der deutschen Sprache*?" Mama's eyebrows drew together in a tight line.

"No, Mama, I say them in English with Regina."

"Ah. *Braves Mädchen.*" Mama took Magdalene's hand and squeezed it tight, conveying maternal approval in a way that touched her deeply.

How long had it been since Mama had called her a good girl? "Danke, Mama."

They bowed their heads and prayed the Our Father prayer. Peace stole over Magdalene. God was surely with them. After all, He had saved Regina. If anyone should be panicking, it was her new friend. She knew what captivity was like. Knew what it was to lose one's family.

"I'd hoped we would not ever have to see this place." Mama sighed.

"Me too, Mama."

The scent of freshly sawn wood, of campfire smoke, and of animals greeted them as they disembarked from the wagon. How long would this place be their home?

After assisting Mama out, Papa came around and helped Magda and Regina down from their seat as Magda's brothers unloaded the wagon. When the last straggler was inside the gates, the bar was lowered with a thump that seemed to jar the hard-packed dirt in the courtyard.

Regina trembled from head to toe and Magdalene wrapped a blanket around her narrow shoulders. "It will be all right, my friend."

Regina remained silent, tucking her chin as she adjusted the light blanket until her face was almost hidden.

Michi ran to her. He had complained when the fort was being built that he wanted to be there to see it. "I wish I hadn't prayed to see this place."

Magdalene wrapped an arm around Michi, who was trembling even more than Regina. "It's not your fault."

The boy wrapped his arms around her and began to sob. "I wish. . . I wish."

"Shhh, it will be all right." An urging in her spirit prompted her to put her fears aside. She had to put on a brave face for her brother even if she was frightened out of her mind. "Your friends will now be right here with you, ja?"

He pulled back and looked up at her, his dirty face streaked with tear tracks. "I should have told Jacob the truth—that you really had hoped he'd marry you."

"How did you know I hoped that?"

He shrugged. "I listened to you and Mama speaking in the kitchen in Philadelphia when you thought I was asleep."

"Ah." She brushed a tawny lock of hair from his forehead.

"If I'd told Jacob the truth, he'd have married you and you'd be safe in Philadelphia."

"Maybe, maybe not." She bent and kissed his cheek. "Do you not think God could have kept me there if He willed it?"

She straightened and her youngest brother's face brightened. "You think so?"

"I know so." Magdalena pressed her hand to her heart. "And He'd not allow you to come to this fort unless it is in His plan."

"Good." Michi ran off toward a cluster of boys who stood around a woodpile. Judging from its size, Matthew Ruckman was tasking the boys to make kindling. That should keep them busy for a while.

Mr. Davis emerged from one of the cabin-like structures in the fort, followed by his new wife. The two hadn't been seen much since their wedding. He'd been busy helping Jacob supply the forts and had been in charge of constructing Fort Holman.

Mr. Davis's strong features contorted as he stared at Regina, whose gaze was firmly fixed on Franz as he carried boxes and bags from the wagon into one of the buildings, presumably where they'd be staying.

Mr. Davis spoke something to his wife and kissed her cheek. He hurried toward them, the fringe on his buckskin shirt swaying to a rhythmic beat.

He stopped a few feet from them, his Adam's apple bobbing as he swallowed. "Regina Tilson?"

She blinked rapidly and cocked her head. "Til. . .son, yes, Tilson."

The stalwart man's face crumpled in anguish. "The Lord has been merciful. My sister's little girl, and the very image of her."

"Uncle?" Regina choked out.

He pulled the young woman into his arms, and she clung to him as he repeated, "Little Regina."

Tears pricked Magdalene's eyes as all around her settlers hurried into their new quarters.

Davis's broad back shook with his repressed sobs. Franz emerged from one of the wooden buildings that lined the fort's interior and joined them. Regina had told them she couldn't remember her surname, but that she'd always repeated to herself that she was still Regina, not the native name the Indians had given her.

Much later, seated across the wood-slatted table from Regina and her uncle and new aunt, Magdalena listened to Davis's story over tea, Jacob seated beside her.

"I've continued as a wagon master all these years hoping I'd find my sister's family. I believed all were gone." Mr. Davis grasped Regina's small hand in his.

"I'm still here." Regina smiled up at him.

"I'm glad."

"Me too." Franz took Regina's other hand and raised it to his lips to kiss her knuckles.

Papa blew out a puff of pipe smoke. "I'd always wondered what drew you to this work, Scott."

"My Williams great-grandfather on my father's side and Scott grandfather on my mother's side, for whom I'm named, settled in Virginia long ago. Both had ventured out into this wild area. But my parents wanted a city life. Years later, with every rare visit to Philadelphia to see us children, my grandfathers regaled us with stories. They eventually encouraged my sister and her husband to purchase land in these 'far blue hills,' as they called them."

"Ja, we also came because of the beauty and the land we'd heard so much about." Papa drew on his pipe.

Unspoken were the words, *but look where we are now.*

The wagon master's wife set a tray of hastily baked bannocks at the end of the table and began slicing them into triangles. Another woman, a Scotswoman and a stranger to Magdalene, carried a crock of jam and some butter to the table. Beside her, Jacob's stomach rumbled loudly.

"Sorry. Nothing to break my fast this morning," he whispered in her ear, his breath warm.

Outside, the women tasked with preparing the supper had to make do. Tomorrow, as was their custom, the midday meal would be more substantial, with enough left over for the evening. This night, they'd receive much the same fare they'd had whilst on the wagon trek to Shenandoah.

Mrs. Davis brought a plate of sliced bannock bread to her husband and new niece. "This will have to hold you until the stew is ready."

"Thank you, dear." He patted her hand with affection.

Regina smiled up at the older woman. "You are kind, Aunt."

"We're blessed to have you."

Mr. Davis's expression grew grave as he spread a scant amount of butter across his bread. "I'd heard stories of a pale-faced, flame-haired maiden who as a young girl had been taken North by the Shawnee, but none of the scouts ever came across her. Not the Christys nor Shadrach Clark nor even Guillame, who was stationed at Fort Detroit."

"Until I was sent to him." Regina managed a shy smile.

"Good that you were." Papa accepted his plated bannock from the strange Scotswoman. "Danke."

"Very good. He is a kind man." Regina's gaze flickered briefly to the Frenchman before settling upon Franz. "An understanding man."

And still grieving the loss of his wife and child.

"You are with family now." Papa reached across the table and patted Regina's hand.

This young woman, raised in the wild and now reunited with family and about to join the Sehlers' large family, would have had a hard time making her way in the city. Even some people in the settlements would scorn her. Regina had admitted that she'd taken several "husbands" since she had first "married" in her fourteenth year. When Magdalene explained that such was not done in their culture, Regina said she hadn't remembered, but such was the custom among the Shawnee. How could the others judge her when the young woman knew no better? Mama had remarked that it was a blessing Regina had borne no children from these relationships, and, as the girl wished to readjust to living among the settlers, it was also a blessing that she'd have no constant reminder of her captivity.

Papa lifted his hand from Regina's. "I will be happy to call you Tochter."

Her fair cheeks grew rosy.

Magdalene smiled at her friend. "And I to call you Schwester." From where he stood, Franz gave her a nod of approval.

Jacob took Magdalene's hand in his. "And how long before she becomes my sister-in-law?"

"Soon." But they must first be released from this fort, and who knew how long that might be.

"Not soon enough for me." He leaned in and kissed her cheek, heat flowing down her neck as everyone at the table looked on.

Uncertain as to what would happen to them, forted in with friends and strangers, and her head light with all of the circumstances, Magdalene leaned against Jacob, convicted of one thing—no matter where they were, this man was her home, and God had brought them together for a purpose.

A red-coated officer entered the building, clutching a leather satchel. "Have you any tea left for me? I'm the new surgeon, Dr. Michael Potter."

Chapter 6

After supper, Jacob finally had a chance to speak privately with his brother's latest surgeon. Of course, introducing him to the women who may require his assistance tending to the wounded had brought a pall over the fort's occupants. And Jacob couldn't shake off the sense of unease that had settled on him like a heavy wet cloak. As if sensing Jacob's concerns, Magda's dog trotted toward him and rubbed against his leg. Jacob bent and scratched Clovis's head.

Where is Magda? Jacob set out to search inside the fort, spotting none of the Sehlers until finally locating Michi sleeping under an overhang on a huge coil of rope. He gently pushed the boy's shoulder. "Where is your sister?"

"Huh?"

"Magda. Where is she?"

Through sleepy eyes, the boy surveyed him, scowling. "Probably with that stupid *Wilde Frau.*"

"You shouldn't speak of her that way. What happened to Regina wasn't her fault." But he knew how some of the settlers were grumbling amongst themselves. It was as though they thought if they welcomed her, it would be admitting that their daughters too could be abducted. And all had breathed in relief to learn that the newcomer was to wed Franz, who lived in the next community.

"She is nothing but trouble. Probably told the Indians to come and attack us."

"That is ridiculous." A comment like that might have earned Jacob a cuff on the ear from his own father.

"I don't like her. I don't trust her—nor the Frenchie either."

"Guillame is your family's friend."

Michi shrugged.

Jacob was sorely tempted to give the boy a good lecture, but such was not his place. "Where do you hear these things?"

Michi's nose wrinkled. "Have not seen my Schwester." He laid his head back down.

Jacob exhaled loudly in frustration. It was already nightfall. Throughout the fort's courtyard, small pots of charcoals burned, lending heat and some dim light to the night.

He wanted to spend time with Magda, to assure her that all would be well, even though he knew it was a promise he couldn't keep. But he also needed to speak with his men in the militia.

Giving up his pursuit of Magda, he crossed the yard to where Matthew Ruckman, his second-in-command, stood sentinel at the front gate. "Did the men inspect the palisades one more time?"

"Aye."

"Good."

"I pray we have no need of my boys." Ruckman cast a weary glance at his sons, who were polishing guns at a table beneath the courtyard overhang.

At fifteen years and thirteen, the two youths should be learning a trade, not fighting off an Indian attack. "They shall be at the ready if needed though?"

"Aye, their mother and I have already spoken with them." Ruckman gave a curt laugh. "Their chests puffed out like peacocks, and now they are lording it over their younger brothers."

They wouldn't be so proud if they knew what such an attack could bring. Cold ash seemed to have settled in Jacob's gut as he recalled the Foyles' gruesome site. "Ah, boys will be boys." If only they could remain such. And if only Dafydd could turn somewhere else for comfort instead of to his silver flask.

Magdalene carried a tray of cornbread from the oven, a beehive-shaped clay structure which hadn't ceased baking since the first week they'd arrived at the fort. The women as well as the men kept the coals going and supplied the wood devourer with whatever they could round up to bake. With the army now encamped with them as well, there were many mouths to feed.

Clanging noises echoed from the courtyard as she set the pan down on the table where Regina was sitting, scooping butter into bowls for the midday meal.

Regina set her wooden spoon down in the larger bowl, which held the huge mound of creamy butter, and pointed. "What are they doing?"

Magdalene followed her gaze. In the fort's hard-packed clearing, Guy and Dafydd raised their swords as they squared off against one another. "I think they are combatting the boredom of their routine."

Every day the scouts, the army, and the militia surveyed the surrounding fields and woods. Every night each group returned irritable, tired, hungry, and weary of the repetitive task. And even though there was much work to be done every day, no one begrudged the men their ways of letting off some steam.

Her new friend frowned. "I think maybe it's something else that spurs them on."

"Maybe."

A red curl bobbed on Regina's ivory brow as she picked up her spoon again and inclined her head toward the next table. "That Scotswoman, perhaps."

Across the room, at another work table, a pretty young blond kneaded bread in a deep pottery bowl. The other women at the table chopped potatoes and onions, rarely looking up. But the Scotswoman surreptitiously glanced in the sword-fighting men's direction.

Magdalene sliced the cornbread into small squares. "They are practicing their skills with the sword too."

"Not much use for swords out here. They need that. . ." She pointed to where the young visiting scout, William Christy, was tossing hatchets at a wooden board, the other young men lined up behind him. Each connecting throw echoed with a resounding thud.

A gentle breeze, carrying the taunt of the verdant spring fields outside the enclosure, fluttered Magdalene's neck scarf. "But I think they enjoy the sword fighting too."

Narrowing her pretty celadon-green eyes at the two men, Regina continued to transfer butter from the larger bowl to the smaller ones. "Guillame clearly has the advantage."

The Frenchman struck blow after blow. But Dafydd kept casting glances in the pretty blond's direction as his men cheered him on from the side, looks that reminded her of those Jacob sent her way. "Being forted seems to have encouraged several romances."

"Yes."

"Jacob told me that Dafydd had planned a proposal to your aunt right before your uncle asked her to marry him."

Regina began to laugh. "Colonel Owens is too young. My aunt may look and cook well, but she is almost old enough to be his mother."

"That is why I did not believe Jacob at first, but who understands the ways of the heart? I certainly don't!" If she did, she'd be married, living in Philadelphia, and likely with child. But she wasn't the type of woman to encourage a man's attentions either, not with Mama sick and her brothers to feed and clothe in addition to her silversmithing.

"Now the colonel wishes that woman would choose him for herself." The way Regina said it, you'd think she believed that any woman was able to choose her husband, as the native women did. No use in correcting her perception.

"Do you think so?" Magda watched as Dafydd rallied and sent Guy moving backward across the yard, the men cheering.

"Colonel Owens watches her over the tables." Regina pushed back a lock of hair from her forehead. "He wants her for his wife."

Magdalene felt her eyes widening. Indeed, Dafydd had intently studied the Scotswoman over dinner. But he'd looked like he was angry rather than besotted.

The muscles in his jaw had twitched. He'd almost glared at the Scotswoman before sneaking drinks from his flask. Jacob had kept casting his brother sideways glances. Perhaps Dafydd was afraid of being rejected and what looked like anger was really fear. Truly, who could understand men?

"Guillame will let him win because of this." Regina pronounced the words as an edict.

Watching, Magdalene had to agree. Guillame, as an aristocrat Frenchman, was practically born with a sword in his hand yet he continued to retreat, his backward steps bringing him nearer the palisades as Dafydd continued to pursue him. "Guillame is a good man. And a perceptive one."

"Yes, but Father God told me this man was not the one for me."

"Guillame has only recently lost his wife." A woman he'd brought with him to New France. "And their child."

"He has a heaviness in his spirit." When Regina spoke like this, it seemed to reflect the language of her captors.

"Yes."

"Not so with your brother, Franz. He is weighed down by nothing." She smiled, set down her spoon, and reached across to touch Magdalene's hand. "And soon we will be sisters."

Who knew when that would be. They could be attacked any day. They could all be killed. Or abducted like Regina had been.

Another hatchet hit the board with a *thwack*.

The clatter of swords continued until Norbert called down from the tower, "Incoming riders!"

Chapter 7

"I t's Shadrach Clark!" Franz cried from the north tower.

Women ceased chopping vegetables and meat, bowls of dough were set aside, and Magdalene stopped cutting the cornbread. The entire yard went quiet, with the exception of Michi, who called out, "What?"

A better question, the unasked question, was *why?* Magdalene's heart lurched to her throat. The young, and esteemed, scout rarely brought good word. William Christy, Shadrach's closest friend, retrieved his hatchet from the board, his shoulders becoming like hatchet blades too, so stiff they were.

Suddenly Norbert let out a whoop. "And the preacher!"

A cheer went up from beneath the covered work area. Regina pressed her hands to her heart. "Praise God, he is finally here."

Reverend Hite's arrival meant all manner of good things. Magdalene beamed across the table at Regina and then up at Franz in the tower.

Her friend sighed. "Marriages performed by a real pastor."

As her heart beat faster, Magdalene drew in a deep breath. Would one of the marriages be her own? In the midst of this turmoil, there was yet joy.

A shadow passed over Regina's face. "But would Clark bring the minister for only such a purpose?"

Of course not. Magdalene pressed her lips tightly together and watched William Christy pace the yard as the men opened the gates.

"The scout must bring word of something," Regina persisted.

Magdalene should find Papa and have him wake Jacob, whose turn it was to sleep after the night watch. But he needed to rest, especially if Shadrach brought news that would require militia action. "Let's go see."

First through the gates, Reverend Hite was greeted by welcomers, all pushing in on him. The poor man's face was ashen but he smiled and waved.

Once inside, Shadrach passed his horse off to Michi and then offered William a quick embrace, whispering something in his ear. A number of the militia surrounded him as William left the group and headed toward the dwellings.

Magdalene and Regina rushed toward Shadrach. Only in his early twenties, he bore evidence of the many years he'd already served as scout, for such endeavors wreaked havoc on the body. He had recovered from his recent injuries, but his leg seemed to hitch up as he walked, and his features were etched in pain.

Hands cupped around his mouth, Franz called down from the tower. "Have you any word?"

"Let me get a drink before I speak with you." Shadrach loped toward the cider barrel, where Mrs. Davis was pouring two mugs full.

Matthew Ruckman elbowed his son. "Go get Jacob Owens."

But Magdalene grabbed Alexander's sleeve as he passed. "Let him sleep."

The youth broke free and strode on and she shot his father a reprimanding glance.

Shadrach accepted the cider from the wagon master's wife and then quaffed it so quickly Magdalene wasn't sure how he'd managed the feat. He wiped his mouth with his sleeve and then his gaze flickered around to each of them.

Magdalene sensed movement behind her and turned to find William Christy accompanying Jacob, who had dark circles under his eyes. His sleep tunic billowed around him and was almost as long as the breeches he wore.

Reaching her, Jacob leaned in and wrapped a warm hand around her arm. "Shad told William that Colonel Christy and his men might arrive soon to render any needed assistance."

A chill shot down Magdalene's spine. "Is there more trouble anticipated?"

"I'm going to bring Shad into the meeting room to discuss this in private." He released her arm. "Please keep this to yourself for now. I shall find out more."

"What about your brother and his men?" Were they in danger even now?

"They were to have encamped only two nights, near my cabin." His lips twitched. "They are expected back tomorrow night."

"And Colonel Christy and his men—when will they arrive?"

"I don't know." He pulled her into his arms and held her so tenderly, that she forgot about asking any more questions.

Was it wrong to be thinking more of marrying Magda than of how an additional army unit might strain their resources further? Not only that, but if Christy's reported concerns of an impending attack, both from the north and the west, were correct, then who knew what could happen? Still, he wanted to make Magda his wife, and soon. Night had come and gone and the morning was fleeing fast, yet Jacob still hadn't been able to speak to Reverend Hite. He crossed his arms and watched as men, women, and children clustered around the Lutheran pastor.

Matthew Ruckman, relieved from sentry duty, crossed the yard and joined Jacob at the edge of the circle. "Too bad there aren't even benches."

"We could arrange some for a makeshift church assembly, but. . ."

THE *Backcountry* BRIDES COLLECTION

Ruckman nodded. "Aye, we have got other things to plan as well."

Augustine Hite raised his long arms and motioned for the people to move back. With so many baptisms, weddings, and other requests, the man had been kept occupied for all but his sleeping hours. One of the militia members had gotten married up on the watch tower, claiming he wanted his wife to always remember that God was watching over them no matter what. It had made quite a spectacle having the pastor, bride, and groom up there with the witnesses crowded below. Jacob had no intention of making such a show of what should be a reverent and deeply meaningful moment.

Beside Jacob, Matthew huffed a sigh. "I'd better help Hite shake some of his flock off of him." He strode toward the clergyman.

What would Dafydd be doing if he were here now? Shadrach had set off that morning to bring news to him and his men. How the scout got his work done, he didn't know. Wasn't sure he wanted to know. And he certainly didn't wish to dwell on the intense deprivations that Clark and the other scouts like him experienced in the backcountry.

Life was short. Jacob had wasted years that could have been happily spent with Magda as his wife. Regardless of what may or may not come, he didn't want any more days to go by without their vows being said.

Jacob went in search of his sweetheart at the work tables. When he found Magda, he slid onto the bench next to her, so close that his thigh pressed against her heavy linsey-woolsey skirt and he felt the curves beneath. When she gave him a warning glance, he scooted a little farther away, but not too far.

"You shall be gettin' an elbow in your side," Mrs. Davis grumbled from across the table.

"Or worse!" Regina, seated next to the wagon master's wife, raised the sharp knife she was using to slice potatoes.

"Be useful." Magda smiled up at him. "Can you pry open that case of dried apples?" She inclined her head toward a nearby wooden crate.

In a moment, he'd opened the container which held not only dried apples, but also several types of beans. He lifted and displayed a string of apple slices.

"Thank you." Magda rewarded him with a smile and a flash of approval in her pretty blue eyes.

"We're trying to get things prepared ahead." Regina chewed on her lower lip. "Just in case both armies end up in here tonight."

"We need a rest." Mrs. Davis raised a hand to her brow. "But I shall go soak those dried apples in cider. They will make a nice tart for tomorrow."

Regina set her pan of potatoes aside and rose. "I need to lie down for an hour or I won't be able to help serve tonight."

Magda's new friend had just spoken the longest sentence Jacob had heard from her. Had that come from the many nights that Franz had spent courting her? Jacob was responsible for the young man, one of the best shots in his militia. What would happen to this young woman if Franz was killed while they were on one of their forays into the surrounding area? Could she overcome it? He allowed himself to imagine the horror that might come.

Lost in his own thoughts, Jacob hadn't noticed that the other two women at the table had left, until Magda pinched his arm.

"Jacob, you would look mighty good in an apron." She pointed to one folded and set on the end of the table.

"Do you think so?" He reached for it and put it on.

When he turned to face her, an impish grin stole across her face. "Ja, I like a man in an apron."

He laughed. "Didn't I wear one many days at the store?"

"That is the man I fell in love with."

Warmth spread across his chest. "And I like you in an apron too. . .Ladysmith." He bent to kiss her tenderly.

Soon they would be man and wife. When she made a low moan, he deepened the kiss. She tasted of coffee and cinnamon and of a future together and a joy that husbands and wives shared with one another.

He finally pulled away. "Why did you not stay in my shop, Magda?"

"I already told you."

"We cannot blame Michi. You did not listen to your heart, my love."

"I know." She ducked her chin. "But I did not feel that calling from God to stay in Philadelphia, especially with no promises from you."

"But you do want to be my wife?"

"With everything in my heart. You must believe me."

"Do you miss it? Our life in Philadelphia?"

"I do. Every day."

Why, then, were they in this wilderness?

Chapter 8

Dafydd, who had returned with his men that afternoon, paced the narrow floor between their cots, three steps forward, three steps back. "The militia will be needed here. At the fort."

Jacob's ire rose. "But we should come out with you and the armies to fight."

"Let's wait until Colonel Christy and his men arrive and see if he agrees." Dafydd stopped pacing and fixed him with a dark gaze. "Shad said a renegade tribe's attacks on homes farther west and the potential of another group joining them from the south was reported to Christy recently."

He hadn't shared that information with Jacob earlier. Why not? Because this small militia alone couldn't withstand the attacks. "What is the militia to do?"

His brother scowled at him in much the same way he had when he'd helped tutor Jacob in Latin and Jacob had struggled. "You're to protect the people here and. . ."

"And what?"

"Be prepared to make this a hospital for those who return injured."

That was presuming the army prevailed. Jacob knew what would happen if the renegades prevailed. "Yes. We'll make ready."

"Colonel Owens?" Franz's voice carried through the curtain that divided their room from the next.

"Yes?"

"Christy and his men have arrived."

"I shall be right out." Dafydd donned his red field jacket.

That night, the fort was crowded to overflowing. Jacob had barely five minutes alone with Magda. The two stole off to a bench pressed against the palisades. He took her hand in his. "I don't know why we're here, Magda."

"Everyone has spoken of the beauty of the blue mountains."

The Palatinate community in Philadelphia certainly had. Every week, German-speaking people had come through his shop, all looking for items they might wish to take southwest with them. And even though they worried that they'd not have the comforts of the city, all had expressed a desire to live in the fresh, clean air, to be in the lovely mountains, and to own large lots of land. But so too had Jacob overheard others speaking of how the Virginians along the coast, the gentry and merchants, were happy to offer cheap land to these newcomers because it meant putting a human hedge between themselves and the Indians.

Magda squeezed his hand. "So many of the people are freed from indenture and want to start a new life—like my brothers. They want to own land, to grow crops to feed their families, to even have a family."

His dream had been to follow her. To ultimately join his brother in their forge. But what would happen to their plans now? He wrapped his arm around Magda and pulled her close. They watched as several couples danced while William Christy played his fiddle. Nearby, men from both armies played card games. What would the next few nights look like inside this fort?

After sunrise the next morning, the two army units went out in silence. Jacob and his brother had exchanged one of their rare embraces. Dafydd had surprised him by the intensity of his hug and by clapping him on the back as he left.

Tasked with manning the fort, the militia waited, but with each day's passing the men grew more restless. Each evening, Jacob paced the courtyard.

On the fourth night after the armies' departure, Mrs. Davis approached him and pressed a cup of cider into his hands. "You need to get some sleep, Jacob."

He hadn't slept soundly since the armies left. "When Dafydd's unit returns."

"Then you think you shall rest?" A furrow formed between her eyes.

"Perhaps." Birds sang their evensong but Jacob couldn't relax. Come the morrow, he'd rally some of his men and head out. The rest would remain to guard the fort.

Alexander Ruckman crossed the yard from where he was throwing his hatchet. He squared off with Jacob, eyes challenging. "Why does William Christy, who is but a year older than I am, get to go off on scouting missions while I am shut up in here?"

Jacob huffed a sigh. "For one thing, I am not your father. I suggest you speak to him."

"But you know how Pa feels."

"Indeed I do, but it is him you must persuade, not me." Jacob ran this thumb beneath his jaw, considering. "But you might wish to know this fact. Young William grew up with the Shawnee for a portion of his life."

The youth's eyebrows rose. "So it's true then, what they say."

"Yes. And he knows the countryside like the back of his hand." Jacob grasped Alexander's shoulders. Soon enough he would indeed be a man. And would have to do what was required of him. "William is already a seasoned scout, yet he almost died from his recent injuries."

Alexander hung his head and Jacob released his shoulders.

"If it's any encouragement to you, lad, you're one of the best shots I've seen." Almost as good as Jacob himself.

"Really?"

"Yes. And I am counting on you to help if those savages breach our palisades."

"Yes sir." The youth grinned, but then his eyebrows tugged together and his Adam's apple bobbed as he swallowed. "Do you think that might happen?"

If he wasn't so tired, Jacob would have barked out a laugh. The folly of youth, thinking they were invincible, yet when faced with the possibility of attack they had their sense of reality adjusted.

"Ho the fort!" The call echoed over the fort's walls.

"Can you see them?" Jacob called up to Norbert, who startled awake. Jacob hurried up the ladder.

He narrowed his eyes, scanning the horizon, as the call repeated, "Ho the fort!"

The fast-approaching dun was Guillame's mount. Attired in fringed buckskin shirt and trousers, the man almost faded into his horse.

"It's Richelieu, let him in!" Jacob called out.

His future brother-in-law shook his head. "I'm sorry. I fell asleep."

"What if the rider wasn't a friend?"

"I will be more vigilant."

"I shall put a more rested man on the tower. Come on down."

The two men descended and Jacob called Alexander over. "Can you take the watch tower for a while?"

"Yes sir!"

Guillame brought his horses to the water trough. From the shine on the dun's coat, the mare had been ridden hard.

"What did you see?"

"Du mouvement partout." Guillame whistled loudly and Clovis bounded toward him. "There is movement everywhere."

"If the armies have not returned here by morning, we'll need to go out to search for them."

"My French army friends continue to stir the Indians to attack the settlers." Guillame shook his head. "This will be my last mission. I have a bad feeling about this situation. Please pray for safety. And be prepared."

Hours later, at daybreak, a rooster crowed in the yard. Not that Jacob needed waking, for he'd not slept. He'd relieved each man, in turn, on the towers. The yard came to life, chickens scratching at the dirt, women gathering up eggs, and a group of his men already arming themselves to leave the fort.

The Frenchman emerged from nearby quarters. He adjusted the hatchet in his belt and sheathed his knife before stepping to a table strewn with rifles and selecting his own weapon. He strapped his rifle across his chest.

Jacob stated the obvious fact. "They've still not arrived."

"True."

Sick in his heart, Jacob knew what must be done, as discussed with the men the previous night.

Jacob made a circular motion to include himself and half of his militia. "We'll head south."

Guillame nodded. "Leave men to surround the fort as well."

Some of the men assembled in the courtyard kissed their wives and children goodbye. He'd told Magda to sleep, but there she came, a shawl wrapped around her shoulders. He opened his arms for her. As he embraced her, he felt her tremble. He bent and kissed her. Would he kiss his precious Magda again? Prickles ran up Jacob's spine. He broke away, stepping back to take her in. She was so lovely even with her hair mussed and covered by her mother's old black shawl. "I will see you soon, my beloved."

Magda nodded, a tear trickling down her cheek. He wiped it away and then wrapped his arm around her.

Nearby, extra kettles of water boiled over the fire causing a sizzling sound and sending up smoke. When Mr. and Mrs. Davis emerged from their chambers, arms stacked high with folded sheets, he knew the tension was felt by all. Those sheets might end up torn into bandages. Would the militia return? If so, in what condition? *Dear God, help us now.*

The hours passed slowly that morning. Magdalene had checked in every cabin for extra blankets, bedding, pillows, and planks to help assemble cots if needed for surgery.

Mrs. Davis had tallied up all foodstuffs that would be needed to make a nourishing broth if the men returned injured. If they returned at all. Magdalene wouldn't allow herself to imagine never seeing them again. Or worse yet, coming upon their ravaged bodies, as Regina had to witness. How did her friend cope with her memories? Why had God brought them here?

Let God hear our prayers as the men face danger.

Suddenly, the bell's incessant ringing echoed in Magdalene's ears. Nearby, Papa assisted Mama up from where she sat tearing clean sheets into strips of cloth for bandages.

Mama came to her and pressed a hand to her shoulder. "No matter what, my Tochter, you must be strong."

Had Jacob and she finally been at the precipice of a new life, only to have that future snatched away? What kind of God could allow such a thing? Such agony? *Lord, forgive me. Lord, help them. Lord, be with us through this all.*

"Let's pray." Mama bowed her head. Her heartfelt prayer, spoken in German, went beyond that which Magdalene had offered up. But she knew, in her soul, that God heard even the unspoken requests.

Alexander called down from the tower. "Injured men!"

Magdalene wiped her hands on her apron and rose, her breath sticking in her throat. Regina ran past her and scampered up the ladder so nimbly that it startled Magdalene. Would the woman be keening in a moment, as she said Native women did when a loved one died?

Jacob, oh God, let Jacob be fine.

Nervous energy surged through the crowd gathered in the courtyard as all ceased their work. Even the ever-present sound of hatchet on wood stopped. Magdalene heard her heart beating in her ears. *Oh God, ever present provider, You put who You need here. Help us.* The sense of being part of something bigger, a future, suddenly opened to her, and a shiver coursed from the top of her head to her toes. They were the beginning of something much larger than simply settlers forted in the Shenandoah Valley. Would she and Jacob be part of that future?

The first entrant inside the fort was Clovis, and the dog charged at Magdalene, but she made him stop and sit. To reward him, she snatched a bone from the soup pile and tossed it to him. Taking it in his mouth, he slumped at her feet as Guillame dismounted.

"*Préparez-vous!*"

Mama gave instructions to the women, who quickly set off arranging cots and covering them with sheets.

Magdalene caught Michi's eye as he milled near the edge of the crowd at the open gates. "Wake the physician!"

She thought she caught sight of Jacob. But when Magdalene couldn't get a clear view, she stood on her bench, relief coursing through her when she spotted him upright, until she recognized that he stumbled under the weight of carrying his brother, a gash ripped through Dafydd's red coat, blood seeping onto the jacket. Did his chest even rise and fall? Was he dead?

Jacob mustered a tentative smile for his sweet Magda as she wiped sweat from his brow. "You're a good nurse."

"I'd say you're a good doctor." She arched an eyebrow at him.

"I'm no physician." And who knew if his efforts would be enough to save his brother?

"But you do know how to sew."

Nearby, Mrs. Sehler patiently stitched up Franz's arm wound. The scent of sulphur, calomel, and brandy filled the air. Amazing how much liquor had been hidden beneath the beds. "Your mother is a talented stitcher."

"I'm sure her hands must be hurting her, but God gives her strength."

And God had given Jacob almost supernatural strength to carry men off the fields after the attack. When he'd lifted his brother from the ground, it was as though another hand had given him assistance, yet there was no one near him.

He handed Magdalene a blood-soaked rag, and she threw it in a communal pail. Groans were met with a sip of whiskey from Dafydd's flask. "I never thought the sound of moaning could be so good." But it meant his brother yet lived. Nor had he welcomed the sight of his brother's flask until now.

"Musical, isn't it?" Magda smiled.

"Not quite, but welcome." He paused midstitch when Dafydd's closed eyelids twitched. He patted his brother's arm. "You've lost a lot of blood, but it is staunched now."

"How's the hot water holding up?" His brother croaked out the words.

"Not your concern, Colonel Owens." Magdalene lifted Dafydd's head and gave him another sip of whiskey. "Michi is in charge of that, and he has continuously hauled hot water in here."

Hours later, Dr. Potter's baritone voice boomed out, "Everyone leave your stations for a respite. We have women who will watch the men."

Regina, eyes filled with tears, moved in quickly to replace Mrs. Sehler, who was mopping Franz's brow.

The surgeon joined Jacob and Magda. "You two are a good team."

"We have been working together a long time." Jacob smiled at his beloved. Here they were, bloodstained, reeking of sweat, and hovering over his brother, whose recovery was yet unknown. They had done all they could.

"Your brother would surely have died had you not repaired his wound." Dr. Potter lifted the bandage and examined Jacob's neat rows of stitches. "I daren't contemplate what would have happened to many of these men were it not for your quickness with a needle."

Moisture clouded Jacob's vision and he blinked it back. Was the surgeon correct? Had he not been there, would his brother have perished? Only God knew. Jacob had simply obeyed Him when the Lord had urged him on to the Shenandoah Valley.

Epilogue

Jacob cast a sideways glance at his sweet Magda as she settled onto the padded armchair in what was now their home. He bent in and kissed her, the aroma of cinnamon and apples sweetly scenting the cabin. He pulled back and took her face between his hands, her deep-blue eyes full of love. "My beautiful bride."

"My handsome husband." She stroked the side of his jaw and then turned her mouth to kiss his hand, her lips leaving an imprint of warmth.

"Can you believe we're finally home?"

"No. It's so quiet here."

Outside the window, the Ruckman boys shrieked in merriment as they chased each other on the green as though nothing had ever happened. But their father would never walk without a limp again. Laughter continued as Alexander caught his brother and removed his hat, tossing it into the air.

"Maybe not so quiet after all?" Jacob chuckled and straightened. "And it's time for the gift I promised you."

"And I have something for you." Magda's husky voice gave him pause.

"My older brother brought me the first fireback made in his forge." Jacob retrieved the crate, set near the fire. "I believe this was meant for me and my bride."

He removed the heavy piece from the crate and unwrapped it. He brought it to Magda, who sat near the window. The Owens family crest, two lions roaring at each other over a rose entwined with a wreath of thorns, gleamed in the midday sun.

Magda ran a finger over the rose garland. "Seems like this is a gift from Llywellyn, not you." Her voice held a tease.

"Is that so?" He bent and kissed her forehead and then set the piece angled on the floor, propped against her chair.

She fished in her pocket before pulling out a silver tablespoon. He recognized it. "It's from my shop."

"Yes, but I paid for it." She cocked her head and handed it to him, the silver warm beneath his fingers.

He turned the utensil over, lettering visible on the back. "Magdalene and Jacob?"

"Yes." She had to have made this before they'd left Philadelphia.

"It's beautiful." He kissed her again, this time more thoroughly and with promise.

She pulled away. "Can you see yourself working in an iron forge?"

"I don't know." He knelt by her. "I do know that every night in Fort Holman, I struggled with the desire to grab you, marry you, and carry you off to Philadelphia."

"There's no guarantee you could've gotten us to Pennsylvania safely." She stroked the side of his cheek. "And you had the militia to think of."

"All I knew for sure then was that we should marry and let God direct our path." He pressed a kiss to his precious wife's hand.

Magda's smile promised a future joined in love. "One road, not two."

"Yes. Our Shenandoah hearts together, forever."

ECPA-bestselling author **Carrie Fancett Pagels**, PhD, is the award-winning author of over a dozen Christian historical romances. Twenty-five years as a psychologist didn't "cure" her overactive imagination! A self-professed "history geek," she resides with her family in the Historic Triangle of Virginia but grew up as a "Yooper" in Michigan's Upper Peninsula. Carrie loves to read, bake, bead, and travel—but not all at the same time! You can connect with her at www.CarrieFancettPagels.com.

Heart of Nantahala

by Jennifer Hudson Taylor

Chapter 1

North Carolina Colony
1757

J oseph Gregory had not yet met her, and already the woman was driving him to distraction. Why would Miss Mabel Walker want to hold on to a wilderness of timber and a sawmill full of dangerous equipment, not to mention the responsibility of all the men who had been under her late brother's employ?

He tilted the letter at an angle to make use of the sunlight through the window behind him. The smell of sawdust drifted through the air and the swadust swirled in the sun's rays from the back of the building where his men worked. Sounds of sawing wood and men's muffled voices floated in the atmosphere. Satisfaction swelled in his chest.

Joe recognized a hint of an apology in his best friend's letter. While Gerald promised he would not return until he secured Miss Walker's agreement to sell, Joe sensed his friend's waning doubt that he would succeed.

Running his forefinger and thumb across his tired eyes, pinching the bridge of his nose, Joe considered his next steps. Something had to be done. He sighed in frustration, unable to understand what drove the woman to such a drastic decision. Perhaps he could find a way to address her concerns, if he could get to know her.

"What do you intend to do?" Ron Johnson broke Joe's concentration from where he sat in a chair across from him. Muscles bulged in Ron's arms and legs, a tall frame that enabled him to tackle large trees and bring them down. He wrinkled his gray hat in his big hands and watched Joe with an intense gaze. "I came straight away to bring you the letter once I saw it was from Gerald. I knew you would want to know what it said." He gulped and raised a brown eyebrow. "Was he able to do what I could not? Did he convince her to sell?"

"Unfortunately, no." Joe shook his head and sat back in his wooden chair, dropping the letter on his desk. He linked his fingers over his middle and considered his options. "I daresay the woman is stubborn. You spent a fortnight trying to convince her to sell and now Gerald has spent another fortnight, and still she refuses."

"Indeed, Miss Walker is unlike any woman I have met. No doubt, she would have made some lucky husband proud—had she married." A fond expression crossed Ron's face with a reminiscing grin.

"Your admiration is perplexing to me." Joe raised an eyebrow, still assessing his friend's behavior. "Especially considering how much trouble she is causing. I need to expand the business if we are going to continue meeting the demand for lumber. New colonists arrive each week, and the first thing they want to build are homes."

"Be assured, I remain loyal to you, sir." Ron met his gaze and leaned forward as he twisted his hat. " 'Tis hard to explain." He gulped and straightened in his seat. "Miss Walker is a higher level of grit. How many women do you know determined to run a group of loggers and a sawmill full of dangerous equipment in the backwoods mountains next to the Cherokee?" Ron lifted a finger and pointed at Joe. "Miss Walker has gumption. 'Tis unfortunate she chose the life of a spinster despite all the would-be suitors determined to call upon her."

"As long as she is determined to hang on to five hundred acres of good timber with a feasible sawmill full of valuable equipment, the suitors will keep coming. It would not matter if she were eighty years old with thinning white hair and no teeth." Joe touched the top of his own head for emphasis. "Greed and opportunity comes in many disguises."

Ron chuckled, relaxed back in his chair, and stopped twisting his hat. "While 'tis true she is the older sister, I do believe she still has all her teeth." He shook his head with a humorous grin.

"So she is fairly tolerable, is she?" Joe leaned forward, pulled out a piece of paper, and reached for his quill. He dipped it in a container of black ink. "My mind is made up. I need to act swiftly before she weds and all her property reverts to her new husband. Miss Walker has left me no choice." Joe wrote out his brother's name in broad strokes. "I need you to carry this letter to Charlie. I am instructing him to take over the sawmill in my absence. Tomorrow morning I will travel to Nantahala myself to deal with Miss Walker. I intend to convince her that it is in her best interest to sell to me."

"Please forgive me, sir, but how will you convince her? Gerald and I have both done all that we could short of trying to marry her ourselves—" He stopped speaking as his eyes widened. "Is that it? Do you intend to woo and marry her yourself?"

"Of course not." Joe stopped writing long enough to give Ron a daring glare. "Do not be absurd. I intend to make her an offer she will not likely be able to refuse unless she is completely daft. You and Gerald were limited to the terms I gave you. By negotiating the deal myself, I can better determine what may change her mind."

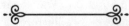

Mabel Walker stood in front of her brother's headstone and breathed in the sweet aroma of the purple and blue pansies she had planted over his grave. The early morning dew carried the fresh scent stronger than any other part of the day, and it was her favorite time to come out to reminisce and remember how good he had been to her and their younger sister, Bethany. After their parents died of the fever on the voyage from England to the colonies three years ago, Avery had taken care of their every need.

"Lord, why did You take him away from us after You already took Mama and Papa?" She whispered the words as she stared at the carved indentation in the gray stone, AVERY WALKER, BELOVED BROTHER. Several sparrows in the nearby trees sang in the soft breeze caressing her face and neck. Mabel closed her eyes to savor the moment as deep sorrow took root. Had he already been gone a whole month? It didn't seem possible. At least they had a gravestone to mark Avery's time here on earth. They didn't even have that for Mama and Papa. She dropped to her knees and pulled at the new weeds growing around her flowers. While her brother had been indifferent to flowers, he had liked the color blue, so she thought blue pansies would suit his memory best. "Lord, no matter how hard I try, it seems as if You do naught to help me. Even the weeds are defying me."

The sound of an approaching horse caught her attention. She turned to see a lone rider coming up the dirt pathway leading to their white two-story home. Zacharia Edwards, her brother's best friend and foreman, came from the direction of the log cabin he rented from her. It had been her family's home during their first year here and served as a great reminder of the progress they had made.

As Zacharia made his way up the grassy hill toward her, Mabel threw the weeds aside and dusted her hands before standing to greet him. She would be forever grateful for the way he had come to her and Bethany's aid during this difficult time.

He wore a black tricorn hat that shaded his brown eyes but did not hide his concerned expression. His full beard and mustache looked trim. Zach's attire consisted of a white shirt and cravat tied at the neck beneath a dark-green frock coat over brown breeches to the knees. His calves were covered in white stockings that disappeared into a pair of black shoes.

"The moment I saw the sight of you upon this hill at Avery's tombstone, I worried you were weeping in grief again, but I see you are well." Zach dismounted, leading the animal toward her with a smile of relief lighting his eyes. "I am glad of it, for I have witnessed your deepest grief these past few weeks." He tilted his head. "You are wearing blue?"

"Make no mistake, I am still deeply grieved, and I fear 'twill always be so." She folded her hands and lifted her gaze to his. "I ripped the only black gown I have doing chores."

"I pray your heart will heal soon. I dislike seeing you in such pain." He stroked his bearded chin as if considering what to say next. "If I may, I have come to escort you to the sawmill. I heard more suitors will be arriving this day, and I do not believe 'twould be good for you to be alone."

"More?" She covered her mouth and glanced back at Avery's grave. "Will it never end? Why can a woman not remain her own or at least be given time to properly grieve?" She blinked several times to keep the threatening tears away. "None of them know me, yet they all pledge their protection and to care for me." She gritted her teeth with resolve. "We all know they only want the wealth and lands my brother worked to build. I do not matter at all." She breathed in the fresh air and set her jaw at an angle. *Do I even matter to God? If I did, would He have not helped me more?* "Allow me time to saddle my horse. I shall ride out to meet them as the independent woman that I am."

"You may not know these other suitors, but you do know me." Zach dropped the reins to his horse and stepped closer. He reached out and laid a hand on her shoulder while placing a gentle finger under her chin. "I have spent these past few years in fellowship with your family, as your brother's best friend, and in his service. I have been a loyal companion to him in life and to his family upon his death. I know you, and you know me. I want the best for you and Bethany, for the business he and I built together." He laid a hand on her cheek. "In truth, I have come to care for you. Marry me, Mabel. We could build a good life together."

The compassion in his eyes was unmistakable, and she did not doubt his sincerity, but his words were very surprising. If Zach cared for her in that way, why did he not take advantage of it when her brother had openly expressed his blessing and wish? A sinking feeling spiraled in the pit of her stomach. He had not voiced his desire for her before because there would have been no lands or business while her brother lived. She swallowed the bitter thought stinging her insides.

Confusion clouded her mind, bringing on a headache. She brushed her hair to the side and dropped her gaze from his. She and her sister depended on Zach, but she wanted things to stay the same. Was it so wrong to want to keep him on as their foreman? She paid him a salary—the same as her brother had. The only difference was the fact that she needed consultation advice from him, and perhaps for this reason alone she should offer him a raise. Could she afford it? She could not very well ask him for advice regarding his own salary. If she refused to marry him, would he leave them stranded? Mabel had more than herself to think about. She had Bethany's welfare to consider.

"I'm not sure how to interpret your silence." Zach blinked as an expression of disappointment crossed his face, and he dropped his hand from her shoulder.

"Zach, please understand that so much has happened in the past month. I am still in mourning. While I am very grateful to you, right now I need more time to heal." Mabel touched his arm. "I hope you understand."

"Of course." He nodded, covering her hand with his and leading her down the hill with his horse following. "Take all the time you need. I will be right here by your side as I have always been."

Chapter 2

Nantahala was a wilderness filled with miles and miles of forest that could swallow a man up for years. More timber surrounded Joe than he could conjure in a dream. He followed the sounds of the river, hoping to reach the sawmill within the hour. He had been told at Skinner's Trading Post that Avery Walker had built his sawmill right on the river—just follow it up the mountain.

Joe guided his horse around a bend and pushed several branches aside to protect his face and neck. The rush of running water skipping over rocks and falling limbs danced to the sounds of birds above and other wildlife nearby. Reflecting on the Cherokee he had met at the trading post, Joe hoped any encounters out here in the wilderness would prove to be just as friendly. The two Cherokee men he had met spoke broken English and were very cordial in giving him directions. They seemed to have known Avery Walker and thought highly of him.

His mind drifted to Miss Mabel Walker. He imagined her to be a middle-aged spinster who had come to enjoy her independence, stern and strict, much like a bluestocking who insisted on meddling in things that should not concern her. It was the only explanation he could figure why the stubborn woman refused a sensible marriage and unburdening herself of her brother's business. Most young women he had known of marriageable age were obsessed with securing their future with a husband. This woman's actions made no sense—unless she had become a middle-aged spinster.

The echo of falling water intensified into rapids, reminding him of a waterfall. The noise grew louder until Joe broke free of the woods. A red building on a rock foundation emerged through the trees. Several horses were tied to a post outside. The morning sun shimmered on the surface of the water as it fell over the edge of a man-made dam into a pool where a nearby red wheel attached to the building churned through the water. The two trees on the right held a hint of orange facing the sun, but the rest of the tree remained green. Joe had seen several trees like them—a sign that the end of September had come and the cool fall would soon be upon them.

As he approached, sounds of sawing echoed through the windows, along with men's voices carrying conversations. Joe dismounted and secured his horse next to the others. He walked over the cobbled pathway to the front and climbed the stone steps where he paused to read a wooden sign above the door on a black iron chain. In red letters it said, NANTAHALA LUMBER MILL—a fitting name. Joe smiled. He had finally found the place.

Stretching out his hand, he pushed open the door. It may have creaked, but he could not have heard it with all the noise on the other side. A mule attached to a pulley moved in a circle to keep the waterwheel outside going. It ground a sharp blade through the center of a log with a single-sash saw. A man shoved the two halves down the long table, while another man replaced it with a new log. Two other men were in a back corner, sawing through a piece of oak with a pit saw. Others unloaded a wagon from the back door and stacked the logs along the side wall under an open window.

Voices carried from above, and Joe looked up to see a loft where three men were in conversation. He could only view the partial outline of the third man. Joe blinked the sawdust out of his eyes, but the scent brought a welcome appreciation and reminded him of his own sawmill back home. He climbed the steps to the loft where he hoped he could make a swift business deal.

"When do we anticipate his arrival?" A woman's smooth but sure voice broke through the background noise. Joe couldn't see her on the other side of the men, but a blue skirt filtered through them. "He is the third one this week. Do we know where he hails from? Perhaps we could send him a message and save him a journey."

"I am afraid it may be too late," one of the men said. "His letter arrived a sennight ago, so I would imagine he is already on his way."

Joe stepped on the landing and cleared his throat to let them know they were no longer alone. All eyes focused on him. He strode forward. "I apologize for the intrusion, but I have traveled a long way to see Miss Mabel Walker for an important business proposal."

"Is she expecting you?" One of the men turned with an unfriendly scowl as he crossed his arms over his chest and glared at Joe. "Any business dealings need to be made with me. I'm Zacharia Edwards, the foreman here at Nantahala Lumber Mill."

"Joe? What are you doing here?" Gerald stepped around the fellow and came toward him. He had an uncertain grin, but his brown eyes brightened with surprise and sincere warmth. A few strands of blond hair fell on his forehead with a visible line of sweat. " 'Twould have been nice to know you were coming."

"I am Mabel Walker," the woman said, breaking through Joe's thoughts before he could answer. She stepped around the other men, her brown hair piled high upon her head with pearl pins. Intense blue eyes assessed him as her gaze traveled down to his brown shoes and back up to meet his eyes again. Her expression didn't waver as a slight smile curled her lips. Intrigued, Joe wondered what amused her.

Miss Walker's smooth skin showed her age to be much younger than he had thought. She was no spinster in the making—at least not yet. This new turn of events put a spin on things. Intelligence lurked behind her eyes. If she were a man, he would know exactly what to say, but since she was a woman, Joe feared he might be out of his depth. Women had no place in business decisions. How was he to deal with her?

He took a deep breath and tried to regroup his thoughts. Too many men were trying to court her. She wouldn't trust him if he joined their rank. Yet Ron and Gerald were not making any progress with a direct approach either. The only way he could change things would be to figure her out. In order to do that, he had to find a way to stay around long enough to get to know her.

"So you have an interesting business proposal?" She walked toward him, meeting his gaze and folding her hands in front of her. "Let us hear it, but I warn you, Mr. Gregory, I may not be in favor of it."

"You may call me Joe."

"No, thank you, Mr. Gregory." She straightened her shoulders and lifted her chin. "As I was saying, do not make the same mistake as so many others. I do not consider a marriage proposal the same thing as a business proposal, nor do I intend to sell what my brother worked so hard to build from scratch. I shan't tarnish his memory that way."

"Even if the offer is so generous that you and your sister could lead comfortable, independent lives into your old age?" She blinked and something in her expression shifted. He needed to know what had caused her to consider his words. Was it the mention of her sister, or the enticement of a comfortable life? "I am quite aware that many women enter into marriage agreements out of necessity. My offer would secure your freedom from that need. An offer of marriage would shackle me as well, so I am not inclined to consider it."

"I take it the two of you know each other?" She stepped back and gestured to Gerald.

"Indeed, Joe is my boss. He owns the company where I work," Gerald said. "'Tis on his behalf I have been negotiating the purchase of your business."

"Ah, I see." She folded her arms and tapped a finger against her chin. "And, Mr. Gregory, what offer do you intend to make that your previous employees were unable to?"

For weeks Mabel had been hearing the praises of Mr. Gregory from Gerald Newman. Now that the man stood in the flesh before her, she couldn't determine if she too should be impressed or disappointed. So far, she could only go by his appearance and a few spoken words.

His green eyes held a depth of color similar to the leaf of a southern magnolia tree—dark and smoldering with what she imagined was a determined and passionate nature. He wore a black felt tricorn hat with gold trim. His silk and velvet coat consisted of a bright salmon color with gold thread trim and embroidery. The waistcoat beneath the outer layer matched, with gold buttons and fall-front breeches with silk twill.

A white cravat hid his neck and white sleeves bloomed from his coat at the wrists. She glanced down at his hosed legs and determined by his muscled calves that he must have put in long hours at his sawmill. Good. That meant the man wasn't lazy and joined in the labor he expected of his men. Avery had taught her to take the true measure of a man by his work ethic. Perhaps all that Mr. Newman had told her about Mr. Gregory was true.

"Mr. Gregory, I believe you have a proposal you would like to offer?" Mabel lifted an eyebrow and waited for a response. She needed to stay focused and not allow herself to be distracted, no matter how handsome Mr. Gregory appeared.

"As you are well aware, I own a small sawmill in the Bethabara area, but I would like to expand my operations by investing in land rich with timber. This will allow me to be less dependent upon coastal lumber companies who keep increasing prices due to high demand for lumber in England. I believe a prospering business such as the one your late brother built will be worth more than the number of years 'twould require of me to build on my own."

Mabel nodded. "That sounds quite logical." She tilted her head to better assess him. "But how would this new knowledge convince me to sell? Why would I?" She took a deep breath and swallowed the gathering lump that always gathered in the back of her throat when she thought of Avery. "I may be a woman, but my brother left everything to me in his last will and testament. He trusted me. In no way do I intend to be careless with the gift of trust he gave me."

"Based on the fact that you have rejected both offers from Ron Johnson and Gerald on my behalf, I imagine this is about more than the money. I suppose you and your brother were very close, and the business is not only a responsibility, but a legacy for your family."

"True, so you see, any offer you could make would be useless. I shall never accept it."

"You wish to be independent so that you needn't commit yourself to an advantageous marriage out of necessity if the business begins to fail in the future." His green eyes searched hers as the meaning of his words sunk deep into her heart.

" 'Tis true. I do not wish to commit myself to a lifelong marriage with someone I hardly know in order to save my sister and myself from destitution."

" 'Twould hardly be necessary," Zach said. "As long as I am foreman, I shall see that the business runs smoothly so that you and Bethany will have what you need."

"Or I can offer you fifteen thousand pounds for the Nantahala Lumber Mill. You would retain the fifteen acres that includes the home where you currently reside, as well as the log cabin that I have been told you rent out." Mr. Gregory stepped forward. "This offer is five thousand pounds more than the previous offer Gerald made on my behalf, as well as including the home and the fifteen acres. You and your sister will want for naught, and there would be no need to marry unless you desire it."

Chapter 3

Joe stepped out onto the front porch of the mill and waited as Gerald closed the door. A slight breeze stirred, brushing the leaves and tree branches together. Puffy white clouds floated across the blue sky. The waterfall poured at a steady pace with the waterwheel in a consistent rhythm.

"I would like you to take me up the mountain to see the loggers." Joe glanced over his shoulder at Gerald coming up behind him. "I need to see how they set up camp and observe how they cut down trees. Have you had a chance to document their process and equipment?"

"Not at the logging camp." Gerald moved down the steps toward the horses. "I made a few notations regarding the work inside the lumber mill, but I have to be discreet. I'm afraid they are beginning to grow weary of me."

"Of course. Now that I have met Miss Walker, she is not at all how you and Ron described her," Joe said while untying his horse.

"Is that so?" Gerald tilted his head and lifted an eyebrow. "Remind me how I described her?" He mounted his brown mare and leaned his hand on the saddle pommel.

" 'Tis what you did not say." Joe slipped his foot into the stirrup and mounted up. He leaned forward, rubbing the animal's neck to calm his restless prancing. "You neglected to tell me of her beauty, young age, and sharp wit. She is no middle-aged spinster. 'Twas quite a surprise."

"A pleasant surprise, I would wager?" Gerald chuckled, nudging his horse to Joe's left. "Women are rare in these mountains, but to find one who is comely with good sense and courage—that is more like a jewel. She is quite dedicated to her faith. Since she took over, three more loggers are attending church. Miss Walker has a way with words that can be quite persuasive."

Gerald eased his horse around the building and stayed by the river's edge as they climbed the gradual incline up the mountain. Joe followed his lead and listened to his friend's chatter as images of Miss Walker played through his mind. Her blue dress brought out her elegant blue eyes to perfection, reminding him of the blooming royal empress trees on his parents' farm in the spring.

"Your business proposal brought relief to Miss Walker. She feared another matrimonial proposal." Gerald shook his blond head with a good-humored grin. "I witnessed four such proposals in the last fortnight. Last week, I heard her say she may never know a sincere proposal without a greedy motive."

"That is unfortunate," Joe said, feeling an unexpected surge of anger on her behalf. Memories of all the parents who introduced him to their daughters for the same purpose sifted through his thoughts. Each time he felt like he walked into a trap, and he couldn't understand why they would not let things progress naturally. Their manipulations ruined any prospective feelings he might have had toward their daughters.

"I admit, I enjoyed meeting Miss Walker. She seems levelheaded, and I do not blame her for rejecting all those fake proposals. Matchmaking is a sorry business. Parents should stay out of it, no matter their good intentions."

"Is that why you have not settled down yourself?" Gerald asked.

"In part. Marriage is a lifelong commitment, and only a fool would rush into it." Joe sighed. "I have yet to meet the right woman."

White canopy tents were assembled among a forest of pine trees. It reminded Joe of the militia tents he had seen as a result of the French and Indian War still raging in parts of the colonies. With the Nantahala Lumber Mill so close to the Cherokee, he feared for Miss Walker's safety if the tribe decided to support the French.

As they passed the tents, they heard sounds of axes hammering against tree trunks and men yelling warning calls. First they removed branches as they climbed to the top of a tree. Once the limbs were gone, they worked on chopping the trunk to the ground.

The timber looked healthy and there was plenty of it. If Miss Walker refused to sell the business, perhaps he could take advantage of a partnership by purchasing better timber for reduced prices. He imagined with his offer, she would be less interested in the cost of transporting her lumber to the coast and competing with high market prices in exportation to England.

A tall man walked toward them. He folded his muscular arms as his dark eyes assessed them. Curly red hair protruded from beneath his gray cap. His formidable frown glared through his thick red mustache and beard. "Are you two new? Did Miss Walker or Zacharia Edwards send you up 'ere?"

Gerald's jaw visibly tensed as he cast a nervous glance at Joe.

"Not exactly," Joe said, meeting the man's gaze. "We first stopped at the lumber mill. My name is Joseph Gregory and this is my foreman, Gerald Newman." Joe nodded toward Gerald. "I own a sawmill east of here. I made a purchase offer to Miss Walker. I'm interested in expanding my operations."

"Did she accept?" The man stroked his beard, glancing from Joe to Gerald in hesitation.

"She has not yet refused," Joe said. "I wanted to get a look at what I have offered to buy and confirm what I have heard about the business. Are you running things? What is your name?"

"I'm Adam Birch. Zach runs things, but I oversee the loggers up here. He spends more time at the lumber mill with Miss Walker."

"How does it feel to be working for a woman? Do the men seem to mind it?" Joe leaned forward with interest.

"None of us like it. 'Tisn't natural." Adam's dark eyes narrowed, and his lips thinned beneath his mustache. "We keep hangin' on, hopin' she might be holding out for a proposal from Zach. 'Twould be the right thing to do. Zach was her brother's best friend and knows the business better than anyone."

"Has Zach asked her?" Joe disliked how Adam insinuated that Miss Walker owed something to Zach.

"If not, he is probably giving her time to grieve." Adam adjusted his cap. "With all the proposals she has received, Zach should act soon before someone catches her affection or winter comes. Cold weather can be hard here in the mountains. Miss Walker and her sister will need help and protection."

"What have been your biggest challenges up here besides winter?" Joe asked.

"Sir, I mean no insult, but unless Miss Walker accepts your offer, I reckon I have said enough."

"Much obliged." Joe nodded and turned his horse. "Where to next?" he asked Gerald.

"I shall take you to Miss Walker's house." Gerald nodded in the direction they had come.

"Why?" Joe tried to ignore the quickening of his pulse at the idea of seeing Miss Walker so soon again.

"She felt sorry for me living out of a tent and offered to rent out one of the extra chambers at the Walker House," Gerald said. "We can ask to rent the other empty chamber for you."

"Lead the way." Joe smiled, realizing how convenient this could be for his plans.

Mabel slowed her horse outside the white church, which also served as a school. The pastor's wife, Mrs. Fern Leland, taught class here. The hot afternoon sun bore down on Mabel as sticky sweat layered her skin against the fabric of her linen blouse. On days like this, she longed for the cool of autumn. Her stomach swirled with excitement now that some of the tree leaves transformed into shades of yellow and orange. If only it would stay fall and not turn into a harsh winter.

The sound of female giggles broke through Mabel's thoughts. Bethany sat on the front steps with her best friend, Esther Leland, the pastor's middle daughter. A rock propped open the front door to the church, no doubt to allow for a slight breeze to pass through.

"There you are." Bethany shaded her blue eyes to look up at Mabel. "I was beginning to wonder if I should go home with Esther."

"Please?" Esther smiled up at Mabel with hope in her bright-blue eyes as red curls hugged her face. She and Bethany were the same age at ten and five, but when together they could be quite mischievous. "Bethany has not stayed with us in ages."

Mabel's heart sank at the reminder that Bethany had not stayed with her friend since Avery's death. Guilt pierced her heart.

"Maybe another time, Esther. I do not wish to leave Mabel alone all night just yet." Bethany touched her friend's shoulder as she stood. "We need more time." She picked up a set of books on the step behind her.

" 'Tis disappointing, but I understand," Esther said in a sad tone. "I cannot imagine what you both have endured. Our family is still praying for you."

Bethany handed her books up to Mabel so she could mount up behind her. Mabel dropped the books in a bag hanging from the saddle. She waited until Bethany's hands were secured around her waist before nudging the horse forward.

"Thank you," Mabel said. "See you tomorrow, Esther."

" 'Bye!" Bethany waved. She squeezed Mabel's waist. "How many marriage proposals did you get today?"

"Let me see, one marriage proposal, and one business proposal." Mabel adjusted the reins in her hands and turned them onto the familiar dirt road to home.

"You rejected both, I hope," Bethany said. "Was the marriage proposal from anyone we know?"

"Of course not. He was another fortune hunter who heard about Avery's demise and thought he would come calling. Zach helped me get rid of him." Thoughts of Zach's proposal from this morning came to mind. "Come to think of it, I actually received two marriage proposals, one from someone we know very well."

"Who?" Bethany shifted, her voice full of curiosity and skepticism. "You rejected him too, I hope."

"You are beginning to sound as if you never want me to wed." Mabel smiled, glancing over her shoulder to see her sister's disturbing frown. "I told you, when I wed, you go where I go. I shall never leave you, and that is a promise I intend to keep."

"I believe you, but I also know that when you wed, everything you own will become your husband's property including our home. 'Twould be best to not marry at all." Bethany tapped her on the arm. "Who proposed?"

"Zach."

Silence lengthened between them. Mabel gave Bethany more time to process the news as they climbed another hill. Their white house came into view. The familiar site always filled Mabel with a mixture of comfort and relief. She hoped Blue Bell had cooked up an enticing meal. Hunger pains gnawed at her stomach.

As they grew closer, Mabel could see two men outside on the front porch rocking in her white wooden chairs on the left side of the steps. The other two rocking chairs on the right remained empty.

"Good afternoon, ladies," Mr. Newman said with a nod.

"Who is that?" Bethany asked, pointing at Mr. Gregory. "Is he the other one that proposed this morning?"

"No, he is Mr. Newman's boss, Mr. Joseph Gregory. He offered to buy the company." Mabel assisted Bethany with dismounting and handed her the saddlebag before dismounting as well. "Mr. Gregory, this is my sister, Bethany." Mabel nodded toward her sister. "Bethany, take the horse to the stables while I deal with our unexpected guests."

"Mr. Newman is not unexpected. You rented a chamber to him." Bethany's dry tone would have annoyed Mabel at any other time, but now Mabel realized she may have made a mistake in providing the man a chamber. Bethany took the reins with reluctance. "Please do not rent out *my* chamber to anyone."

"Bethany, go." Mabel pointed toward the stables a short distance from the house. Mabel walked up the gray wooden steps and paused by the men. "Mr. Newman, it appears you have brought us an unexpected guest. Even though I offered you a room for rent, I hope you understand that this is our home and not a boardinghouse."

"I do, Miss Walker, and I apologize for the inconvenience. There is not an inn within a three days' ride. I did not know what else to do. Mr. Gregory is my boss. The proper thing is to give up my chamber to him."

"That is not agreeable." She glared at Mr. Newman. "I rented that room to you and my agreement is with you." She turned to Mr. Gregory, placing her hands on her hips. "As for you, I suppose you must have someplace to sleep. Consider it my Christian charity. I shall rent out a cot to you in the attic for the same price Mr. Newman is paying."

"The attic? I thought you had another chamber," Mr. Newman said, giving Mr. Gregory a nervous look. "Surely the cot would be more suitable for me since he is four inches taller than me."

"Gerald, 'tis fine. Miss Walker is right, I came without writing ahead to warn anyone. This is the best solution." Mr. Gregory gave Mabel his full attention, his green eyes targeting her. "I heard you are a woman of faith. I'm glad to see I was not misinformed. By the way, have you given my business proposal any further thought?"

"Not at all." She sighed, brushing her hair from her eyes where a few strands had fallen from her pins. "Today has been quite busy. After you both left, we had another stranger arrive." She nodded toward the front door. "I take it you have met Blue Bell and her son?"

"The cook?" Mr. Gregory grinned. "Indeed, Gerald introduced me to Blue Bell, but I have not yet had the pleasure of meeting her son. The Cherokee I met at Skinner's Trading Post were very pleasant. Blue Bell is charming and speaks excellent English."

"She should. Her late husband was English. He had no family in the area and her own family refused to take her and the boy back. They saw her marriage to him as a betrayal."

"That is unfortunate," Mr. Gregory said, his tone more sympathetic and sincere than she would have guessed him to be.

"Yes, well, not all Cherokee families disown their children. 'Tis the same with white families."

"I understand," Mr. Gregory said.

"I should tell you that we will have dinner within the hour in the dining room. We are different than other households. Blue Bell and her son John always join us. They are like family."

Chapter 4

Joe's quarters in the attic were cramped. He had to bend over to keep from hitting his head on the beams. His calves hung off the end of the cot, but he would not complain. It was better than being outside on the hard ground with all the annoying insects. He had no wash basin, and he needed to clean up before dinner. Time to visit the well between the house and the stables.

After washing his hands and arms up to his elbows, Joe followed Gerald to the dining room. He stopped at the sight of Zach at the end of the table facing Miss Walker at the other end. Why was Zach here, sitting at the head of the table as if he were the man of the house? Bethany sat beside her sister, across from a young man who looked like Blue Bell. Two empty seats were beside him. Blue Bell sat on the other side of Bethany. All the places were set and the food already on the table.

"Go ahead, Mr. Newman, Mr. Gregory, take your seats." Miss Walker gestured to the empty chairs and folded her hands, bowing her head. "Zach, would you please say grace?"

"Of course." Zach nodded, unfolding a napkin and placing it over his shirt. He waited for Gerald and Joe to sit down then bowed his head and closed his eyes. "Dear Lord, please bless this meal that has been prepared for us. We thank You for Your provision and all that You do for us. In Jesus' name, amen."

There was a chorus of "amens" around the table and then the bowls were passed around. John handed Joe a platter of homemade biscuits, which he was eager to try. He passed it on to Gerald. His gaze strayed back to Miss Walker. She intrigued him. It bothered him that Zach was here. It shouldn't matter, but it did.

The room was painted grayish blue with white molding dividing the top from the bottom. A cherry-wood china cabinet filled the corner, but the other two walls were adorned with double windows with navy-colored drapes and gold trim. A canvas painting of a wine bottle with fruit hung in the center wall in a gilded frame between the windows.

"So Zach, I understand you proposed to my sister this morning. Why did you wait so long when you have been here with us for years?" Bethany asked, spooning a pile of mashed potatoes onto her plate and handing the bowl to Joe.

"Bethany!" Miss Walker's voice cut through the room and her blue eyes glared at her sister like shards of glass. "Enough. 'Tisn't the proper time or place to discuss this."

"Why not?" Bethany shot a look at her sister and turned to Zach. "If he is now after your wealth, you should at least know about it." She twisted her lips and narrowed her blue eyes at Zach. "I always thought you were different, but I suppose I was wrong."

"Bethany, there are things you are too young to understand," Zach said. He opened his mouth as if to speak again, but nothing came out. An awkward moment passed. Zach cleared his throat. "Bethany, unlike the others, you know me. I should think that would count for something."

"It does count for something, Zach. You know we are very grateful for all your support this last month." Miss Walker bit into a chicken leg and chewed. More silence permeated the room.

Alarm slammed into Joe as he tried to act normal and reached for a bowl of beans and spooned them onto his plate. The marriage proposals she had been receiving from strangers didn't concern him, but Zach was a different matter. Unlike the others, Zach knew her well and how to wear down her defenses.

"Mabel, I thought you said we would observe the proper grieving time for Avery." Bethany dropped her fork and it clanked against her plate. "I do not understand why things cannot continue as they have always been. Zach, why can you not continue working for Mabel as you did for Avery? Why must marriage be part of it?"

"If it makes you feel any better, Mabel did not give me an answer. She needs more time to properly mourn. Now, I would like to change the subject until Mabel and I have had time to discuss this in private." Zach picked up his cup and took a swallow.

"The food is delicious. What is this yellow item?" Joe pointed to a long round yellow thing he had never seen before. "And how does one eat it?"

" 'Tis corn." Bethany brightened with a smile and picked the corn up with both hands. "You eat it like this." She put it to her mouth and bit into it, scraping off the top layer. She chewed and swallowed before saying, "The Cherokee taught us how to grow it. Blue Bell has the best corn of anyone around."

Joe copied her example. Surprised by the burst of juice that exploded in his mouth, he chewed in delight, happy he had successfully changed the topic.

"I tried it for the first time last week," Gerald said. " 'Twill be one of the things I miss when we leave Nantahala. What does that word mean anyway? Where did it come from?"

"It means land of noonday sun," Blue Bell said. "It is Cherokee, from my people. With mountains, sun not shine in heart of Nantahala until middle of day."

"And is that where we are? The heart of Nantahala, I mean?" Joe asked, looking up at Blue Bell's dark, sparkling eyes. While her black hair lay straight past her shoulders, a touch of gray layered each temple.

"I like to think we are," Bethany said, picking up her fork and spearing her beans.

"Gerald took me up to see the loggers today. I met Adam Birch. He seems very knowledgeable." Joe took a swallow of his water. "I wonder, do you ever do any log driving down the river?"

Everyone stopped eating and drinking. A strange silence came over the table. Had he said something wrong?

"We did," Miss Walker said, blinking back moisture as a sad expression crossed her eyes. "We had a logjam recently, and it took six men to break it up. One of them was caught in the current and in danger of drowning. Avery jumped in to save him and lost his own life in the process." She swallowed hard and took a deep breath. "If you hear anyone calling him a hero, 'tis because he is."

"I'm sorry, I did not mean to upset you," Joe said, wishing he had never asked the question. He disliked seeing her so unhappy.

After leaving Bethany at the schoolhouse, Mabel rode to the lumber mill to begin another day's work. Dread pooled in the pit of her stomach at the crowd of men gathered around the waterwheel. It wasn't moving. Fear slithered up her spine as she dismounted and rushed over to learn what happened. As soon as the men noticed her, they parted to clear a path.

Zach and Adam Birch waded through the water and worked together to pull out a huge piece of wood that had been shoved into the waterwheel. The moment they pulled it free, Mr. Birch's arm almost got caught, but Zach dropped the wood and pulled him free in time. The two of them ducked under to grab the wood and bring it to shore. Whispers and murmurs carried through the crowd as Mabel tried to make sense of what had happened. They sloshed through the water as the two of them made it to the edge and hauled the log onto the bank.

Zach made his way out of the water and climbed onto the bank with Mr. Birch close behind. They both breathed rapidly as water dripped from their soggy clothes.

"What happened?" Mabel rushed forward. Zach's brown hair pressed against his scalp in disarray. Beads of water layered his mustache and beard as his breaths slowed. A few men slapped him and Mr. Birch on their shoulders and backs in hearty congratulations for removing the jam.

"Someone tried to break the wheel. It is not possible that a log could have gotten lodged in there on its own," Zach said. "If there had been a storm last night, I might have believed it an accident, but 'tisn't the case. This was deliberate and evil."

Mabel glanced at the wheel over Zach's head. It still wasn't moving. She tried to swallow the fear rising in her throat, but it rose just the same. "I do not understand.

How could this happen?" Her voice broke, but she managed to keep the tears away as she clenched her jaw.

Lord, I pray this is not happening. Please do not let the waterwheel be broken. Mabel prayed the silent prayer as she listened to Zach. These days it felt like her faith hung on a thin ribbon of hope.

"Someone had to cause this," Zach repeated, pressing his hands to his knees and breathing deeply.

"I agree," Mr. Birch said from behind them. "A log that size cannot get stuck inside a waterwheel without help."

"Are you all right?" Mabel asked, touching Zach's shoulder. Guilt coursed through her as she realized her first concern should be for her men, more than the survival of her business. She leaned back and touched Mr. Birch's arm. "And you?"

Both men nodded.

"I hope the wheel 'tisn't broken," Mr. Birch said, wiping water out of his eyes. "We need to get the mule moving to see if 'twill run again."

"Good idea," Mabel said, turning to a young man on her right. "Go inside and hitch the mule to the pulley."

He nodded and hurried off in the direction of the lumber mill.

"How do we know Mr. Gregory is not responsible for what happened?" Zach reached out a sturdy hand to squeeze her arm and gain her full attention. A mixture of surprise and disbelief swirled through her as she tried to clear her mind to think clearly.

"He could not have done it," Mabel sighed, jerking her arm free. "He rented a room from us, and he was at our home in his chamber last night."

"Unless you can explain his every move throughout the night, you have no definitive proof, Mabel." Zach lowered his voice and leaned toward her ear, covering her hand with his. "He could have slipped away while you slept at any time during the night."

"Be reasonable." Mabel shoved his hand away. "You cannot accuse a man of this deed because he is new to the area." She placed her hands on her hips and met his brown-eyed gaze. "For we both know I am surrounded by men who believe I should marry and turn over the running of the business to my new husband. They are of the opinion that women have no place in business. Is that not what they are saying? How do we know one of them did not do it?"

"And ruin their ability to provide for their families?" Zach pressed his palm against his forehead and shook his head as if in disbelief. " 'Tis true that many of them resent working for a woman. Trust me, none of our men would have done this. They cannot afford to destroy the only job available for many miles."

"True." Mr. Birch straightened from examining the wet log lying on the ground. "Forgive me for sayin' so, but you should have more faith in your workers, Miss

Walker. We work hard and put in long hours. Most of us feel the lumber mill may not be as solid now that your brother has passed on, but we stayed, and we have been loyal."

"I'm sorry, Mr. Birch." Another wave of guilt crashed through Mabel as his words echoed in her mind. "I did not mean to imply any distrust, but I have heard the grumblings and complaints about my unmarried state." Her gaze shifted through the curious faces watching her. She folded her hands over her chest and tried to regroup her thoughts so she could better explain. "I was not referring to men such as yourself who have proven your loyalty. My doubts concern the newer men who dislike working for a woman." Her eyes strayed to the wet log lying on the ground. "Perhaps they did not intend to ruin the business or their jobs, but to merely intimidate me into marriage."

"Mabel, I find it to be more than a coincidence that Mr. Gregory offered to purchase the business, you refused, and now someone tried to destroy the success of what you refuse to give up."

"No, he and Mr. Newman were in their rental rooms at my home. One of us would have heard them leaving. I do not believe he would try to ruin a business he is in the process of pursuing. That would not be in his best interest."

A man hurried from the lumber mill and spoke to Zach.

"The wheel is broken," Zach said, glancing at Mabel with an apologetic expression. "The men inside tried to get the mule to move the waterwheel, but it would not budge. It will need to be repaired."

"I shall check Avery's records to see who he hired to build it," Mabel said. If she wanted the men to see her as the rightful owner, and believe that she was strong enough to run the business without a husband, they had to see her making sound decisions.

"Yes, but we may not have the funds to hire them after we pay the men this month," Zach said. "We may have to find another way."

"We can do it." A familiar voice spoke from behind the crowd. The men stepped aside to reveal Mr. Gregory and Mr. Newman. She had not noticed their arrival during the chaos. "I worked on the crew who built the first waterwheel on our family farm." Mr. Gregory walked forward with a confident swagger. "I shall take a look and give you an estimate before the end of the day."

"No need." Zach stepped forward, his voice stern and full of warning. "I'm sure we can find someone we know and trust to make the repairs."

Memories of Avery having to wait several months for the builders to arrive from Virginia came to mind. Mabel was younger then and uninterested in all the details. Should she trust any of the local men around here? Would Avery have hired someone so far away if anyone in the area could provide the kind of quality work they needed? Mr. Gregory was not here then, and as long as the wheel remained broken, she would be out of business.

Lord, I pray I'm not making a mistake. She whispered the words in her heart as she walked toward Mr. Gregory. Her heart pumped faster until she thought she would become dizzy.

"Let us discuss the details and see if we can come to an arrangement." Mabel offered a smile of confidence she didn't quite feel, motioning to the lumber mill.

Chapter 5

Over the next three days, Joe and Gerald worked with Adam to restore the wheel. Zach seemed too preoccupied with business matters to help. As Joe and Gerald approached the mill, Zach headed out in the direction of the logging camp. Joe's horse snorted and flipped his tail. Miss Walker whirled, her cautious expression relaxed, and she waved in greeting.

"I see Zach is already hard at work this morning," Joe said, nodding toward Zach's form disappearing into the woods by the river. Joe dismounted and secured his horse by the pole next to Gerald.

"Yes, I asked Zach to gather all the loggers and bring them to the mill this morning," Miss Walker said. "I need to make an announcement. 'Twould be nice if I could tell them that the wheel has been fixed as well. Are we ready to test it?" Miss Walker shielded her eyes from the sun as she looked up at him. Her bright smile revealed a row of pearl teeth. His pulse quickened as her blue eyes glistened with enthusiasm.

With a rare moment away from Zach, Joe allowed himself the liberty of appreciating everything about her. She wore a straw hat with a green ribbon braided through the material over a white cap. Brown curls slid from beneath the material framing her face around her temples and smooth cheeks. A linen handkerchief of white tucked along the neckline into a solid dark-green bodice transformed into a lighter shade of green at the waist with curved tabs. Her yellow petticoat contained stitched oak leaves. The bottom of the gown was embroidered with a floral print in the same oak leaf stitching. Her attire consisted of sturdy material for work and free movement, but also had the appropriate quality for a lady of her station.

"Mr. Gregory, is the wheel ready?" she asked again, blinking up at him.

Guilt besieged him at studying her so openly. His attention snapped back to her question. "Please, you may refer to me by my given name, Joe." Everything about her kept tempting him from his business.

Forcing himself to focus, Joe rubbed the back of his neck. "I apologize, my mind strayed for a moment." He offered a smile of apology. The last thing he wanted was for her to think he didn't take her seriously. Joe swallowed his discomfort and met her gaze. "Indeed, yesterday after you left, we managed to finish all the needed repairs and remove the obstructions that caused the delays. The wheel is ready."

He rubbed his hands together to spur a bit of heat back into them. Today was the first morning it actually felt like fall with the first frost of the season.

"I shall do the honors," Gerald said, the warmth of his breath forming a cloud around his mouth. He turned and strode toward the lumber mill. The pebbles on the path crunched beneath his heels. "I will do anything to avoid getting in that cold water this morning," he said over his shoulder.

"Let us hope and pray this works!" Joe called after him. He disliked the idea of getting back into the cold water as well.

"I cannot call you by your given name if you do not call me by mine," Miss Walker said, moving to stand beside him. Her arm touched his, and he could feel the warmth from her small frame. He liked being near her. "Please, call me Mabel. After all, you are the only bachelor around who has not offered me a fake marriage."

"Come now, Mabel, I am certain there are a few more chaps around who could still make you an offer." Joe's heart pounded like a man on the run. He took a deep breath in an attempt to calm his irrational pulse. He gave her a teasing grin and winked.

She laughed, and the sound sailed through the air like a harmonious melody. Unexpected warmth filled his chest. She happened to be the first woman he could relax around without fearing a matrimonial trap awaited him. With all the recent challenges she had faced, Joe felt a connection with Mabel.

"Well, *Joseph*," she said, emphasizing his name. "I appreciate your direct approach. You came with the intention of buying the mill, and when I rejected your offer, you never tried to manipulate your way through the sanctity of marriage. Instead, you came back with a better offer—each time." She lifted a finger and shook it at him. "And *that* is to be commended."

A groaning and creaking noise shifted through the river. They turned and rushed to the river's edge to watch the wheel as it began to slowly turn. After a few moments, it picked up speed and churned through the water at a regular rhythm like before.

"You did it!" Mabel couldn't hide her excitement as she clapped with delight.

"Of course I did." Joe watched her bounce on her heels as her enthusiasm became contagious. "I promised, did I not? I had to keep my word."

"Yes." She clutched his arm. "And I am very grateful."

Her eyes widened as she looked down at her hand gripping his arm. "I'm sorry." She started to pull away, but Joe covered her hand with his, not wanting her to let go.

" 'Twas my pleasure. I hope you will allow me to stay and hear the announcement you intend to make?"

"You may." She nodded. "In fact, I could use your support." She scraped her teeth over her bottom lip as she looked up at him. "Ever since Avery's passing, Zach has paid the men their salary on my behalf. I feel it is time they begin seeing me as the owner and come to realize I do not intend to marry out of convenience. I must show them I am strong enough to run this business."

A mixture of admiration and fear swelled up in Joe's gut. He pressed his hand against hers with a reassuring grip. "I take it Zach does not know what you have in mind?"

"He does not." She shook her head and shifted her gaze back to the running wheel. "I know he will be upset, but he as much as the other men must realize I do not intend to marry my brother's business away—not even to him."

"In that case, I would not miss this for anything."

Mabel pressed a quivering hand to her stomach as the logging crew lined up along the river by the waterwheel. The men wore various expressions ranging from annoyance to mild curiosity. She lifted her chin in determination and concentrated on how to best phrase her words.

Joe leaned over to Mabel and whispered, "Hold your head high and remember you are doing this for Avery."

She straightened and scanned their faces to show her strength. "As you all know, someone tried to destroy our business by jamming a log into the waterwheel. I hired Mr. Joseph Gregory and Mr. Gerald Newman to attend to the problem." Mabel gestured to both men standing on her right then to the waterwheel. "As you can see, it is now running as well as ever."

"Do we know who did it?" one of the men asked.

"No, not at this time." Mabel shook her head. "You are here because I want to personally inform you of what happened. Work at the mill can now resume. Please know that your jobs are safe. I intend to keep this company going and will look out for our crew as faithfully as my brother did." She turned and reached out to Mr. Newman. He handed a small wooden box to her. "The other reason I asked you here is to pay you for the quality work and long hours you have put into the Nantahala Lumber Mill. I'm very grateful for your loyalty since my brother's passing."

Some of the men looked down at their feet, others cleared their throats and shifted their feet in discomfort. A few watched her with unchanging expressions. It was hard to read their mood and know where they stood. She took a deep breath and pulled out the piece of paper where she had carefully written down each man's name and his agreed upon pay.

One by one she called their names. She met each man's gaze, thanked him for his service, and handed him his pay. Most of them were civil and nodded with a grunt of thanks.

After they had all collected their pay and gone back to where they stood, one man stepped out and cleared his throat. "Miss Walker, I do not mean any disrespect, but 'tisn't right for a woman to be runnin' a lumber mill company. This is a man's business."

The tall logger stared at her with a critical expression that burned in his dark eyes. Mabel remembered his name, Dale Hendrix. The other men nodded and murmured in agreement.

"First of all, Miss Walker is not your boss," Zach said. He shoved his hands on his hips and walked down the line of men, meeting each gaze with an intimidating stare. "I'm your boss as I have always been." He pointed at Mabel. " 'Tis true that Miss Walker now owns Avery's company because he set it up that way to provide for his family in the event of his death. Most of you have wives, mothers, and daughters, and you would have done the same thing."

"I would provide for my woman by putting the business in a man's hands to run things properly. The way it should be. I would have named my brother," Mr. Hendrix said.

"Avery did not have a brother, but he had me, and he knew I would continue running things as I did when he was alive. Nothing has changed." Zach shifted his weight to one leg and adjusted his tricorn hat. "I advise Miss Walker in all her business decisions. I assure you, things are as they should be. Give her the proper time to grieve over her loss. I expect you men to be loyal through this difficult time." Zach lifted a finger and pointed at them. "That, my friends, is the proper thing to do."

"Zach, I cannot work for a woman." Another man spoke up. " 'Tis been over a month now. I have to move on if things are not goin' to change within a fortnight."

"Men, I assure you things will not change in a fortnight." Mabel stepped forward, her voice firm with determination. "I do not intend to tie myself to a husband I barely know for the rest of my life so you can feel more comfortable with me owning this company—a company that Avery intentionally left to me. Many of you knew and worked for my brother. There was naught he asked you to do that he would not have done himself. Is that not how he lost his life? He died trying to fix a logjam in the river because he did not want to risk your lives." She swallowed back the rising emotion gathering in her throat.

"Miss Walker, while it may not be customary for a woman to run a logging business and sawmill, not all of us feel this way," Adam said. "The younger men have no other mouths to feed but their own. They can roam from job to job and town to town. The rest of us are older and wiser. We have families to consider and homes settled here. There is not another lumber company for hundreds of miles. As long as you give us the pay we are due, we will be fine with you owning the company until you find a proper husband."

"Thank you." Mabel folded her arms and looked at each face, trying to determine who would stand with her. "I will not try to force anyone to stay. If you feel you cannot work for a woman, leave now."

Mr. Hendrix and one other man stepped out of line. Mabel waited, hoping no more would join them, but her heart dropped to her stomach when another man came forward. As Adam had pointed out, all three of them were quite young and most likely unmarried. She glanced at the rest of the men who remained in line. "Is there anyone else who would like to join these three?" She waited, but no one else moved.

"You three have your pay. I owe you naught else. You made it very clear that you do not wish to work for a woman, and I have every intention of remaining the owner of this company. I release you. Collect your things from camp and go. You are no longer welcome on this land."

Mr. Hendrix strode toward her, but paused when Zach moved to her left and Joe stepped to her right. He tightened his lips in anger, his dark eyes glinting. "I will be happy to leave." Mr. Hendrix clenched and unclenched his fists at his sides and turned to stalk away. The other two men simply turned and followed.

"I thank the rest of you." Mabel lifted her chin and ignored the churning inside her stomach as she forced a polite smile. "You may go back to work." She stood still as she watched them leave. Conversations murmured among them.

"Are you all right?" Joe asked.

Mabel released a deep sigh and let her shoulders droop. The outcome had not been what she had hoped, but at least it was now over. She wanted to cry and let out her frustration at the unfairness of it all. Instead, she swallowed back the rising lump and gave him a grateful smile. "Yes, I will be fine. I would like to be alone now. Perhaps a walk would do me some good."

"I do not believe your being alone would be a good idea considering what just happened," Joe said, concern evident in his green eyes. "At least not until those three are gone. We still do not know who tried to break the waterwheel."

"As much as it pains me to agree with Mr. Gregory," Zach said, nodding, "I think he is right." He glanced down at her and touched her elbow in a reassuring manner. Still reeling from the conflict, Mabel did not withdraw as more confusion clouded her mind. She didn't want to encourage Zach, but neither did she want to push him away. She needed him, especially if the men disliked her so much and Joe and Mr. Newman would soon leave.

"I do not wish to leave you alone, Mabel," Zach said, "but I believe it would be best if I make sure those three men leave without causing any trouble. Adam will need to keep a close eye on the others to make sure there is not any more dissention."

"She will not be alone," Joe said. "Gerald and I will stay here until you return. As you pointed out, we still do not know who broke the waterwheel."

Zach gave Joe a hesitant look and glanced back at Mabel for her reaction. She nodded. "Go on. I shall be fine. I am in good hands with Mr. Gregory and Mr.

Newman. I would not allow them in my home if I felt otherwise."

"I give you leave to call me Gerald," Mr. Newman winked at her. "We are business partners now."

"As soon as I see those three off the property, I shall return to check on you." Zach rubbed her arm before walking toward his horse. He mounted up and took off, circling around the mill and up the mountain.

"Well, I still intend to go for a walk." Mabel sighed and looked at Gerald and then Joe. "I need to clear my head."

"Gerald, keep an eye on the men inside the mill. I shall escort Mabel." Joe held out his elbow with a reassuring grin. "Shall we?"

Chapter 6

A s much as she hated to admit it, Mabel felt safer with Joe by her side during her walk. She had known the men disliked working for a woman, but their animosity was much worse than she had imagined. She startled at a sudden rustling in the branches above them, unaware she had squeezed Joe's arm until his other hand covered hers in a gesture of reassurance.

"Do not worry. 'Tis only a few squirrels playing." His thumb circled the top of her hand. "I promise, as long as I am here, I will not allow any harm to come your way."

Mabel looked up into his green eyes, struck by the sincerity in his expression. An unexpected warmth fluttered through her, swirling in her stomach. She could feel her cheeks heat with embarrassment. Not once had Zach ever made her feel this way.

"I'm sorry. I assure you, I am not usually so anxious. The events this morning managed to unsettle me a bit. I am hoping a walk will help ease my nerves." She looked down the path in front of them and noticed the fall colors. A few leaves had already fallen from the trees and scattered about the countryside.

"No apology necessary." His arm brushed her shoulder as his boots crunched twigs beneath his shoes. "If you wish for me to leave you to your thoughts, tell me so at once and I shall refrain from speaking. I did, however, want to express my regret at what you experienced this morning and let you know that you have my full support."

"That is very kind of you," Mabel said. "In fact, talking about it may help me work out my thoughts. That is, if you do not mind being my confidant." She glanced down at his hand still covering hers as they walked.

"Of course, I would be honored. Whatever you say will remain between us unless you give me permission to share it," he said. "I thought addressing the men yourself and giving them their pay directly instead of having Zach do it was a clever idea. It established your ownership and authority over not only them, but their boss. You showed strength that you are not afraid to face them, and integrity in being perfectly open and honest with them."

Mabel felt a flush of pleasure at his words. "And as you own a successful sawmill company for nigh on five years now, I trust in your good judgment." A whiff of sawdust lingered from the dark-brown vest he wore over his linen shirt, and she relished in the scent of him. The aroma of a light touch of pine always accompanied him. "I realize I have much to prove to them. At times, the thought of it overwhelms me, but not as much as the thought of binding myself to someone for the rest of my life—someone I do not care for as I ought."

"Ah, in that I agree with you. I have lost count of all the mothers and young ladies who have attempted to ensnare me over the years." He chuckled. "A successful business definitely brings out the matchmakers in society."

Mabel smiled, trying to imagine him keeping all his admirers at bay. Glancing at his finger to ensure she had not missed a wedding ring, she exhaled in relief as a satisfied peace poured over her like liquid balm. The she gulped at the realization that a man's marital status had never mattered to her—until now.

Not only was Joe a successful businessman, but a confirmed bachelor. Perhaps he could enlighten her with advice on how best to remain single regardless of everyone's attempts to trap her into marriage. He could teach her about running a proper business. Ever since proposing, Zach refused to answer her questions and merely assured her over and over that he would take care of everything for her.

"I simply wish everyone would stop giving me advice on who I should marry and what is right and proper. They are so convinced a woman cannot run a business— even all the women at my church have said something to that effect." Mabel paused and looked up at Joe's profile. His brown hair was gathered into a black ribbon at the back of his neck. In spite of the black tricorn hat he wore, his dark curls bounced as he nodded and listened.

"I am going to be honest, I doubt there is anyone here in the colonies who believes a woman should be running a lumber mill." Joe stopped walking, pulled both her hands into his, and gave her his full attention. "Since I have been here watching you show up each day making decisions for the company in your brother's place, I am now convinced you have the potential to prove the rest of us wrong."

"I am one woman. It seems that the whole world is against me. Having three of my men quit this morning makes me question myself. And then there's the waterwheel. I wish I knew what my brother would do." A deep ache squeezed her heart as it always did when she thought of Avery.

"Avery would not be in your situation, now would he? You are only facing these particular challenges because you are a woman." He tightened his grip on her and moved a finger under her chin to force her to meet his eyes. The sparkle of determination in his green gaze stirred a kindling of hope in her. "The business decisions you have made appear to be quite sound. All I have witnessed, and the letters Gerald and Ron have written about you, convince me that you are levelheaded, a fast learner. You possess a strength and courage I have not seen in a third of the men I meet. Do not let them win."

"I intend to keep trying, but there are things I need to learn, and Zach has appointed himself as the decision maker over all things related to the company. I fear in his desire to protect me, he does not share business details with me that he should."

"As much as it pains me to defend Zach, I feel I must in this case. You are still grieving for your brother, and it may be that he is merely trying not to burden you further." A slow, encouraging smile graced his lips beneath his brown mustache. " 'Tis a different kind of loyalty, but I can see where it may cause you frustration."

"I hope you are right." She glanced down at his hands still holding hers. While he had held onto her much longer than was proper, Mabel did not mind. He followed her gaze and let go, offering her his elbow. She placed her hand on his arm, and he led her in resuming their walk.

The birds chirped in the trees above them. A breeze lifted a few orange and yellow leaves from nearby trees, sending them sideways in the air, and dotting the green grass in various places. Mabel breathed in the fresh air, enjoying the landscape around them.

"You mentioned I had been in business for five years, so I am led to assume you read my business proposal. What are your thoughts?" Joe asked.

"I believe it is the best offer I have received thus far and much more tempting, since it does not come with the offer of matrimony." She laughed, but he remained silent. An awkward silence passed between them as the sounds of nature grew louder around them. "I'm sorry. I do not mean to imply an offer of marriage from you would be a horrible experience. I am certain you shall make a wonderful husband for. . .someone." She rubbed the back of her neck to smooth out the sudden knots forming. "You were honest with me, and so now I need to be forthright with you. I never intend to marry or sell my brother's business. 'Twould not matter what offer you make."

"I know. As soon as I met you, I realized you are emotionally attached to the lumber mill. Such an attachment is what my parents had hoped I would develop for the family farm." He shrugged and shook his head. "I did not have the stomach to plow one more field, milk one more cow, or slaughter one more hog. Timber is my future. If these colonies are to grow and prosper, lumber is the way to make it happen, but for my parents, my business was never good enough. My older brother thrives on the farm, and so he is their favorite."

"I wondered if you have any brothers or sisters," she said.

"One older brother and three younger." Joe tilted his head toward her ear and lowered his tone to a timbre. "I wanted a little more detail on what you thought about the proposal, but since it will not matter and you are not about to change your mind, I have another idea."

"Such as?" Curiosity bubbled in her chest as she looked up at him and was struck by how handsome he looked as the sun cast a golden globe around him.

"I accept that you will not sell the company, but I think we would both benefit from a partnership. I would like to purchase lumber from you at a fair price, and I could offer you some new sawmill equipment that would make your work at the mill faster and easier." He patted her arm. "So, are you interested?"

Joe rode to Skinner's Trading Post as soon as dawn broke the next morning. As he traveled through dark woods, the rising sun tinted the sky with a shade of light gray. He felt grateful Blue Bell insisted he eat a plate of scrambled eggs and toast with a cup of coffee. A satisfied stomach did not distract him as much as a grumbling one.

After a thirty-minute ride, the wooden building came into view. A couple of horses were tied to a post out front. Skinner, the owner, stepped out onto the porch and struck a match to light his pipe. He took a few puffs and smoke filled the air around him as he breathed out. He lifted his pipe with a nod in Joe's direction.

"You are out an' about early this morning," Skinner said. He tilted his head to the side, and the tail on his beaver hat fell over his shoulder. The hat didn't hide the long scar across his forehead. On his last trip here, Joe learned that Skinner's scar served as a constant reminder that while he considered the Cherokee his adopted family and even wore their buckskin clothes and moccasins, he had suffered a scalping from them when he was young. The man knew an act of forgiveness that others spent a lifetime trying to find.

"I came to see if I had any letters from my brother," Joe said, dismounting his horse and climbing the three wooden steps.

"Not only that, but a fella dropped off some wood thing with a blade in a wagon. Also, a letter came for Miss Walker." Skinner took another puff and shook his head. The wrinkles around his brown eyes creased when he grinned. " 'Twas too big for the trading post. I had to store it in the barn. Come on." He gestured for Joe to follow him back down the steps and around the corner. "I want you to tell me what this thing is," he said over his shoulder, leaving a trail of pipe smoke for Joe to walk through.

Inside the barn, Skinner pulled back a canvas cover revealing the equipment Joe had instructed his brother to send. With the knowledge that Mabel might still refuse to sell the business to him, Joe developed a backup plan and prepared a business offer that he hoped she would accept. He smiled and pulled back the canvas even further, revealing the saw blade lying beneath the equipment. It had arrived sooner than he anticipated.

"This, my friend, is the new vertical-system pulley saw that is powered by the waterwheel without a mule. Of course, I shall install some more turn wheels inside Miss Walker's mill with some belts and pulleys, but this system will run better and smoother, without the need of an animal." Joe slapped Skinner on the shoulder with a wide grin. "This is the future. I first witnessed one of these during my travels to New England last year. I had to invest in one."

"And Miss Walker agreed to this?" Skinner blinked as he walked around to view the equipment from the other side of the wagon. "Did she agree to marry you then?" He looked up at Joe with wide, concerned eyes. "I never thought she would give up the place. Truth be told, I was hopin' she would stick by her decision."

"No, I did not ask her to marry me." Joe shook his head. "I'm not ready to settle down like that. I did offer to buy the business, but she turned me down—flat." He sliced his hand through the air for emphasis. "But after coming up here and seeing what a fine job she is doing and all the quality timber on her land, I would rather do business with her than her competitors on the east coast. They keep raising prices to compete with England."

"The sorry devils." Skinner raised a fist. "They know we cannot compete with the likes of the mother country. They should give us colonists a better deal. 'Tis because of greed like that we continue to be so dependent upon England."

"Well, Miss Walker is giving me a good deal, and in return, I am helping her with new equipment and a better process to make things easier at the lumber mill." Joe flipped the canvas back over his equipment and secured it with heavy rocks.

"An' that is how it should be." Skinner stepped back out of Joe's way and adjusted his beaver hat.

"Skinner, I would be obliged if you would let me use the wagon to get this equipment to the mill."

"Of course, anything for Miss Walker. She is like the granddaughter I never had." Skinner leaned forward and lowered his voice. "If you are doin' business with her, I think you should know that yestereve a few men came here an' I overheard 'em talkin' about a logger strike that will force Miss Walker to 'er senses."

"What are they hoping to force her to do?" Fear slithered through Joe's chest as he thought back to the day three of her men quit. "Are these men still employed by her?"

"Maybe." Skinner scratched his temple with a thoughtful frown. "I reckon I may not know all the men in her employ."

"Was Adam Birch one of them?" Joe asked, trying to determine who could be trusted.

"Adam does not have time for that kind o' nonsense," Skinner said. "These were younger men." He tipped his head and gave Joe a stern look. "You had better warn Zach. He will know what to do. He is sweet on Miss Walker and will make sure no harm comes to 'er."

"In that case, I had better get my horse hooked up to this wagon and get going," Joe said, not bothering to share his concerns about Zach with Skinner. Concern for Mabel's safety caused his heart to pound. "Do you know when they plan to do this?"

The old man shook his head and Joe sprang into action. He had to hurry.

Chapter 7

Mabel came down to break her fast and was surprised to learn from Blue Bell that Joe had already left for Skinner's Trading Post. Zach arrived after Gerald announced he would stay behind to help John with his chores around the house. Gerald promised to take the boy hunting later that morning. Mabel was grateful to have a mentor as nice as Gerald take up time with John. Since Avery's death, Zach had not had the time and no one else came around.

Zach insisted on riding with Mabel and Bethany to the schoolhouse. Bethany chatted about her friends at school, the upcoming harvest festival, and her struggles with arithmetic. After they dropped her off at school, Zach and Mabel rode in silence. As long as they did not talk, she could pretend they had not quarreled about her partnership with Joe throughout the past week.

They arrived at the mill with the rising sun casting a golden glow against the red buildings. The running falls continued to splash over rocks, a sound she always found enticing and soothing. Three squirrels frisked around each other and then ran to a nearby tree as she and Zach halted their horses. They shook the branches, and a mixture of orange and brown leaves floated down around them as she dismounted.

"I shall take the horses to the water to drink and will get the mule from the barn." Zach reached out to take her horse's reins. Mabel handed them over in silence, trying to ignore the awkward discomfort between them.

She wished he had never proposed. Was his anger from his disappointment at her rejection or because of not getting the business? She watched him lead the horses to the river. Six months ago, she would have never questioned Zach's motives, but Avery's death had changed things. It had changed her. She no longer knew whom she could trust.

Mabel pulled her shawl tight around her and walked toward the mill. She breathed in the crisp, cool air as she made her way up the pebbled path leading to the front porch. A light dew had fallen across the land, causing the blades of grass and the leaf tips to glisten in the sun's rays.

The heels of her shoes clicked on the stone steps. Mabel pulled the key from her skirt pocket and unlocked the door. It creaked and groaned as she opened it. Movement across the floor caught her attention and she paused. She blinked to allow her eyes time to adjust to the dim light. Golden streaks slanted through the windows across the wood floor, but prominent shadows lurked all around.

Another movement to her right caused her to look in that direction. An orange-and-brown snake with a diamond shaped head rose up to watch her—a copperhead. Mabel gulped and stifled the gasp threatening to leave her throat. A movement to her left caught her attention and she shifted her gaze. Fear spiked through her heart at the sight of another copperhead. A third snake slithered across the floor toward a pile of wood where she saw a fourth snake lying across the top of the pile. A fifth snake lay curled on a wood table.

Saliva pooled in her throat as her hand went clammy against the doorknob. Frozen with fear, Mabel didn't move for a few moments as she gathered the courage to slowly back away. She had no idea how many poisonous snakes were in the mill, but she felt certain this many would not have found their way inside without help from someone.

"Lord Jesus, be with me," she whispered as she backed up. When she was safely through the doorway, Mabel slammed the door and locked it with fumbling fingers. She trembled and breathed in rapid pants. Had someone tried to kill her? She pressed her hand to her forehead. What was she to do? Zach would know.

"Zach!" She screamed his name. "Zach!" She hurried down the steps.

Zach ran out of the barn, his brown eyes wide with concern as he rushed toward her. "What is it? Are you all right?" He grabbed her by both arms and looked her over. "Mabel, answer me! 'Tisn't like you to be afraid. What happened?" He glanced around as if looking for a sign.

She took a deep breath to calm her racing heart. "There are at least five copperheads in the mill, maybe more."

"Five? Are you sure, Mabel?" Zach let go of her arm and stroked his beard in thought. "Did you accidentally leave the door open? Did you check the back door?"

"No, I did not leave the door open," she answered, not bothering to hide her irritation. "We checked the back door before we left yesterday, but I am not about to go back in there now." She pulled away from him, crossed her arms over her chest, and paced back and forth. "Zach, this was no accident. Someone did this on purpose."

"Let us not jump to conclusions, Mabel." He rubbed the back of his neck as he glanced up at the sky. His tricorn hat shifted and he had to adjust it. A deep sigh escaped him. "Although, I have to admit, five snakes in one night is unlikely."

"Of course it is!" Mabel continued to pace as her mind pursued a number of scenarios and suspects. Who could be so cruel that they would risk her life? Someone hated her. Did they have that much animosity toward her just because she was a woman and she dared to run the company her brother had left her?

"I shall be right back." Zach walked toward the barn.

"Where are you going? You cannot leave me here!" She followed him, afraid to be alone.

"I'm going to find a tool to catch them," he said.

"Do not catch them. Kill them!" Mabel's voice rose in anger, as she clenched her fists at her side. "I want them dead. Every single last one of them."

The sound of a wagon rolling down the dirt path and the *clip-clop* of a horse's hooves caught Mabel's attention. She turned and propped her hand over her eyebrows to shield her eyes from the sun. Joe sat on the wagon bench with his back straight and a set of reins in his hands. Relief coursed through her and a strange comfort eased her taut nerves. Where had he gotten a wagon? Even in the short time she had known him, Mabel realized she felt safer with Joe than she did with Zach. The realization slammed into her like a lance in a jousting contest.

"It looks like Joe is back." Zach laid a hand on her arm and waited until she looked up at him with her full attention. "Stay here with him. I will let you know when it is safe to go into the mill."

She nodded and stood wringing her hands as she waited for Joe to roll to a stop in front of her. Three more riders came up the road at a steady, slow pace. The mill workers had arrived. She wondered if any of them could have been responsible. The thought passed through the shadows of her mind, fleeing as fast as it had come.

"Whoa!" Joe called to his horse and secured the reins around the hook in front of the bench. Within seconds, he hopped down to the ground and strode to her, dipping his head in concern. "What is wrong? I know something is bothering you. I can see it on your face." He glanced toward the barn where Zach had disappeared. "Did you and Zach have another argument?"

"No." She told him about the snakes, and by the time she finished, the other mill workers had dismounted from their horses.

Zach came out of the barn with a rake and two shovels. He handed them out to the mill workers. "I suppose Mabel has told you all what we are dealing with?"

"I'm ready to catch me a viper!" one of them said, stomping off in the direction of the front porch.

Zach hung back and glanced from Mabel to Joe. "Please stay out here with Mabel and keep her safe, but if you will, walk around the building and see if you can find an opening where they may have gotten the snakes inside." He turned and strode to the porch where the other men waited by the front door.

"For what it is worth, I agree with you." Joe stepped forward and offered his elbow. "Someone put those vipers in the mill. I'm concerned you are in danger. Will you accompany me on a walk around the building?"

"Indeed, I would like to determine who did this." Mabel placed her hand on his arm and fell into step beside him. More leaves dropped around them as the men's voices floated through one of the mill's windows. Mabel pointed to it. "Look, that window is propped open by a stick. We forgot to close it when we left yesterday."

"Even though it is about eight feet off the ground, it would not be impossible to place a snake on the end of a stick or pole and shove it through the open window." Joe covered her hand with the warmth of his. "Well, now we know there is at least one access."

"True, but who did it?" she asked, gripping his arm tighter. "Is there any way to know who is responsible?"

"We may never know, Mabel." Joe's soft tone soothed her ears. "But we will do our best to keep you safe. I promise." They reached the back of the building. Joe tested the doorknob, but it was locked. "Let us keep walking, shall we?"

"Yes, please. I do not care to go back inside until those snakes have been captured and disposed of."

He guided her on a path by the river. After a few moments of silence, he reached into his vest. "By the way, Skinner asked me to deliver this letter to you. The postman dropped it off a sennight ago. Perhaps some good news will cheer you up and help you to forget all of today's nonsense."

Mabel accepted the folded parchment paper and broke the seal on the letter from her largest customer, hoping it was a new order for more lumber. As she read the contents of the letter, the pit of her stomach sank in disappointment. Tears stung her eyes, but she swallowed and blinked them away. Drawing a deep breath, she folded the letter and resisted the urge to crumple it up in her fist or tear it to shreds.

"Mabel, what is wrong?" Joe asked, leaning toward her. She avoided his eyes and clenched her teeth until she had gathered enough courage to speak again in a calm tone.

"It appears that I have lost the largest customer we have." She bit her bottom lip, wishing she could have foreseen this. "Apparently, they refuse to conduct business with a woman."

Over the next fortnight, Mabel appeared to have gotten over the snake scare, but she grew withdrawn from everyone and her behavior concerned Joe. She still worked beside them in the sawmill and showed genuine interest in the new equipment that Joe and Gerald worked to install. Even Zach couldn't hide his curiosity as he asked questions and offered to help. Now that the mule was no longer needed for the mill, Mabel took him home and gave him a stall in the stables. He would be a field mule during planting and harvesting seasons.

They sat around the dining table with a warm meal after a hard day's work. Joe scooped a spoonful of black-eyed peas from a bowl Bethany handed to him. She sat on his left and gave him a wide grin.

"All my friends at school are talking about the new equipment you installed at the mill," she said to Joe. She glanced over at her sister sitting at the head of the table. "Mabel, I think the men who have given you a hard time for running the business are going to be sorry. You wait and see." Her proud tone was unmistakable.

Joe watched Mabel for a reaction. Her gaze dropped to her plate and her cheeks turned a shade darker as if she was ashamed to receive any kind of praise from her sister. His heart lurched as a deep ache wrenched through his chest. Mabel had every right to be proud of what she had accomplished in the wake of her brother's demise. She had managed to keep the business going, defied a whole community who set themselves against her, and persevered through the sabotage of others.

Shame filled him with remorse as he took a biscuit from the platter in the middle of the table. When he first arrived, he had been one of those men who believed she had no business trying to run her brother's company. He believed she should sell it or marry just like everyone else. Now that he knew the woman behind the lumber mill, he had gained a new respect for women and had come to feel something very special toward Mabel. The thought of leaving this place filled him with a sadness he couldn't explain. Yet he knew he would have to leave. He couldn't stay here forever.

"Now that I have seen it in action, I do believe it is going to make a big difference in what we can produce," Zach said, sitting at the other end of the table facing Mabel. "We are much obliged to the both of you for bringing it to us." Zach nodded to Joe and then Gerald before lifting his glass of water and taking a long swallow.

Mabel cleared her throat. "That reminds me, Joe, after dinner, I would like to see you in the study. I have a few more questions I would like to go over before you and Gerald leave."

"Certainly," Joe said, wondering what else she could possibly ask him. Mabel had been quite thorough in her inquiries over the last fortnight. It had given him the perfect excuse to spend more time in her company.

Zach cleared his throat. "Mabel, I'm sorry, but I will not be staying. I'm going to continue my nightly routine of riding up to the mill and making sure no more mischief is happening."

"I understand, and I'm very grateful to you, Zach, but is it still necessary? I thought we decided that the responsible parties must have been the men who left the company?"

"Most likely, but we cannot be completely sure," Zach said. "It helps me rest better at night."

"I wish I could say that knowledge makes *me* sleep better." Mabel turned to her sister. "Do you have any more homework for tonight?"

"No, I finished it before you came home," Bethany said.

"She spent the rest of her time teaching me how to read," John said from across the table with a wink at Bethany. Her cheeks turned pink.

"He refuses to go to school, and I believe he should know how to read," Bethany said, shrugging her shoulders.

"I'm glad he is willing to let you teach him, as long as Blue Bell supervises the teaching," Mabel said.

"I not let them out of my sight," Blue Bell said. "They sit here at the table while I cook." She placed her dark hands flat against the table on each side of her plate.

"I am going to miss this place, but 'twill be nice to get back home again," Gerald said, before biting into his biscuit. "Hmm, I will especially miss these delicious biscuits, Blue Bell."

"You're welcome." Blue Bell gestured to the platter. "You want more?"

Gerald held up a hand and shook his head. "No, thank you. I'm stuffed as it is."

"Well, I think I shall be off." Zach took the last bite of his steak and finished drinking his water. "The meal was as tasty as always." He stood and nodded to Mabel and then Blue Bell. "Thank you for supper." He turned and walked out of the dining room, his steps echoing down the hall.

"I believe I will finish packing, unless you need me in the study as well?" Gerald wiped his mouth with a napkin and lifted an eyebrow in Mabel's direction.

"No, I believe I only require Joe at this point," Mabel said, laying her fork down on her plate and pushing it away. "Gerald, I want to thank you for all you have done for us. Not only have you thrown yourself into working at the mill when you did not have to, but you have spent valuable time with John and taught him things no one else has taken the time to teach him."

"Miss Mabel, I can now hit the center of the target Mr. Newman set up for me. The bullets are no longer hitting the trees in the woods." John's dark eyes lit up with enthusiasm as he turned to Gerald. "I wish you would stay and teach me some more things."

"If it is okay with Mabel and your mother, I might come back for a visit," Gerald said. "Now that we are going to be business partners with Mabel, I'm sure we will need to come back from time to time."

"Of course, that would be lovely." Mabel dabbed at the corners of her mouth and laid her napkin by her plate as she scooted her chair back. Her gaze shifted toward Joe. "When you are ready, I shall be in the study."

"I will join you in a moment," Joe said, picking up his water and gulping it down to hide his eagerness. As she walked out of the dining room, he was tempted to hurry after her, but he forced himself to remain in his seat and take another bite of his steak. He chewed, but it no longer held the taste he had experienced moments earlier. His appetite had disappeared along with Mabel.

His mind raced through scenarios, trying to find another logical excuse to stay longer. The thought of leaving brought a heaviness to his chest that he wasn't used to experiencing.

Joe took another bite of his steak and noticed Bethany staring at him. She propped her chin on her palm and leaned toward him. "You like my sister, do you not?"

Swallowing with difficulty, Joe grunted in discomfort. "What do you mean?" He touched a hand to his throat, wishing the steak would finish going down. He wondered why she kept staring at him as he reached for more water.

"You know what I mean." Bethany scraped her teeth across her bottom lip as if trying to decide what to say next. "Why did you not ask her to marry you like the other men?"

Joe coughed, setting his glass down and turning to give her his full attention. "I suppose it was because I was not ready to get married, and we did not know each other well."

One corner of her mouth twisted, and Joe couldn't tell if she was satisfied with his answer. She blinked blue eyes up at him, and he saw once again how much she and Mabel looked alike, although Bethany's locks contained a darker shade of brown than Mabel's.

"Thank you for not trying to marry my sister and take her away."

The quiet words took Joe by surprise. Why had he not seen it before? The wary way Bethany always watched him was because of the fear she carried. It wasn't because she didn't like him. He searched her expression in an attempt to understand her better, and saw only innocence on her face. He hoped that losing both parents and a dear brother so early in life would not cause her to be cynical later in life.

"Bethany, I can promise you, no matter who Mabel weds, she will never leave you behind or allow you to be separated from her," he said. "And no man who truly loves her would ask it of her."

"Listen to Mr. Gregory," Blue Bell said, rising to her feet. "He smart man."

"I told you not to worry," John said. "Miss Mabel would take you with her. My mother and I are the ones who need to worry. If Miss Mabel's new husband hates the Cherokee, we could end up homeless again."

"Hold on," Joe said, glancing from John to Bethany. While she had been acting a bit odd since the snake incident two weeks ago, Mabel still showed no indication that she wanted to be a bride. He could only think of one person who might be able to persuade Mabel to change her mind. "Has Mabel agreed to marry Zach?"

"Not yet," Bethany said. "Mabel told me she thinks of Zach like a second brother. I think she likes you."

"How do you know?" The question popped out before Joe could hold it back.

"Bethany!" Blue Bell gave her a warning look as she collected the discarded plates.

"What? I am not saying anything wrong." Bethany lifted her palms up and shrugged. She turned back to Joe. "Mabel knows you wanted her land and business, or you would have not tried to buy it. She does not understand why you did not try to marry her like the others, but I think your answers are reasonable."

"In that case, I'm glad I passed the sister test." Joe pushed his plate back and stood up. He paused, looking down at her. "Was this a sister test?"

"Perhaps." Bethany stood beside him and leaned over to take his plate and stack it on top of hers. "As long as you make my sister happy and do not take her away, you pass the sister test."

Chapter 8

The mid-September evenings brought a chill into the house. Mabel rubbed her cold fingers together as she bent over and waited for the tiny fire to build in the stone hearth. Since the study was built for Avery, she missed him most when she was in here. Two candles burned on each corner of her desk, causing shadows to bounce on the wood-paneled walls. A floor-to-ceiling bookcase was on the left. It had taken them two full years to fill it. Two windows with heavy gold drapes filled the wall across from the bookcase.

Footsteps sounded on the hardwood floor at the door. Mabel turned to see Joe standing in the doorway, his shoulder leaning against the doorframe. She stood and pulled her ivory-colored shawl tight around her. She gestured to a cabriolet chair with a plum-colored cushion seat and back containing floral stitched artwork. The wood-framed armrest and legs were carved with roses. He came forward, his steps turned silent as he crossed the square rug in the center.

Mabel sat in a matching chair across from him and listened to the growing embers crackle and pop. Two candles also had waving flames on the mantel. Over the last few days, she had grown uncomfortable at the thought of Joe leaving. Not only had his presence here filled a lonely void that her brother's death had caused, but he alone had managed to carve a special place in her heart that Mabel feared she may never get back.

"Thank you for joining me. I have come to a decision and I feel you are the first person I should inform." She folded her hands in her lap and gazed into the fire. "You must know this has not been an easy decision for me to make, but I fear I am left with no other choice."

Joe scooted to the edge of his seat and leaned forward, linking his fingers between his knees. "Mabel, you have not been yourself lately. I pray you have not made a hasty decision that you will later regret." He paused. "If I am the first one you are telling, then it may not be too late to change your mind. If you have not told Zach, you do not owe him any explanation when I find a way to make you change your mind."

"What does Zach have to do with this?" Mabel turned from the fire to meet his gaze. "How could you know what I mean to discuss before I have had a chance to share it?"

His tense shoulders and the concerned expression with unusual lines around his green eyes relaxed as he took a deep breath and breathed it out slowly. "I'm sorry, but I assumed you had changed your mind about not wedding Zach."

"No, of course not." A few strands of hair fell over Mabel's forehead and into her eye. She brushed them aside and smiled as the glow from the fire flickered across his face, making him look golden. "Remember the letter I received a fortnight ago informing me that we had lost our biggest client?"

"I do." Joe straightened in his seat and crossed his feet at the ankles. He rested his elbows on the armrests. "Has anything changed? Did you receive a new letter?"

"I have added the sums, and without the income from our major customer, I cannot pay the loggers. I would only be able to pay the mill workers and a few loggers." Hearing the words spoken aloud made her ears sting. She had tried to ignore the truth and could find no way out. Every possibility ended with the same result. "I'm afraid I am done for. The men will get their wish. A woman will no longer own the company and pay their wages."

"Mabel, I am so sorry for this. I have witnessed how hard you have worked to continue what your brother built." Joe shook his head and rubbed his chin in thought. "You said you have made a decision. What have you decided to do?"

"To sell the company, the land—all of it—to you."

"My proposal was only for the business land. You and your sister are to keep this parcel of land and live here for as long as you want. I would not dare take away your home."

"I have not told the others yet, but I do not wish to remain here and pretend to be part of a community that turned their backs on me after my brother died. I intend to leave and never return. The dream of coming to the colonies and building a better life began to die with my parents' deaths on the voyage over, and what was left of it died with my brother. I thought I was doing what God wanted me to do by taking on the business and continuing what my brother had started, but with the way things have turned out, I realize I must have been wrong. There are too many painful memories of this place for me to bear."

"Where will you go? What will you do?" Again Joe scooted to the edge of his seat and leaned forward. His lips turned down in a frown, and his brown mustache seemed to make it even more prominent. He reached out as if to touch her hand then hesitated and pulled back.

"With the profits from the land and business, I shall purchase passage for Bethany and myself, and we will go back to England. My grandparents are still living. We have other family there as well, aunts and uncles." She gave a sardonic laugh. "I daresay we will be better cared for there than if we were to remain here in this wilderness of the Nantahala."

Joe jumped up from his chair and paced back and forth in front of the fire. His agitation made her nervous, but she clenched her hands and tried to remain calm. She had been as open and honest as she dared. The only piece of information she had left out was that this place would no longer hold any reason for her to stay once he left. Over the last few weeks, he had made life bearable again, and the thought of watching him walk out of her life now that she had come to know him left a void she could not quite explain. She had never felt this way about anyone before.

"I wish you would reconsider." Joe leaned against the mantel as if in pain. He dropped his forehead on top of his knuckles. "I realize it may seem like God has abandoned you, but He has not. What if God sent George and me here to help you keep the business going?"

"You came here to buy it."

"Yes, but not like this," he said.

"I thought you would be pleased. This whole time you have wanted to purchase the land and business." Confusion pressed against her brain until a small headache began to form behind her eyes and across the top of her head. She touched the palm of her hand to where the pain radiated. "Can we not negotiate a new deal that includes the house, the cabin, and the rest of the land?" She cleared her throat. "And it would need to include a provision for Zach to continue renting the cabin from you. 'Tis the least I can do for him. When he finds out I have sold everything to you, I believe he will be upset, as he worked alongside my brother and helped build up the business."

"Then why not sell it to him?" Joe turned, keeping his right hand on the mantel and propping his other hand on his hip.

"He does not have the funds, and I need to go back to England and have enough to start over again. My sister and I will need to depend on my grandparents for a place to stay, but I do not want to return penniless and be a complete burden to them."

"Why go back at all?" Joe rubbed his dark eyebrows. "Simply accept the first offer I made and stay here." He lifted his head and gestured around the room. "There is no need to risk your health with another voyage across the sea to England."

"I have told you why I wish to go back to my homeland." Disappointment spiraled through her core. If Joe refused to support her decision, she would have no ally in this endeavor, for she already suspected Zach, Blue Bell, and John would be against it. She imagined Bethany loathing the idea of leaving her friends behind, especially Esther. The pastor's daughter and Bethany had grown inseparable over the last three years. "Please. . .I need your support in this." Her words fell into a whisper.

Joe groaned while massaging his left temple. His agitation increased Mabel's anxiety as if each nerve had tightened into a violin string. She shivered in spite of the warmth from the fire. Was he angry? She lowered her gaze to her lap as she dug her nails into her palms, unsure of what to do or say next.

"Mabel." Joe said her name in a soft timbre, an intimate tone that tugged at her with a longing she could no longer deny. "I am sorry, but I cannot support your decision to return to England."

"But why?" she asked, wishing she had more control over the desperation in her tone. "Does this mean you intend to retract your offer?"

" 'Twould if I thought it would keep you here, but I realize I do not have that power." In two strides, he bent in front of her and reached for her hands with a sure grip. Her fingertips tingled as she resisted the urge to cling to him. "Mabel, I have not spoken of my feelings for you because I know how you have been flooded with a number of marriage proposals of late. You knew I had come here with the intention of purchasing your business and the land accompanying it. I feared you would think ill of my intentions if I were to declare myself."

Joe lifted one hand to tilt up her chin and searched her face like a man looking for an oasis. His green eyes sparkled with orange specks reflecting from the firelight. Shades of gold and gray shadows flickered across his face. The sincerity in his expression and tone ignited a hope she had not dared entertain until now.

"Mabel, your decision has changed everything. You have already offered me the purchase of the business and land without the benefit of wedding you, so I hope you believe me when I say I would like to court you. I cannot do that if you are in England." His thumb lightly caressed her chin. "Please believe me. I am not like those other men. I have no ulterior motive other than I have come to care very deeply for you."

Her despondent spirits lifted in renewed hope as she absorbed Joe's words and prayed she would not mistake his meaning. The tender way he stroked her chin sent a current of heat to her heart. She looped her fingers through his and raised her other hand to cradle his cheek. "If you are sincere, then I believe you have just given me the one reason I might need to stay. I must admit, I was beginning to dread how empty this house would feel after you leave tomorrow."

"You believe me?" Joe asked, his lips curled into a grin, and she realized he had recently trimmed his brown mustache.

"I want to," Mabel said. "Lately, it seems as if the whole world has been against me. Even Zach put a contingency on me. He promised to give me the grieving time I needed, and then he expected to marry me so he could have everything. I realize he helped my brother build the company into what it is today, but that does not mean I should have to give up the rest of my life for it. I do not love him—not like a woman should love a husband."

"What about me?" He leaned his forehead against hers. "Do you think you could ever love me like that?"

"You are the first man who has made me feel as if that is possible." Mabel laid her hands against Joe's chest and could feel his heartbeat increase in a rapid rhythm.

"Please, do not leave tomorrow."

"I will send Gerald on his way," Joe said. "I need him to check on how well my younger brother has handled my business in my absence. I do not intend to risk him being in charge for too long."

"I would like to meet your brother," Mabel said.

"And you shall, that is, if you do not go to England," Joe said.

"Then do not leave tomorrow," Mabel said. "Stay here in Nantahala a little longer."

"I think I can manage that. We will have a lot of business to discuss, but first we shall discuss *us*." Joe eased both hands around her cheeks and tilted her head until her lips met his.

Joe's kiss was tender as the soft hairs of his mustache tickled her skin. Mabel breathed in the scent of him, a mixture of pinewood and sawdust. Jubilation lifted the heaviness that had been burdening her chest the past fortnight. If she had known that Joe was the remedy, she would have taken action much sooner. He deepened the kiss, and her fingers curled around his cravat at the light-headed feeling that came over her.

He pulled away, gazing into her eyes with a slow grin. Their breaths were erratic and rapid. If she had been standing, her knees would have buckled by now. His thumbs circled her cheeks in a light caress that she cherished.

"Mabel, you frighten me," he said.

"Why?" Alarm pounded inside her heart. Those were not the words she would have expected to hear after their first kiss.

"Because you make it impossible for me to think of anything else but you. Because I would be willing to do anything to put a smile on your beautiful face. Because I think I have lost myself. Because you now hold all the power over me. When I do return home, my heart will stay in Nantahala."

"Then you should be glad that I am a God-fearing woman," she said. "For only a woman with a weak mind would take advantage of that much power." She slipped her hands around his neck, entwined her fingers through his curls, and pulled him close for a second kiss.

Jennifer Hudson Taylor is an award-winning author of historical Christian fiction and a speaker on topics of faith, writing, and publishing. Jennifer graduated from Elon University with a BA in Journalism. When she isn't writing, Jennifer enjoys spending time with her family, traveling, genealogy, and reading.

Her Redcoat

by Pegg Thomas

Dedication

This story is dedicated to the Quid Pro Quills, composed of Robin Patchen, Jericha Kingston, Kara Hunt, Marge Wiebe, Candice Patterson, and Jodie Wolfe. Without you ladies, my dreams of publication would have crashed and burned long ago. You have pushed me—many times kicking and screaming— to be a better writer. Perhaps even to be a better person. My life is much richer for knowing you.

And to Michael, my husband of *mumble* years. I couldn't have asked for a better man to share my life with. You've supported me through every harebrained idea, put up with every critter I dragged onto the farm, and been with me every step of the way on this crazy writing journey. I love you best.

Acknowledgments

A special thank-you goes to Monique Linseman for helping me with the French words and phrases. High school French class was more than a few years ago. Your help was greatly appreciated.

For I know the thoughts that I think toward you, saith the LORD, thoughts of peace, and not of evil, to give you an expected end.
JEREMIAH 29:11

Chapter 1

Laurette Pettigrew's father limped away from their cabin and was swallowed by the tall pines and budding brush of the surrounding forest. She was alone. Months of isolation stretched before her.

A wet nose pressed against her clenched hand. Laurette relaxed her fingers and tangled them in the wiry hair around the tall dog's ears.

"We are on our own, my friend." Her voice broke the early morning stillness. "We are banished from the settlement."

Charles Pettigrew owned a trading post in the settlement outside of Fort Michilimackinac. Since the death of Mama last fall, Laurette had helped Papa. They'd lived in the simple room tacked onto the back of the trading post. She'd cooked and cleaned and, on the rare occasions a redcoat visited the post, she'd hidden in that room. Until yesterday, when reports came that the *voyageurs* had been heard. Their boisterous voices carried over Lake Huron, oars striking the water in rhythm with their songs, announcing their arrival.

Papa had left the trading post in the hands of his apprentice and hustled Laurette back to the cabin two miles south of the fort. At least he'd stayed the night with her. One last evening before the loneliness closed in.

"Papa, how can you leave me?" she whispered into the stillness. Because the voyageurs would stay for many weeks, until gold and crimson edged the leaves again. Harsh men, strong men, men her father didn't trust with a daughter old enough— past old enough—to be married.

She turned toward the cabin, its logs sturdy and straight, bark overlapping on its roof to keep out the rain and snow. What had always been her home had now become her prison. Or it would be if she followed Papa's orders to remain here all summer.

She entered and scraped the last of the warm rice porridge into a shallow wooden bowl. "Here, Marie." She set the bowl on the hard-packed dirt floor. "We will fish for our supper, which you will enjoy much more, *n'est-ce pas?*"

The dog wagged her tail as she ate.

Laurette washed the few dishes, including the bowl when Marie was finished, and then scanned the inside of the cabin. They'd had to chase a squirrel out last night that had wintered inside. It would take a full day to clean everything. But even clean, it wouldn't be home without Mama.

She dropped onto the bench. What to do first? Elbows on the table, she rested her chin on her hands. What did it matter? Marie jumped onto the smaller bunk on the cabin's back wall, turned around three times, and lay down. Laurette squashed the urge to do the same. To lie down and wait for summer's end, for the voyageurs to paddle away, for Papa to come and fetch her. To be part of the small settlement again. To end this time in exile.

Laurette rose and opened the satchel she'd packed in haste before leaving the settlement. From the center, cushioned between her folded skirts, she pulled out a book. Its leather cover was cracked, the edges tattered. She opened it, its yellowed pages stiff and fragile. Her mother had treasured this book, even though she couldn't read it. How often had she watched Mama rest her hands on the leather cover, her lips moving without sound, at peace with herself? The book wasn't magical. Mama hadn't believed in mystical things, unlike their Ojibwe friends. She'd believed in Jesus. The book told about Him.

If Laurette could read the words printed there, maybe she wouldn't be so lonely here this summer. Maybe she'd find that peace Mama had found and be content with Papa's absence and her solitude.

Or maybe when the Ojibwe returned to their summer village, Waagosh would present her with another option, one he'd hinted at last fall.

-❦————❦-

Henry Bedlow stood at attention at the end of his cot in the fort's infirmary, doing his best not to cough.

"You have been here for a fortnight, and all you have accomplished is to lie on that cot and consume the king's provisions." The regimental surgeon paced in front of Henry. "You require movement to rebuild your muscles. If you do not get yourself into some semblance of fitness, you shan't be worth a pile of rotted beaver pelts to this regiment. Is that understood?"

Henry waited for the surgeon to either continue with his current diatribe or launch into a new one. Heaven knew the man had an arsenal of them. He was one of the many soldiers Henry wouldn't miss when his time of service was completed.

"Walk thrice around the fort each morning and thrice each afternoon until further notice, taking in the fresh air and exercising your limbs. Not inside the fort where you would be in the way of our industrious soldiers, but outside the palisade."

To the north, beyond the fort's high wooden sides, stretched a strip of beach that went as far as the eye could see to both the east and the west. The forest to the south was like something out of medieval times, deep and foreboding, stark with winter's lingering grip. Henry had been awed by the sight as he'd disembarked from the canoe that had carried him to Fort Michilimackinac. These were certainly nothing like the gentle woodlands of his native England. Concealed in its darkness were heathen tribes—the same savages who had sided with the French in their recent war against the Crown in the American colonies.

The surgeon smirked, his pale lips pulled thin and his eyes narrowed. "Worried about the Indians? Good. 'Twill keep your feet moving." He motioned toward the door. "No better time to start than the present. Dismissed to walk."

Henry snapped a salute and then relaxed for a moment after the surgeon moved on. As much as a man could relax who'd just been told to walk among the heathens of this untamed land.

"He were a mite rough on ya, if ya ask me." Willie Harris raised himself on his elbows from the cot next to Henry's. "Like ta see him marchin' 'round outside the fort."

"He is correct, however." Henry tugged at the belt that kept his breeches on his gaunt frame. "I shan't improve without some meat on my bones."

"There's puttin' on meat, and then there's fattenin' ya up for the animals out there." Willie jerked his head toward the south. "If the four-legged fail to get ya, the two-legged will."

Henry couldn't argue with that. He'd seen a few Indians from the window of the infirmary, warriors dressed in a haphazard combination of animal skins and cloth clothing, some with feathers in their hair, some with little hair at all, just a circle at the top that grew out into a tied-back lock. He'd heard Indians painted their skin garish colors, but not those he'd seen.

Of course, you couldn't believe half of what was said. To hear some of the soldiers talk, Indians were all eight feet tall with legs like tree trunks and pointed teeth like a cat. Those Henry had seen were average height and lean, even wiry-built men. Of course, he'd not been close enough to see their teeth.

Like it or not, one did not disobey orders in the king's army. He tied thick wool leggings over his breeches and hose and grabbed the well-worn red coat he'd been issued so many months ago. He pulled his hat from its peg on the wall and snugged it onto his head then slung his musket over his shoulder.

"Marie!" Laurette's voice bounced back from the dense woods near the creek. "Marie!"

Nothing moved in the forest, no brown, brindled coat flashing between the trees. Even the birds were rendered silent by Laurette's call. The fish secured on her willow twig had long since stopped their flopping. Where was that dog?

The needle-strewn ground between the trees absorbed any sound her moccasins made as she trotted along a narrow path made by woodland creatures. The last she'd seen of Marie, the dog had been poking around the brush in this direction. Laurette slowed to a walk. This path led to the fort. Prickles danced along her arms.

With the British in the fort these past two years, Laurette had given it a wide berth. They were disrespectful of the land and the people on it and known for their acts of cruelty. What if one of the soldiers spotted the big dog and shot at her for sport? *Non.* Marie was all she had.

Laurette sped down the trail, pushing between a pair of pines, their wispy needles brushing her arm in a feathery touch. She stopped to listen. Waves broke against the shore, crashing onto the packed sand and smooth stones of the beach. That she could hear them meant she was close to the fort. Too close. Papa would not be happy. But she must find Marie.

Something stomped through the brush to her right. She ducked against the nearest tree, its low-hanging branches shielding her. Marie wouldn't make that much noise. No woodland creature would, nor any returning Ojibwe. Gooseflesh pebbled her skin despite the heavy wool of her coat. Her breath frosted in the cool air. She slowed her breathing and moved nothing but her eyes as the creature approached.

A flash of red through the trees sent her heart racing. Moments later, a red coat came into view. She had to lock her knees to prevent their trembling. How many times since the British soldiers had arrived had Papa told her not to approach the fort? The same number of times that she'd assured him she wouldn't. And she'd meant it. Everyone knew how cruel British soldiers were. How much they hated the French. She and Papa were Métis, but they spoke French. Would a British soldier know the difference? Or care?

The soldier drew nearer, swatting brush out of his way, stomping on everything in his path, making more noise than a bull moose in full rut.

A brown blur caught the edge of Laurette's vision. Marie! She willed the brindled lurcher to stop, but the dog raced on silent paws straight toward her and into the path of the oncoming soldier.

The man uttered a cry and raised his musket.

"Non!" Laurette launched from the protection of the pine. Marie bounded to her side and turned to face the intruder. The hair on the dog's back raised as she growled.

The soldier lowered the muzzle of his gun. "*Qui êtes vous?*"

Startled at his use of her native language, she answered without thinking. "*Je suis Laurette Pettigrew. Et vous?*"

"Henry Bedlow, *à votre service.*" He sketched a stiff bow.

His French carried a strange accent, but the words were clear and non-threatening. He was skinnier than a spring weasel. Bones jutted over the hollows of his cheeks, his shoulders poked against the red wool of his coat, and the thick leggings did nothing to disguise his stork-like legs. His face lacked color other than the red splotches that rode high on each unshaven cheek. More telling than all that, the lackluster golden-brown eyes, a shade she'd never seen before, said that this man was ill and had been for some time.

He leaned against a tree and dragged in labored breaths.

"You are not well." She reached for him but pulled her hand back, fear battling with her healer's instincts.

"I'm recuperating."

He had the deepest voice she'd ever heard. It rumbled its accented French in a pleasing way. His light-brown hair hung in lank strands beneath his hat, neither tied nor braided. A small scar marred his upper lip. He was tall. Perhaps even taller than Waagosh, the tallest man Laurette knew.

He doubled over, and a wracking cough shook his frame. She could almost hear his bones rattle. A man so ill should be in bed. "What are you doing out here?"

When his coughing passed, he barked a short laugh. "I have been ordered to walk for my health by our regimental surgeon. He prescribed me to walk each morning and afternoon."

"If you live that long."

Humor sparked in those odd, light-colored eyes, giving them a bit more life.

"Aye, we shall see which arrives first, the cure or the kill." He glanced around the woods and then back, measuring her. "Where did you come from?"

She cocked her head and eyed him up and down in return.

He raised an eyebrow.

How much should she tell him, a British soldier? Nothing at all, that's what Papa would say. She should run. He'd never catch her. There were few who could, even when they were healthy. But something about the rumbly-voiced man wouldn't let her feet move.

"You should return to the fort. It is not safe here, especially for one who wears the red coat."

He straightened and scanned the surroundings. "I thought it safer to walk among the trees. Less likely to be seen than if I walked near the fort's walls."

She smothered a grin, but not fast enough.

His eyebrow lifted again.

"Nobody needs to see you. You make enough noise to be heard across the straits."

He coughed again, then a grin tugged at his lips, matching the humor in his eyes. "I suppose there's truth in that. My feet are slow to do my bidding. The trees give me something to rest against."

"They also hide the Ojibwe and the Odawa."

"The Indians?"

She nodded.

"Are you one of them?"

Papa said the British hated the natives of this land. Would he hate her for the blood of her ancestors?

"My papa and I are neither Ojibwe nor white. We are. . ." She shrugged. "We are Métis."

Chapter 2

Whatever Métis were, this one was beautiful. Her black hair was straight and sleek, hanging free in front of her linen cap and framing the perfect oval of her face. Intelligence sparkled in eyes the color of strong coffee. Wild roses would wish for the color of her full lips. A dimple played coy on her cheek. Her wool skirt was a nondescript brown that blended in with the winter-dressed trees around them. Her coat, which reached almost to her knees, was a greener shade. She might have been a wood sprite escaped from a fairy tale except for the fish dangling from her hand and the long-legged, snarling dog at her side.

If he weren't committed—however reluctantly—to His Majesty's service for the next four years, he'd want to know more about Laurette Pettigrew. But he wasn't interested in the type of dalliance so many of his fellow soldiers engaged in. He rubbed the back of his neck. It wouldn't do if one of them found her here.

"You should not be so close to the fort."

"I was searching for Marie." She ran her fingers through the wiry hair around the tall dog's ears. A lurcher, a cross between a sighthound and a terrier of some sort, were popular back in England, but this was the first he'd seen in the colonies. "She slipped away from me this morning."

"You should go before anyone else sees you."

"*Oui.*" She took a step back.

Was that regret in her eyes? Wishful thinking on his part. No doubt it was wariness. He pulled in a deep breath and didn't cough. The rest had helped. He should be able to make it back to the fort's gate on the water side before his strength gave out. His legs wobbled as he moved away from the tree.

She stretched her hand toward him. "Can you make it back?"

"Of course." And if he tumbled to his face in a briar patch, he didn't want her there to witness it.

"You should stay near the fort. The Ojibwe will return any day, and they do not like the British."

"Would I not make a fine arrow's target, walking in the open next to the palisade?"

"You make a fine target here. Your noise will draw them from a mile away." She turned, and then looked over her shoulder. "I must go."

She and the dog melted into the forest.

Henry flinched when the barb—which was nothing more than the truth—hit home. He was a bookish London boy flung into the wilderness. What did he know about survival here? Nothing. That slip of a woman lived in a place too dangerous for him to walk. Shame crawled along his shoulders.

The surgeon had been almost correct. Even should he regain his health, he'd still be useless to the regiment.

Laurette fled the red-coated soldier. It wasn't the man that had her running, it was her reaction to him. Had she really jumped in front of his musket? What would Papa say if he found out she'd spoken to a redcoat? She cringed and slowed to a ground-covering trot. Marie loped at her side.

"I had to, n'est-ce pas? He might have shot you." She reached out and Marie nosed her hand without either of them breaking stride. "You were a very naughty girl, running away like that. What would I do if something happened to you?"

She'd be entirely alone.

Her thoughts returned to the deep-voiced soldier. Papa had said the British were cruel men, mad to kill whoever got in their way. She'd seen no cruelty in the depths of his eyes. No madness either. She'd seen illness and something else, despair maybe. He'd made no move to touch her. Although his illness had obviously stolen much of his strength, he was still a large man and could have threatened her. But he hadn't.

Why had she not been more afraid? What was there about Henry Bedlow that had appealed to her? Not his looks, although with a few good meals, a bath, and minus that red coat, he'd be handsome enough. Had she been drawn to him because of his illness? She'd been tempted to touch his face. The red splotches on his cheeks may have been fever. He'd mentioned being under the care of a surgeon, although what kind of healer sent a man out to—

A shadow slipped from between two trees and stepped into her path. Laurette's heart leaped to her throat as she skidded to a halt on the damp needles that carpeted the trail. Then the shadow moved and the sun glinted off the hammered copper pieces decorating the ends of his long hair. Waagosh.

"You startled me." Laurette pressed her hand to her chest as Marie bounded to the Ojibwe man and circled him, tail lashing in greeting.

He stood with his arms crossed, his legs braced. A deerskin tunic decorated with dyed porcupine quills stretched across his chest. An otter cap was pulled low over his forehead, his glittering eyes black in its shadow. Deerskin leggings hugged the muscled length of his legs. Every inch of him defined strength, health, and confidence. The complete opposite of Henry Bedlow.

"Why did you speak with the redcoat?"

Laurette caught the edge of her lip between her teeth. Could this man be the same one who'd hinted about her becoming his wife last fall? He didn't look like a prospective bridegroom. He looked furious. The intensity of his gaze pushed her back a step. She stretched herself to her full height, which came just short of his chin.

"Because he spoke to me."

His nostrils flared, and his lips pulled into a straight line.

"You will not speak to the redcoat again."

For reasons she couldn't begin to express, the need to defend the British soldier almost slipped from her tongue, but she bit it back. "I am sure we will never meet again." Unless she went back to the fort.

Waagosh nodded then left her standing alone on the trail.

Marie nosed her hand. Not quite alone.

She looked back over her shoulder before continuing to the cabin. Her father had left, her dog had returned, and she'd met a redcoat who didn't appear at all evil. And Waagosh had returned. Not with tender words or soft eyes, but as every inch the warrior he was. Was he still interested in her? Did she want him to be?

Henry made it to his cot before collapsing. He had no idea how long he'd slept when a medic banged his way down the row with cups of soup for everyone. A jaw-popping yawn shook him the rest of the way awake. He rubbed his eyes and pushed himself up to sit on the edge of the cot.

"Welcome back." Willie sat with his splinted leg straight out before him.

Henry grunted and took the tin cup filled with lukewarm soup. The medic handed him two ship's biscuits and moved on.

Willie sniffed his cup. "They put somethin' different in it today." He sniffed again. "Hope 'tis better than the last."

Henry dropped his two biscuits into the soup and waited for them to soften. He looked around the room which housed only a handful of men. Frustration gnawed at him. He'd always been healthy. He'd survived the smallpox outbreak that had taken his family. He'd survived the horrendous conditions at the work-house. And he'd even survived the interminable voyage across the ocean in a leaky vessel not worthy of His Majesty's fleet, seasick for the entire voyage. Then, weakened by his poor sailing abilities, winter fever had claimed him from the moment his feet had touched the colonial shore.

He coughed and rubbed his chest. It still hurt, but there was improvement.

"Glad the Indians left ya be." Willie slurped a mouthful of his soup.

"I saw none." Best not mention Laurette Pettigrew to anyone at the fort, not even Willie.

Willie fished a biscuit from his soup. After a futile attempt to bite off a piece, he let it sink into the cup again. "They get harder every day."

Henry looked into his cup. "At least these lack weevils. Remember those on the ship?"

Willie grunted, and the two finished their meal in silence.

His soup gone, Henry stretched back on his cot.

Miss Pettigrew's face hovered in his mind's eye. Where had she come from? There was a small settlement outside the fort's walls, but that spread to the east, close to the shore. He'd met the girl behind the fort. Of course, she could have walked around it like he had. She'd said she was looking for her dog, a wire-coated lurcher, no less. Not one of the Indian dogs who closely resembled their wolf ancestors. She denied being an Indian, but she'd been almost dark enough. And that hair, such blackness surely gave her origins away. He rubbed his unshaven jaw. He'd trained for the army with an Irish lad who had hair as dark. Still, she was a mystery.

Henry rolled to his side. He had no business thinking about a woman. He was little better than a prisoner, trapped on a frontier fort at the end of civilization. Some blokes dreamed of serving in the king's army and winning glory on some distant battlefield so they could return home a hero. Those blokes hadn't been forced into service to avoid prison. And returning home was impossible. Nothing short of the muzzle of a gun would entice him to set foot on a ship ever again. He'd better find a place to belong here in the colonies.

The minutes ticked by until the surgeon made his afternoon visit to the infirmary.

"Time to walk, Bedlow."

Henry sat a moment on the edge of his cot while the room tilted around him.

"Dizzy again?" The surgeon grabbed Henry's chin and looked into his eyes. Then he snorted. "You are dragging this out longer than anyone I have ever seen. 'Tis winter fever and spring is but a stone's throw away." The surgeon straightened. "Walk. Nothing else has worked." He moved down the line.

"Wish I could walk with ya, Indians or no. This cot gets harder by the minute." Willie glowered at his broken leg.

"Surgeon said 'tis healing well. I expect you shall be on your feet in no time." Not that Henry knew anything about healing, but his words brought a smile to his friend's face.

"Sure and why not. This will not keep a good Englishman down." Willie touched his forehead in a jaunty salute as Henry left the building.

His friend's words followed him out for his walk. *"A good Englishman."* That wasn't a label anyone would apply to him. Henry brushed the red wool of his coat. He wasn't good at anything except maybe book learning. A lot of good that would do him on the frontier.

Chapter 3

Laurette ran her hands down her midnight-blue skirt. The thick fabric would be too warm to wear much longer. She grabbed her embroidered jacket from the bed and tugged it over her stays. The colorful stitching added a festive touch to the dark-blue background.

Memengwaa, Waagosh's sister and Laurette's best friend, hadn't seen this outfit that Laurette had sewn and embroidered this past winter. She traced a red butterfly with her finger, and then a brown bear. Memengwaa, whose name meant butterfly, was a member of the Ojibwe's Bear Clan, the clan of protectors and healers. The surrounding flowers and leaves Laurette had embroidered were depictions of those with medicinal properties. Both girls had been trained as healers by Memengwaa's mother. Laurette picked up a leather satchel with a blue cloth band across its front decorated with the same embroidery. Memengwaa preferred to wear the soft deer-skins of her people, but she'd appreciate the satchel and accept it as a gift.

Marie at her heels, Laurette left the cabin. The sun had traveled halfway to its zenith. Any frost had long since melted away. The scent of the forest awakening from its winter sleep greeted her, and the mustiness of last fall's decaying leaves warred with the subtle hint of buds yet unfurled.

She trotted toward the fort. It was almost on the way to the Ojibwe village. It wasn't far out of the way, at least. Waagosh would be angry if he found out she'd returned. Papa would be furious. But then, Papa wouldn't approve if he knew Waagosh had hinted to her about marriage either.

Twisting and turning along the path, Laurette covered the two miles to the fort. She stopped near where she'd met the redcoat. Had he taken her advice to walk closer to the walls? The sun's angle was almost exactly as it had been when they'd met yesterday. She moved forward, placing each foot on the damp earth, avoiding twigs and dried leaves. Marie stayed close by her side. When the gray timbers of the palisade came into view between the trees in front of her, she crouched and waited.

A tingle of anticipation that she couldn't deny held her in place.

The scuffle and crunch of boots announced his arrival. He walked along the forest's edge, not next to the palisade. His position left him within sight of the fort but gave him the option to dive into the forest for cover if needed. He was adapting, and that made her smile. She waited until he drew abreast of her.

"Monsieur Bedlow."

He jerked, his musket snapped from his side to his chest, his eyes searching the trees.

Laurette stepped from behind the shielding pine, her heart beating a frantic pulse near her throat. What was she doing?

He stepped into the trees before glancing back toward the fort. Then he moved toward her. "Mademoiselle Pettigrew?"

His face was newly shaved, his hair combed and gathered at the nape of his neck with a leather tie. A more natural color rested on his cheeks.

"You feel better, oui?"

He ran his hand across his jaw. "Cleaner, at least." He glanced at the fort again, a pucker creasing his brow. "This is not a safe place for you."

She averted her gaze. Did he think her too bold?

"But I am glad to see you." His voice dropped into a deeper, more intimate rumble.

"I am on my way to visit a friend."

"In the settlement?" He waved a hand to the east, where a collection of cabins and Papa's trading post were hidden by the fort's walls.

"Non." She lifted her chin toward the west. "The Ojibwe village. They have returned for the summer."

"You are friends with the Indians?" His eyes widened.

She shrugged. "A few of them."

"I have been told they are very dangerous."

"They are, they can be, if you do not respect them and their ways."

He scratched above his ear, tipping his hat to one side. "Respect that they kill people?"

"Only people who invade their land."

He looked toward the fort and grunted, then shot a glance back at her. "Have you invaded?"

"Non."

"But you live near here—" He snapped his mouth shut and blinked a couple of times before focusing on her again. "Do you live with them? Are you, that is, do you belong to—" A wariness entered his tone.

He thought her an Ojibwe's woman? She shook her head, braids bouncing on the front of her coat. "Non. I live with my papa." At least, she had until the voyageurs had returned.

"Who is your papa?"

She retreated a step. "Someone who does not trust the redcoats."

"And you? Do you trust us?"

Papa wasn't the only one who told stories about the British soldiers. Her whole life she'd heard the stories told by trappers and traders, Ojibwe, French, and Métis. They could not all be wrong. And yet. . .

"I think perhaps that people are people, no matter what color coat they wear. Some are good, some are not good, and some are bad."

He looked at the fort again. "That is why you must not come so close to the fort. You are correct, some are bad. Some are very bad."

"Are you bad, Monsieur Bedlow?" Such boldness. She almost wished the words back. Almost.

"I hope that I am not, Mademoiselle Pettigrew. While I know you should stay away for your safety, I admit that I would very much like to see you again. Does that make me bad? Or just selfish?"

Warmth exploded across her cheeks.

He tipped his head and studied her for a moment. "The sentry will wonder why I have not resumed my walk. I worried them yesterday when I was out of sight for so long. I must go, lest they come in search of me this time."

"I should leave as well."

He reached toward her, and when she didn't move, he took her mittened hand and squeezed it, bowing from the waist. "Be safe."

She nodded, the best she could do with the lump in her throat. He turned and walked away while she stood as rooted to the forest floor as the towering trees around her. What spell had this man cast over her? Why did the redcoat's voice, so different from the singsong cadence of her Ojibwe friends, make her body vibrate with its timbre?

What an utter fool he was. Henry had no business talking to any woman that way. He was a soldier, obligated to serve the Crown until discharged, and that not for four more years. He should have sent her off with a stern warning and been done with it.

But she'd been waiting for him, even after seeing him at his worst yesterday. The same unexpected encounter that had prompted him to bathe, shave, and tidy his appearance for the first time in weeks. Almost as if he'd hoped she'd return, but how could he have?

He finished his round of the fort with a final glance into the woods. Did she linger? Did her dark eyes follow him? An utter fool indeed, 'twas more likely an Indian with an eye to his scalp who watched him from under those trees. His skin crawled beneath his coat. He quickened his steps and made it to the gate before a coughing spasm bent him over.

Laurette reached the Ojibwe village, and Memengwaa came running to meet her, no sign of censure on her face. Her brother couldn't have told her about the British soldier.

"Waagosh said he saw you in the forest." Her friend greeted her with a hug. The scents of wood smoke and herbs lingered in her braided hair.

Laurette pushed back to arm's length and looked her friend up and down. "The winter has been kind to you." It had. She fairly glowed. "Marriage must suit you."

Memengwaa pushed one of her braids over her shoulder and pointed toward the village. "I have our wigwam set up and ready for our first guest. Come. Waagosh and Niigaanii speared fish this morning. We will eat well."

They fell into the familiar pattern of their friendship, as if the long winter months had never happened. Memengwaa exclaimed over the embroidered satchel while Laurette exchanged her worn moccasins for a pair Memengwaa had sewn and decorated with shells. They'd settled near the fire at the center of the wigwam, tending the roasting fish and sharing memories of Memengwaa's mother, when Waagosh and another man entered.

Memengwaa rose and stepped to the man's side. "This is Niigaanii."

The man made no move or sound to acknowledge Laurette, and Memengwaa did not share her name with him. Her friend gathered the turtle shells stacked in a corner, and Laurette joined her. They parceled out fish onto each shell, serving the men near the fire first, and then sitting together at the back of the wigwam.

Laurette refused to meet Waagosh's eyes when he glanced at her. He hadn't told his sister about her meeting with the redcoat, but his displeasure hung between them like a physical thing. How much worse it would be if he knew about this morning's meeting.

"Is he not as handsome as I told you?" A blush added a rosy glow to Memengwaa's dusky skin.

"He is." Niigaanii came from another Ojibwe village, one that wintered near Memengwaa's, many days travel to the south. Her friend had talked about little else last summer than her intended and their upcoming marriage.

"And my brother, is he not handsome as well?"

Laurette flicked a glance at Waagosh. His head was turned, his profile strong and proud. Any woman would agree. It would not be difficult to give her heart to such a man, if he weren't Ojibwe. As much as she loved her friend, and as much as she had adored their mother, Laurette didn't think she could fit in among the Ojibwe.

Perhaps there was too much French blood in her. She believed in the God the Jesuits spoke of, the Jesus in her book, not the spirits of the Ojibwe. She believed the stories her mother had told her of Jesus. The Son of God. A gentle Man, not a warrior.

Waagosh was a warrior. There was much to admire in that, and much to fear. The stories told around the fire by the Ojibwe elders, stories of battles, had always disturbed her. Her mother had said that the Ojibwe looked at life differently than the Métis. That difference created a barrier between her and her friends. She could come and visit, but she would never truly belong.

Memengwaa nudged her, snapping her thoughts back to the present.

"Since our mother's death, I have looked after Waagosh. But my brother is restless. He should seek his own woman." She stared at Laurette.

"Your brother is very handsome, as you say, but I do not know. . ."

"He could be your husband. He would like to be."

"So you have said, but he has not." Laurette raised her hand, palm out. "Not since he returned. And that may be for the best, as I do not think I could accept him."

Unless the loneliness drove her to it. Whether she fit in or not, at least with Waagosh, she wouldn't be alone.

Her friend snorted and set her turtle shell aside, displeasure written on every inch of her face. Niigaanii looked toward them, his gaze locked with his wife. The stoic warrior's eyes took on an unexplainable gleam. Laurette turned her head. What would it be like to have a man look at her that way?

Henry Bedlow's tawny eyes teased her thoughts. Why had she felt safe with him? He was an enemy of both French and Ojibwe, and therefore of the Métis as well. Yet she'd felt more comfortable with him than she did with—

She glanced at the fire. Waagosh stared at her. She'd known him almost her whole life, but she'd never felt as comfortable with him as she did with the British soldier she'd encountered in the forest.

Perhaps it was best that she did as Papa wanted and remained at the cabin this summer. She squeezed Memengwaa's arm and thanked her for the meal and moccasins, then slipped out of the wigwam. Marie rose from a patch of sunshine where she'd been lying. In moments, Laurette was running through the forest toward the cabin. If only she could run away from all the uncertainty stirring within her.

Chapter 4

Although he scoured the forest's edge for the next three days, Henry caught no glimpse of the lovely Métis woman. He'd let the sentries know that he preferred to walk in the shelter of the trees rather than be exposed in the open near the fort. They thought him daft.

He continued to improve each day, so perhaps the surgeon had known what he was talking about. Henry had inquired about the Métis and learned that they were a mixed-race people, mostly French and Ojibwe. Offspring of the first trappers and Indian women, they'd found themselves rejected by both sides of their lineage. Over the years, they had banded together and become their own people, many speaking both languages and often working as interpreters and guides. When he learned that the trading post in the settlement was run by a man named Charles Pettigrew, he expanded his daily walks to include a loop through the settlement. He even stopped in one day, but left after a quick perusal of the merchandise.

On his last lap around the fort that morning, something brown flashed between the trees. A deer? He lifted his musket, heartbeat quickening, and froze. Fresh meat was always welcomed by the cook. The creature bounded back into sight and a different kind of excitement sluiced through his veins.

Miss Pettigrew's lurcher, for he doubted there could be two such dogs in this remote backcountry, ran for the pure joy of it. Her head high, her tongue lolling out the side of her mouth in a canine grin. If she saw Henry, she ignored him and made a beeline for a huge soft-needled tree with reddish bark. Before the dog reached it, Miss Pettigrew stepped into view.

Henry sucked in his breath. He'd almost convinced himself that she'd been a figment of his imagination, a fever dream from his illness.

Her unbound hair, free of its linen cap, fanned around her like a shawl, its inky darkness a foil for her oval face. A hesitant—or maybe wary—expression clouded her eyes.

Neither of them moved for several heartbeats.

He cleared his throat. "How do you do?"

A shy smile lifted the corners of her lips. "I am well. And you?" She walked toward him, her hand resting on the head of the lurcher.

"I thought you had taken my advice to stay away from the fort."

She caught the edge of her lip between her teeth. His stomach tightened. Had she any idea how appealing that was?

"You are unhappy to see me?"

Nothing could be further from the truth, but saying so would only encourage her and put her in danger. And yet, the words spilled out against his will. "Non. I have watched for you each time I have circled the fort."

Her dimple deepened, her dark eyes shone.

The combination affected his breathing. "I must keep walking. Surgeon's orders, you understand."

She nodded and strode forward, then stopped and looked back at him. "This way, n'est-ce pas?"

He hastened to her side. "You cannot walk around the lake side of the fort. You would be seen. There are men who would—"

"I will leave you there."

He snapped his mouth shut and strolled beside her for a few moments, savoring her company, comfortable in her silence. They approached the edge of the forest near the beach far too soon. They stopped, side by side, staring out over the waters of the straits, where the two mighty lakes, Michigan and Huron, met and mingled.

"The water is exceptionally blue today and so calm it is hard to express it with words." She pushed her hair behind her ear.

"It makes me wish I were a poet, that I could capture this moment in words and write them down."

She gasped and clenched a fistful of his coat sleeve. "Can you read and write?"

Desire burned in her eyes, but he wasn't foolish enough to think it burned for him. "Of course. My father was a scholar. He tutored the children of a wealthy family and his own children as well."

"This is why you speak French, n'est-ce pas?"

"Oui. As well as a bit of Latin and German."

Her mouth formed a small circle, drawing his eyes like children before the chocolatier's window. He swallowed.

"I wish I could read."

"I could teach you."

Her hand tightened on his sleeve.

"I have a book. It was my mama's. It tells the story of Jesus."

She had a Bible? Out here? "Is it written in Latin or French?"

Her brow puckered and she shook her head. "I know not."

Of course, how would she? "I'd like to see it."

"I will bring it tomorrow."

She tucked that edge of her lip between her teeth again, and he knew he was lost. She was returning tomorrow. This exotic creature clinging to his arm could have his heart at the twitch of her finger.

But even if she did, that did not release him from his service to the Crown.

The next morning, Laurette waited at the eastern edge of the forest behind the fort, bouncing on her toes as if she'd never learned to conceal herself in the woods, Mama's book pressed into her breast, secured beneath her crossed arms. She was early, but how could she stay away? Today she would learn to read.

The sun inched its way above the trees.

Marie wandered off and came back several times, but Laurette couldn't pry her eyes from the fort. Two soldiers walked around the corner of the palisade, and she dropped to the forest floor. Where was Marie? A nose nudged her shoulder and she heaved a silent sigh while slipping her arm around the dog's neck. The soldiers didn't approach the forest. They walked to the forest gate and entered the fort.

So intent on watching the two men, she'd missed Monsieur Bedlow's appearance. Marie lifted her head, drawing Laurette's attention to him. Tall and slender, his step was more measured today, his shoulders straighter. He cleared the distance between the fort and the forest without a cough.

When he entered the trees, she rose, and Marie bounded toward him.

"She sees me as a friend." The rumble of his voice warmed something deep in her middle.

"As do I."

He stopped, and something flashed in his eyes, something she didn't understand. More warmth fanned out from her middle, not at all unpleasant.

"Do you?"

She nodded and then lifted the book in her arms. "I have the book."

He took it, splaying one hand underneath. With the other he caressed the cover. "A Bible." He turned it sideways, and the book opened in the middle. "Written in French." He glanced at her. "Perfect for teaching you to read."

Her toes curled in her moccasins, and her fingers curled into her skirt. "Father Denis said it is not good for a woman to read." She gathered the edge of her lip between her teeth. Would he change his mind now? She'd debated telling him that throughout her restless night.

He closed the book and her heart dropped. "A priest is just a man, mademoiselle. Even he can be in error."

Blood rushed behind her ears. She reached out to the nearest tree to steady herself.

"Are you ill?"

"Non. I am overcome. Overjoyed."

Crinkles fanned from his eyes. He was, without doubt, a very handsome man. "I am happy to teach you. I am not good at much else." He waved a hand toward the fort and then the woods. "Not a good soldier, not a good woodsman. A truly terrible sailor. Teaching, however, is something I can do."

"And today you will teach me to read."

His deep chuckle pulled her in like a flame pulled a moth. "It will take more than one day to learn to read. But today we will start."

More than one day? Of course, what had she been thinking? Had she learned all about healing in one day? Had she learned to gather and preserve or tend her garden in one day?

He pulled a flat piece of slate rock from one coat pocket and a piece of white stone from another. "We must walk as you learn, or I will be missed." He slipped her book into his coat and then held up the slate. "I will write out the letters on this."

She fell into step beside him, amazed as he drew white lines and gave them names. It would take many days to learn. Many days of meeting with Monsieur Bedlow.

That meant many days she would not be alone.

They'd made a good start on learning her letters, and he already looked forward to her visit tomorrow, as long as he could keep her out of sight of the fort. He'd reversed direction at the fort's water gate, which allowed them to walk back and forth through the forest without her being visible to the sentries. Today's walk had flown by even though he'd walked slower than ever before.

Henry returned to the fort and did his best to ignore the blank stares of the Indians who sat near the gate. He scratched his scalp. The Indians didn't seem to worry Major Etherington. He'd heard that Charles Langlade, a fur trader of mixed French and Indian heritage who still lived in the fort, had warned Major Etherington that the Indians were not to be trusted. But it was said that the major had scolded Langlade and ignored the warning.

Perhaps the major was right. And yet, where yesterday three Indians had loitered near the commander's house, today there were four. He paused at the door to the barracks and glanced back at the gate. How many had been there yesterday? The day before? He'd never counted, but not as many as sat there now.

Soldiers who had fought in the war just finished, those in colonial forts such as Michilimackinac, told gruesome tales. Painted Indians drinking blood scooped from the chests of the fallen, scalping men still alive, cutting out hearts that still beat. Henry entered the barracks and dropped his musket on his bunk. Such tales were doubtless embellished with each telling. He scratched his scalp and coughed.

He sat and rubbed his chest. It was better. Daily walking was helping as was the warmer weather. Being in the barracks was a nice change from the infirmary too. Soon he'd be drilling again and taking his duty on the upper walkway around the palisade. But not yet. His jaw cracked with a yawn, and he stretched out on his bunk. Raven locks flowing toward a piece of slate filled his mind as he drifted off to sleep.

Had ever a morning dragged on so long? Not that Laurette could remember. She had practiced every letter on the slate, using a stick to scratch the image in the dirt while saying the name aloud, just as Monsieur Bedlow had shown her. How soon until she knew enough to begin reading? She lifted her hands as if holding a book and used one finger to turn the imaginary page. The only person she'd ever seen hold a book to read was the Jesuit priest, Father Denis, who had lived in the settlement until the French forces had pulled out. On Sunday mornings, he had read in a language she didn't understand, but even so, she'd sat spellbound after Mama had explained that the words he spoke were written on the pages.

In her little-girl mind, it had been magic. Later, Papa had explained about writing and reading. Papa could sign his name, which was all he'd ever learned. Mama hadn't been able to do even that. But, oh, how proud Mama would be if she knew that Laurette was learning.

She reclined onto her back, disturbing Marie, who snoozed at her side. The dog laid her head on Laurette's shoulder. Leaves on the hardwoods had begun to unfurl, reaching toward the sky, creating dapples of sunshine on the brown leaves littering the ground.

Not unlike her life. Her old life with Mama at the cabin, visiting the Ojibwe, learning about healing, gathering and storing for the winter, waiting for Papa to come home. That life was over, dead like the leaves moldering on the ground. But the new leaves sprang forth, tender and shining, soon to replace those discarded below. Her new life was pushing through the old, adjusting to the changes. Mama was gone, Memengwaa was married, but Henry Bedlow was here, and he would teach her to read.

She sat up, earning a disgruntled look from Marie.

"How can I rest, when my mind is full of letters and my heart is full of. . ." What was her heart full of? A tall redcoat.

The distant cracking of underbrush brought her to her feet. He needed to learn to walk in the woods. She would teach him that while he taught her to read. A good trade. Not one that Papa would approve of however. She shoved that thought aside as he grew closer.

"*Bonjour*, Monsieur Bedlow."

"Mademoiselle Pettigrew." He inclined his head, and her heart pattered behind her ribs. "As we are to be studying together, perhaps you should call me Henry."

"And you shall call me Laurette."

"Oui. I would like that. Very much."

One side of his mouth lifted in a questioning smile. She'd been caught staring. What would Mama say? She cleared her throat. "I have been thinking. I would like to teach you something while you teach me to read."

His brows rose. She almost giggled. He must be wondering what an uneducated woman such as she could know that he did not.

"I will teach you to walk in the woods so that you do not sound like a whole herd of stampeding elk."

"That is something I would very much like to learn."

For two passes of the fort, they exchanged letters for demonstrations. When he snapped a twig, she set it back down and demonstrated how to avoid it. When she mangled a letter, he leaned toward her and repeated it, so that she could watch his lips make the sound. Perhaps once or twice she mangled a word just to bring him nearer.

On the final pass, they walked in silence for a distance. The companionable silence of two people who didn't need words between them.

In the quiet, the brush of leather against leaves caught her ear. She grabbed his forearm and shook her head as he opened his mouth. Pulling him down with her, she slid into a crouch beneath a midsized pine whose limbs still brushed the ground. He followed without a sound.

Ojibwe men trotted past them, not more than ten strides from their tree. There must have been a dozen of them, all young and grim faced. When the last one's copper hair ornaments came into view, she sunk even lower. Why had they been to the settlement? And why were they so somber?

When they had passed, she eased out from the tree.

"Who were they?" Henry unfolded his length from their hiding spot.

"Ojibwe."

"Where are they going?"

"Back to the village. The real question is, what were so many doing at the settlement?"

His eyes met hers, and a tremor ran the length of her spine. Not in a good way.

"You must return to the fort. Make haste."

"But what about—"

"They would not hurt me. That last one. . ." She couldn't tell him about Waagosh. It was better if he didn't know. And much better if Waagosh didn't know that she'd met with Henry. Again.

Chapter 5

Four days of lessons and Henry's pupil could write her name and recognize a few dozen words. She thrilled over each new word almost as much as she praised him for each silent pass through the forest. She waited for him in the mornings and returned again in the afternoons.

Never had he enjoyed life more.

It couldn't last, these idyllic days, because with each one his strength grew. His cough had all but disappeared. In good conscience, he should report to the surgeon and ask to be reassigned to his regular duties. That's what a good soldier would do.

Henry left the fort and stepped under the dense covering of trees. Laurette waited for him there, her piece of slate clutched to her breast, her eyes shining.

"Bonjour, Henry."

"Bonjour, Laurette. What has you looking so eager this morning?"

"Last night I looked at Mama's book. I tried to find places I could read. I found some words I knew and could put together. But I could not understand this part." She thrust the slate at him. She'd copied part of the Bible in her tiny letters, squeezing it onto the slate.

He glanced at it, then back at her. "You have discovered the Psalms."

"What are they?"

Could anything be more enjoyable than discussing the Psalms on a perfect day with this delightful woman by his side? He told her about the poetry and praises in the middle of her Bible, and time slipped away. On their third pass through the woods, she grabbed his arm and dropped into a crouch. He squatted beside her. Something moved ahead of them.

"Return to the fort," she whispered.

He hefted his musket and searched the dense underbrush ahead. "What is it?"

"Not what, who. Make haste."

"And leave you alone? I cannot do that."

She laid her free palm against his cheek and turned his face toward her with surprising strength. "It is not I who am in danger. Go." She shoved his arm away and sprinted in the direction of the movement.

He opened his mouth to call after her, but didn't. She had disappeared.

The hair on Henry's forearms stood at attention. Whether from her touch or the implication of danger, he wasn't sure. Nay. Not implication. The danger was real, almost tangible. A cold sweat broke out under his coat. He backed away, musket to his chest, until he came to the clearing around the fort. Laurette was friends with the Indians. She'd said so.

Had she just saved him from one of them?

Laurette ran without looking back toward the flash of buckskin she'd glimpsed between the trees. No crashing followed her, and Henry wasn't good enough yet to run silently. He must have listened to her and returned to the fort. She kept herself between him and whoever waited ahead. Waagosh wouldn't shoot if she were in the way. At least, she didn't think he would. Her heart hammered against her ribs. What if it wasn't Waagosh?

She came to a tiny clearing and turned in a circle. Marie ran toward her right as Memengwaa stepped into view. The dog circled Memengwaa, but was ignored. Her friend's dark eyes bored into Laurette's.

"What were you doing with that redcoat?"

The brief flare of relief that it wasn't Waagosh disappeared under her friend's accusing stare.

"He is teaching me to read."

Memengwaa crossed her arms, making the resemblance to her brother more pronounced. "You have seen this man before."

It was an indictment.

"Oui."

"A redcoat. Why would you do this?" Disbelief warred with anger in her tone, her brows drawn into a formidable line.

Why would she? Henry didn't fit the mold of a redcoat. He spoke French. He was. . .kind. And handsome since he'd cleaned up and regained his health. His eyes lit up when he saw her in a way that played havoc with her pulse. And he was teaching her to read.

Memengwaa sliced the air with both hands. "You must not see him again."

"But I—"

"Waagosh has been waiting for you to notice him. You are a year older than me. It is time for you to choose a husband as I have done. Waagosh is a patient man, but it is time."

Laurette shook her head. "It is impossible."

"It is not." Memengwaa took a step closer. "My brother is a brave man, very strong, and a good provider. He is handsome. I know you see that."

She did. In her girlish thoughts years before, she'd even wondered if he would notice her in that way. Perhaps even hoped for it. But now, as a woman, she wanted more. She wanted to be where she fit in, and she knew that wasn't with the Ojibwe. How to explain that to her friend?

"Why are you looking at a redcoat when such a man is yours for the taking?" Frustration colored her friend's voice.

"Because I cannot accept your brother."

"Tell me why."

Laurette ran damp palms down her skirt. The last thing she wanted to do was alienate her friend. "We do not see things the same way. We do not believe in the same things."

Memengwaa tilted her head, confusion in her eyes.

"I believe in the God that the Jesuits taught of."

"The Jesuits." Scorn filled her friend's voice. "They fled before the redcoats. They were cowards. Who believes a coward?"

"I did not say I believed in the Jesuits, I said I believe in their God."

"I believe in many spirits, and so does Waagosh."

It wasn't the same. Her heart told her it wasn't but gave her no words to help her friend understand something she barely understood herself.

"Stay away from the redcoat." Memengwaa all but spit the word. "It would be best if Waagosh never found out."

"He knows."

"If he knew, he would kill that one."

Fear drained the warmth from Laurette's body. Memengwaa was right. Henry was in danger because of her. The sun dimmed, and the birdsong quieted around her.

Laurette turned and stumbled toward her cabin. Memengwaa called after her, but she didn't respond. One thing she knew for certain—she could never see Henry Bedlow again.

Chapter 6

The mingled scents of tobacco, cured hides, and bear grease greeted her when Laurette slipped into Papa's trading post. Three traders in their striped coats haggled with Papa at the long counter, their tight bales of furs as yet unbundled at their feet.

She shouldn't have come. Papa wouldn't be pleased. But she couldn't stay another day alone at the cabin. She couldn't. If not Henry, she must see someone or she would go mad. The past week had taught her one lesson—she couldn't live alone.

A man wearing a bear claw necklace of the Sauk tribe squatted against the wall across the room. His dark eyes latched onto Laurette. She kept her head high and avoided his glare. A pair of Ojibwe men examined hatchets and knives along the side wall with their backs to her. The taller man's familiar height and copper hair ornaments forced the air from her chest.

Waagosh.

"Laurette." Memengwaa stood next to the newly replenished display of yard goods, her eyes soft and seeking.

"Laurette?" In contrast, Papa's near bellow drew the attention of everyone in the long room.

She cringed.

"Do not leave until I am finished here." Papa's beard bristled across his frown.

She nodded and then joined Memengwaa, keeping her back to Waagosh. One man frowning at her was quite enough. She didn't need to see another face of disapproval.

"We parted with harsh words." Memengwaa fingered a length of fine wool that hung from a bolt. "You have not returned to the village."

Neither had her friend come to her. "Non."

"I regret the sharpness of my words that day."

Laurette offered a sad smile. "You love your brother. This I understand."

"Nothing would make me happier than to have you for my sister." She pressed her hand to her breast. "My words came out wrong, but the reasons were from the heart."

While Laurette loved her friend and had cherished every moment with

142

Memengwaa's mother, it didn't change the fact that she wasn't Ojibwe. Visiting them was one thing, living among them would be entirely different.

"You honor me with such thoughts." Laurette shook her head. "But I cannot do what you wish." Not even to stop the loneliness that was grinding her spirit into the ground.

"Because of the redcoat?"

"He was teaching me to read. To be something more than just…than just…"

Sadness crept into her friend's eyes. "Than just an Ojibwe bride?"

"There is something inside me that longs for more."

"And you think the redcoat can offer more?" Memengwaa frowned. "Can he provide for you more than my brother? Keep you safer? Love you more?"

Waagosh had stayed away from her since his return. Perhaps he too had come to realize they were not well matched.

"Laurette." Papa shouldered his way to her side through the growing crowd of customers. "What are you doing here?"

Memengwaa slipped away.

"I needed to be with you." She glanced out the window at the settlement and then back at him. "To see people."

His face relaxed, a sad glint in his eye. "I wish you were not alone so much, *ma petite bichette*, but this is how it must be. Keep Marie near you. She will protect you as well as keep you company."

She nodded, unable to meet his eyes. He didn't understand.

"Come. I will see you back to the cabin."

"Non. I will return."

He glanced at the traders and nodded. "Oui. I will come to see you as soon as I can. I will bring you something special when I do."

She wasn't a child anymore, but Papa couldn't see that. A treat wouldn't fix the loneliness. It wouldn't fill her heart or teach her to read.

It wouldn't stop the longing every thought of Henry brought.

He hadn't seen her in a month, but that didn't keep Henry from scanning the forest from his position along the top of the fort's palisade. Not that he could have seen her if she'd been there, hidden in the trees. The surgeon had canceled his walks and ordered him back on duty. He'd had no opportunity to search for her, no way to learn what had happened to her. Had she been taken captive, injured, or worse? He'd toyed with the idea of speaking to her father but rejected it, knowing the man's opinion of the British.

An opinion Henry was beginning to share.

Major Etherington seemed more concerned with his daily grooming than the fact that the fort housed forty soldiers while being surrounded by ten times that many Indians. The hair rose along the back of Henry's head every time he passed the Indians who lounged around the fort's gates. Hair he was fond of, that he'd like to keep in his possession. He rubbed his scalp with one hand and gripped his musket with the other.

He'd never wanted to be in the army. He knew he wasn't soldier material. But when he'd gotten in that scuffle at the workhouse and knocked the overseer unconscious, the magistrate hadn't cared that the oaf had beaten a young girl half to death for falling asleep at her work station. Henry's choice had been between the army and prison. For once, being fluent in French had worked in his favor, as had his size. A smaller man would likely have been thrown into prison with no choice. It must have galled his captain to have watched his frame dwindle under first seasickness and then winter fever.

Now he spent his days drilling on the parade ground, patrolling along the top of the palisade, and polishing brass buttons and buckles that nobody but the local Indians would see. Indians who, in his opinion, were allowed far too much access to the fort. He scratched his scalp again.

Shouting in a heated stream of French erupted outside the commanding officer's house. A man dressed in the striped coat fancied by fur traders waved his arms as he stomped away. It was Charles Langlade, a man who was well-known and well-liked by the Indians even though he continued to live inside the fort with its British soldiers. Major Etherington watched from the doorway. Langlade's words filtered up toward Henry. Although he could only make out bits and pieces, Mr. Langlade was obviously not happy with the fort's commanding officer.

Henry shrugged. Who was?

Another soldier strolled his way along the walk, his head bobbing above the sharpened points of the fort's wall, the same sharpened points that only covered Henry to midchest. The soldier grinned and jerked his head toward the buildings below. "Off you go."

Henry tapped the brim of his hat with two fingers before scaling down the nearest ladder, relieved to have his shift over. He crossed to the barracks and entered.

"There ya be." Willie stood and stretched. "Been waitin' on ya."

"What for?"

"To help me test my leg." Willie did a slow jig with a decided limp around the tight confines of the barracks. After a setback with infection, his friend was up and about. It was good to see.

"Did the surgeon declare you healed then?"

"As good as. So you and me are goin' to the settlement to celebrate. I'm buyin' the first pint." Willie winked.

The local tavern stood next to Pettigrew's trading post. Henry had passed it on his walks but hadn't been inside. He laid down his musket and flexed his shoulders. It might be good to get out of the fort for a few hours.

"Did you hear the shouting a few minutes ago?" he asked Willie.

"Who could miss it?" Willie pulled on his coat. "But I cannot understand a word of that Frenchie talk. Come on."

Henry followed his friend out the door and through the fort's gate leading toward the water. Lakes Michigan and Huron converged in front of them. White-crested waves lapped against the shore. Seagulls squabbled over something near the rocks, their raucous cries rising above the surf. Henry stopped and breathed deeply, enchanted anew by the clean air of this region, so different from the black smoke of London or the briny odor of its waters. It smelled like. . .freedom.

Willie stopped and looked back. "Hurry up. I been waitin' for ya all afternoon."

Henry trotted to catch up. As they approached the settlement, colorful bits of red and yellow cloth brightened the ever-present leather that covered most of those who ambled or lounged along the street. The settlement was straining at its seams. Where had all these people come from?

Three soldiers in their red coats walked toward them, the one in the middle listing precariously from side to side. The tavern must be doing a brisk business today. Willie quickened his limping steps. Henry lengthened his stride to keep up.

The tavern sat squat and dark, a building made of logs like all the others, its steep roof covered with wide strips of bark held down with split logs. Smoke rolled from its wattle and daub chimney.

A flash of blue drew Henry's attention as his friend stepped into the tavern.

Laurette. Relief flooded him.

She shut the door to her father's trading post. Her eyes widened when they met his, their coffee depths twin pools he'd be happy to drown in. He took a step toward her, but she whirled and ran in the other direction.

What had he done to cause her to flee from him?

He glanced around. Two Indians watched him from across the street. Their flat expressions might mean anything, or nothing. Had she avoided him to protect him? Again. The thought chafed against his pride. He tugged the hem of his coat a bit straighter.

"Henry!" Willie stood in the tavern doorway with a pewter pint in each hand. "Are ya comin' or not?"

At least he knew she was safe. And that she was avoiding him. For his own good? Because her father disapproved? Or had he somehow disappointed her? Like he'd disappointed everyone in his life since the death of his family.

The outing lost its luster, but that was no reason to disappoint his friend.

Not trusting the voyageurs, Laurette doubled back to be certain she hadn't been followed, and then she ran the rest of the way to the cabin. After slamming the door shut behind her, she fell onto her bed. Marie climbed in beside her, washing the salty wetness from her mistress's face.

Laurette hugged Marie, the wiry hair rough against her cheek. After a long moment, she sat up.

"I cannot live like this, my sweet. I cannot."

Marie stretched out beside her with a contented sigh, apparently convinced that the crisis had passed. If only that were true. Instead, weeks of loneliness and sadness stretched before her. Seeing Memengwaa again, knowing that she now had a husband and would probably have a baby by next summer—

She stood and banged a pot onto the table before scooping a handful of wild rice into it. With a huff, she pushed it aside. Why cook a pot of anything? She wasn't hungry. Restless energy, not at all depleted from her run home, begged for release. She pulled her gathering basket from its shelf.

"Come, Marie. We will look for something fresh. We don't need much for our supper, just you and I."

The dog at her heels, Laurette left the cabin and headed north toward a place where wild strawberries grew. It was early yet, but there might be a few. If it was close to the fort, what did it matter? Henry didn't come into the forest anymore. She'd checked after a few days of avoiding him. She'd seen him once along the top of the palisade, no doubt fully healed and on duty again.

Hours later, with the sun's rays beginning their descent, Laurette's basket was filled with fresh greens and a handful of tiny strawberries. She brushed her hair back and looked around. Where was Marie?

Something moved through the trees to her left. She followed the sound, even though Marie wouldn't make that much noise. She grew closer, then tucked her basket beneath a tall tree to retrieve later, moving silently without it. A flash of something red sent her heartbeat skittering. Could it be?

Drunken laughter reached her and she froze. Words passed between those ahead, words she didn't understand. Then a voice penetrated, deep and rumbly and not at all slurred. She crept forward.

Four men had stopped along the trail that led from the settlement to the fort's forest gate. Why were they here? Why didn't they walk along the lake as most did? One of the men lay on the ground. Henry grabbed him by the back of his coat and hauled him to his feet.

Laurette edged closer. Displeasure radiated from Henry like heat from a fire. Her breath caught at the comparison of his tall, upright carriage next to his disheveled companions. He wasn't like the others. She'd known that from the first. If Papa could see this—

A low growl caught her attention, as well as Henry's. He swung his musket from his back. The other men laughed and pointed at him, too drunk to hear Marie's warning. But why was she growling. . .and why wasn't she by Laurette's side?

She moved toward the dog, keeping out of sight of the soldiers, trusting that Henry would recognize Marie in time and not shoot.

"What is this?" He spoke to the dog in French.

Marie whined, but she didn't move.

Something behind her did.

Chapter 7

Henry's heart dropped to the floor of his chest. Marie's growl slipped into a whine. He wanted to yell at the dog to keep growling, to protect her mistress.

He didn't think Willie would accost Laurette, but the two soddened soldiers with them were another story. One crashed into Henry's shoulder as he stared at the lurcher.

"Whaz thawt?"

Ale fumes rolled from him in sour waves.

"A dog. Probably belongs to someone at the fort." Henry clamped his hand on the man's shoulder and tried to turn him around.

The drunken soldier resisted, pushing Henry away with surprising strength considering he tottered with the effort.

"I seez sumpin behindz it."

Willie joined them, pulling the other drunken soldier with him, but the man flopped to the ground when Willie stopped.

Henry scanned the dense foliage behind Marie. Nothing moved. "I do not see—"

Something clinked, a metallic sound at odds with the forest. Henry froze.

The soldier pushed past him and Marie growled again but retreated.

"Willie, stay with that man." Henry pointed to the soldier passed out on the ground.

"You might need—"

"We cannot leave him here. He's helpless."

Willie frowned but nodded, sober enough to comprehend the danger. If these other two hadn't been so tipsy, they could've gone back to the fort through the water gate. But no, they had imbibed beyond their tolerance and were trying to sneak in the forest gate, opposite of where they thought their captain was. And Henry, great fool that he was, had agreed to help them.

Henry charged after the other man. Laurette, it must be her, was leading them deeper into the forest.

" 'Tish a woman! Wesh can have ush a good time."

Blood pounded in Henry's ears as he caught up with the soldier, standing almost on top of a woman sprawled in the ferns. Henry raised his musket, bringing the butt down on the side of the man's head. The soldier jerked and then went limp, collapsing in a boneless heap. But Henry didn't spare him a glance. He knelt before the figure on the ground. She had a steel trap clamped on her ankle. The woman lifted her face, pain etched around the fear in her dark eyes.

It wasn't Laurette.

Something moved to his left. He raised his musket. Marie bounded toward whoever was approaching. He lowered the weapon a notch.

Laurette stepped into sight. With a small cry, she rushed to the other woman's side. "Memengwaa." She looked up at Henry and then down at the trap, its teeth dug into bloody flesh. She looked back at Henry. "Help us."

He cast a glance at the soldier. Noisy breathing meant Henry hadn't inflicted anything more than a headache on the man. Which he would've had anyway, given the level of his inebriation.

Dropping the musket, he approached the women. Marie whined again, her tail wagging uncertainly, hair standing at attention along her back.

"Do not worry, Marie. He will help our friend."

The Indian woman said nothing as he knelt. Blood dripped onto the grass. How she had managed to run from them with that steel trap on her leg was beyond him. She glared, the pain in her eyes not masking her hatred. Laurette's presence must have eliminated her fear.

He cleared his throat. "This is going to hurt."

Laurette nodded. The Indian woman narrowed her eyes and clenched her teeth. She understood French.

Henry bent her leg until her foot was level on the ground and he could get a firm grip on both handles of the trap. It was a fearsome thing, meant to do great damage. And it had. But somehow it had missed the vital tendons at the back of the woman's ankle.

"When I get the trap open, pull her leg out as quickly as you can." At Laurette's nod, he squeezed the trap's handles with all his might, releasing the grip of its jaws.

The Indian woman gasped. Laurette had to ease the teeth out of the flesh on one side. Henry hung on, sweat popping on his forehead. Once the foot was released, he let the trap snap shut and threw it as far into the woods as he could.

The Indian woman scooted away from him.

"Hold her."

Laurette grabbed the other woman's arm.

Henry pulled a handkerchief from his pocket and wrapped it snuggly around the wound. "Get her back to her village."

"I will." Laurette glanced at the soldier who was now snoring enough to wake the dead. "Will you be in much trouble?"

"He shan't remember anything tomorrow. But I must get him back to the fort."

She nodded, her dark eyes full of. . .something he couldn't define.

The Indian woman tried to stand. Laurette assisted her, then glanced back over her shoulder. "I am in your debt. Memengwaa is as a sister to me."

"I did little enough. Make haste. And be safe." He should remind her to avoid the fort. But how could he when he wanted nothing more than to see her again?

Laurette had cleaned Memengwaa's wounds, and now her friend rested in her wigwam, her foot elevated and wrapped in moss lined with a mixture of healing herbs. Laurette was amazed that the damage hadn't been more severe. If they could keep infection at bay, her friend should heal without a limp, although she'd carry the scars for the rest of her life. Laurette pushed strips of willow bark into a pot of hot water and set it aside to steep.

Niigaanii rushed through the opening, Waagosh behind him.

Waagosh stopped near Laurette as Niigaanii knelt beside his wife.

"What has happened to my sister?"

"A trap."

"Where?"

"Near the fort."

Waagosh gripped the tomahawk at his belt, his mouth pulled into a flat line. But he held his tongue.

Niigaanii did not. He spoke in rapid Ojibwe. Laurette knew enough of the language to make herself understood, but couldn't follow the singsong flurry of words that volleyed between husband and wife. Niigaanii's body language and tone left no doubt of his anger. Memengwaa's response was slower, but no less angry.

Waagosh stiffened with each word. "Redcoats chased her?" His fury lashed through the wigwam.

"One did." Laurette raised her chin and met his furious gaze. "Another stopped him and freed your sister."

His eyes narrowed to slits. "Who was the one who set her free?"

"The same soldier I have spoken to before. He knocked the other man unconscious and then sprung the trap to free Memengwaa."

Waagosh would never accuse her of lying, but it was clear that he wanted to deny her words.

"It is true." Memengwaa spoke in French. "Laurette's redcoat stopped the other man and released my foot from the trap."

"Laurette's redcoat." Waagosh almost growled the name.

She took a step back as emotions flickered across his normally stoic face.

Niigaanii spoke, his voice more controlled this time, and Memengwaa answered him before turning to Laurette.

"Thank you for seeing me returned to the village. You should go now, before the sun sets."

Laurette turned to Waagosh. "If she becomes fevered for more than a day, or if the fever is high enough that she is confused, fetch me."

He grunted.

"Come, Marie." The dog rose and padded out the entrance behind her. Waagosh joined her and walked in silence. He slipped behind her as the trail narrowed to a deer path.

She spoke over her shoulder, "You do not need to accompany me. I will not go near the fort."

"Who knows how far the redcoats are encroaching into the forest?"

A chill raised the fine hairs of her forearms. Perhaps an escort wasn't a bad idea after all. Where had that trap come from? It was long past the time of trapping for furs. Had it been overlooked by a careless trapper? Not likely, since traps were expensive and hard to replace. More likely, it had been maliciously set along a well-traveled path. But who would do such a thing? The redcoats. They weren't all like Henry. He'd warned her that some were very bad. She rubbed her forearms.

Waagosh touched her shoulder and she stopped. He towered over her, his strength evident in the width of his shoulders, the roped muscles of his crossed arms. She need fear no redcoat when he stood beside her.

"If the redcoats have penetrated the forest, they may find your cabin."

"I will be careful."

"Your father will be gone much."

"I have Marie."

He looked off into the distance, then shifted his gaze back to her. "Return to the village." He paused. "With me."

"I cannot—"

"I would protect you."

The dark intensity of his eyes unsettled her. He was asking her to stay with him as his wife. To become Ojibwe. To be safe, protected by him, provided for by him. Maybe she could have said yes if he had asked last year. . .before she'd met Henry Bedlow. She shook her head.

He let loose a long breath, which ended in a hiss.

"Is it the redcoat?"

She shrugged. "It is more than that. I long for. . .something. A different way of life. A place to belong where I fit in. I am not Ojibwe."

"You are not British."

"Non. I am not." Nor was she French. Was there anywhere she truly belonged?

A hawk cried in the distance, then Waagosh started for her cabin again. She fell in step behind him this time. He wouldn't make that offer again, and her refusal was sure to change her relationship with Memengwaa. Disappointing her friend weighed heavily on her heart. The stiff, solid back of Waagosh saddened her as well.

They reached the cabin as the forest swallowed the last of the sun's rays. Waagosh turned to her, blocking the door.

"Stay away from the fort. Stay away from the settlement."

There was something in the darkness of his face that unnerved her. "Why?"

"Anger rises toward the redcoats."

"Ojibwe anger?"

He nodded. "Ojibwe and others."

Fear curled around her middle. "Papa?"

"Charles Pettigrew is a friend to the Ojibwe. He will be left alone. You will stay here."

It wasn't a question. It was a command. One she'd be foolish to ignore. She nodded, and then he was gone. What had he warned her away from? What was going to happen?

Chapter 8

Five days had passed since Waagosh had walked away from the cabin. Five days Laurette had battled her desire to leave against his warning. Five long days. She dug the hoe into her small garden patch, jabbing it deep into the loamy soil. It didn't help. Neither had second-guessing her answer to Waagosh nor poring over the Psalms to practice her reading, trying to sound out new words.

Marie lay stretched in a patch of sunshine, oblivious to the unrest in her mistress's soul. If only Laurette could lie in a patch of sunshine and be so content with her life. If only she didn't long for more than this. She kicked a clod of dirt out of her way and carried the hoe back to the cabin. Marie rose and padded after her.

"We will fetch my gathering basket. I left it close to the fort, but it is my favorite."

Marie cocked her head, one ear perked and the other laid back as if questioning her mistress's motives. Laurette couldn't deny, even to her dog, that what pulled her to the fort had nothing to do with a favorite basket. With a huff, she leaned the hoe against the cabin wall.

She was going to the fort against Papa's wishes—again—and now against Waagosh's warning. Against her own good sense. But she had to see Henry, or at least be near him. Even though the most she could do was watch him on sentry duty above the fort's wall.

She pulled off her linen cap and tossed it inside. The light-colored head covering might draw unwanted attention. "Come, Marie."

Each step she took into the woods was faster than the one before until she was running. Her braids streamed out behind her, bouncing off her back as she ducked low-hanging branches. Tiny flowers littering the woodland floor released their delicate scent to mingle with the earthy odors of pine and moss. A partridge launched from a bush as she raced past, stirring the air with its flurry of wings. Two black squirrels scampered up a tree, the last just inches ahead of Marie's nose.

Laurette slowed as she neared the fort. Sweat slicked her back and forehead. She gulped in the fragrant air and pressed her hand against the stitch in her side. Marie stayed beside her, tongue hanging from the side of her mouth.

"It feels good to run, n'est-ce pas?" She ruffled the dog's ears.

Her basket lay where she'd left it, its contents wilted. She dumped it out and hesitated. She should go straight back to the cabin. Her heart tugged her on toward the fort. When the palisade walls became visible through the trees, she wrapped her fingers around the long hair on Marie's neck.

"Stay with me."

She crept from tree to tree, watching for any movement ahead, watching the ground before her for any sign of a trap. A sentry patrolled the top of the palisade. He was tall, his shoulders visible above the points. Her heart tripped against her ribs. If only she could see his face.

The man made his circuit back and forth on the side of the fort not directly across from her. It was impossible to say if it was Henry or not, but for a little while, she let herself believe that it was. Would he wave if she showed herself? Would he sneak out to see her? Would he take her in his arms? Would she let him?

What would it be like to have a man come home to her each evening?

Lost in her imaginings, she almost missed the light tread of someone moving through the forest. Marie whined. Laurette pulled back from the edge of the forest, working her way past the path that led to the fort's forest gate.

A whistle trilled, and Marie lifted her head. She bounded toward a large man strolling down the path.

Papa.

He stopped and spread his arms. "Laurette, where are you?"

"I am here." She stepped into the path.

"What are you doing so close to the fort?" He lowered his voice from its normal boom to as close to a whisper as Papa could get. "Have I not told you it is too dangerous?"

"Oui, Papa." She gripped her basket's handle in front of her with both hands, her head bowed. "I am very happy to see you. I have been. . .lonely."

"Oh ma petite bichette." He clicked his tongue. "I am sorry. This last week, it was too busy for me to come. What is good for my pocket is not always good for my daughter. Come." He held out his elbow, and she slipped her hand into it. "We will go home."

"Oui, Papa."

"You listen to your papa now. You must stay at the cabin. You must not come to the settlement, the fort, or even the Ojibwe village."

"Why?"

"The settlement, she is like a keg of powder waiting for the spark." He shook his head. "It is not good. You should not be here. Trust your papa."

She did. Hadn't Waagosh told her the same thing? She trusted him too. Laurette cast a glance back toward the fort, which was long out of sight. Would she be able to stay away? Or would loneliness—or something stronger—drive her out of the cabin once again?

That was the last time Henry would play Good Samaritan to his fellow soldiers. He didn't even like most of them, drunken louts lacking both manners and morals. He may have come out of the workhouse, but he hadn't been born there. His father had earned a good living and taught his children well. His mother, a God-fearing woman, had taken them to church on Sundays and read the scriptures to them in the evenings. If they'd survived, how different his life would be now. He wouldn't be stationed at the end of the earth in a fort surrounded by heathens who wished him and all the king's soldiers dead.

At least his week of extra kitchen and garden duties had ended, punishment for his role in hauling in the two drunken soldiers. No one had questioned the sizable lump on the one soldier's head, not even the soldier himself when he awoke. His memory hadn't extended past the last pint he'd imbibed at the tavern. When they'd been caught trying to sneak into the fort, Willie was the only one who'd given Henry a sideways glance during his explanation of what had happened. Henry had returned to Willie with the soldier over his shoulder and told Willie they'd chased the dog until the soldier had tripped and fallen. He wasn't sure his friend believed him, but Willie wasn't one to go looking for trouble.

"Will ya be goin' to the settlement with me then?" Willie pulled on his boots.

Or maybe he was. Henry bit back a groan. "To the tavern again?"

"Aye, well, maybe for just one pint." The good humor twinkling in his eyes was hard to ignore. "I'm sick of these fort walls."

That Henry could understand. A week of guard duty followed by hoeing between the sprouting turnips and cabbages had Henry eager to be away from the confining logs as well. His heart pattered an extra beat or two at the thought that Laurette might be in the settlement. She hadn't left his thoughts for long in the past week. The way she'd rushed to the Indian woman's side, the way she'd turned back to thank him, the trust in her eyes.

"Are you listenin'?"

Henry blinked. Willie stood by the door, toe tapping.

"Pardon me. My mind was—"

"Chasin' the wind. Have I not seen that same look on your face for the past week?"

"I'm coming." Henry grabbed his musket and slung it across his back before Willie could launch into any speculation about his lapses of concentration.

They exited the water gate and Henry filled his lungs with the fresh air blowing off the sparkling water. "I could never grow tired of this."

"You? The same man who hung over the rail of the ship the entire crossin'?"

"Just the ocean crossing. Once we set sail on the lakes, I was fine."

"Other than coughing fit to throw a lung, you mean."

"Other than that."

Willie grinned. "I'd hop the next ship home if I could."

Henry groaned out loud this time. "I shan't return at all if I can help it."

"You would stay here?"

"Not here, not exactly, but somewhere in the colonies. There is no one back in England pining away for Henry Bedlow." No one at all.

Willie shrugged. "I'm on the first ship home that the captain points me to."

They strolled to the edge of the settlement that looked very different than it had one week ago. Voyageurs lined the street and lounged in front of the buildings. Colorful cloth caps, striped coats, and loud French voices filled the space that last week had already seemed crowded. Now it overflowed. How many more would come to trade?

Henry stopped and stared, trying to see everything in the moving mass of humanity.

Willie stopped beside him. "Where did they all come from?"

Henry's scalp crawled. For every man dressed in the cloth and hide garb of a trapper or a voyageur, there were twice as many with feathers tied in their hair. No redcoats moved among the masses. Not one.

He took a step back. "I have a bad feeling about this."

"I know what ya mean." Willie wiped the back of his hand across his mouth. " 'Twouldn't hurt me feelin's any to be comin' back another day."

"Aye." Henry swallowed. "I believe we should report this to Major Etherington."

"Do ya think he will listen to the likes of us?"

Henry turned and hiked back down the path to the fort, ignoring the creeping sensation marching double-time between his shoulder blades. The major might not listen, but he should. He most certainly should.

Henry prayed that Laurette was somewhere else. Somewhere safe.

Chapter 9

An entertainment?" Henry snapped his mouth shut. Was the major deranged? He certainly wasn't listening to anyone. Henry and Willie had reported the conditions in the settlement to their captain, who had gone to the major. Not that it had done any good. How could the man not feel the tension in the very atmosphere surrounding the fort?

"A sporting event of sorts." Willie buffed his boots to whatever shine they had left in them.

" 'Tis daft," Henry said. The fort was surrounded by hundreds of Indians who'd been allowed to stay by a commanding officer who wanted to be entertained.

Willie shrugged and then looked up. " 'Tis a welcome diversion, I say. The game is played with some sort of a ball and sticks. Nothin' like cricket, I'm told."

"I have heard 'tis a game played to prepare their young men for war, and to keep their warriors in fighting shape."

"Ya can hear all sorts of tales around here." Willie blew on his boot and rubbed it with his shirt sleeve. "But I say watchin' a game will improve morale. That would be a good thing."

Henry almost envied Willie for his state of optimism. He certainly didn't share it. But rather than argue, he strapped his musket across his back and left the barracks. He wandered to the forest gate. The doors stood open, guarded by a pair of soldiers who leaned against each side of the opening, facing each other. Even Henry, poor soldier that he was, knew this was foolish. The dangers lay outside the fort, where the sentries should be looking. He cast a glance over his shoulder. Seven Indians gathered near Mr. Langlade's house. Maybe the sentries were right to stand where they could see both directions at the turn of their heads.

He stepped through the gateway.

"Where are you going?" one of the sentries asked.

"For a walk."

"It do be a fine day," the other sentry said. "Watch your hair."

The two men laughed. Henry smiled, although it took concentration on his part. He was a fool to walk outside the fort. Why be worried about an Indian sporting contest and then step out alone where who knew how many Indians lurked?

Because she might be out there.

That truth brought home all the old wives' tales about love and common sense. He couldn't possibly love Laurette Pettigrew—he didn't know her well enough. But something inside him was convinced that he could, if given half the chance. As it was, she stole into his dreams at night and occupied too much of his thoughts during the day. Just three days ago, patrolling along the palisade, he could almost feel her out there somewhere, the pull was so strong.

He was an idiot. A besotted idiot.

But he wasn't stupid. He turned and walked back into the fort.

She'd managed to stay near the cabin for just three days this time. Each successive day found her ranging closer to the fort as she gathered medicinal herbs to dry for the coming winter. Gathering herbs and edibles kept her busy. But busy wasn't enough. Her soul cried out for companionship. For a place among people where she would be useful and. . .loved.

The urge to visit Memengwaa tapped her several times a day, but the thought of seeing Waagosh squelched it. Had she done the right thing, turning down his offer?

Laurette leaned against the rough bark of a tree. She bowed her head and waited for the words to come, words to ask God for deliverance from this lonely existence. Only they didn't come. Deep inside, her spirit groaned without words. She opened her eyes and allowed that silent groan to fill her and replace the words she couldn't find.

Marie's head jerked up, ears perked. Her tail swished against the ferns.

Laurette crouched beside the tree and put her hand over Marie's muzzle. Movement caught her eye. A line of buckskin-clad men filed past, heading from the settlement in the direction of the Ojibwe village. They were deep in the woods, at least a mile from the fort on a little-used trail. There must have been three dozen at least—the young men, the warriors. A line of women followed, maybe half as many as the men. What did it mean?

Papa's warning rang in her ears as the last Ojibwe slipped from view. She waited several minutes and then stood.

Marie, released from her mistress's hold, bounded forward, her tail lashing.

What if she followed the Ojibwe? Fear spiked through Laurette. She dashed after her dog, afraid to call out lest the trailing Indians hear her and question her presence.

Instead of following the Ojibwe, Marie turned the other way on the path, straight toward an Ojibwe woman who leaned against a tree.

Laurette stopped a few paces from her friend.

Memengwaa looked at her. Heavy wrappings covered her injured leg, but her color was good, her eyes sharp and bright.

"It is good to see you well, my friend."

"For that, I have you to thank." Memengwaa gestured to her leg. "Today is my first day walking any distance."

"And yet you lag behind the others."

Her friend's eyes widened. A worried frown wrinkled her brow for a moment and then was gone, her face a blank mask. What was she hiding? They'd known each other far too long for Laurette to be fooled.

"What is happening? Why are so many Ojibwe moving through the forest?"

Memengwaa pointed to the basket at her feet, half filled with healing herbs. "It is the time to gather."

"Women gather, not warriors. Why were the warriors here?"

Memengwaa's voice dropped to a whisper. "Go home, my friend. Stay away for many days."

Dread pooled to a knot in Laurette's stomach. "Why?"

"Because you are as a sister to me. Trust me." Memengwaa looked in the direction of the fort.

"Will there be an uprising at the fort?" Dread turned to fear. Fear for Papa. Fear for Henry. Fear that, once started, the uprising could take on a savage life of its own. Would any of them be safe?

"Go home. Stay home." The pleading in Memengwaa's dark eyes did more than her words could. Laurette turned and fled.

The men in the barracks talked of nothing but the baggataway game tomorrow between the local Ojibwe and Sauk warriors. From the sound of it, hundreds of warriors would meet between the settlement and the fort, where the ground was level and cleared of trees. Most of the men were looking forward to the entertainment. Life on an outpost like Fort Michilimackinac was nothing if not monotonous. Still, a fair number of men grumbled about the risk of such a gathering of Indians at their very door.

Henry was solidly in their camp. He'd been scratching his scalp all day.

Was Laurette safe? He'd spent the evening alternating between congratulating himself on his good sense in not entering the forest and berating himself for not taking the chance. Had she been nearby? He hoped not. He hoped she was far away and would stay there. Who knew what a horde of Indians might do to a white—or even partly white—woman.

With luck in his favor for once, he was scheduled off-duty until tomorrow evening. He'd go to Pettigrew's trading post in the morning. Perhaps she was there. At least he could speak with her father. He ran a finger around the collar of his shirt. He wouldn't be well received.

But he had to know that she was safe.

Chapter 10

June 2, 1763

After a night of tossing and turning, Laurette splashed tepid water on her face. She'd finally fallen asleep toward morning, and slept much later than usual. She pulled her nondescript brown skirt over her shift and shrugged into a short jacket close to the same shade. Her fingers fumbled in their haste to braid her hair. She left her linen cap on its peg near the door. With her moccasins tied, she checked the looking glass. Nothing light or colorful stared back at her. Perfect.

Marie rose when Laurette put her hand on the door. The dog's ears perked.

"I do not know if we will return. I do not know if anyone will return."

She slung a satchel over her shoulder with a change of clothing, a blanket, a small pot to cook over a fire, a cup, a knife, some pemmican, and her mama's book. She slipped through the doorway and secured the latch behind her. Her mother's image sprang to mind. Her fingers lingered on the wood before she patted the door and turned away.

The sun was well above the trees, the pine branches danced above her, their wispy needles sighing in the wind. She settled into the ground-eating trot of one born in the wilderness, placing each foot with care to make no sound. Today of all days, the urgency for silence pulsed within her.

Despite the warnings, she couldn't sit in the cabin and wonder what was happening. Ugly images from her dreams threatened to choke her. She'd never witnessed an uprising, but she'd heard stories. Stories told around the Ojibwe campfires in the evenings. Stories that even now raised the hairs on the back of her neck.

As much as she admired the Ojibwe people, her friends and neighbors, she could not understand that part of them. The part that gloried in the battle. In the killing.

She shuddered without breaking stride.

Papa knew something was happening, but he couldn't know what. If he did, he would have come home last night. Whatever it was, it was going to be bad.

Memengwaa's eyes still haunted her.

It would be very bad.

The Indians had been gathering for days, but that morning, Henry was astounded by the ocean of bodies outside the fort's walls, some mostly naked and many painted. Others were wrapped in blankets. How they could stand it on such a warm morning, he had no idea. As soldiers carried out benches to seat the officers, Henry shouldered his musket and walked through the forest gate before turning toward the settlement. There were fewer Indians on this side of the fort, but still too many for comfort.

He quickened his step as he passed a trio with faces and chests painted. They carried sticks with a webbed basket on one end used to play baggataway. Talk was that they painted for games as well as war, and this was to be a game, after all. He breathed a sigh of relief once past them. They'd ignored him altogether. Perhaps Major Etherington had been correct all along.

The settlement was deserted. Would Pettigrew be at the fort to watch the game? That hadn't occurred to Henry when he'd left. He paused outside the trading post's door. Even with a whole night to prepare, he still hadn't a clue what to say to Laurette's father.

Lord, I could use Your help right now. He opened the door and entered.

The long, low-beamed building was empty of people except for a bear of a man behind the counter. He looked nothing like Laurette, but who else would be there except her father?

"Monsieur Pettigrew?"

Thick graying eyebrows rose above the man's gray-bearded face before he gave a brief nod.

Now what? He swallowed.

"Monsieur, I have come to ask after your daughter."

The man bristled like the porcupine sentries had found and teased a few weeks ago. One sentry had gotten too close and came away with a hand spiked with quills. From the look of Laurette's father, Henry had much more to fear than a handful of quills.

"What do you know of my Laurette?"

"We have met and spoken a number of times." He raised his hands as the man charged around the counter. "In no way improperly, I assure you. But I fear for her."

Nothing softened in the man's menacing posture.

"The fort is overrun with Indians, mostly men. The major—" He bit off his words. He would not gossip, not even about Major Etherington, no matter how justified. "The major has assured us that this is just a friendly game, an entertainment."

"Your major is an imbecile."

Pettigrew wasn't a man to mince words. So neither would he.

"The Indians are painted—"

"They wear paint for the game, but what has this to do with my Laurette?"

"I have seen her near the fort on a number of occasions. Can you assure me that she is somewhere safe? Somewhere far away? All these men—"

The door to the trading post opened, and Laurette slipped inside, the lurcher by her side. She stopped, her mouth opened, eyes flicking between Henry and her father.

"Papa. Monsieur Bedlow."

"You know him, do you?" The growl from her father brought a flush to her cheeks.

"Oui, Papa."

"A redcoat comes to ask after your safety. Why is this? What have you not told your papa?"

If displeasure could heat a room, Henry would be cooked through by now.

"He came to ask after my safety?" Her eyes were unfathomable from across the room. "I have come to ascertain yours, Papa."

Pettigrew grunted. He looked around his trading post, at the wall where tomahawks and knives had been displayed when Henry'd been here weeks ago. It was empty.

"Perhaps I should disappear for a few days." His shoulders slumped. "There will be looting when it is over. All will be lost."

"I will help you carry what we can." Laurette turned to Henry. "Monsieur Bedlow can assist us."

Her father stiffened. "Non. We need no help from the likes of him."

"Papa." She came forward and grabbed her father's arm. "He is not like the others. He will help us." Her dark eyes shimmered in the low light. "Will you not, monsieur?"

"I will." He'd agree to anything when she looked at him like that.

"Ah ma petite bichette, they are all the same. The redcoats, they are not to be trusted." He looked Henry up and down. "Even if this one speaks French."

"He can be trusted. He saved Memengwaa from an attack. I was there. I saw."

Pettigrew scratched his beard.

"And he was teaching me to read."

The silence that followed her statement was thick enough to stop a musket ball.

"You have met with him often?"

"I have. He is a good man. We can trust him, Papa, I promise."

Would he believe his daughter? Henry racked his brain for something to say but came up empty. If her father wouldn't believe her, there was nothing Henry could add to sway the man. Time slowed to a crawl. Sweat gathered under Henry's hat and trickled down his temples. The itch in his scalp intensified.

A roar came from the fort. The game had begun.

Her father retreated behind the counter. He pulled a coat and a pair of breeches from the shelves behind, and thrust them at Henry.

"Change." He picked up a pair of moccasins and added them to the pile. "Hurry." He nodded to a room at the back of the store.

Henry stared at the clothes, then at Pettigrew. "Why?"

"You cannot blend into the forest dressed in red and white."

If he were caught out of uniform, he'd be lashed for it. Another roar rose from the fort. Nobody would notice he was gone until he was back and into his uniform again. If assisting Laurette's father to move his trade goods to protect them from looting also kept her safe, he'd do it.

He'd do anything to keep her safe.

Papa tossed cookware, clothing, blankets, spices, pemmican bags, gunpowder, lead, and whatever else he could fit into three oiled canvas packs. Worry creased his cheeks above his beard.

"What is going to happen, Papa?"

"I do not know for certain, ma petite bichette, but the anger rides high in the hearts of the Ojibwe and the Sauk. Together. . ." He shook his head. "We must get you away."

"And you too."

He paused, then grabbed another blanket. "For a few days, oui. But I will return." He gestured around the room. "This is all I have." He tapped his bad leg. "I can no longer spend my days kneeling in a canoe with the voyageurs. This is my life now."

"Then we will return and rebuild if we have to."

"Not we." His eyes clouded. "This is not the place for you. I know that. I have known that for a long time, but I could not let you go."

"Papa, non."

Henry came from the back room. Clad in the cloth breeches that were a little short and a fringed buckskin coat of the frontier, he looked nothing like a soldier except for the musket in his hands.

"Come, we must make haste." Papa thrust an otter hat at Henry, handed them each a canvas pack, the smallest one to Laurette. Henry stuffed his uniform into the top of his pack. Papa strode out the door, his limping gait not hindering them as they escaped the settlement.

"Where are we going?" she whispered.

"You will see. Stay close and stay quiet."

She glanced back at Henry. At his nod, she turned and caught up with Papa, Marie at her side.

The game's roar rose to a cacophony of shrieks.

"What—?" Henry stopped. "That sounds like an attack."

Papa turned and cocked his head. "Baggataway is a savage game to prepare the men for war. It can get out of hand. We must get Laurette away. Come."

Relieved that it was just the game and not an uprising after all, Laurette glanced at Henry. He hesitated, indecision etched on his face.

"Come," she said. Would he stay with them? Help them? He glanced behind and then came toward her. She hurried to catch up to Papa.

The game's noise dwindled with distance, until the only sounds were squirrels chittering from the branches overhead and the chirp of a bird.

They continued deeper into the forest southeast of the fort, in an area Laurette had never explored with Mama or with Memengwaa. They passed through several boggy areas, topped a couple of ridges lined with hardwoods, and moved beneath acres of pines. Sweat ran down her back, and her legs strained with each incline. Papa had picked up a stout branch and used it as a walking stick, his limp more pronounced and their pace slower. They halted at a burbling creek, its clear water shaded by hovering cedars.

Dropping to his good knee, Papa scooped a handful of water to his face. Henry joined him, pulling off his hat and splashing water over his head before taking a long drink. Laurette knelt and drank, watching Marie wade into the stream and lap up its cool goodness.

Papa pointed to a rocky outcropping above the stream. "There is a cave there to hide the packs."

Henry climbed the moss-covered stones and slid his pack into the cave before reaching back for Laurette to hand him the others. Under Papa's instruction, he rearranged a few fallen branches to hide the opening.

Papa grunted, then jerked his head to the east. "Around the bend of this creek, there is a cabin."

"Out here?" She peered into the wilderness. "Who lives there?"

"Father Jacques."

Laurette's mouth dropped open. "The hermit priest? He is real?" She'd heard tales of him, but never thought them to be true.

Papa nodded. "He is very real and very old."

Henry mopped the sweat from his brow. "How can he live out here and not be in danger from the Indians?"

"The Ojibwe, Odawa, and Sauk know he is here. He means them no harm. They see him as the holy man he is. They respect him."

"Will he keep your goods and Laurette safe?" Henry asked.

"Non." Papa stood. "He will marry you."

Chapter 11

Henry staggered a step, dizzy as the blood drained from his head. Was the old man delusional?

"Laurette." Pettigrew took his daughter's hands and drew her to her feet. "There is nothing here for you. You do not belong with the Ojibwe, no matter how much Waagosh makes eyes at you."

Henry's back stiffened. Who was this Waagosh to be making eyes at Laurette?

"Oui, your papa has seen this."

"I do not wish to marry Waagosh."

That was a relief.

"I know, ma petite bichette. You must follow the Métis west. Your place is there. You are a healer, and a healer is a valuable part of any community. Go there. Help our people."

"Your place is there too, Papa."

"Non. My place is here. As with Father Jacques, I am respected. And needed. The tribes need the trade goods the white men bring. They do not realize it yet, but their old ways have changed forever. They have grown dependent on the goods I supply. They need the cooking pots, metal knives, the muskets and powder. This is my place."

Pettigrew turned to Henry. "My daughter says you have taught her to read. This is a good thing. The Métis need someone to teach them to read and write."

"I would be honored to teach them when—"

"You have also been with my daughter, alone, without my approval." His beard bristled, and he glowered at Henry. "For this, you will marry her. My Laurette, she is not some camp follower."

"Of course she is not, but—"

"You will marry her and take her west. Teach the Métis to read and write. Teach my people how to deal with the British."

"But—" Would the man not allow him a full sentence?

"And you, my daughter." Pettigrew turned his back on Henry. "You will marry this man, travel north to the *Saults de Sainte-Marie*, and from there join a group of voyageurs heading west. As a married woman, you will be safe with them. The

Métis have congregated near the *Riviere Rouge du Nord*. Go there. Join our people. Be happy."

"Come with us, Papa." Her voice was thick with unshed tears that pulled at Henry's heart even as his mind whirled with everything her father had said.

"Non. This is where I belong."

Father and daughter stared at each other as if suspended in time.

Henry cleared his throat. "There is something you have not considered."

Laurette's heart tore in two. Papa was sending her away, and Henry's stiff tone left no doubt that he didn't want to marry her.

"What have I not considered?" Papa's scowl would have intimidated most men, but Henry only tugged his fringed coat straighter.

"I'm a British soldier. I cannot desert my post."

"Your post is gone."

"What do you mean?"

Papa drew his hand down his beard and gave the end a tug before meeting Henry's gaze. "By now the fort has been overrun."

Henry's face paled. "I must return."

"It is too late."

Henry took a step back. "Even so, I must return."

Papa grabbed hold of Henry's coat. "There is nothing to go back to. The game, it was a ruse to cover an attack."

Anger surged from Henry's clenched jaw to his balled fists. "You knew. You knew and you did not warn the major."

"He is not *my* major. And besides, I did not know until this morning when the women came. They entered, stripped my wall bare of weapons, and left without a word or offer of payment."

Henry tried to shake him off, but Papa hung on like a bulldog, his walking stick falling to the ground. Marie barked and circled the two men.

"There is nothing you can do," Papa said between clenched teeth.

"I have to try."

"There were at least four hundred warriors. How many soldiers did the fort have?"

"Forty—nay, thirty-nine." Henry's shoulders sagged, his face grayed.

Papa leaned against Henry, his hands still clutching the fringed coat. "By now, the officers have been captured and the rest killed."

"I have to see for myself."

"Then you will die. Who will take Laurette to the Métis? Who will keep her safe?"

Everything inside Henry wanted to be that person, but he had a duty to his fellow soldiers. "You will have to do it."

"My leg, it will not hold out much longer. It will be days before I can travel again."

Only then did Henry realize the grip the old man had on his coat was not only stopping him, it was keeping Pettigrew upright, his weight on his good leg. He might be lame, but at least he was alive. What of Willie and the rest of the soldiers? "My place is back at the fort." Anger still flowed with every beat of Henry's heart.

The sea of painted bodies that had covered the field next to the fort, the benches to seat the officers, the open gate—the picture was burned into Henry's memory. There was no way the soldiers could have survived an attack. Their shrieks would haunt him. Shrieks he'd foolishly believed were part of a game.

Laurette deserved to be safely away, but— "I cannot marry Laurette."

She gasped, her stricken face wrenching his heart and making it difficult to breathe.

Pettigrew tightened his hold on Henry's coat. "Why, when there is nothing left for you here?"

"I am not Catholic." He pushed the words past stiff lips.

Monsieur Pettigrew shrugged in that eloquent way only a Frenchman, and apparently a Métis, could. "Father Jacques is old. What he does not know will not bother him. So we do not tell him this."

"And it will not bother you?" Most Catholics would rather lose an arm than marry a daughter outside of their faith.

"My God, He is bigger than this difference, n'est-ce pas? He brought you here, of this I am certain. He brought you when my daughter needed a husband, someone to take her away, someone to keep her safe. The someone He sent was you."

If only Henry could believe that. "How do you know?"

"Because this I have prayed for."

Such faith stood before him in this bear of a man. It was humbling, but could he be right? Was it God who had urged Henry to leave the fort this morning?

He pressed his hand to his forehead and closed his eyes with thoughts of Willie and the other soldiers. The truth pressed heavily against his chest. They were all gone. He opened his eyes and met Pettigrew's, filled with wisdom and an infinite sadness. The old man nodded.

There was nothing one lone soldier could do.

Henry glanced at Laurette, who studied the shells on her moccasins.

There was something he could do. As her father said, he could take her far away and keep her safe. He vowed that he'd be a better husband than he'd ever been a soldier, but only if she agreed. And she couldn't agree until he asked. Pettigrew released him as he moved in front of her.

"Laurette?"

She flicked her eyes up in a damp glance before she cast them back down.

"Laurette." He tipped her chin and held it until she raised her eyes. This moment shouldn't have been possible. He should be lying dead with the others at the fort, not toe-to-toe with this incredible woman.

Laurette had held her breath as Papa and Henry talked. Could this be true? Would she soon be wed and on her way west? Was this what God, the God of the book secured in her satchel, had planned for her?

Henry said her name then held her chin, sending a quiver through her. She met his eyes.

He cleared his throat. "Please understand that I wish this was under different circumstances. I wish we would have met somewhere else. Somewhere more civilized where I was free to court you properly. But even so, I know this is what I want. I hope it is what you want as well. Will you marry me?"

Papa would have given her to him, as was his right, but Henry was asking. A wrinkle creased the wide expanse of his forehead, and his gaze flicked from her eyes to her lips and back again. His thumb caressed the point of her chin, sincerity in his eyes.

She summoned the breath needed to answer. "I will."

Henry's thumb moved from her chin to brush her bottom lip. Her entire body thrummed like partridge wings against the wind. Henry pulled her into his arms.

"Bah! There is time for that after the marriage. Come." Papa turned, but not before Laurette caught a glimpse of a smile hidden beneath his beard.

"Before we follow him." Henry's arms tightened around her. "Know that I will love you and care for you as long as we live. No matter what our future holds, we will meet it together."

Ignoring Papa's hobbling retreat, she leaned toward Henry. He lowered his lips to hers in a gentle touch that flared into a scalding heat. He murmured her name against her mouth in his rumbly voice. She'd never heard anything so beautiful. He pulled back, and she pressed her face against his chest, his heart racing beneath her ear, his hand cupping the back of her head. She loved him.

Wherever he went—that's where she belonged.

Historical Note

On June 2, 1763, the uprising at Fort Michilimackinac dealt a blow against the British that was part of Pontiac's Rebellion. Ojibwe and Sauk chiefs had meticulously planned their attack. With hundreds of warriors staging a game of baggataway—the game that would evolve into our present-day lacrosse—the British soldiers were caught completely off guard. Ojibwe and Sauk women, wrapped in blankets too warm for the day, sat near the gate to watch the game. One of the warriors tossed the ball to the fort's wide-open gate. The players—estimated at as many as five hundred—rushed the fort as their women stood and dropped their blankets, exposing an arsenal of knives and tomahawks. Most of the soldiers were killed. The officers, including Major Etherington, were taken as hostages and later traded for ransom. But the victory was short-lived when the British returned some three thousand strong the following spring.

Pegg Thomas lives on a hobby farm in Northern Michigan with Michael, her husband of *mumble* years. A life-long history geek, she writes "History with a Touch of Humor." When not working on her latest novel, Pegg can be found in her garden, in her kitchen, with her sheep, at her spinning wheel, or on her trusty old horse, Trooper. See more at PeggThomas.com.

A Heart So Tender

by Debra E. Marvin

Acknowledgments

A thank-you to author Carrie Fancett Pagels for her love of colonial history and for her dream to create this collection. My childhood fascination with colonial cooking and brick ovens aside, I'd like to thank two Social Studies teachers who brought New York history alive: Eugene Bavis and Ronald Porray. As always, I wouldn't be doing this without my critique partner and daily sounding board, author Susanne Dietze.

And, most of all, I'm thankful for the desire and creative ability given to me by a creative and loving God.

Author's Note

Sir William Johnson's Great Gathering lasted through much of the summer of 1764 and is an event never duplicated in our history. While Susannah, Arch, Captain Porter, and Mrs. Browning are purely fictional, much of the story and its characters are not. The current stone blockhouses at Fort Niagara are used in this story, but were built after 1764, replacing the timber redoubts. Another fictional tweak is the addition of rooms on the third floor of "the castle"; I believe the space was used for storage instead. What is unequivocally real is the rich history of my home state. Lastly, if you are curious, here are a couple pronunciations: Karawase (Kara-wah-say), and Kahente (Kah-hen-tay).

Chapter 1

A Lake Ontario breeze trifled with the Union Jack overhead, but failed to cool Lieutenant Archibald Waters' frustration. Very little could. The lookout above the blockhouse provided a broad view from thirty feet above Fort Niagara's rolling terrain. The July sky and endless blue water was preferable to the increasing number of Indian encampments surrounding him.

"Things are about to get interesting, Private Dawes. A favor, please. You will see that the troops arriving from Oswego are kept unaware of our dwindling stock."

"Rum, sir?"

"No. Sultanas. Or it will be the last of decent puddings until winter."

"Oh, aye sir."

Arch crossed to the other side and gazed upriver until shouts drew his attention to where a large party exited the woods. Wagons, riders, and two fine carriages.

And so the mighty Sir William Johnson had arrived.

This foolishness before Arch's eyes was Johnson's doing. Hundreds of invited guests might swell to a thousand. Chippewa, Maumee, Huron, Chickasaw, Toronto, Cayuga. All because the Iroquois Confederacy's westernmost villages of Chenussio Seneca had sided with the Ottawa Chief Pontiac's rebellious ways. If Johnson failed to bring about reconciliation, there would be no safe home along the frontier.

Sir William Johnson, hero in the Battles of Ticonderoga and Fort Niagara, had been rewarded with a baronetcy, and now, as the Indian Counsel for His Majesty King George, he planned to stay on until he'd brokered treaties with every tribe.

Below, on the open grounds east of the fort, where British and French blood had spilled five years earlier, an altercation—sharp words and a shove—raised Arch's ire as though he'd taken the blow himself. Too many braves, too many century-old conflicts for his liking. The last thing he could stomach today was a fight between two of these haughty warriors.

The approaching party was close enough now to confirm guests of some importance, or at least white-skinned visitors, for it was well-known that even Johnson's Mohawk consort and mother of his youngest children, Molly Brant, rode horseback.

An occasional blinding flash of sun leapt off polished metal as the fort's regiments stood in precision formation. Johnson, a big Irishman, stepped out of his carriage, grinning and eager. The second carriage produced a gentleman dressed in black—certainly no soldier—and then the woman he assisted. Arch met Private Dawes's eyes. Things were getting interesting.

Given her frame, she was young. And lovely. A collective shift of interest rolled through the onlookers when she moved forward, nodded to Lt. Col. Browning, their commanding officer, and then turned her head to take in the impressive sea of British soldiers, frontiersmen, and native warriors who'd suddenly stilled.

A gust from the lake played with the golden curls at her delicate neck.

Was the man in black a fool? Whether his daughter or young wife, what kind of namby-pamby would bring this portrait of perfect British femininity to an outpost packed with lonely soldiers, much less the expected massing of warrior chiefs and braves from thirty tribes?

A thin, well-dressed youth with a queue of thick black hair and skin as dark as some of the assembled Indians stepped out behind the young woman and stayed close at her side.

She spoke to him then turned her head up to consider Arch as though he'd called to her. Her appraisal continued as she moved forward with the group, and he returned it until her angel face and her dress the color of his mother's bluebells disappeared from sight into the fort's gatehouse below.

Who the blazes was she, and why would any man in his right mind bring her here?

Susannah Kimball forced a serene smile as she searched faces for another woman. An army wife, a chief's woman, a laundress would do. The officer in charge, a lieutenant or colonel—she'd already forgotten—moved Father and Benjamin into the cooler shade of the gatehouse. She'd never seen so many people in one place since she and her parents arrived at Boston harbor. Now, ten years later, Indians no longer frightened her, but the number of them and so many uniformed soldiers left her uneasy.

"My wife will join us later," the commander explained. "I'm afraid one of the women—a camp follower—is"—he searched for the word—"indisposed."

A female complaint or impending birth? "I look forward to meeting her, sir."

"Let's get you inside the fort and get you settled into what its French builders called 'The Castle.' We had two cells in the garret prepared when word came the baronet was bringing guests. I apologize for the minimal comforts."

Sir Johnson was the sort of man who drew attention by simply entering a room. He'd requested her family accompany him, and Susannah now understood that his political power here at Niagara equaled his sway in the Mohawk Valley. Every named tribe knew of him, and, pray God, respected him. Johnson had a hand on the older commander's shoulder. "Browning, my friend." Johnson's Irish accent had thickened after such a tiring journey. "I'd have you choose your most trusted officer to watch over the Kimballs."

"Of course." The lieutenant colonel in turn addressed her father. "Follow me." Then to Susannah, "My wife has a woman who will. . ." He shrugged. "See to your needs."

Relief shot through her. "Thank you, sir." Her eyes had barely adjusted to the bright sun when they entered the "castle's" dark interior. With high, finely crafted ceilings and impressive stonework, a castle it was. Taking them down a hall, Browning bade them to sit in the commander's study where Father and Ben took the proffered chairs out of politeness. After days of rough trails since leaving their cabin near Johnson Hall, she declined out of compassion for her bruised bottom.

A boyish private brought them weak cider.

"Send Lieutenant Waters to me," commanded Lt. Col. Browning.

"Yes sir."

Susannah gladly left the conversation to her father while she studied the dark interior and high arching woodwork overhead. What little daylight made it through the deep-silled windows diminished with a soldier's arrival.

He swept his hat off, glancing smoothly around the room before saluting the officer.

Susannah stared.

"You asked for me, sir?"

"Yes, Lieutenant Waters. See that Sir William's guests are made comfortable and allowed as much freedom as possible inside the fort. I expect no problems, but their safety is your responsibility, and you will remain available to them at all times." Lt. Col. Browning gestured with one ink-stained hand. "This is Mr. Kimball, his daughter, Miss Kimball, and his. . .son, Benjamin." Browning's clumsy introduction was not unlike most they encountered outside of Johnstown, for Ben was clearly of Indian birth.

Sir William reappeared. A man strong enough to command troops, summon and dismiss chiefs as he pleased, and, with an officer's title as well, he risked little chance of resistance from this soldier.

But resistance flashed in the lieutenant's eyes.

In the way of big men, Sir William slapped the lieutenant on the back. "Ah, then. I couldn't have made a better choice myself. How are you, Waters?"

"I am well, sir," came the reply.

Lt. Col. Browning relaxed considerably. "Our regiments are honored to be part of this historic event, sir."

"It will be that, I assure you. I am not going to leave until I've done everything I can. So get used to me." Sir William's laugh filled the room. "Now, I'm going to stretch my legs, and leave you and Lt. Waters to see to my friends."

She'd seen this soldier, this Lt. Waters, judging them from up in the blockhouse when she'd arrived. Well-groomed, and unsettling in his spotless uniform tailored to his impressive frame. But if he disliked his new job as nursemaid to her family, he was not alone. Would she have his formidable company without respite?

Father remained composed. "I thank you, Lieutenant. I expect my girl here needs some time to herself, so if you'll see us to wherever they've taken our trunks. . ."

"Of course. Follow me."

Father did, with Ben behind him and Susannah watching when she could peek around Ben's shoulders. Waters stopped once to quietly ask another officer what he was supposed to do with their visitors. His polite words did not match the tension in his movements.

At the end of the dark, uppermost floor, he directed Father and Benjamin into a tiny room. Tiny until she saw hers across the hall.

Exhaustion left her disadvantaged when she passed under the lieutenant's intense gaze. Only when she was across the threshold did she raise her eyes to his. "Thank you."

He tipped his head, his brown eyes giving no relief. When he'd finished his appraisal, she felt she'd been found lacking.

"The Indian woman, Kahente, will help you. Send her for me should you wish to leave your room. Do not. . ." He cleared his throat. "That is to say, I shall be accompanying you everywhere you go. Your father as well."

"And Benjamin?"

His eyes shifted toward the other room. "When possible."

She had long ago decided she owed no explanations regarding Ben. "Be assured, Lieutenant, I do not make a habit of living in fear." *But you? You frighten me more than any red-skinned man I've met.*

Chapter 2

Inside the room smelling of leather polish and shaving soap, Susannah smoothed the gathers below the stomacher pinned to her blue silk dress. There would be hours yet before she could be relieved of these heavy layers. Before she had time to latch the door, a short, dark woman, enviably dressed in simple homespun and apron, stepped inside carrying a pitcher and a glass.

Susannah introduced herself to a woman old enough to be her mother—if Mother were still alive. "Tell me your name again, ma'am."

"Kahente."

Kahente went to work unpacking the trunk, while Susannah downed the cool water. If she'd once anticipated this adventure, the feeling had faded with reality.

The Indian woman tipped her head toward the chamber pot, not expecting Susannah to be too shy to wait for privacy.

She wasn't.

Ten minutes later, she felt capable of facing the long afternoon ahead. And the redcoat.

A knock at the door rattled the hinges. At the second, more urgent interruption, she opened it to Lieutenant Waters. He removed his hat and tucked it under his arm.

She must admit, the man had a talent for scrutiny. "Yes?"

"Sir William requests you tour the fort before this evening's meal."

Trust Sir William to keep them busy.

"We have one hour until they gather." Susannah cleared her throat. "Yes, that's fine. Thank you." The hall window behind him framed a view of blue lake and the occasional white-capped wave. Miles and miles of open water filled the air with a peculiar, inviting freshness.

Quiet conversation floated into the passageway from her menfolk, contrasting with the rabble of a British regimental company camped below the mullioned window.

She couldn't seem to move.

"You will want a hat, Miss Kimball."

"Yes. Of course." She turned for it, reddening. He thought her a tenderfoot, and she was proving him right. Better though that he discounted her rather than trip over himself to gape as some of the other soldiers did.

Father and Ben joined them in the narrow corridor. "Will you dine with us as well, Lieutenant Waters?"

"I expect not."

That should have relieved her.

He directed her ahead, then hurried to precede them down the steep stone steps. Once outside, he played the guide, explaining the layout of the fort, its armaments and fortifications. Freedom, however, came with the price of a thousand eyes on her. It was Sir William's fault for telling her to wear her bright-blue dress "*to liven up the place.*" It seemed she had succeeded.

Listening to the officer's deep voice had her guessing at his place of birth. A different part of England than Father came from. With the men's attention diverted by Ben's eager questions, she studied Lt. Waters as he stood half-turned from her, his hand behind his back.

"Do you wish to see the kitchens, Miss Kimball?"

Susannah startled, darting her gaze away, as if she hadn't been admiring the tails of his officer's coat and the blue breeches above his shining black boots. "I should rather see the view from up there." She pointed to the spot from where he'd watched them arrive.

Tiny lines appeared at the corner of his eye, as if he had once been fond of laughter. "I was keeping it for last."

If he thought her answer unexpected, so did she find the sudden warm smile transforming his face.

He glanced at Ben. "Your brother will like it."

"This should be a splendid view, Susannah." Father draped a hand across her back. "And doesn't it feel good to be out walking again? Don't tell the baronet, Lieutenant, but even his carriage began to feel like a box rolled across stones."

Once up the narrow stone steps, a pitted stone floor with half walls all around and a protective roof made an excellent sentry station.

"I never saw such a thing!" Ben darted from one side to another, acting more like the fourteen-year-old boy he was than the proper young gentleman Father cultivated at home. "Look! There's a ship approaching."

The endless blue brought to mind the ocean crossing years prior, yet her attention slipped to the landscape outside the walls. The encamped visitors wore all manner of skins, feathers, beads, and paint. Ponies and makeshift tents clustered around small fires.

Her redcoat joined her at the half wall. "You do realize that their camps will grow by the day?"

She turned to face him, determined to prove her point. "You needn't be concerned on my account. I am comfortable among the many Mohawk people at home.

It does none of us any good to declare each stranger an enemy."

"I meant no disrespect. But even so you must admit—"

"They desire peace as much as we do. Or perhaps I should not speak for you. It sounds like you anticipate trouble."

A snort of doubt escaped him as his hand drifted to the hilt of his sabre. "It is my place to do so." He turned back to Father. "How long is your stay, Mr. Kimball?"

"We come and go at Sir William's discretion."

She wouldn't allow him to addle her. "I hope we do not impose on your time longer than necessary."

"Daughter. The lieutenant is only doing his job."

Perhaps, but the pulse beating above his neckcloth told her she wasn't far wrong.

Waters took a deep breath and studied the wall. "It is only that I don't believe this is a place for women, Miss Kimball."

"But I am not the only one, after all."

When he chuckled, she found him examining her from shoes to hat.

"But you, Miss Kimball. . ." He glanced at Father. "You rather stand out in a crowd."

The wide brim of her bergère hat had the advantage of hiding her face. "Perhaps you'd rather I stay in my room."

"That would make my life easier."

She turned, shocked at his rudeness, until she saw the humor narrowing the corners of his mouth and those captivating eyes, while he continued to look straight ahead, a model for military precision. Susannah put gloved fingers to her mouth, fighting the urge to laugh out loud, so surprised was she at his teasing.

Father came close enough to give her a nudge, his eyes merry once more. "What number do you give these gathered, Lieutenant?"

"Lieutenant Colonel Browning counted three hundred but expects a thousand strong by the time it's over. But it's the wayward Seneca whose attendance is most needed after—" A glance at Susannah stopped him.

"We know about the massacre at Devil's Hole," Father assured him. "The Chennusio Seneca chiefs traveled to Johnson Hall."

Surveying the campfires, Lt. Waters' mood returned to its earlier darkness. "Then you know our concerns." He took a deep breath. "I will do all I can to keep you safe."

"Splendid. Splendid. I wonder if we might go down by the lakeshore. Benjamin is quite eager."

The lieutenant turned to Susannah, "I can take you back to your room first, if you'd like."

"Why ever would you think such a thing? I'm as interested as Ben."

Father's laugh held a hint of warning. He removed his hat to push back his graying hair. "You'll find my daughter has a mind of her own."

"That's what I fear, sir."

The telltale lift of one of the lieutenant's brows made her thankful she had a hat to hide under.

"Not to worry, Lieutenant. While she is a bit headstrong, she is not so foolish as to take chances with her safety."

Seeking an end to their discussion of her, Susannah started down the narrow stone steps. Father had no business talking about her in such a way.

Her wide skirts weren't practical for such a stairwell, and her flimsy shoes would do little good on a rocky beach. But she would suffer more bruises rather than complain in front of that cocky soldier.

Upon her first step into the sunlight, he offered his arm. Refusing would be impractical—and impolite—and she was glad of his assistance along the steep, winding path. Nevertheless, she promptly pulled away as they neared the water and picked her way to where traces of waves gave up to the shore. She removed her gloves and, copying her brother, picked through smooth stones, wishing her stays gave more freedom of movement.

Two bare-chested Indians in breechclouts approached. She knew too little to recognize their tribe, though the strips of leather beadwork tying their leggings in place were unusual. The younger of the two greeted Ben while keeping a wary eye toward the soldier now at Susannah's side.

Her brother's ease with the Mohawk language served him well at home, but he either did not understand all of the young warrior's words or he heard something he didn't like.

When the older man, wiry and weathered, came close and reached toward her, the lieutenant's hand swung up hard to block him.

"Do not fret, Lieutenant. He only wants to touch my hair." Keeping her eyes cast down, she pressed her guardian's hand away and waited.

Encouraged, the warrior raised dark fingers to touch the pale curl resting upon her shoulder. He laughed when it sprang back in place, murmuring something to his young companion, and even grinned at the lieutenant.

Ben's continuing conversation amused the pair, but Susannah would need to chastise the lieutenant later. Even though she was not proficient in the language, she knew his protection had been taken by the Indians as affection, or ownership.

The two Indians parted, passing around them and continuing along the rocky shore.

She must prove to the lieutenant he need not be so full of mistrust. If she were one day able to accomplish her dream of new schools along the frontier, she must learn to deal with such men.

"You handled yourself well with the strangers, son." Father's gentle words were much the same since the once frightened boy had come to them.

"Susannah will leave us someday. Marry and go off?"

Heat rushed up exposed skin and Susannah stepped in front of Ben, forcing him to meet her eyes. "You mustn't say such a thing. You know we will work together."

Ben's high spirits faltered. "That is wishful thinking, sister."

Maybe so, but she refused to accept it. Ben had few places where he was accepted unconditionally, and she would not let him down.

"Yours won't be an easy path," Father agreed. "But that is not how wisdom comes. Trust that the Lord will help you accomplish much good for your people and for our family."

Did Ben's blood family walk here among hundreds of native people? It was thought he'd been born Seneca. Had his father been among the group responsible for the massacre?

The gentle ripple of water and Ben's delight in the lake made up for her wet shoes and soggy hems.

He'd become a replacement for her brother, the much-anticipated child whose death took her mother as well. If he'd lived, would she feel this need to make up for all that Josiah Kimball had lost?

Arch lingered inside the airy vestibule, watching the setting sun color the face of the north blockhouse, thinking of his son.

"Lieutenant Waters! Come quick."

Arch spun around to see only the retreating backside of his best sharpshooter, a very impatient Private Riley. "Captain Porter's ordered Snyder whipped, sir."

No doubt for some ridiculous reason.

Arch carefully folded away the childish drawing he'd been studying, a constant reminder of his child. Merritt's penciled sketch of a father and son parted by an ocean made Arch feel strongly closer to the boy, while still too far away.

"I can't keep stepping in, and I won't leave my post."

"You're the only one he listens to."

"Not likely." Porter had gone from trusting Arch with his life to accusing him of undermining him. "Who's to do it?"

"Hayes."

Arch shook his head in disgust. Of course. While it was common to have the drummers dole out lashings, Porter knew this set young Hayes to lash his best mate.

"Insubordination?"

"That's what Porter's saying."

Arch surveyed the empty hall, yet still lowered his voice. "Go then. See if Lieutenant Nichols is about. It's nothing I can change." Not yet. Captain Porter had lost control once he'd lost the men's respect, acting the tyrant one moment, confused and illogical the next. His anger grew with every Indian's arrival. The truth was, Arch was plenty ready for promotion, and it wouldn't take more than a few words to Major Wilkins or a letter to General Gage to finish the captain's career. He'd have witnesses to the captain's growing incompetency.

But nothing more could be done during the upcoming weeks of what Sir William called "The Great Gathering."

Back outside the private meeting room, he didn't wait long until the door opened. Sir William, Lt. Col. Browning and his wife, four of the visiting chiefs, and the fort's translator, Jean DeCouagne, sat back as the dining table was cleared. This time, catching the intriguing Miss Kimball's attention, he smiled.

She was pure bliss to gaze upon.

The beauty didn't exactly wave or return the sentiment, but at least she didn't frown. He'd been blunt with her, after all, but he was not as horrid as she no doubt considered him. While her opinion shouldn't matter, and no female in his care would be in such a wild place, he'd liked having the warriors on the beach believe she was his woman.

The meeting room door closed again behind Private Dawes, doubling as footman today. "Have you heard?" Dawes whispered. "The lassie's goin' t' sing. A voice like an angel, I reckon. That face, and that—"

"Enough! I'll not have you discussing Miss Kimball's. . .attributes."

"But you can't stop me from thinking about her."

Arch shouldn't have grinned. "Go on. Get to work."

"Aye sir." The private whooped and ran off.

The tumult outside brought Arch's mind back to Porter. The whipping had begun.

This was not the time to air discipline problems. Porter's uncontrolled frustration over the events at Devil's Hole deepened with each new encampment outside the fort. A man unable to lead with a clear head could get them all killed, and if Porter was allowed to interact with the Indians in his current state of mind, his short fuse could lead to a dangerous situation.

Arch rubbed his jaw.

Until then, there was Miss Kimball to consider.

She'd be singing for them, would she? Even the thick stone walls and door wouldn't cheat him out of hearing that.

Chapter 3

S till exhausted from days of travel and the oppressive heat, Susannah rose from her seat at the long, crowded dining table. Performing set her nerves jagged, but at least it put an end to the trivial conversations of gentlemen eager to engage her attention.

The practical Mrs. Browning had been seated too far down the table to allow any opportunity to speak.

How she longed for time alone before she faced the task she'd set for herself.

Her family was part of Sir William's plan to show what he'd done for both Indian and pioneer families—a working system of schools, churches, and communities not unlike an English country squire's. The Mohawks prospered under Johnson's friendship, and the white settlers lived in peace.

This outpost, bursting with men on edge was—just as Lt. Waters implied—no place for her, but not for the reasons he thought. The surly lieutenant had all but called her naive, foolish. Had he so little knowledge of what women in the colonies were made of? She was as strong as the women in each backcountry family they'd met, and she longed to be as wise as the grandmothers to whom the tribal elders looked to for guidance.

Except she planned to do it without a husband.

So far today, she'd felt like a prized mare at auction and longed to be away from them all. When she made a move to stand, the men on either side of her rose at once, offering her an arm, while a third called to her from across the table.

"Thank you, but the lieutenant waits for us."

"Arch Waters is used to waiting, Miss Kimball," said the taller of the two men beside her. "It is a soldier's true occupation."

"You will find me much better company," the other offered. "I am quite accomplished on the pianoforte, should you need a partner."

"I will keep that in mind, sir. Now if you'll excuse me." She slipped through the crush of officers and chiefs and out into the hall. Lt. Waters waited right where she'd seen him last, but he offered no greeting. Had she imagined that earlier smile?

The sandy-haired officer had followed her out. "What will you be singing for us tonight, Miss Kimball?"

"A duet with Benjamin."

Not to be left out, the more obnoxious of her dinner companions frowned. "He speaks English?"

"Yes, of course. And Mohawk." Not one of the men at the table had addressed Ben during the meal, except for Sir William himself, who teased him to take more food. "His Latin is significantly better than mine, and perhaps yours as well?"

Nothing more was said, and she glanced behind her to see Archibald Waters following. Whether he liked it or not.

The diners moved slowly, for the tribal representatives hesitated, unfamiliar with the unexplained move from room to room as was the British custom. Indeed, who would not prefer to be outside and away from this stuffy group?

The room where she was to sing was no larger than the dining room but had little furniture. It filled quickly. Benjamin came to her side and squeezed her hand just as she had his when they were younger. Now he stood a good few inches taller.

Johnson waved an arm, the broad cuff of his coat heavy with stitchery. "Gentlemen and Mistress Browning!" His voice rose in volume. "For those just joining us, Mr. Josiah Kimball here is headmaster for our Mohawk school and tutor for many of the families. This, as you no doubt know, is his gracious daughter, Miss Susannah. They, along with Kimball's ward, Benjamin, are my guests to witness these historic meetings. What better way to enjoy our new and broadening friendships and trust, than with good food and drink, honest conversation, and now, this delightful entertainment."

Genial agreement filled the room.

"Miss Kimball and Benjamin have made a name for themselves throughout the valley and Albany. During their time here, they hope to find support for new schools to continue the success we've had at Mohawk Castle." He nodded at Father. "Have I missed anything, Josiah?"

Father came forward, flushed with excitement at this unusual audience. "It is an honor for us to be here. Sir William believes in the virtues of an educational program for all children, as well as music and a study of God's Word. And now..." With a nod, Father raised a pitch pipe to his lips and blew one short note.

They began with the most difficult song, and though they sounded pleasing, Susannah was thankful of Ben's perfect pitch. She stared ahead at a flickering sconce, unable to look at her audience, though curious how the visiting chiefs and warriors reacted.

Nor could she consider meeting the intense gaze of Lt. Waters.

They moved on to a short hymn translated to Mohawk. The many syllables always challenged her, but she finished their short program alone with a lively English ditty.

Then it was done, and her relief allowed her to enjoy the encouraging applause. Even the visiting chiefs smiled, though they didn't join in the strange custom.

No longer able to avoid Lt. Waters, she accepted his appreciative nod. He'd told her she stood out; if she did, so did he. For her, he might have been the only man in the room.

Mrs. Browning bustled over, bright with delight. "How I envy your talent. As you can imagine, I shall keep those songs in my heart to recall at will. We have nothing like this here. The men sing their songs, but you two. . ."

Benjamin's face shone. "Thank you, ma'am."

"You must tell me your plans, young man. Will you be working for Sir William one day?"

Ben glanced at Susannah. "We plan to teach, like our father."

"And instruct music as well as the practical studies?" Mrs. Browning clasped her square neckline. "Why, there must be any number of families who would do well to hire you. I have friends in Tarrytown. Unless you prefer the city."

"Actually, we hope to open an Indian school along the frontier."

The older woman's mouth dropped. " 'Tis a noble idea, but you are both so young."

"I am already one and twenty," Susannah explained, fighting the old frustrations. "So many my age have. . ." A home and children. "Much to show for themselves."

They began to move toward the door, the room too warm by half. At once Lt. Waters was at her side as if he needed to reassure himself she'd come to no harm among her admirers.

"You must have enjoyed that, Lieutenant." Mrs. Browning tipped her head to take in the three of them. "But now you all must pardon me. One of the women is. . ." She leaned closer. "About to deliver. I promised to help the old midwife, but I couldn't bear to miss such an evening."

Once she'd left, the Lieutenant wasted no time. "Your father suggested a walk while he speaks with the baronet." He nodded toward the main entryway and ushered them out. "The lake breeze will help shake off this heat."

"May we go down by the water again?" Ben asked as they stepped out into the much fresher air.

Lt. Waters scanned the area before venturing farther. "I prefer we stay inside the fort tonight. The blockhouse again?"

His constant vigilance was beginning to make her nervous. "Do you really have a concern?"

"Outside the camp, I have much less control over what happens to you and your. . . brother."

My brother. Yes. Must she explain how Father had taken the abandoned boy in to raise as his own?

Ben couldn't hide his frustration. "I am not afraid to go beyond your walls."

"Which is explained by your age and lack of experience."

Ben stopped walking. "Then I will return to the room."

The lieutenant remained firm. "Are you in such a hurry to return to those stuffy confines?"

Susannah touched Ben's arm. "Come. The air will do you good."

He pulled away, his eyes narrowed. "I can find my way."

Lt. Waters stepped in front of him, causing Ben to look up.

"That may be, but it doesn't change my responsibility for you. And rushing off is inconsiderate of your sister."

Ben exhaled loudly but complied, and headed for the blockhouse.

Susannah slowed, drawing the lieutenant to drop behind. "I believe had he been born my brother he would still struggle at his loss of freedom. Did you not chafe at the bit when you were his age?" She glanced ahead, her heart feeling fragile. "I'm afraid this gathering might be more difficult for him than we realized."

"That won't change in his future."

Frustration rode up the length of her back. "He's had a good education, Lieutenant."

"I am sure. But where will he use it?"

Something in those dark-lashed eyes chased away her last clear thought. "Use what?"

"His schooling. The Latin."

"You can't be against education, Lieutenant."

He kept an eye on Ben. "He may do well in Johnstown, but he'll always be a curiosity elsewhere, regardless of how he's dressed or how proper his English."

How dare he say such things?

If only he wasn't right.

"Miss Kimball. Do you think he would ever feel comfortable back with his own people?"

His own people? "He is and always will be my brother." She had no more use for this conversation and hurried to catch up before she lost sight of Ben in the milling crowd.

With little effort, Lt. Waters stayed at her side, studying her. "What if being here makes him want to leave what you and your father have given him?"

She heard no challenge in his words. Just concern. And he'd voiced the very thing she'd feared. "I imagine he's curious, but—"

"Of course. At fourteen, I too longed for the opportunity of living as these people—his people do. Living in the forest. Warring. Enough so that I left school and convinced my father I needed to be an officer rather than a scholar."

Yes. Bloodshed. "And here you are, Lieutenant. Having done the very thing.

How has warring, as you put it, lived up to your dreams?"

"That is a conversation I don't believe you want to hear, Miss Kimball. But I did leave home, and Ben may feel the same way."

"That will be his decision."

"And in five years?"

Goodness! Just when she'd thought better of him! "His education, his time with us, will help many people. *His people*, if that suits you better." That was it then. They'd never agree on the subject. Yet, one glance up from his neatly tied neckcloth to his intelligent dark-brown eyes. . . The man was grinning at her.

It wouldn't make up for his stubborn opinions.

He tipped his head toward the Indian camps. "You've come here to promote new schools. For them?"

"For girls. When Indian and English children play and learn together, they become friends." Maybe she'd misread him.

"Then you intend to make proper little English girls out of them. Good church-going ladies?"

She should have known better than to think a man who preferred killing Indians to befriending them would support such an idea. "You have a very narrow view, Lieutenant. Things are different where I come from."

"Yes, I'm sure they are." He turned away. "You've not lost your closest friend to a massacre, then arrived too late to do anything but recover what was. . ."

"No, I haven't." She touched his sleeve. "But Ben has seen worse."

"Susannah! Come up here!" Ben waved from up in the blockhouse.

A brazier spit out a shower of sparks behind the lieutenant. He looked at her, waiting.

"Ben was just a child when a group of white men killed his mother and grandmother. His father had been missing and the three of them were traveling to his mother's village. Perhaps he'd have been happier raised by another tribe, but I believe we've done right by him." Such injustice always stirred her; she glanced around and lowered her voice. "There are many children who lack the blessing of being raised by their parents. Most often it is due to war. Warring. The thing that has kept you busy since you left home. We are not replacements, but Father is good to him."

The lieutenant removed his hat. He didn't seem so convinced of his own opinion anymore. Maybe something she'd said had sunk in.

"You are right, Miss Kimball. The age is difficult for any boy. I've made it worse by treating him like a child and I will apologize."

"You've made no secret of your dislike for his people."

"Not all, no." He looked off into the distance. "But friendliness toward them doesn't come easily. And if the Chenussio Seneca arrive, I shall have to face the very men who slaughtered my friend. Would you rather I played you false, miss?"

"I'm sorry you lost your friend. It was a horrid event. An act of war, yet making war is what men do when it means protecting family and a way of life."

They both watched Ben lean over to look down at the riverbank.

"I don't judge your father. I see he is a good man, but, unlike the commander, I would never bring my wife here, or a daughter."

She shifted away, taken aback. She hadn't considered that he might be married. That was good. He had a wife. Maybe that was for the best, given his surly moods. "And what does she say about that?"

"She would have agreed."

Would have? He'd spoken so quietly she turned to study him. His eyes were unreadable in the deep shadows along the stone building. She'd ask more, but they were mounting the narrow stairs to where Ben kept watch and the soldiers on duty chatted. At the top, she joined them in their protected view.

Benjamin's earlier mood had brightened, and he eagerly pointed out what he'd seen, leading her from one side to the next—the endless lake, the opposite shore of the river, and the camps and small fires where men of every ilk waited. Lt. Waters waited quietly, and when Ben had finally had enough, they returned silently to the castle. Father waited in the entryway and ushered her brother ahead. "Thank you, Lieutenant. I expect that has satisfied him for the moment. And thank you for seeing to my family. Good evening."

"I don't. . ." The lieutenant's words trailed off.

Susannah stopped at the door. "Lt. Waters, I'm sorry for the loss of your friend. There's no cause—"

He spun around, grabbed her, and forced her behind him with such speed, she yelped.

They both looked to the threat. It was no more than one of Johnson's backwoodsmen, inebriated. Susannah knew him to be a ranger, but his habit of decorating himself like an Iroquois hadn't helped.

She pushed away from the lieutenant's grasp, away from the shock at his touch and from how she'd clung to the broad expanse of his back.

He was at once by her side. "I'm sorry, Miss Kimball. Did I hurt you?"

"No." She raised a hand, needing him away from her. "Please. I'm fine. Let me go to my room."

He looked at her hand, then raised those dark lashes to look into her eyes.

Please. Just let me go. "I know the way from here."

He gathered the part of her shawl that had slipped from her shoulders and carefully replaced it, his fingers brushing her skin. "Allow me to know you are safely in your room."

She nodded, too flustered to argue, and continued with him at her heels. Her heart rate didn't slow. Inside and climbing the dark staircase she had to ask. "Your wife. Was it. . . ?"

"Lung fever. A simple cold and she was gone. Three years now."

And nothing he could blame but the weather.

Behind her, the solid sound of his boot steps stopped long before she reached her doorway.

"Wait."

Susannah leaned back, speechless as he approached, then hurriedly entered her room. She was still looking away when he removed himself.

"I wanted to be sure. I. . . Anyway, Kahente has prepared the room. I shall send her to attend to you."

"Thank you."

He didn't move. "Miss Kimball, please look at me. Have I distressed you so much?"

She met his gaze, unable to hold back a grin at his accuracy.

His eyes were wide with true regret, before she sighed. "Accept my apologies. Tomorrow, I hope to have the opportunity to change your opinion of me. Perhaps we might even be friends for the time you must endure my company."

Susannah nodded, fighting the urge to touch his arm to reassure him. "I think that is wise. Good night, Lieutenant." She waited at her door as he walked away.

Again his footsteps paused. She held her breath.

"Tonight. . .has been a fine evening."

She could never have expected to find his words comforting. He didn't move. Father and Ben's quiet conversation in their room reminded her that a proper young woman would not let a man linger in her hallway. Certainly not near her bedchamber. But she would make this moment last. He'd take more than his presence when he left her tonight.

"I've kept you long enough." He came closer.

Inwardly she sighed, thankful the meager candlelight hid both their faces.

"I apologize for my—"

"No," she whispered. "There's no need. You wouldn't be much of a soldier if what happened to your friend didn't anger you."

He glanced at Father's door. "But I was wrong about the boy. You and your father will see he finds his way in both worlds."

She focused on where the leather strap to his munitions pack crossed the pewter buttons of his officer's coat. That was, until a lock of dark hair fell forward from his brow, loosened by the constant removal of his hat. In that unguarded moment, she saw beyond the uniform, the soldier's detachment, anger, regret. Arch Waters was more than she'd allowed him.

He could use a friend.

They could both benefit from a confidant.

"Good night, Lieutenant. I really must get some rest."

When he didn't reply, she raised her gaze to his. And then he backed away, donned his hat, and became a soldier once again. She watched him go, staring long at the spot where he'd disappeared, leaving an emptiness there and in her chest.

Chapter 4

Susannah carefully latched the door before heading to her narrow built-in bed. After never-ending days in a carriage, she'd been paraded about, forced to endure a stuffy dinner, and asked to sing as entertainment. But the words she'd sung hadn't touched her, hadn't given her the restoration she'd needed.

She could drop straight off to sleep, fully clothed. She'd never been so exhausted, nor felt so alive.

This wasn't supposed to happen.

Not here. And not with a hardheaded, hard-hearted soldier.

This wild, impractical racing of her heart when Lieutenant Archibald Waters was near—and he was almost always near—might be what she'd heard about but never believed in.

It couldn't be real, only fleeting, precarious, and thoroughly exhilarating. When she returned home, he'd still be here, tied to the regiment.

Her heart would be safe.

Was this then what made Mother willing to leave her family in England to follow a man she hardly knew? To give up everything to marry and bear his child? Yet that man hadn't been there when the next child, his very own son, had struggled to be born. Josiah Kimball hadn't witnessed the hours of torment or seen the blood, nor arrived in time to say goodbye.

Susannah would never forget that day. The whispers, the crying, the acceptance on the midwife's face when she'd told a nine-year-old Susannah that her mother's death was a sad but common one.

The woman had called it "the price of love."

Silent tears ran down Susannah's cheeks. Mother's face had faded from her memory, and, while Father had never remarried, she wondered if he too had forgotten.

A knock at the door was so light she might not have heard it without the latch's metallic rattle. She wiped the back of her hand across her cheek. "Yes?"

"I have tea for you."

Susannah admitted the short Indian woman. A patch of white streaked down one side of her thick, black hair. Kahente had no use for subtlety and looked Susannah over. She took back the mug and set it down, letting her rough hand settle on

Susannah's shoulder. "Come, girl."

Susannah had no will to resist and felt Kahente work at the ties cinching her *robe a l'anglaise,* while Susannah unpinned her stiff bodice and stomacher. She left the untying of her petticoats and stays to the skillful old Indian. When layers of silk, cotton, and linen clothing lay in a pool around her feet, Susannah stepped out from its center.

Kahente encouraged her to sit. "I work the hair." Nimble fingers removed the pins, letting the bulk of hair drop down her back. Kahente collected Susannah's hairbrush and returned on silent, leather-clad feet. She gathered Susannah's hair in one hand and began to work the brush through the length of it. "It is like the sun." The gentle pressure on her scalp lulled Susannah and made her heart break all over again at the loss of a mother she'd never needed more.

Kahente stopped and Susannah glanced back at her.

"Why do you cry, songbird?"

"I'm so very tired."

"And alone."

Susannah turned away. "No. The God I sing for. He is with me always."

"And your mother?" Kahente tapped at her own chest, just above the biggest shell of her beaded necklaces. "She is with you here as well."

Susannah could only nod.

The old woman continued working at her hair. "I am your mother tonight. I have lost a daughter. Your God understands what we need."

Tears flowed freely, and, trying as she might, Susannah could not keep quiet, even after Kahente, no longer a stranger, wrapped her in her arms.

When she could, Susannah pulled away, nodding that she was through with tears. "Yes. My Lord understands and has reminded me of His love through your ready arms. Thank you."

"When you have your own child, your mother will come to you, speak to you. You will know much about her then."

Susannah understood, but the knot of fear came too close to the surface. "No. There will be no children for me."

Kahente pushed her back by the shoulders to examine her.

Susannah raised her eyes.

"But you are young, and strong."

"I will not marry."

"How do you know such a thing? You say you will never love?"

Not if it meant what had happened to Mother. She would live alone rather than risk dying that way. Why did no one understand? "I will teach, instead, and I've already learned that my pupils will become my many children."

"And the songbird will never sing for a mate?"

Susannah stood and folded the rest of her clothing. She reached for the teacup but knew her hands were too shaky to hold it. "There is more to life. Not everyone marries." She kept her back to the old woman, even when she heard Kahente go to the door.

"Sleep well, child."

A wonderful sentiment, but Susannah wondered if sleep would come at all.

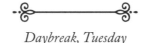

Daybreak, Tuesday

Great white gulls rode the currents of Lake Ontario's breeze, their arguments a noisy chatter Susannah preferred over the hundreds of men outside her closest window. Fort Niagara's perch high above the water also managed to keep the odors of a large encampment downwind.

She'd eaten breakfast with Mrs. Browning and learned that the childbirth she'd attended had gone well. Susannah had stood far too long at the upper window when Father came to her side.

"Come walk with me, daughter."

Concern filled her chest at the tone of Father's voice, but she quietly followed him downstairs, past Lt. Waters' dedicated post, and out of the building, where a busy fort made it hard to be overheard.

From that upper window, she'd watched the lieutenant return to the castle at dawn while the sky sang with pinks and golds and the crowded camps of the courtyard listened in silence.

Father stopped her, making sure she looked at him. "I know that the woman Kahente was with you. But what caused your tears last night?"

She glanced around, reassuring herself no one had heard. "It was nothing."

"You are no longer my little girl, but I still worry. I'm afraid there are many dishonorable men that would do you harm."

"You know I would never put myself in danger."

"No, but if you insist on teaching, it will be along the coast. I was wrong to let you consider the frontier." His gray eyes took in the tumult around them before resting again on her. "If the famed warrior Farmer's Brother and the Chennusio Seneca don't answer Sir William's request, a split in the Iroquois confederacy will destroy this tenuous peace."

"But there are too few willing to teach in a mission school. Far fewer will work among the Indians."

"For good reason."

"But Father—"

"The Mohawk school is an experiment, at best. Without the support of the missions board and Sir William, few care to see Indian children schooled. Even the chiefs argue."

"But it is what God has called me to. I know it. And I love the Mohawk people."

"I can't discount your reasoning, but until you marry, you will listen to me."

What was happening? "But I have to teach! That is why I wanted to come here. You know that." She'd sought to never disappoint her father, but if he continued to press her thus, she would have to stand against his wishes. "What about Benjamin?"

"We will talk about this later."

Yes. Because Lieutenant Waters waited nearby. How much had he heard?

The tension inside the fort had simply unsettled Father. He would never prevent her from missionary work.

"Until you marry." He'd never said that before. It was always supposed to be the three of them, working together, a family. And now he was ready to send her away?

Father rubbed his face. "I'm going to my room. I'm suddenly quite tired."

She didn't like the color around his mouth today. "Where is Benjamin?"

"He is with Sir William. Learning diplomacy, I hope."

He was more worried than he'd let on. "I will always watch out for him."

"And when I'm gone, who will watch out for you?"

Chapter 5

Wednesday's Dawn

On the morning of the third day, Susannah was unable to remain in her room any longer. When the commander had called it a cell, he wasn't far wrong. Yesterday, after convincing Sir William that she and her father needed a day to rest, she'd taken her meals in the room and managed a hip bath—a long process and not without its challenges. It had helped that the Lord had provided an afternoon of heavy rain.

The two times she'd ventured downstairs to find Kahente, Lt. Waters was watching the stairwell. She'd convinced herself that her thoughts of love were owed to his good looks and stubborn gallantry. After all, she didn't know him, and wouldn't. There couldn't be love without friendship—not a love to last.

Today she felt more herself. She descended the stairs and now stood chatting with the supply officer, a pleasant Scotsman.

Lt. Waters watched from where he waited along the wall.

Sir William burst into the storeroom. "Ah, I'd begun to suspect you were hiding from me, Miss Kimball."

One look told Susannah he had something in mind for her. Benjamin appeared behind him.

"I've arranged a great surprise. You'll be mightily amazed. Of that I'm assured." He turned and waved Benjamin off. "Go get your things, lad. Don't worry. Your father will be joining you." His sharp eyes scanned the room. "Lieutenant Waters?"

"Yes sir?" Waters stepped forward.

"Maximillian Mueller, the solicitor at German Flats, and his uncle, a Mr. Schwerter-Bach, arrived yesterday and wish to view the falls. I'm sending at least two of my Mohawk guards and, thanks to Browning, four men of your company." He paused, and his eyes never left the lieutenant's face. "I have no concerns for safety, you understand?"

It was more of a challenge than a question. Sir William blinked, but Lt. Waters remained impassive.

The baronet turned back to her. "It would be a shame to have you come this close and not see the falls of the mighty Niagara. A sight even King George desires. Though it means a few hours in the carriage, mine is the most comfortable. Mrs.

Browning has overseen a boxed lunch, but you'll return before supper. With great stories for us, sure as I'm born." He reached toward Susannah and placed a fatherly hand on her shoulder. "Oh, and now that I've had a chance to hear Josiah's hopes for your future, we will soon discuss what I can do to help."

"Yes sir. Thank you." But today? Now? After a week of travel? Thank God she'd had a day to rest. The baronet turned away, his limp more noticeable as he left the room.

She hurried past Lt. Waters to peer down the hallway for signs of the others, and allowed herself a deep sigh. "You don't care for Sir William, do you?"

"My opinions of anyone hardly matter."

She laughed. "But you definitely have them. Tell me, you think this trip wrong?"

"I don't care for the journey on such a hot day, nor the route, but I daresay we'll be safe enough. I'll see to it. Even Cornplanter, the tribal chief, wouldn't be so foolish as to attack the baronet's carriage."

Good. "If you are for it, I can find no excuses." She glanced back at the man behind the counter. "I find I'm eager to see the falls. Here, the river seems loathe to move."

"It's a grand sight, lass."

The lieutenant waved her forward, and she stopped in front of him before starting up the stairs. "You may stay here while I gather my things. I am safe enough, unless you think I can escape your oversight by way of an upper window."

"I imagine you've already searched for just such an opportunity."

She laughed, risking a glance at his face. Genuine amusement only made him more attractive.

Fifteen minutes later, Susannah sat inside Johnson's carriage. Father did not look rested, but said he would not miss the chance. The smaller of the two huge Germans, Herr Mueller, sat in the middle with Susannah and Ben squeezed in by each window. Across from them sat Father and Herr Schwerter-Bach, the latter taking up more than half of the cushion.

Sir William's slave Harry rode alongside, a choice she envied, as the strong scent of a dirty powdered wig and body odor deepened with each mile.

A fair number of soldiers, Lieutenant Waters among them, also rode alongside, ahead, and behind. Two Mohawks, Blue Sky and Buck, passed by her window, moving to the front.

"Sir William tells us you vill like to work among the Indians," said Herr Mueller. "Missionary work, *ja*, Miss Kimball?"

"Teaching English, and understanding of world history, as well as Biblical studies."

He shook his head. "My, my. And music. Do you play the pianoforte?"

"She does," added Benjamin, mischievously catching Susannah's eye.

Mueller stroked his pointed gray beard. "Singing is a *gut* way to learn language, and language—English of course—promotes peace among ze people."

"Do you honestly think so, sir?" Susannah asked. "That there will be peace if you continue to bring in new settlers? They reduce the hunting that the Indians depend on."

He was surprised by her question. "Oh, ja. Their chiefs depend on our trade goods now. Don't you agree, *Onkel* Verner?"

The still silent Herr Schwerter-Bach shrugged.

Herr Mueller was missing her point. "Yet it is their warriors that most highly disagree with relinquishing land."

"You must forgive my daughter's zeal, gentlemen. Susannah dear, you must let Mr. Mueller form his own opinion."

Her father's warning stung, betraying everything he'd taught her about intellectual conversation. She offered her seatmate a smile before looking back to Father. "If I was your son instead of your daughter—"

"Precisely. And if you were not as lovely and kind as your mother, I might not have encouraged you this way."

While he no doubt meant it as a compliment, his timing was poor. Father had not once ever hinted at any resemblance to her mother, and now he did so while chastising her in front of strangers.

She glanced across the German's broad chest where his massive arms rested on his belly. Ben sent her an understanding nod. It seemed everyone's emotions rode a knife edge. She was no different.

Once on a wider portion of the trail, Arch maneuvered his mount next to the carriage, hoping to casually look in on Miss Kimball. She gazed out, but didn't seem to see a thing. Whatever stole her thoughts, saddened her. The next time he looked, she saw him and turned away. Her earlier enthusiasm for this outing was gone. He needed to take more care in his manner with her rather than let his frustrations cast a shadow.

Although he disagreed with the great gathering of tribes, he had to admit that it could mean an end to the killing on the frontier. Johnson was a savvy businessman, a successful—if untrained and undisciplined—soldier, and skilled in accurately reading people while having a general respect for all he encountered. So far his methods seemed to be working.

A young Indian boy—a favorite of Sir William's—scrambled down from one of the Mohawk's mounts and on to the back of the carriage. Looking like some half-dressed, wild-haired footman, the imp's antics reminded Arch of his son. His parents had succeeded in seeing Arch and three brothers through childhood with all their limbs, but Merritt's proclivity to get himself into scrapes surely wore them out and exceeded Arch's ability to discipline him from another continent.

At times, the deep ache of missing his son only exaggerated the emptiness inside. Was soldiering worth being parted from the boy? Merritt, at seven years, was growing too fast and in need of an active father, not a tired grandsire.

Far ahead, horses crested a small rise visible through the trees. Arch's back stiffened as he motioned to those behind him then reined his horse closer to the carriage. "Indians approach, gentlemen." He hoped his tone offered reassurance to all as he joined the soldiers of his company at the front of the procession.

Both Mohawk scouts' postures proved they'd seen the approaching party, but they showed no concern. They wouldn't.

"Seneca," one announced.

He counted three.

Having to revisit the site was bad enough, but to encounter the same butchers so close made his blood boil. But he couldn't afford to let his anger rule. He'd been given responsibility for the Kimballs at the fort and now led them to face his enemy only a mile from where they'd massacred eighty.

"Hold up."

Arch looked back at the carriage driver's shout. A door opened and Herr Mueller crouched to step out.

"I vill talk to them."

Arch spun his horse around and went back. "Are you sure, sir?"

"They must understand we are a party under the protection of Sir William."

Sir William was not God.

But neither was he. What if something happened to him?

God protect her.

Those accompanying the carriage arranged themselves ahead of it while one of the Mohawks walked forward with the German. Arch reined in next to Miss Kimball's window. She might say she wasn't afraid, but the look on her face proved otherwise.

He dismounted and opened the carriage door. "Please do not worry." He glanced at Mr. Kimball and Ben, then the other German. "Sir William will be pleased if this means Farmer's Brother has deigned to attend."

Mr. Kimball reached across the carriage space and took his daughter's hand, while Arch's fingers sought the reassurance of a weapon in his belt.

He waited at her door as Mueller, with the Mohawk's help, tried to communicate. It didn't last long, and the three Seneca mounted and began a path straight through the Fort Niagara party.

Sweat trickled down his temple as Arch stared straight ahead, fearing his own response. The second brave stopped next to him and Arch could not miss the fact that the man's eyes were on Miss Kimball.

"Woman. It is you."

She looked from her father to Arch, before acknowledging the warrior, but she didn't speak.

Word had traveled fast of the yellow-haired songbird.

"The lady is not your concern."

Smiling, the Seneca ignored him, though he must know some English.

Miss Kimball leaned out the open door to speak. "Sir William waits for you, sir. It is good of you to attend him. Good for all of us."

He frowned. "But you. You not stay?"

"We will return to the fort by evening," she said, her voice agreeable and stubbornly unafraid.

Arch's anger stoked. She did not owe this man any answer, nor any kindness. "Go on. Leave us."

The brave turned his sharp eyes upon Arch, laughed, and rode on.

Arch returned to his saddle, but couldn't shake the anger in every breath. The carriage shrugged and rocked as Mueller climbed back in. Arch prodded his horse on, done with trying to figure the woman out as she watched the warrior depart. Was her interest in their world, her familiarity with them, all because she sought a wild brave as a husband? He knew white men who preferred the beauty of an Indian wife.

Her supposed lack of fear might have been admirable in someone else, but not a fair young woman in his care. What did it matter? His responsibility would be over when she went home.

He watched the Mohawk boy leap up behind one of the scouts. The boy exhibited heated animation as he complained to the older man.

When Arch heard *Yonterennothiyo*, the Mohawk word used for Miss Kimball, "she who sings beautifully," he deftly urged his mount to join them. "Is there trouble?"

The old brave's eyes crinkled in amusement under the woven fabric he wore like a turban. "Karawase not like the Seneca looking at his woman. Woman he will marry."

The boy pounded his chest with pride.

Arch laughed aloud for the first time in days. "Your woman, eh? Well, I didn't like it either." He gestured to the boy. "Come." The boy climbed across then settled behind Arch in the saddle. Letters from his mother said his son Merritt was also agile. Arch signaled to the carriage driver that he was going on ahead then addressed the boy. "Tell me your name again."

"Karawase."

"Hold on." When small but strong arms were snug around Arch's waist, he urged the horse into a gallop, until they came to the twisting descent at Devil's Hole.

He pulled up, ordered the boy down, and dismounted.

Arch wasn't ready to forgive what he'd seen that day. He wasn't sure when he would be, but his anger had eaten at him far too long, and he needed to be done with it. He planned to spend his life in the army, but he'd be no better than Porter if he didn't leave Niagara's memories behind.

He wanted an extended leave that would allow a return to England. With his wife gone three years, Merritt needed more than letters from a missing father.

Miss Kimball's words returned. *"There are many children who lack the blessing of being raised by their parents. Most often it is due to war."*

Yes, and he'd made that choice.

Arch squatted down to touch the footprints of the Seneca's unshod ponies, then landed upon them when Karawase jumped on his back. The boy's raucous laughter kept a surprised Arch from reaching for his knife. Untangling himself proved difficult until he finally shrugged the boy off, pinning him to the coarse earth. "Stay away from my woman."

"She is mine, *Anglais!*"

Arch let the boy up. Rather, Karawase sprang to his feet. Arch shook his head, laughing, and rose to dust himself off. "Let's go." He collected his horse's reins and offered the lad a hand up. Turning back to rejoin their party, the gelding set his own pace and conveniently returned to Miss Kimball's side of the carriage.

She leaned forward, her face brightening at their return, and opened the door enough to speak. "Is it much farther, Lieutenant?"

Arch glanced over his shoulder at the grinning Karawase. "Worth the wait."

She nodded. "Father showed me a painting of Niagara when we visited New York, many years ago."

He looked across the carriage's green interior. "Perhaps you'd like to ride back with the scouts on the return, Benjamin?" Then, belatedly, he deferred to Mr. Kimball. "If your father agrees."

At his father's benevolent nod, Ben brightened. "Oh yes. I'd like that."

Arch was rewarded with Susannah's appreciative smile. When Karawase removed Arch's hat and placed it on his head, her laughter was heartier than he'd expected.

"What about me, Anglais? I ride with you."

"You, my friend, may have to ride in the carriage with Miss Kimball so she might explain the benefits of an English education."

The boy's frustration waned once he realized the benefits.

Arch grinned. He'd too long been busy being angry. He'd been going about this all wrong and was determined to win more smiles from Susannah. He reclaimed his hat and dipped his head. "We shall see you at the falls, Miss Kimball." With his best attempt at a charming grin, he set the horse into a gallop.

"She likes us, boy."

"My woman," argued Karawase.

"We'll see about that."

Susannah peered forward, all but pressing her face to the smudged glass. Smoke rose in the distance. "I think there's a fire ahead."

"Oh, I hope not." Father moved cautiously to look out toward the river gorge. "We've come so far."

The chance to walk would suit her, so she was much relieved when the carriage slowed and the soldiers dismounted.

One opened the carriage door. "We walk from here, miss."

She took the soldier's hand as she alighted. Father was next; Ben all but knocked him over in his rush.

"What about the fire?" she asked.

"No fire, miss," the soldier told her, smiling. "Listen."

It was not smoke she'd seen but mist, just as the faint distant thunder meant the rumble of the falls was near. She glanced around for Arch and a path through the trees.

"Are you ready?" he asked, coming to her side. "I promise this is a day you won't forget."

Yes, Arch Waters. And it's more than Niagara.

Their route here had rimmed an ever-deepening gorge. Now, on foot, the well-worn path opened out to a full view of the precipice. A torrent of wild, rushing water raced to drop with such power it pulled her toward it. Ben obeyed the call. Susannah shrieked and one of the men put a protective arm out to stop him, though no one ventured closer than twenty paces. Including an island perched on the edge, the river must be hundreds—no, thousands—of feet wide. Only by looking across the chasm to the other shore could she see how far the white curtain of water dropped.

Herr Mueller came to her side. "Vat do you think, Miss Kimball?"

"I am half frozen with fear, yet I can't look away."

This prompted a tale of his visit to waterfalls in his homeland, and Susannah found his English faltering the more he spoke of Germany. Behind her, the carriage drivers chatted as they unloaded food baskets and blankets. Father whisked her away from their ever-droning companion, but Mueller and his silent uncle followed them toward their meal of bean and bacon porridge, cold duck, and buttered brown bread.

She was in awe.

The soldiers spoke among themselves. Karawase and Blue Lake joined Arch where he'd found a downed tree trunk to sit on. After days of forced companionship, he was likely glad to relinquish sole responsibility for her.

Not once did he look her way!

Herr Mueller called Arch over to join them for fresh berry tarts. "I have yet to see your Captain Porter, ze man of such courage at the Battle of Carillon."

"They call it Ticonderoga now, sir. And yes, he was honored for distinguished service." One of the other soldiers snorted and was rewarded with a sharp look from the lieutenant. "I will give him your regards, sir."

Later, she joined Arch for one last look across the waterfalls. So much beauty, yet his appreciation of it would forever be spoiled by the angry destruction of life downriver.

Soldier he might be, but she appreciated the education and intellect she'd not found among most men she'd encountered.

He brushed a dried leaf off his sleeve as if also brushing away the difficult memories, then offered a tentative smile.

"Lieutenant Waters, I've hardly seen you since we declared our friendship." She hesitated, then went on. "I've never found myself feeling so free to be honest with someone and say what I wanted to say."

"Only with me?"

"Well, yes. I can't account for it. I think of you as Arch, so I've been afraid I'd say it aloud, as if it's a secret we share."

"I'm honored."

That smile she'd worked for would stay locked in the memories of this day. He replaced his tricorn as they strolled toward the carriage.

"You've made an impression on Karawase."

He studied her for a moment. "I realize now he is from your village."

"He is what we would call a cousin to Sir William's children."

One of the soldiers called to him.

"They are ready to go."

"Yes. Unfortunately." She dreaded the pending hours of travel.

Together, they watched one of the regimental soldiers give up his mount for Ben and climb on the back of the carriage. Arch had not forgotten his offer and had arranged for the exchange.

"I expect you'd like to have a son someday."

"I have a son, Susannah."

His words made it difficult to breathe. She didn't see Father until he touched her arm.

"Come along. We've taken much of their time."

"I'll be right there." She turned back to Arch. "I should not have assumed otherwise. I should like to hear about him."

Arch retrieved a paper from an inner pocket and handed it to her. "I believed my job was to provide for him by serving the king, but now I'm not so certain."

She studied a child's drawing of a son and a proud, smiling British soldier. "It's wonderful. I wonder that you haven't remarried."

"Do you?" His eyes searched for something other than Susannah to look upon. "Excuse me," he said, hurrying past her. "We must not keep them any longer."

Susannah rushed to where Father waited to help her into the carriage.

What had gone so wrong?

Chapter 6

A rch rode ahead of the excursion for the first hour, certain the return trip would feel twice as long, with regret for company.

Benjamin Kimball, atop a steady roan gelding, stayed close by, and, while unlikely his first time on a horse, his inexperience showed.

Those few moments with Susannah were sweet—until he'd bolted when she'd mentioned remarriage. It was something a friend would ask, but his thoughts of her went beyond friendship.

These hours away from the fort, the day's relaxed company—the Mohawks included—made Arch wonder if he'd been too ready for trouble.

"I know what my people, the Seneca, did."

Arch's hands tightened on the reins. He'd been completely unprepared for that.

A hank of long black hair had loosened from its queue and fallen forward to curtain Ben's dark eyes. "The massacre."

Arch took a deep breath. "We are all tied to that day in some way. Your heritage does not make you one thing or another."

"But you've killed others? Did you not regret it?"

He'd thought once he might have to explain that subject to Merritt, but had never figured out what he would say. He kept his eyes ahead. "Not at the time, but I hope I never need to do so again."

"Then why are they—my people—considered so evil? Have they not done only what you have?"

He studied Ben, who in turn kept his attentions on the trail. "I can't answer that. Not for you and not for myself. Your sister has convinced me your education gives hope for both sides. To do that you will need to learn to think for yourself."

Ben met his gaze. "When will your anger leave you, Lieutenant?"

Arch rode on, considering the question. "I don't know. I may have to leave here first."

"To your home?"

That would help. "Does your father speak of it?"

"Never. But Sir William tells us about *Ire*-land and *Eng*-land both. I should like to see these great places."

"Then you should. I'll suggest it."

"No."

Arch was surprised at the strong response.

"I don't like going on the water."

A snort of amusement became shared laughter between them. "If you find another way, let me know." Arch had crossed the Atlantic and sailed to the Caribbean and back. But sail again he would, when it was time to go home. A moment later he realized Ben had dropped back to join the Mohawks teasing young Karawase through the carriage window.

Much later, their journey over, Benjamin Kimball rode into the fort, straight-backed and confident.

Arch dismounted in time to see Susannah exit the carriage and, a bit unsteady, take a soldier's hand. Giggling, she came to Arch. Pride filled her eyes as she watched her brother. "If he becomes a soldier instead of a scholar, it will be your fault, Lieutenant Waters."

He returned her smile, relieved she'd put aside his earlier awkward response.

Benjamin Kimball would hardly make a soldier. "His riding will improve, but I'm sorry I wasn't able to extend the same invitation to you." He leaned closer. "And even sorrier you had to endure the trip with Herr Mueller. No wonder his uncle remains silent."

"I considered getting out and walking, if you must know. God bless Father. He carried the conversation while I feigned sleep."

Arch handed his reins off to a private and stayed at her side through the crowded fort. "You *can* call me Arch, you know."

The color rose on her cheeks, but she didn't reply.

The noise inside the castle spoiled the day's peace and his hard-won ease fled when he saw the three Seneca scouts lounging in the counsel room.

When will I be free of this?

An hour later, he was back to waiting outside the dining room while she was within. He kept busy with thoughts of why she'd asked if he'd remarry. Other than it seemed to be a favorite topic of women.

When the door opened, he didn't like what he saw. Whether by choice or not, Susannah sat next to the handsome Seneca scout who'd made a point of his interest. Johnson was telling a tale that had the whole room laughing, including those murderers from Devil's Hole.

Mr. Kimball was first out the door. "Ah, Lieutenant Waters. Good, you're here. Susannah has agreed to sing for our guests before they leave tonight. Come along."

No, he didn't think so.

He couldn't blame any man for finding her attractive, but must it be this particular warrior?

Arch clutched Mr. Kimball's arm. "You must not allow that Indian to look at her so."

Mr. Kimball chuckled as he looked up at Arch. "Who has control over the attractions between men and women?"

Arch couldn't believe it. "He is far too familiar with her—"

"He has been to our village, Lieutenant, and she has done nothing to encourage him. It is her nature to be kind. He—"

"You would let her go with him, marry him?"

"Oh my dear fellow. Is that what you think?" Kimball leaned closer, his gray hair falling forward. "She likes her niceties far too much to live as a warrior's wife, especially as she's adamant she'll never marry."

Arch wanted to shake the man out of his amusement.

Kimball must have noted. His smile vanished. "You've taken your role quite seriously. I fear I must learn to see her as a grown woman and not my little girl. I've failed at trying to be mother and father to her."

Arch regretted his tendency to bluntness. "You've done well, sir. Make no mistake."

Susannah enjoyed his company, but he had no right to thoughts of how it would be to court her, when he couldn't even care for his own son. Her sole desire was to work among the Indians, to teach them about God and never marry.

Just as well. Arch wasn't a favorite of the Iroquois or God.

For the first time since he'd been told to guard Miss Kimball's safety, he left his post early and headed for the blockhouse. The view overlooking the fort normally improved his mood, but tonight too many fires burned in Indian camps.

Susannah's interest in teaching Indian girls was admirable but she was naive to think she'd be safe. Was she expecting to make them Christians by spending her days among them? Living without a family of her own and on the perimeters of theirs?

Like you? Watching over the lives of others?

He needed sleep

Inside the officers' barracks, Arch paused by Captain Porter's room and glanced through the partially open door to gauge his commanding officer's current mood. Porter faced the wall, his head dropped forward.

The man was crying.

Arch stepped back, desperate for a silent retreat.

He'd cried. He'd cried plenty when his wife died, but here? A regimental commander? He hastened to escape before Porter realized he'd been overheard.

Arch stripped off his belts, buckles, and straps and shrugged out of his coat. In his dirty shirt, long red waistcoat, and blue breeches, he dropped to his cot and began the process of brushing his jacket, a mindless chore that generally set him up for a good night's sleep, something he'd need given both Porter's problems and his own inability to keep a clear head over Susannah.

She'd suggested friendship. Nothing said he couldn't also love her. He sat back, frustrated. It would be hours before his mind allowed sleep. Arch threw on his coat and went out into the night.

Men's voices and the rattle of a door latch drew Susannah out of a heavy sleep. She glanced about, confused at the hour, for she was still dressed. Evening, or dawn?

It was Father's voice she'd heard. "Thank you for telling me, Lieutenant."

Even with the departing boots, she let her heart rate settle before opening her door. "Is something wrong, Father?"

"Nothing, my dear. Nothing but regrets."

They showed in the lines about his mouth. She glanced at the other door. "Is Ben inside?"

Father shook his head.

"Were we wrong to bring him here?"

He took her hand. "No, but I was wrong to think I could keep you both with me forever. Benjamin must find where his place will be, and for that, it is good he's here, but. . ." He ran a hand through his untied gray hair.

"Has he done something?"

Father's shoulders sank but he smiled. "He's been in a fight with one of the other. . .young men."

She closed her eyes. It could be about anything, but most likely it was about being an Indian raised by the English. "It is to be expected at his age, is it not?"

"Still, I may have done him a disservice—"

"No. He's had so many opportunities—"

"But no mother. You both needed a mother. I thought I could make up for it, but I was wrong."

She rested her head against his shoulder. "We've done well."

"You need a mother now more than ever, my child. I can't advise you on things of the heart."

"How many times must I tell you that doesn't concern me?"

"I too didn't plan to marry."

She looked at him as if she'd somehow misheard him. "But you—"

"I loved your mother more than I ever thought possible. I didn't choose to. I had no desire to take anyone, much less a gentle woman like her, away from her family. And then she never saw them again. We planned to go back so you might spend time with your grandparents and attend a girls' school."

"Did she not want to come to the colonies?"

"Oh daughter. There's so much I've not shared. My loss was so deep, I denied you the chance to speak of her."

Her heart beat like a wounded bird struggling to flee. "Then may we again speak of her?"

Footsteps echoed up the stairwell and they watched. "Of course. I'm so sorry."

Ben appeared, his shirt torn and bloodied. Father frowned but spoke no rebuke, not that she'd expected one.

"I have caused you pain, Father."

He waved Ben closer and put a hand on the back of his neck. "You are a boy becoming a man. While I hoped this trip would be educational, I know it has also been difficult for you. That is what pains me."

Ben's mouth tightened. "No. It is good we've come."

Susannah could wait no longer. "What happened?"

"I learned what not to say to a Chippewa." Amusement broadened Ben's mouth into a grin—until he grimaced and touched his bleeding lip. "Good night, Father."

Much relieved, Susannah took a step toward her room.

"Wait. Both of you." Father grasped at her hand. "The revelation that one day you will both leave me has left me at a loss. Yet I would never stop you from what God has in store. I'm proud of you both."

Susannah placed a gentle kiss on Father's cheek and turned to Ben. "And you will be hard-pressed to rid yourself of your older sister, no matter the path you choose."

Ben nodded.

"I already wish to return to Johnstown," Father admitted. "I have not Sir William's energy. He would have us talk with every chief that comes to call, and this may go on for weeks." He stepped back, glancing toward the open window. "But, we must enjoy what we can of it." His tired eyes were warm with affection. "Get to bed, son."

"Yes sir."

She wished them both a good evening and closed her door.

They had not traveled for days only to turn around and leave, but she longed for the quiet of her home as much as she'd once longed for this chance to see the frontier.

But she'd never imagined it would be like this. So many warriors.

And one particular soldier.

How could she feel anything toward a man she hardly knew? Three days was nothing, but it was three days that had changed her. In her naiveté, she simply decided she would never fall in love. Any man she'd found attractive had only been that—an agreeable form, and handsome face. Never had her heart been so engaged. Perhaps these feelings had given her much-needed insight into why people did the things they did. Even Mother and Father.

She must learn to trust God for her heart, and her life. Men and women fell in love, they married, they had children. Love had to be worth the risk. If childbearing was the deadly occupation she'd thought, it hadn't slowed the population.

She'd kept fear as a constant, silent companion. Now Arch offered new friendship—he'd made her laugh and feel free to feel courageous in all things. Except one.

A soft tapping at the door proved to be Kahente, come to help her undress.

The woman hummed softly as she worked at the pins supporting the weight of hair off Susannah's back. "Your father is a good man?"

"Yes, of course." What an odd question.

Kahente brushed out the long hair with strong fingers. "Then why does he have no wife?"

Susannah looked over her shoulder, hiding her amusement at the softness in the woman's eyes. "Do you know of such a woman?"

Chapter 7

The Kimballs broke their fast with the commander and his wife.

Sir William had reluctantly agreed to Father's request to return home before him, but it could be weeks yet before they'd leave. The idea of schools among the tribes was a worthwhile cause, but to be paraded each night before the visiting elders of one or another tribe grew tiresome. Sir William intended to broker a peace treaty with each attending tribe, no matter how long it took.

"I agree you can't be expected to stay as long as the baronet," Mrs. Browning continued. "But I'm dreading the day you leave. Why, the men will mope about for days." She reached out and covered Susannah's hand. "You must promise to write. I long to hear of your success with teaching and of the day you marry." She let go, turning to her husband, "Darling, tell me now you'll let me travel to her wedding."

Susannah leaned back in her chair. "I—" But it was pointless to argue. No one believed her. She didn't believe it herself anymore. If she was to truly trust God for her future, she couldn't very well lay down the rules He was to follow.

It was easier to agree. "I will miss your company as well, ma'am, and look forward to seeing you again one day."

"I fear my wife has had more than enough of this frontier life." The colonel spoke to his guests, yet his eyes remained on his lovely wife. "I hope to return her to England in the next year, and then join her soon thereafter."

The lieutenant colonel might be a tough commander, but it seemed he had no hope of overruling his wife. Mrs. Browning had her husband still besotted after years together and now took his hand. "I never meant to marry a military man, and he knew it."

But that was different. The woman probably had no goal but marriage.

I have been called to teach.

Or, that was her excuse.

One that fit with her determination to never marry.

Oh Lord. I've let my fears guide me, rather than trusting You.

The meal ended and, though she tried to hide her impatience to speak to Arch, Father engaged him the moment they exited the dining room.

"Lieutenant. I've spoken to Sir William, and he agrees your devoted service must be rewarded with an end. We are well settled in now, and there is little danger here for any of us. I appreciate your help with Benjamin last night, but I believe he's learned something from it."

The lieutenant nodded. "I stepped in too late."

"No," Father disagreed. "He would not have appreciated it, and he needed those consequences."

"Very well, sir. But please call on me if you need me, and I insist that Miss Kimball does not leave the fort without me, or one of the guards."

Other than a quick glance her way, Arch gave little reaction to the news. She fought the urge to tug at his sleeve and pull him out of his maddening military aloofness.

Friends, that was all.

Just as she'd wanted.

Yet her meager morning meal sat like a stone in her stomach. Very well. "And I will thank you now, Lieutenant, for I know how you've taken such care to honor your orders." She offered him a smile she didn't feel. "It must be a relief for you to return to your regular duties."

"I'm not so sure, Miss Kimball." He bowed his head then made a sharp military exit from the room.

They both knew they had no future together.

She would keep Arch in her heart—a love without the risks and heartache. She couldn't stop her feelings for him, much as she'd tried.

She'd decided after Mother's death that she must never leave Father alone. To be the best daughter. To make up for him not having a wife and son.

What did God want for her? Not every woman married; not every wife bore children. But was this desire to teach hers, or the Lord's?

Despite every argument chasing around against it in her head, she wanted more time with Arch.

The following day, Arch was summoned to escort the Kimball family upon their visit to a camp of elders from Kanadasegey, a village by one of the long lakes. Johnson asserted that, despite being Seneca, they remained loyal to the British.

The baronet had managed to convince the village chief to take the Kimball family with them upon their return to Kanadasegey, then provide safe escort on to Johnstown. Arch had asked to accompany them, but Lt. Col. Browning, no doubt suspecting the motive, said he was needed at the fort.

It was better for all involved to let Susannah go.

Preferably before Captain Porter's irrational hatred for the Indians ignited trouble.

When it was time to leave the fort, Arch felt all eyes on them as they walked through the Indian camps, but Mr. Kimball looked no more worried than if he were visiting neighbors for a Sunday dinner. Lieutenant Colonel Browning had explained that Ben had been born Seneca, but no one knew from which village his mother had traveled. Would these people today, with their devotion to family, have heard of this and want him back?

He snorted. When had he'd begun to see these people through Mr. Kimball's eyes? People with flaws and weaknesses and strengths, just like the English. Children misbehaved. Grandmothers scolded and forgave. Around him people chatted, laughed. Young men and women from different villages eyed one another.

Then there was the young Mohawk boy named Karawase determined to marry a lovely English woman whose hair shimmered like sunshine on the lake.

The songbird.

Susannah.

Arch watched as Mr. Kimball, assisted by one of Johnson's Mohawks, spoke with the elders. One of the clan mothers placed a small amulet around Benjamin's neck. Many around the campfire studied Susannah—her smiles and laughter were enough to keep anyone intrigued.

Her beauty, so enhanced by that tender heart, made him as vulnerable and foolish around her as was young Karawase.

He had nothing to offer a wife. A motherless son in England they'd never see, a life in a fort at best, or alone while he remained with the regiment. Avoiding marriage was easy in a world almost void of single women. Why, he couldn't ask Susannah Kimball to marry him and then send her alone to England. Even if this shaky peace with the French and the Ottawa warrior Pontiac continued, would Johnson's treaties stand?

Many colonists wanted the British army's protection, but not the British king's rules and taxes. Talk of liberty had begun.

So much of the future remained uncertain. After all, his own regiment was recently in Martinique and could be five hundred miles away next month. He desired to be more than a father in name to Merritt, but could he again be a husband? And if he left the army, what could he do? His father's position with the House of Commons had gone to his older brother, and Arch had long ago quit the idea of managing the family estate.

But the idea of never seeing Susannah Kimball again made him forget every practical reason against loving her.

Arch watched Benjamin approach. After witnessing the boy's thrashing last night, he expected embarrassment on Ben's part.

"Your anger at my people," Ben said evenly. "Are you still holding it as tightly?"

Such thoughtful questions proved Arch had falsely judged him at their first meeting. "Not as tightly as I was, but I don't know that I've forgiven those who—"

Ben touched the small leather pouch hanging around his neck. "The clan mother said this amulet is for wisdom. She was wise enough to know I need it."

Arch chuckled. "Who doesn't? Wisdom allows us to think before we act. A difficult skill indeed for a boy your age. You are not losing your faith in Kimball's God, are you?"

"No—"

"Do you not pray to Him for such things? Wisdom, patience?"

"Susannah said you do not believe."

The air escaped his lungs so fast he slumped. Of course she would think that. "She is mistaken. My reluctance comes not from doubting God, but from failing to understand His ways."

"Like the massacre?"

Arch nodded.

Mr. Kimball waved farewell to the camp and joined them, placing an arm around Ben's shoulder.

With every breath, Arch envied the fatherly gesture.

How tall was Merritt? Would the boy even recognize him—if he survived these months along the frontier? Or would they stay strangers?

The day's clouds teased the first drops of rain.

Mr. Kimball turned a kind but haggard face to Arch. "Thank you, Lieutenant Waters. I appreciate your patience."

It was then that Susannah locked arms with her father. Arch's feelings for her might make no sense, but he couldn't ignore them. Nor could he miss the vulnerability in her that tore at all the reasons why love was not to their advantage.

Only when they'd returned and he considered the sentries, did Arch realize that when he should have been most alert for Susannah's safety, he'd been thinking of how much he would miss her.

She leaned close. "Thank you."

"For what? Not growling at the Seneca chief?"

She batted his arm. "For your concern. For speaking with Ben. He looks up to you." Her hand fell away. "You must be a good father."

He looked away to avoid the admiration in her eyes. She truly was naive. "You may be well schooled, Miss Kimball, but if that's your opinion, you have a lot to learn about life."

The devastation on her face forced all air from his lungs, but he rolled on, over the delicate seedlings of their friendship—of their love—before they could grow too deep. "It is good your leave-taking is not far off and you will return home with your dreams intact."

Her eyes widened before she dropped her gaze and moved away. One step faltered before she took her brother's hand. With so tender a heart, she would need God's protection at home as much as she did here. Arch's heart had long ago grown hard, brittle, and now its shattering in his chest made it hard to breathe.

Upon reentry through Fort Niagara's gate, Arch would have breathed a sigh of relief, but for the ghostly pale of Susannah's face.

The Kimballs returned to their rooms at the top of the castle, with little to say. The schoolmaster must have heard Arch's comments; Susannah surely had understood his message. *Go away, you're too foolish.*

Too trusting.

Arch's gut ached with emptiness.

His sharp words were meant to protect her. To make her wary of the selfishness of men and the darkness he often felt inside.

Maybe he'd said them to protect himself. He felt vile with selfishness, and selfishness was something she'd never understand. He'd lashed out at her undeserved praise.

Susannah Kimball was devoted to seeing the good and the possible in each human being, while he judged all with the assumption they were no better than he inside.

The hate he'd nurtured for the treacherous Chenussio Seneca rivaled what they'd done in battle. He and Captain Porter had made names for themselves, though Arch had taken no pleasure in ending men's lives. He'd come out a leader despite his inexperience, and counted killing as part of his job. The army meant survival of a way of life for those he'd signed on to protect.

His hatred toward the Seneca ambush had made him long for an equal or more brutal revenge.

Yet she did not believe that even they lived only to kill.

Were they not soldiers in their own way? Yet wouldn't they too prefer peaceful villages where they could love their women, raise their children, and die as old men in their beds?

He'd begun to believe it. The old men wanted the wars to end, and today he felt like an old man.

At twilight, Arch climbed the steep, narrow stairs and paused at the end of the center hallway when the old woman, Kahente, exited Susannah's room.

She glared at him as she passed. Well deserved.

He sat on the top step before making a decision, then paced the hallway, stopping only when he heard muttering from her room. It was best she was angry at him, but not like this.

He knocked. "Miss Kimball."

The wait seemed endless.

"Yes." The word was as fragile as a butterfly floating on the other side of the door.

"May we speak?" Suddenly there wasn't enough air in the hall to ease the tightness in his chest.

"Give me a moment."

He waited at the end of the corridor, then turned at the sound of her light steps. She moved like a soft breeze, and the glow of a single sconce set a halo around her hair.

He gestured down the steps. "The air in here. . . I know it's still raining but—"
But I must apologize.

She nodded, and showed she'd come prepared with her cloak, her eyes wide, red-rimmed and expectant.

Not angry.

In a military post manned with multiple companies from multiple regiments, assorted hangers-on essential to the everyday operation of feeding, clothing, and arming a British regiment, plus Bradstreet's new arrivals from Fort Oswego, where could he take her to tell her what he must?

The rain riding the gentle winds brought a quiet over the fort and its encampments.

"Come with me. I won't. . ." The words fell away. When he offered his arm, the undisguised trust in her touch nearly undid him. If he looked into her face now, he'd have to take her in his arms and hold her until they both forgot the pain his words had caused her.

They hurried like young lovers to the lake side of the northern blockhouse, out of wind and rain. He moved closer. "I owe you an apology."

"I won't argue with you."

How ready he'd been for just that. Arch had faced armed enemies with more courage. He tugged on his neckcloth and continued, encouraged by the warmth on her face. "I am so sorry, Susannah, but I have much to improve as a father, much as I've been a poor friend to you. But these few moments have meant so much." To finish, he must do better than this. "I still believe it is best you leave. And I can't pretend that just waiting about day and night hasn't been tiring."

She looked up with forgiving eyes.

With such kindness, he found it difficult to swallow. "I was quite wrong to advise you on your life and to have said it in such a manner. I may not understand your generosity of spirit, but I admire it."

Together they scanned the horizon. The lake had disappeared into a gray haze.

She turned back to him. "I know you find us foolish with our hopes for peace. I don't blame you for wanting to return to duties other than nursemaid."

He shook his head to disagree, but she'd told the truth.

"You are right to think me innocent, Arch, and I admit there is much to learn, but I still intend to teach. I'm praying for guidance."

"My faith—" He knew by the way she searched his eyes, she wanted to hear that his trust in God matched hers. But he couldn't lie. "My frustration here was not for those orders. I would gladly guard you from harm for the rest of your life."

She stepped away, cupping her face, then covering her ears.

He ran his hands over his head. He was only making it worse. "While I have little to offer you, nor could I ever hope to be the man you deserve, I must tell you I would change it all if I could."

"Stop, please."

If he tore away their friendship and its safety, his heart would have nothing more to hide behind. Nor would hers.

He stepped closer, speaking into the white cap atop her head. "My orders were to protect you, not cause you pain. If I wasn't a soldier. . ." He took her by the shoulders. "I wish you would look at me. Just promise me you won't marry into the Iroquois."

Susannah pulled away. "As I don't intend to marry, you need not worry."

"You may change your mind. What of that Seneca who would so willingly take you to wife?"

That did the job. She spun around, a whirl of scarlet cape, pink cheeks, and pinker lips that he would never have the chance to taste.

"I have been speaking to him of my faith and of the importance of education. I've almost convinced him to send his daughter to me for schooling."

"That is all?"

"Of course. My heart is full for the Iroquois people, but I am not so noble as to give up my warm house in the winter. I can hardly cook or sew."

"Really?"

"Yes. I would not make any man a good wife." Susannah's face warmed with amusement.

"I think you want me to disagree."

"Oh Arch. Really now."

"I will disagree. Because you will marry. Just take your time in choosing a husband, Songbird, so I can believe you've found the worthy man."

All the color left her face.

He reached for her.

She moved farther away.

"I don't care for the man I've become, Susannah. You, your friendship, made me long for different things and for that, I'm grateful."

"I need to go back now." She turned from him, her back stiffening. "I appreciate your candor. I will pray the Lord helps you heal from that terrible day."

What had he wanted? Some profession of love? A proclamation that love mattered more than anything else? "I believe it will happen as I learn to forgive." He smiled. False, but it would have to do. "I shouldn't keep you out in this weather."

She took hold of his arm as the rain picked up, and he returned her as far as her corridor but went no farther. How he wanted to take her in his arms and take away the need for any words.

Instead, he took her hand, brushing her knuckles against the pewter-buttoned facing of his coat. Just above his heart. "It has been my good fortune to have had these days with you, and I will remember them long after you've left."

He released her, hoping an honest, dignified exit made up for the last time he'd walked away. But there was little point in pretending that his heart was not breaking with every step.

Chapter 8

Susannah closed the latch behind her and made for the edge of her bed, careless of her sodden cloak.

Arch would be out in the rain now, striding away, showing nothing on his face of what had just happened. And something had happened. His touch still lingered on her fingertips. She brought them to her heated cheek. Every beat of her heart said he cared for her. Maybe not love, at least not so soon, but why had he so eloquently sent her off with encouragement to marry?

Being a soldier hadn't stopped Lt. Col Browning. Why, most officers had wives at home.

This constant yearning to be near Arch would pass. After all, what did they share? But if she left without asking him to forgive his enemies, to let faith heal his heart, then her regret would forever darken the memories of his sweet words.

Susannah quietly opened the door, waiting for her eyes to adjust to the minimal light from the stairwell, and hoping her footsteps would not wake and worry her menfolk.

But Father's door squealed open. "Is Benjamin with you?"

"Why no. He's not in bed?"

Father leaned heavily against the frame. "I'm feeling poorly, daughter. Would you ask the lieutenant to find your brother? He's probably watching the ships' lights out on the lake. I do hope he hasn't gone down to the docks."

She nodded, but wouldn't let him see her worry. "Go back to bed. He'll be fine."

"Why is your cloak wet?"

"You will have to guess while you take yourself back to bed. Don't worry."

But Arch was not waiting at his post near the bottom of the steps. For the first time in days, he wasn't there.

Had he gone on to his barracks? Who did she dare ask?

The rain had stopped. In fact, streaming clouds opened up wide bands of dark starlit sky to the west. Without a moon, only firelight lit the way. No wonder Benjamin had escaped into this fresh, damp air.

He'd be safe, wouldn't he? What if he'd seen her with Arch? For that matter, how many others had?

Joyous fiddle music came from the Highlanders' camp. Along with the reel, men's laughter filled the air.

Without the excuse of searching for her brother, she had no idea what she'd say to Arch, when moments ago, she'd been unable to speak.

Whatever their differences, couldn't they be overcome?

She'd first try the area behind the munitions building where a good view of the docks might have drawn her brother.

A mistake. She'd gone too far when she saw a red-coated officer in a woman's arms. A woman who had no fear of men in dark corners.

Not Arch, but her face heated at what she saw.

She spun to flee and bumped into a man whose face remained hidden under his hat. His white shirt gaped open, adding to a disheveled appearance.

Fear froze her ability to think. She drew her cloak closer and gave him a wide berth.

His hand clamped down on her arm at the last.

"Get away!" she demanded, yanking free.

He recaptured her, trapping her protests with a foul hand, then shoved her against the stockade wall. The impact shocked the breath out of her.

"Come on, love. Just a kiss."

She batted at his head, pulling at his hair until the twisting of her other wrist made her fear it would snap.

In a blur of motion, she was freed. A guttural grunt meant he'd taken a blow to the gut.

She fought to get clear of the fray; her wobbly legs didn't help.

Her attacker lay in the mud, dazed, with no visible wound.

Standing above him, a powerful Indian with a shock of thick hair and feathers atop his head. Even in the near dark she could see he wore bands of white shells around his upper arms, and a tunic of red.

He'd finished with the ruffian and studied her.

She couldn't speak.

An eruption of shouts and movement sent her swinging at the first man to touch her.

"Susannah!" Arch's voice was raw. So was the flash of knife blade as he rushed headlong toward her gallant defender.

"Stop. It wasn't him!"

Arch Waters didn't.

"Stop!" She lunged for his arm, nearly taking an elbow to her face, then spun around to face those gathered. "Make him stop," she pleaded as the two circled each other like mad dogs. "That man saved me."

A second, then a third redcoat grabbed Arch.

Chaos swirled around her. She had to get away before the shaking in her legs made it impossible to stand. "Stop it, all of you!"

"Miss Kimball, is it not?" asked a redcoat. "Are you injured?"

She winced in answer. "That man," she said, pointing, "on the ground. He tried. . ."

New torchlight showed the face of a young brave rushing toward her.

Then Arch grabbed her shoulders, his chest heaving. "Susannah."

"Sister!"

She turned to the young, bare-chested Iroquois facing her. "Ben?" She reached for him, but stopped at what she saw. Blood seeped from a deep scratch across his chest and upper arm.

"Stop right there!" A British officer leveled his pistol at the chest of the Indian who'd saved her.

Arch lunged, grabbing the man's arm. "Don't."

The wild-eyed officer wouldn't quit. The pistol waved about as Arch managed only to steer him away.

She buried her face in her brother's shoulder.

"It's over, Porter," she heard Arch say, and dared to look. But it wasn't over. They wrestled for control of the gun until the officer's body slackened. Arch grabbed the firearm and pointed at the man on the ground. "There is the man in need of the lock-up, Captain."

Ben held Susannah tight as they watched soldiers drag her attacker away.

The red-shirted Indian—one she'd never met—paused at her side.

"Thank you."

He nodded and disappeared as quietly as he'd arrived.

Ben gave her up as Arch reached out to pull her close.

Susannah clutched her aching wrist. "If he hadn't—"

"I know."

Her legs were failing her. "I must sit down."

Arch swept her up, carrying her through the gathered crowd.

She was safe.

He set her down inside the castle's entry, then squatted before her. "Are you injured?"

"It's my wrist."

Arch's eyes remained sharp with frustrated anger. "Why were you outside? Did he pull you into that dark corner?"

"No, I was looking for you." Her body felt rigid as she fought to stop the shaking in her legs. "And for Ben."

He shifted his weight, looking her over again, and took one long, deep breath.

"What will happen to him?"

"I don't know, but I'm taking you to the surgery."

She wiped at her mouth, wondering why she tasted blood on her lip. *Blood.* Fear rushed over her again. "Where's Ben?"

"Right here, sister."

She reached for him, wanting to chastise him for wearing no coat. "Why are you bleeding?"

"It is nothing."

"Tell me!"

"Stickball is not a game for women."

She leaned back against the rough stone wall, weak with relief, wanting to laugh. "Go tell Father where you were and that I am with Arch." She glanced at Arch. "I mean Lt. Waters. Tell him I am quite safe."

Arch's attention never wavered. "I told you not to leave your room without me."

"Did I not just say why?" She softened at the ragged worry on his face. "I tried to catch you."

He rose and sat next to her, the heat of his body drawing her toward him. "You've caught me, all right." He pushed loose hair back from her brow. "Are you sure that's what you want?"

She leaned her head into his hand as it trailed down her cheek. "I don't know what I want." Embarrassed, she closed her eyes and placed her hand over his. And winced. "Other than for you to forgive them."

"I will. I'm trying. God help me, I'm trying." He made to pick her up. "Off we go then."

"No. Allow me to walk."

"Are you sure? I rather enjoyed the alternative."

She took his arm and stood, testing first one step and then another until she felt steady enough to continue.

She'd never felt better.

"Susannah."

His words were soft gifts in her ear as he leaned close. "Must I ask your father permission to court you before you allow me a stolen kiss?"

"If you are truly a gentleman." She heard him chuckle. "Or you will at least wait until we are quite alone."

His head tipped back with freed laughter. "When will that be? I will not have leave until the fall, and if I come courting to your village, I fear we will never be left alone." His eyes took in the crowd. "Much like this. And there will be that rascal Karawase."

She studied him. "You said you had nothing to offer me. And I've told you I wouldn't marry." Grinning, she walked on. "Only, I believe I shall always wonder what might have been."

She nodded to the two officers staring at her as they passed. She touched the back of her head to find she'd lost her cap. Her hair? A fright. Torches affixed to each side of the doorway allowed her to see that her clothes looked like she'd been thrown from a horse.

The surgery was unoccupied.

Arch looked back out the door. "The surgeon can't be far."

She reached up to touch his jaw, then closed her eyes.

Arch's lips brushed her forehead, her cheek. "Susannah. All my doubts have disappeared. I don't know why I. . .oh never mind." His lips touched hers, ever so gently.

A man cleared his throat.

She straightened like a startled doe.

"I wanted to make sure you were both safe," laughed Lt. Col. Browning. "I can see I'm too late." His face sobered when the surgeon appeared behind him. "I will let your father know what happened, miss." Then to Arch, "I need a private word, Waters, when Miss Kimball is back in her room."

Arch knocked and entered Browning's study, unsure of what to expect.

"I have deemed Captain Porter unsuitable for duty. I'm afraid he's never recovered from what he witnessed at Devil's Hole. He will be returning to New York, and you will accompany him. You may take two privates of your choosing. I hate to lose you now, but I know of no one else whom he trusts."

"I would argue he trusts me less than anyone."

"Then you are wrong. He asked for you. Porter will take leave immediately. He requested you take his place as captain. He may one day return to service but that, thank God, will not be my decision."

"When will this happen?"

"You will leave at dawn tomorrow. The less said in front of the men, the better. I will advise General Gates by courier."

"Tomorrow?"

"I can't have him here any longer." Browning came around his desk. "You could have seen Porter disgraced, but you have quietly led the men, despite his irregularities."

"I don't deserve your praise, sir. I had all I could do not to expose him."

"I should have seen to it at the first." Browning's shoulders sagged. "Go speak to the men you will take with you, and prepare to leave at dawn."

"Aye sir."

"I know what this will cost you. I will speak to the Kimballs and give them your regrets. If God wills it, you will see her again. My wife reminds me that it was

I who ordered you to protect her. Perhaps she might be impressed upon to marry a captain."

"Then I believe I have a most important letter to write." He returned Browning's smile. "Before I go, will you pray with me?"

Chapter 9

Johnstown, New York
October 1764

Susannah stacked the three Bibles on her desk and glanced up at the knock. "Come in."

Lieutenant Archibald Waters filled her schoolroom's doorway. She clutched the table at her side. Mrs. Browning had written to warn her, but seeing him now...after so long...

He removed his hat. "I didn't mean to frighten you."

"No, I'm sure you didn't. But I've had to brave the world without you at my side for eight weeks. You really must give a lass warning when you're going to kiss her and disappear with nothing more than a quickly scratched note."

"Would you like me to leave?"

She came to him and reached for his hand. "What do you think?"

"That you believed me when I said I would find you. And that you will be willing to accept my healed heart." Arch brought her hand to his mouth and kissed her fingertips. "And that if you considered that moment in the surgery a proper kiss, I have some educating to do."

She felt her face redden.

"So, should I talk to your father?"

She nodded, her heart breaking with joy and sadness. "He has been asking about you."

"He's disappointed I left as I did."

"No. I don't think that's it." She led Arch out of the school and across the commons, reluctant to release his hand. His grip tightened. Before entering her house, she turned. "Oh Arch. Prepare yourself. He is not well."

"I can see you're worried. Where is your brother?"

"Sir William has sent him on to Connecticut. Father fears Ben will come home if he learns how poorly he is."

"Connecticut?"

"The baronet has arranged for a tutor who will in time take him to London. My brother will return to be a solicitor for the Haudenosaunee and, Father hopes, a leader as well." Susannah touched a finely beaded necklace at her throat. "Ben has found the family he lost so long ago."

"I see." Arch frowned. "It must be difficult for you."

"No, he is still my brother. He dares not forget it."

She opened the door, offering Arch a smile against his growing concern. "Father? I've brought a visitor. May we enter?"

"Come in." Father pushed himself up in the bed, his eyes brightening upon seeing their guest. "Lieutenant. You've made it."

"I'm sorry it has been so long, sir."

"We understand you are not at liberty to come and go." He eyed Susannah. "What are you waiting for, daughter? Go prepare our tea."

"Now?" She met her father's eyes and was encouraged to see the old sparkle returned. Perhaps she should have encouraged him long ago to take a wife. The woman at the fort, Kahente, would have been willing enough. "Very well."

The lukewarm water in the kettle needed time to boil.

She paced.

What were they discussing? She could hear the rumble of the lieutenant's half of the conversation, but couldn't catch the words without listening at the door.

She was sorely tempted.

Arch was here. As he'd promised.

Her hands shook, but when the tray was ready, she carried it in to the table next to Father's bed. "What did I miss?"

"Musings of humble men," teased Arch. "Perhaps we can discuss it later. I'm curious to see the blockhouse Sir William had built next to his mansion."

"You do seem to be fond of them. Is that why you've come?" She handed Arch a cup of tea.

He took it, grinning, and set it right back down. "I came to see you, Susannah."

Father coughed. "This is foolishness. Take her outside and be done with it."

"Father, are you sure?"

"Must you always challenge me?"

Arch took her hand. Right in front of him. But Father was still grinning when they stepped outside.

"Lead the way, Miss Kimball."

With Johnson due to arrive later this month, most of the village was busy with harvest, but the few that remained around the commons stood in small groups, watching. She glanced up the hill to the blockhouse. Built for protection, there seemed to be little need for it these days. But it would do.

They climbed the steep, narrow stairs that reminded her of their first evening at Fort Niagara and the days when he'd been there each time she'd looked for him.

And then there was that interrupted kiss.

He joined her at one of the blockhouse's open portals. "Over there is the great river." She glanced at him, but he wasn't looking where she pointed.

"Your father, well, I'm the—it was mostly my idea." He laughed, squared his shoulders, and started again. "I can't promise anything but my devotion. Your father is not well, and it would please him to see you marry. Well, marry *me*, that is."

"He is always after me to marry."

"You still resist the idea?"

"And I should marry you because of his failing health?"

"You should marry me because I love you, and I will do anything to make you happy. Come with me to England. I will see that you speak to anyone and everyone about the benefits of schooling frontier children. Regardless of their skin color and parentage. You can do more for the Iroquois there, than you can here."

"This is. . . Wait." She took a deep breath. "Tell me again why I should marry you? As it can't be for new schoolhouses, nor only for my father's peace of mind."

"Because I love you. You've made me over. That won't change if you won't have me, but please consider it." He dropped to one knee. "Susannah Kimball. Will you be my bride and allow me to watch over you the rest of our lives?"

"And Merritt?"

His gaze dropped, uncertainty on his face. "And a mother to Merritt. Please don't tell me you wouldn't be the best possible choice in that regard. It is a lot I ask."

She laughed. "And if there were more children?"

He glanced up at her, wide-eyed, hopeful. "Are you sure?"

"I longed to prove to everyone I had no fear of the frontier, but I almost allowed another private fear to keep me from you."

"Then I would love all my children equally, unless one daughter was particularly like her mother."

She stepped closer and touched his hair, then pulled him to her, holding his head against the beating of her heart. "And it would help if I returned your feelings?"

His eyes opened wide. "Well, yes, of course. Very much so."

"Then, yes."

"You'll marry me? You would not prefer a great Seneca warrior?"

"No, Lieutenant."

"It's captain now. For now."

"For now? Whatever do you mean?"

He stood and took her hands. "I mean that when I resign at the next opportunity, I'll be a poor second son again and I will take us all home to England until the colonies return to peace. There, I'll be running my father's concerns and no longer taking orders from anyone."

She laughed out loud, bursting with joy. "That's what you think, Captain Waters!"

Debra E. Marvin tries not to run too far from real life, but the imagination born out of being an only child has a powerful draw. Besides, the voices in her head tend to agree with all the sensible things she says. She is a member of ACFW, Sisters in Crime, and serves on the board of Bridges Ministry in Seneca Falls, NY. Besides Barbour Publishing, she is also published with WhiteFire Publishing, Forget Me Not Romances, and Journey Fiction, and has been a judge for the Grace Awards for many years. She blogs at Inkwell Inspirations and Colonial Quills. Debra works as a program assistant at Cornell University, and enjoys her family and grandchildren. You can find her obsessively buying fabric, watching British programming, and traveling with her childhood friends. See more of Debra at http://debraemarvin.com/.

A Worthy Groom

by Angela K. Couch

Dedication

To my father-in-law, a wonderful grandfather to my children.
To my husband, one of the kindest men I know.

Chapter 1

The first shovelful of dirt struck Samuel's crude hickory box, but Lorinda Cowden didn't flinch. Each scoop of the shovel, each dull thud of the earth returning to its hole, unfurled her spirit from its long confinement. But with the dirt over her husband's grave barely turned, it was a sin to celebrate her freedom. Not while her mother-in-law gripped her hand and wept the loss of a son. Lorinda lowered her lids over dry eyes and placed the tips of her fingers over her mouth. Her stomach churned. She had gone without breakfast this morning and felt that loss more than Samuel's.

Another sin.

But could the Lord fault her for her loathing of men?

"Oh my poor girl." Prudence Cowden looked to Lorinda and stroked her hand.

Fighting the need to pull free of the sobbing woman, Lorinda raised her gaze to the sun, already escaped from the haze of the mountain ridges and working its way higher above them, promising warmth. The morning had been spent, and there was work to do. She'd excuse herself to return to the cabin she had helped Samuel build. She planned to live out the rest of her days scratching a living from their land. Alone.

Before she could open her mouth, Dougal Cowden, her father-in-law, stepped over to them. His oldest son, Abner, was in his wake. Dougal shouldered the spade with which he'd buried his youngest and aimed a glare at his wife's tears, though she hurried to brush them aside.

"We shall have to decide what to do with the extra fields. Heaven knows I have enough work on my own land, as do the boys."

"Do not concern yourself." Lorinda sucked in a breath to fortify her resolve as she faced the elder version of her husband. "I can manage them well enough on my own." She still did not succeed in meeting his gaze.

He answered with a low grunt. "I don't know about that."

"I worked as hard as Samuel to build our farm. Have I no right to it?" She had married Samuel two years earlier and followed him through the Blue Ridge Mountains to this river valley where her sweat had watered the ground almost as much as the rains.

"Go on and let her fend for herself if it please her," Abner huffed. He carried more of his mother's physical traits, lighter hair and greener eyes, but his temperament was all Cowden.

"Cowden men are full of gunpowder but have little fuse." That's what her mother-in-law had told her the first time the bruises had been visible. *"You must strive harder to not upset him."*

Lorinda had strived. But as with her father, Samuel's flares of anger seemed more dependent upon his mood than her best efforts to keep him satisfied with his meals, his house. . .with her. She hugged her ribs, aching from blows given moments before he'd stormed out of the cabin to meet his end, his horse falling on him.

Now she would be free.

Thank Thee, Lord.

Even her prayer was a sin.

Her brother-in-law was still speaking. "Let her have my land though. Samuel's should stay in the family."

She clamped her jaw and forced herself to look at him. She had been the one to find the fertile strip of earth fed by a stream running with the clearest water she'd ever seen, and unnoticed when the men had first chosen their homesteads. Ever since, Abner's jealousy of his brother's land had grown with each season. "I have lost my husband, and now you wish to force me from my home—all that remains of him?"

Abner Cowden continued speaking to his father as though Lorinda wasn't present—as he always did. As Samuel had done. "She can keep the smaller cabin as I still need mine for my family, but the land is too good to leave idle. I could—"

"You cannot have my land!" Lorinda's voice rose with a boldness she'd not felt before. Then it broke with a sob, and hot moisture spilled down her face. She swiped the tears away. She had no use for them. Shortly after her marriage, she'd given up crying along with any dreams she'd had of being cherished and loved by her husband. She needed to be strong this time and not let men decide her fate. . .but another sob choked her.

"Now is no time to be discussing our plans for Samuel's land," Dougal reproved, "with his widow standing over his grave." He patted her arm with the warmest gesture she'd ever received from the man. "Go on up to the cabin. And don't worry yourself. We'll see that you are looked after."

Lorinda drew back a step. The last thing she wanted was to be "looked after" by another Cowden man. "I ask only to be left alone."

Abner again overrode her. "A couple of families are returning to North Carolina. We should send her home."

"No!" There was no way to keep the word from exploding from her throat. When Lorinda had first married Samuel, it had been to escape her father's verbal lashes, applied at the slightest fracture of his law. She hadn't imagined being married to a man could be much worse, but she'd paid the price of her ignorance. Still, she had worked as hard as Samuel, and this was her farm as much as it had been his. "I will not leave."

Her vision again swimming, Lorinda gathered her dark skirts and rushed through the glen to the cabin. *Her* cabin. She closed the door and barred it. Hopefully everyone would return to their own homes and leave her be.

Another wave of nausea swooshed within her, and she pressed a hand to her stomach. She frowned. Despite the busyness of spring, her stays no longer fastened as tightly without discomfort. She hadn't paid it much mind, but the rocking of her insides gave her pause. And what of the tears? Fresh ones escaped at the mere thought of what they might mean.

"Oh Lord, please no." Surely He wouldn't do this to her after allowing a brief taste of liberation. What was the likelihood of Samuel's father allowing her to continue alone on the land once his grandchild arrived? She refused to be forced into another marriage.

Salisbury, North Carolina, May 1771

Sun warm on his head, Marcus Cowden tapped the hammer against the edges of the iron splinter until they smoothed and sharpened. Satisfied, he tossed it into the growing pile of headless nails and set to work on the next one. Mundane work, but he had plenty else to occupy his thoughts.

Hinges creaked, followed by the thud of his father's boots from inside the shop. He steeled himself and continued tapping out nails.

"You cannot sit on the fence forever, lad." Though hushed, Father's voice had not lost its raspy edge. He laid a musket across Marcus's outside worktable. "You may not agree with the tactics of the Regulators, but this is a war, and you won't be able to hide from that for much longer."

"I'm not hiding." The force of Marcus's hammer flattened the nail, and he turned it over to repair the damage done. He reined in his temper and measured his strength.

Father's large hands jerked him up and shook him. "The governor's general, Waddell, and his two hundred men who stopped here yesterday are on their way to Alamance. And they have been reinforced." His face reddened and his nostrils flared. "A thousand men, Marcus!"

Marcus turned his face from the assault of stale breath laced with the fetor of ale, his grip tightening on his hammer. He caught himself and quickly released the tool to the ground. "I'll not go."

He tensed his jaw against the blow he knew would come and hardly flinched when it did. He had surpassed his father in both height and strength by the time he had reached twenty-two, and the last four years had only added in his favor. But he'd not fight back. He couldn't risk losing control of himself. Again.

"I have enough work to do here."

Father cursed as he took up the musket and stalked to where his horse waited. "I'm ashamed to call you my son." He threw the clipped words over his shoulder before mounting. "You're no Cowden."

Marcus clenched his hands at his sides as his father spurred the horse to a gallop. If only he wasn't a Cowden and could put aside the rage heating his blood. He stooped and picked up the hammer before tossing it on the bench. Walking cooled his temper the quickest. Walking, and children. He strode toward his sister's home.

The simple cabin sat on the edge of the village, and the land surrounding stretched into barnyard and fields beyond. It seemed the ideal location and life to him. The sound of airy giggling swept away some of his frustration, and he slowed his pace. Near the barn, Sarah knelt in a small pen holding balls of yellow fluff, her two young'uns gathered around.

"What do we have here?" Marcus asked.

A chorus of squeals momentarily deafened him and sent the tiny chicks scurrying. The children assaulted him, and he swept his four-year-old niece over his shoulder and two-year-old nephew under his arm. Sarah's gaze snagged on his face and her smile faded away. She stood and stepped out of the enclosure.

"What set Pa off this time?"

"The Regulators. Guess there's a fight brewing. He rode off to join them."

"I heard. And should have guessed as much." She frowned, resting a hand over the swelling of her abdomen, proof that their family would soon be joined by another. At least she had married well—a kind man who made her happy. "Do you think there will be a battle?"

Marcus nodded. The tensions had been building to that over the past couple of years. "I don't reckon it can be avoided now."

"But you disagree with the Regulators."

"No." He hated the unfair taxation and corrupt, heavy-handed sheriffs as much as his father did. "But there must be another way. Besides vandalism and violence."

She turned and beckoned him to the house. "Let me put a cool cloth over that bruise on your jaw. I have something to show you."

Marcus toted his niece and nephew with him, adding an extra spring to his steps until they giggled and fought to squirm free. He let them down to the floor of the cabin. A chair groaned as he plunked onto it and then perched a child on each knee. Sarah brought both a wet cloth and a folded sheet of parchment.

"What is this?"

"A letter from Uncle Dougal."

That focused Marcus's attention. They had heard nothing from Pa's brother and his family since they left the area two years earlier to settle farther west. On the other side of the mountains. Unbroken, untamed frontier. "How did you get the letter?"

"Pa asked me to read it to him. He did not wish you to know of this—told me to burn it, but I think you should make the decision for yourself."

Like Pa, Marcus had never taken to reading, but. . . "What decision?"

"Samuel is dead. His horse slipped down a ledge and crushed him. He leaves a wife who is—"

"I wasn't aware he had married."

"I heard something about it. A girl from Alamance, shortly before they left. Otherwise I know nothing of her. Other than now she is widowed and with child."

Unfortunate, but how did any of this concern him?

"She needs a husband, and the child needs a father."

"They want me to. . ." Marcus slumped against the rigid back of the chair. Inconceivable. And impossible. "How could I go?" Even if he wished to, his duty as eldest was to stay with the family, to continue at the smithy, to protect his younger sisters from their father's ire.

"It was Jon they asked for. They probably hoped for his return. But I think you should go. You hate it here."

Yes, but he had more reason to protest.

She held up her hand to silence him before he managed a single word. "And you needn't concern yourself about us. I have already spoken to Pa about the girls staying here with me to help with the children. We shall fare well enough. Think of yourself for once. What do you want?"

His own land. To make his own choices. His own family.

No, too much of the Cowden blood ran through him.

"Don't think that way, Marcus," Sarah chided. "You are not Pa."

Heat crawled up his neck. She read him too well. But then, this wasn't the first time they had discussed his reasons for not taking a wife. He remained unconvinced. She didn't understand how deep and unceasing his anger ran. Yes, he had learned to lock it in, to control himself, but he still feared it—feared inflicting himself on a woman or child.

"How can you say that after what I did to Jon?" He was the reason his brother had left seven years earlier, never to look back. He was the one who'd beaten his own brother senseless.

"Oh Marcus. . ." She shook her head, her eyes sad.

He shifted to a safer argument. "Even if I wished to, I could not go. Pa would never agree to it. And if he discovers 'twas you who told me of the letter. . ." Her husband would offer some protection from the wrath, but there would still be consequences.

"Then don't wait. Leave now. You deserve some happiness."

But would happiness await him in the wilderness? He'd never liked his cousin. How could he expect to like the man's widow?

Chapter 2

Ignoring the ache pulsing through her abdomen, Lorinda swung the scythe in smooth motions, its blade skimming an inch above the ground and bringing down even swathes of grass. The hay needed to see her stock through the winter. The summer heat lay heavy over the valley, making each breath a labor. Or was it the growth of the child within her that made each chore progressively more difficult?

Lorinda paused to stretch her back. It ached even more from mowing than in the past. No doubt the added weight at her middle—and this at only five months along from her estimation. She'd kept her approaching maternity from Samuel's family for almost three of those months, but planting had not been easy with her insides constantly swimming. Dougal had caught her retching into the brush alongside the field, and the next day his wife had descended upon her, demanding answers, already guessing about the baby.

"Lord, please let no one come." Her prayer every time she thought of her father-in-law's insistence that he would see she and Samuel's child were provided for. With the thought came a wave of illness—despite being past the time of sickness. He had written to his brother almost two months ago, inquiring after a husband for her. One she didn't want. One who might arrive any day.

"Please let no one come."

The callouses and blisters marring her palms pinched against the smooth handles of the scythe as she tightened her grip and set back to work. Surely a kind God would answer her pleas and let her provide for herself.

Her stomach tightened, a pain circling low as though to remind her that she had more than herself to consider. Why now? Why would God grant her a child when it meant giving up her freedom?

She continued working, ignoring the waves of discomfort contracting around her middle. She had too much work to do to let herself worry if the pain was part of a normal pregnancy or not. She'd not made it this far with her last.

"Lorinda!"

The scythe's curved blade dug into the ground. Dougal Cowden never visited her while the sun still provided light to work by. He'd taken to checking on her once a week on the Sabbath, but never in the middle of the day.

Lorinda turned, the hollow behind her knees weakening. "What has happened?" *Please tell me you have received no news.*

"He has come." Her father-in-law had the audacity to smile.

The three words pummeled her. "Your nephew?" Her voice had no volume, but he was close enough now to hear even her whisper.

"Not the one I expected, but his elder brother. Abner is off to find the parson. With your time approaching and the situation being as it is, he has already agreed to waive the banns."

"I won't." She managed to mouth the words.

" 'Tis what Samuel would want." Dougal crossed his thick arms over his chest, glaring down at her. "Someone to keep his wife and raise his son. Who better than his kin?"

Who better, indeed? And what would Dougal Cowden do if the child was a girl? But now was not the time to suggest he might be mistaken—now was the time to refuse to be forced into a marriage to a man she didn't know and who had every likelihood of being just as heavy-handed as Samuel.

"I won't." She managed a little volume this time, though her voice crackled and broke.

His fingers bit into the tender flesh of her arm. "You will do what is best for my grandchild."

"I won't marry again."

She winced as he gripped her other arm and shook her. "Stop being a sentimental female and think of someone besides yourself. My nephew has come all the way from North Carolina to provide for you and Samuel's child. I'll not turn him away, nor will you shame me in front of him. You will do as you're told, do you understand?"

Her well-rehearsed words clogged her throat, but she forced two out. "I won't."

Fire lit her face under his palm.

"If you don't, you will have nothing, do you hear me? I will take this land, the cabin, everything. You will have no place in this valley."

No place anywhere. Nothing. But what of Samuel's child? His son? Would they allow her to stay until after the babe was born and then force her to leave alone? Without her baby? She didn't dare ask. Did she dare refuse him again?

She'd never truly been free.

I won't!

And yet she felt herself nod, the motion painful, reaching deep and snuffing out what little remained of her dreams.

Dougal did not allow her out of his sight more than it took to change her gown to one less worn and soiled. Not a word passed between them on the trail to the cabin Samuel had helped his father build. The wagon's axle's creaked, begging for grease, singing the demise of the hope she had tried so hard to cling to. All for naught.

The wagon jostled to an abrupt stop, and Dougal jumped down and came to her side. She couldn't look at him, couldn't move, even though she sensed the anger boiling within him.

I won't.

But what good were the whispers of her heart?

The cabin door opened, and a man stepped into the opening...filling every inch of it. A shudder zipped through her. Was this the Cowden they wished to bind her to? Though not more than half a span taller than Samuel had been, his shoulders had breadth his cousin's had not known. And his arms—at least twice as thick as Samuel's. He studied her a moment before stepping out and offering her a hand down from the wagon's high seat.

Breath in her throat, Lorinda could only stare at the strength evident in those large, calloused hands.

"This is Marcus Cowden," Dougal stated, standing near. "He was a blacksmith."

A blacksmith! No wonder the powerful shoulders and arms. She could picture him swinging a hammer...or a balled fist. One blow might be her last.

"I can't." Couldn't risk herself or her child. Samuel had done enough damage. She'd already lost one baby because of his anger. But this man...would surely be the death of her too.

"I can't?"

Marcus wasn't sure what the young woman meant by her words. He stood willing to help her down from the wagon if she would give him her hand, but she held both arms protectively across her swollen abdomen. As though he were the threat.

For some reason, he had expected her farther along and had wondered if the baby would have already arrived before him. But no, and judging from how much his sister had shown with her pregnancies, he guessed they had several months to settle in and become acquainted with one another before their family grew.

Family?

He'd not yet properly met the lady.

"You are Lorinda?"

Not the most eloquent greeting, but words were the least of his current concerns. She appeared younger than he'd expected, not much over twenty to be sure, and yet her eyes—rings of gray and brown and green—seemed so much older. And glistened, red marring what should have been white. As though she'd been crying. . . or teetered on the verge.

"Yes, this is Lorinda," Uncle Dougal said, shoving past him. "Come down here, girl, and greet your groom." He tugged her arm until she complied and allowed him to lift her to the ground.

Marcus's heart sank to his trail-worn shoes. She was not here of her own free will. She had no desire to marry him—seemed intent to not even look at him.

"Perhaps it would be best if. . ." He almost called her Mrs. Cowden, but that was too strange for his tongue—not if he was to marry the woman in the next few hours. "Perhaps Lorinda would like to walk with me, give us time to become acquainted while we wait for the parson?"

Her jaw stiffened, but Uncle Dougal shooed them on their way.

Marcus offered his arm, but she kept her hands tucked across her stomach, head ducked. One cheek wore a pink blush, a contrast to the ashen hue of her face. His gut clenched. It was a look worn by his own mother and sisters too often in the past.

Horses whinnied as their hooves beat out their approach from the trail. His cousin Abner and a middle-aged man with a heavy beard and buckskin garb.

"Thank you for coming, Mr. Ainsley." Uncle Dougal extended a hand as soon as the man's feet touched the ground. "Let us be done with this. I'm sure we all have work waiting on us."

Mr. Ainsley, presumably the parson, though not looking an iota like one, nodded and turned to where Marcus stood with the young widow. "This is the nephew you sent for?"

"This is Marcus, and all's agreed to."

Was everything agreed to? Marcus had yet to hear a word from his soon-to-be bride, and he got the impression she would rather be anywhere but standing beside him. The fear in her eyes he knew too well. He couldn't let this happen—couldn't let her be strong-armed into a marriage she didn't want. Protectiveness surged within him. He knew the temper that raged through Cowden men, knew the mark of a palm across a face. His uncle was just as much a brute as his own father. Had Samuel been any better?

Probably not.

"Lorinda, move closer to Marcus." The backcountry parson waved his hand.

Lorinda. The name suited her well, her dark tresses knotted on the back of her head, her eyes rich and fathomless.

"Lorinda!" Uncle Dougal's yell made her flinch, and she took the required step.

Marcus balled his fists, his own anger rising with an all too familiar heat. He needed to tell them he'd changed his mind and had no plans to stay or marry this woman. But then what would become of her? Who would protect her or the child she carried? What would stop her father-in-law from finding another man to take his place?

He couldn't walk away. . .for her sake.

Chapter 3

N *ot again!* After months of not catering to every need of a man, fearing his wrath if she did anything not to his liking...

Lorinda hurried into her cabin, her ears attuned to the heavy trod of boots behind her. Her *husband*. Though she'd been weeks now without her stomach constantly swimming, bile climbed the back of her throat. She braced against the stone fireplace and swallowed the bitterness. Tried to.

"A fine cabin."

The rumble of bass bit like a lash to her back. This cabin was his now, not hers. Despite all her work, slaving to plant the fields and care for the animals, in minutes she had lost all to him. She could claim nothing for herself.

"I...I think I shall take some time and get to know the lay of the farm." He stepped back out, closing the door behind him.

Lorinda turned and eyed wood planks, thin cracks of daylight marking the edges of the door. He might as well be a thief making away with everything. Even her. Marcus Cowden. As big as an ox and likely just as strong.

Well, he could have the cabin. He could have the fields and every last sprig of grass and wheat. He could have the chickens and cow. But not her. She wouldn't stay here and endure another Cowden and his anger. She wouldn't be the target of his wrath. Nor would she allow that man near her child.

Thoughts racing faster than she could move, Lorinda hurried to the door, to a hook holding a leather pack. Samuel's gelding was hers now, and she would load him with everything she would need for her journey east. The trail would be easy enough to follow—it had to be. As for the future, she would worry about that once she arrived back in North Carolina. All she knew at the moment, or cared about, was an escape. They had stolen her home, but after months of freedom, of not being afraid, she wouldn't look back—wouldn't return to living under that oppressive, black cloud.

The pack stuffed with foodstuffs and clothes, she rolled a blanket on top and peeked out the door. No sign of Mr. Marcus Cowden. She darted to the woods and hid the supplies behind summer foliage. On the way back to the house, she paused at the smokehouse for a cut of ribs from the young hog she had butchered the week before. She'd provide Marcus with one meal and pretend all was well. As soon as he slept, she would make her escape. She would be too far gone to be found by morning.

Would God fault her for leaving her husband of only hours?

She didn't want to think about that right now.

The ribs and some grits were almost ready by the time Marcus's shadow filled the door once more. The glint she had seen earlier in his eyes had softened as had his jaw. No doubt pleased with his new farm—even if he hadn't been with his new wife.

He moved toward her. "You did not wish for this marriage."

"I. . ." How easy to fall back in the habit of saying whatever she thought expected of her—to appease him just as she had Samuel. "I managed well enough on my own before now."

"And in another few months? Do you not wish for help once the baby comes?"

She could not deny the worry pinging her heart as her time crept closer, and with the pains she felt more and more frequently, but any help he offered came at a price. "That basin on the edge of the table you can use to wash for supper." She turned away and dropped the ribs onto a pewter plate, then scooped steaming grits on beside it.

His footsteps neared then paused. Water sloshed. "I am only here to help."

She stole a glance into his blue eyes and lowered brows. His eyes were darker than Samuel's had been, and his nose straighter, but he was still all Cowden. "Nothing more?"

Satisfaction swelled when his gaze dropped to his hands and the now murky water. "You have recently lost your husband, ma'am. It would be insensitive to speak of my hopes until you have been given sufficient time to mourn."

"That is not required. Speak your mind so there are no misunderstandings between us." She passed him a towel in need of darning. Much in the cabin had fallen into neglect and untidiness with her focus on the fields.

As he dried his hands, he moved around the table in the opposite direction, putting distance between them. Was he nervous? Bashful? That was something she had never sensed in Samuel. "I know we had not met before today—before a few short hours ago—but we have our lives ahead of us yet. What I wish for is a wife I can cherish, care for, protect."

How agreeable his words sounded, and the gentleness with which he spoke them, but hadn't Samuel promised her similar before they'd wed?

"I want a family—to raise your child as my own along with brothers and sisters." He looked at her now, intent and questioning, as though he were asking permission for his desires. But a deeper shadow lurked in those blue eyes of his.

Lorinda's head grew light before she realized she'd not taken a breath since he'd begun to speak. The earnestness in his declaration stirred something within her, but she pushed past the sensation. Samuel had been as capable in his earnestness. But familiarity and the frustrations of life had brought out another side of him—one she'd quickly learned to despise.

Instead of answering, she slid the plate across the table along with a fork and knife. Better to busy herself with their supper and her plans to leave than let herself again be drawn in by words dripping with honey.

Marcus sat but kept watching her, setting her nerves on edge—more so than they already were. She poured water into his mug, then sat down across from him to focus on her own meal. Silently she said grace, used to keeping God to herself.

"I won't hurt you."

His words jarred her eyes open.

"I know you have been hurt. But I swear. . ." His large hands lay open on the table, calloused palms up as though with an offering. "I swear I will never raise my hand to you."

Brooding eyes, tight lips, and something she didn't recognize buried in his expression. How easy it would be to gather some semblance of hope and determine to stay, to give him a chance—this marriage a chance. But she'd played the fool already.

Weeks of travel through the Appalachian Mountains and a hurried wedding stole any hope Marcus had of keeping his eyes open longer than the sun's residence in the sky. As soon as the light sank away, so did he. . .onto a quilt on the floor.

What better place for a bridegroom?

He hardly felt like a married man, only an intruder, but he had expected something more on his wedding night. Like a pillow. A mattress. A woman who didn't shoot arrows with her eyes.

Marcus rolled onto his side, facing away from the bed his "wife" occupied, elbow tucked under his head, and let himself drift.

Time. Time would heal all and bring trust. Maybe even love. He had to hold to that hope, even as consciousness slipped away, taking him to a world of unsettled dreams where footsteps scurried, hinges creaked, and a horse whinnied.

Marcus jerked awake and fought through the fog to separate dream from reality. He sat up and looked to the bed where blankets laid flat. The chairs at the table were also abandoned.

Dragging a hand over his eyes, he tried to blink away the sand and exhaustion that still clung to his limbs. His mind slogged forward. Perhaps Lorinda had slipped out to relieve herself. Not unlikely in her state, but the thought of her alone in the darkened wilderness left him uneasy. Who knew what wild animals prowled? Marcus rose and lit a candle.

The door creaked as he opened it, reviving the memory of his dreams. The horse's whinny. He should check on the horses. Muggy warmth hung in the night air, but otherwise all was still. He moved to the corrals where his sorrel mare nickered and pawed the ground, anxious.

"What is it, girl?"

And where was the gelding that had been there earlier?

"Lorinda?"

Nothing.

Fully awake, Marcus darted to the cabin to make sure he hadn't missed something. He lit a lantern, but all lay just as Lorinda had left it before they'd retired.

Hurrying back to the corral, he called her name again and again, but with no reply. The gelding's saddle and a bridle were gone from the barn. Lorinda had left. No other answer presented itself. And only one choice remained.

"Come on, Arrow." He didn't bother with a saddle, just a bridle, and then gave the horse her head, hoping she would follow the gelding wherever he'd gone. Hugging low to the sleek neck, he raced to the trail, and then along it until a shadow dodged into the trees ahead of them. He followed.

"Lorinda?"

"Stay away from me!" Her breathless answer lifted the panic from his chest.

"Where are you going?"

"Anywhere away from here." Her horse balked and tried to reverse course as the woods thickened.

Marcus dropped to the ground and grabbed the reins. "Why?"

"You have the farm and land—everything you could want. Leave me be!" She kicked the horse, and it pressed forward, its broad hoof catching the end of Marcus's boot. Pain spiked through his smallest toes.

He bit back a curse. "I'm a blacksmith, not a farmer."

"Then why come out here?" She tried to maneuver around Marcus, but he pulled the reins tight and forced the horse to comply.

Marcus held his tongue, not so sure of the answer anymore. The thought of land had initially attracted him, but yesterday, walking around the farm, he'd been honest enough with himself to admit to knowing little about farming. He had also thought it noble to journey into this back country to care for this woman and her babe, but he'd obviously been mistaken about that as well. As far as the woman was concerned, he was a villain.

Keeping hold of the gelding's reins, he mounted Arrow and headed back the way they had come, only overshooting the cabin by a few yards before Lorinda corrected him, mumbling the needed directions.

Horses again in their corral for the night, Marcus hauled the pack that had been fastened to the gelding's saddle to the cabin. Lorinda waited for him there, stoic behind the table, hands cradling her stomach protectively, the lamplight betraying raw fear.

"To the bed with you," he grumbled, waving her to comply. And waiting until she did.

She removed only her shoes then slipped into the bed and pulled the covers up to her chin.

"Move over." He sat on the edge until she scuttled to the far side. . .which really wasn't very far.

He almost smiled, but mostly it felt too good to lie down and not move. "Now I won't have to worry about you slipping away and me not knowing."

"If I promise not to leave, will you return to the pallet you made up on the floor?"

Marcus shook his head. He'd slept on the lumpy ground for more than a fortnight of travel, and he was too tired to go anywhere tonight. Besides, she was his wife now, and sooner or later they both needed to accept it.

Chapter 4

Late morning sun streamed through the open door along with a brisk breeze by the time Marcus opened his eyes again. The journey through the mountains and last night's romp through the forest had taken more out of him than he'd realized. He remained on his back, staring up at the rafters, as he let his mind finish waking. This cabin in the middle of this lonesome wilderness was his home now, and a woman named Lorinda, with the prettiest doe eyes he'd ever seen, was his wife.

Lorinda.

He jerked up and looked about. Where was she?

Grabbing his boots, he stumbled out the door and into blinding sunlight. How he'd managed to sleep so late, he wasn't sure, but if she'd left again, he might not catch up with her. He jogged to the corrals first where both horses gazed at him with disinterest as they swatted flies with their tails. Relief almost barreled him over, affecting him much more than he was braced for. Her not leaving meant they were making some progress, didn't it?

Marcus wandered around the farm for the next half hour or so before he found his bride swinging a scythe against thick hay in an outlaying field. Hanging back, he watched her. She moved with smooth rhythm, her head tipped slightly as each new swath fell. After a minute, she paused and leaned into the long arched handle to catch her breath. One hand lowered to the roundness of her middle.

The gesture was enough to jerk Marcus from his musings and set him out across the field. He hadn't come to ogle, but to help and protect. To provide for. While he'd not had much experience with farming, it couldn't be much more difficult than bending a horseshoe into the perfect arch.

Lorinda's wary gaze slowed him as he neared, but he extended his hand. "This isn't work for you."

She kept her hold on the scythe. "I managed well enough before you came." Bitterness sharpened her words.

"Mayhap. But now you don't have to." He drew the tool away from her. "And you have that baby to consider."

She stepped back, but still lingered. "The farm is yours, and you may do with it as you like. . ." Another step distanced her. "But why stop me from leaving? I am nothing to you."

"You are my wife."

"You never saw me before yesterday. You feel nothing for me. Let me go."

Marcus eyed the knee-high grass and flexed his hands over the handles of the scythe. "If you really wanted to leave, I could not have stopped you this morning. Yet here you remain."

He glanced up to see her deepening frown. So leaving again had occurred to her.

"Lorinda. . ." How strange her name felt on his tongue—to speak to her as though they had known each other for more than a day, as though they shared a more intimate bond.

She is your wife.

How much more intimate could a bond be?

She was staring at him, her wide eyes reminding him that he had yet to finish his thought.

"As I said before, I did not come all this way for mere land. I came because I wanted my own life, a home of my own, and a family of my own. I believe God led me to act on that letter my father received." He prayed that was so. "If you wish it, I will see you safely back to North Carolina, but if you agree to stay, I promise you two things."

"Do not make promises you won't keep. . .*husband*." Lorinda fell back another step.

"I keep my word, *wife*." He refused to give in to his own fears.

"I do not want your promises." She sounded panicked. But why? Why be afraid of promises?

"But you deserve them." Marcus set down the scythe and closed the distance between them by half. "I promise I will never lift my hand against you—I will *never* hurt you." *Lord, please help me stay true to this.*

As though sensing his own uncertainties, she inched away.

Marcus stiffened his resolve to never become his father. "I promise that while there is strength in me, I will work to provide for you and your child." And any children that resulted in their union, because while nothing scared him more, he did want children around him, surrounding him with laughter and innocence. And now that he paused to consider it, he'd not complain if each and every one of them looked just like their mother. The same dark waves, and irises now the color of fresh honey but brimmed by a soft green that gave her eyes such depth.

"I have plenty to do back at the cabin." Lorinda's declaration yanked Marcus from his contemplation, but before he could think of anything more to say, she scampered off the way he had come.

He stared after her departing figure, a simmering frustration whitening his knuckles. How long would it take before he won her trust. . .never mind her heart? Because he wouldn't settle for a marriage in name only. He wanted what his sister had found with her husband. A partnership and devotion. Love.

Lorinda halted as soon as she reached the cabin and leaned into the wall. Within her, the child gently prodded against the pinch in her side, reminding her she had more than herself to think of. But how could that bear of a man stand there and make such promises? Yes, he would probably provide for her well enough—he seemed very capable. Was no doubt strong enough. But to look at her with such tenderness and try to convince her that he was different from every other Cowden she'd met. . .

How dare he?

How dare he spout words of tenderness and promise? Just as Samuel had.

How dare he look at her with such sincerity, as though apologizing for every hand lifted against her? In the beginning Samuel had even apologized, leading her to believe that he was capable of change.

She refused to allow herself to fall for the same ploy—refused to open her heart to more. But how dare he invoke hope?

Lorinda pushed away from the wall. She would not let that man affect her. Giving him no reason to be angry, while staying out of arm's reach, was the best she could do for now.

As she stepped into the cabin, a dull ache tightened around her abdomen. Maybe it was a good thing he had taken over mowing. Her body did not seem to appreciate the repetitive swing. All would be well now.

Yet it was impossible to turn thoughts away from the memories of her last pregnancy and its abrupt end.

Lorinda punched down the dough she had started that morning and shoveled more coals over the Dutch oven containing their evening meal. How the man had slept so soundly with her busy in the cabin, coming and going, was beyond her, but it had given her time to study him while he so peacefully lay there. This new husband of hers was a handsome man with hair the color of freshly hewn cedar and features definite, but kind.

If only she could trust him.

Lorinda paused to lean into the table and breathe. The ache had diminished but only a little. Perhaps if she lay down for a few minutes all would settle and she could fix their midday meal before Marcus came in hungry. Samuel was always grumpy when his meal wasn't waiting for him. Maybe sitting for a moment would suffice.

The solid chair braced her up, and she folded her arms and rested her head on the table. Deep breaths, and all would be well.

Swinging the scythe was more work than Marcus had anticipated. Or mayhap his body was simply unaccustomed to the motion. He didn't care to consider he might be doing it all wrong. Mopping the moisture from his brow, he leaned the scythe against the wall of the barn and ducked inside. Not a large building, but well-built— the workmanship almost intimidating. For years he had honed his skills as a black-smith, the wielding of steel and iron into anything desired. What use was that skill now with their lives dependent upon fields and stock?

Unless he could trade his services as he had in North Carolina.

Marcus eyed the breadth and length of the barn. There was no reason not to construct billows and benches for his work. Surely there were others in the settle-ment or neighboring ones that had use for a smithy. Horses to shoe. Wagon wheels to repair. Tools, nails, and even household items he could mend and supply.

Anticipation rippled through him, and he turned from the barn. All things in good time, but there was no reason not to mention his ideas to Lorinda. Perhaps including her in his planning would assist in gaining her trust.

He stepped into the sunlight and something crackled in the brush across the yard. Branches snapping back into place. Twigs breaking underfoot. Marcus peered into the shadows. The hair on the back of his neck rose with the sensation of being watched, though he saw no one. Surely Lorinda had not wandered off again.

Marcus made it halfway to the cabin before he felt the urge to turn back. The horses moved restlessly in the corral, ears flitting as though to catch every sound on the breeze. Maybe he was imagining things, but all the same, he'd fetch his musket from the cabin before exploring.

The door sat open and he jogged inside. "Lorinda, what have you for wolves or bears around these parts—"

He stopped short at the sight of his bride leaning into the side of the table, breathing heavily, pain twisting her lovely features.

Chapter 5

P anic spiked through Lorinda as Marcus's boots pounded against the ground and his large form blocked the sun's entry. Indecision thundered in her chest. Remain still and risk his anger, or hurry with dinner and risk losing her baby?

Oh please, Lord, not again.

"What happened?"

Warmth braced her shoulder, and she clamped her eyes closed against the prickling of tears. She wouldn't cry, wouldn't let him see the terror ripping her heart open. The cramping had increased, becoming too similar to what she'd felt when losing her first child. *Please, Lord. Not again. Leave me my baby.*

"Are you hurt? Did you fall?"

She could hear the anxiety in his voice, raising its pitch. But why should he care? He'd known her less than a day, and this child was not his.

"Let's get you to the bed. Can you walk?"

Lorinda nodded, but couldn't find her voice. If she opened her mouth a sob might escape. Samuel hadn't liked her crying. Tears had only spurred his temper. He'd blamed her for not being able to carry the child, while she had blamed him for striking her. She'd thought he had harmed their baby, but what if he'd been correct—what if she couldn't carry a child? What if she lost this one too?

Strong arms slid around her, bracing her up, and she leaned into Marcus's hold... unable to contain the moisture pressing from under her eyelids. It trickled down her cheeks.

When he laid her on the bed, she dared a glance at him. He leaned near, brows peaked with concern. For her?

His large thumb smoothed across her cheek. "What happened? Are you in pain?"

Lorinda managed a nod as she rolled onto her side and braced her stomach against another wave of cramping.

"The baby?"

More tears. She couldn't stop them, nor the doubts that God would hear her any better than the last time. The cramping would continue to worsen, deepening. And then the blood. There would be no way to stop it, no way to stop her body from rejecting the child it had formed. Except last time had been earlier. She hadn't yet felt her baby moving within, tiny hands and feet tickling her from the inside.

"*Shhh.*" The deep croon carried no chastisement, only comfort. Marcus lowered to his knees beside the bed and combed strands of hair from her face. His other hand drew the covers over her. "Is there anything you need?"

This baby to stay inside me for another four months.

All she wanted. But there was too much work demanding to be done. She couldn't very well lay here indefinitely—and certainly not for months. Only to delay the inevitable? "I need to finish the bread. And your dinner. I've not fixed your dinner." Had he eaten anything that morning? The man was probably famished.

"You're staying where you are, *wife.*" His mouth curved like he wanted to smile, but his lips remained tight. "I can manage everything else. You have pushed yourself too hard. Rest."

Lorinda allowed herself to relax into the pillow. Maybe she could afford a little while. But what would tomorrow bring? How long before Marcus tired of her laziness and learned to resent her just as Samuel had? Just as her father had.

"*You are a good girl, and I love you.*" Mama's words glowed at the very center of her heart where she had tucked them away, but they had little effect against all the other voices. The ones that told her she was lazy and worthless. The ones shouting that no one could love her.

A baby might have changed all that. A baby would have loved her, and she would have loved it—just as Mama had loved her. A baby would have helped Lorinda understand that love.

But surely God didn't love her. . .or He wouldn't be taking this baby too.

Most of the day passed before Marcus felt able to leave Lorinda's side. He had knelt until his knees ached, and then pulled a chair near until she started fretting about the dough again. Bread dough was the least of his concerns, but to appease her, he insisted on shaping it into loaves and cooking it as she directed. He stayed close until their evening meal was finished, and then took it from the coals and forced a generous helping down her throat. In bed. She claimed the pains had subsided enough that she could sit at the table, but then she'd only feel the need to start working again, and risk hurting herself more.

No, better she stay abed a few days—or however long needed—until all was well with both her and the baby. Until then, he would tend to the animals and the cooking as well. He'd done his share in the past, though he pitied her palate.

The sun sank toward the horizon, brushing the top of the towering hickory edging their land to the west. He moved toward the corrals, musket in hand. All seemed quiet now. The horses grazed with their heads low, only glancing at him briefly as he walked past. According to Lorinda, the cow needed milking first and foremost. She had put the cow out to pasture that morning, but the animal could be left in the barn overnight. Only, maybe he was looking in the wrong pasture, because he didn't see a cow.

He climbed over the rail fence near one of the angled braces. Looked like the cow was there after all, resting at the far end of the pasture in the deeper grass. He was almost to it when he noticed the extended back legs, stiff, unmoving. The cow's eyes stared blindly. Blood stained its neck, its throat slit.

Musket gripped, Marcus searched the woods. In vain. Whoever had done this had fled hours earlier. But had been there, watching him.

Marcus stalked back to the barn. He set aside his musket and harnessed his mare. They had lost the cow, but could not let the meat go to waste. By the time he'd dragged the carcass to the barn and hung and cleaned it, darkness blanketed the farm and forests beyond. He listened as he worked, straining to hear past the breeze rattling the tops of the trees and the restlessness of the other animals. He led the horses into the barn for the night and hung the cowbell from the bar securing the door closed with the hope that it would give him some warning if anyone came creeping about. The futility of it settled in the pit of his stomach. He'd been nearby when the cow was killed and hadn't known it.

Frustration built as Marcus started toward the cabin. How could he keep the farm safe and Lorinda in bed? How could he be everywhere at once?

The cabin door swung with too much ease, slamming closed behind him. Lorinda flinched. He needed to be careful not to alarm her. She had more important things to worry about, like resting and getting well. He could feel her gaze steady on him as he set the gun on the table and poured water into the basin to wash his hands.

"Is that blood on your sleeve?" Her timid question tightened his chest.

"Aye." Lying would only delay the truth and do nothing toward building her trust.

"Why do you have blood on your sleeve?"

"The cow is dead."

"You killed my milk cow?" Her eyes widened at him.

"No. I don't—"

"It was healthy this morning when I milked."

Marcus buried his hands in a threadbare towel. "Have you had any trouble with Indians of late?"

"Very little." She pushed up higher on the bed. "You think Indians killed it?"

"I don't know what to think." He threw the rag on the table and took up the musket again. He'd clean it and keep it loaded. "Its throat was cut."

"Its throat. . . ?" The horror in her voice also showed in her eyes as her hand rose to her slender neck.

"Been dead for hours."

"Who would do such a thing?"

"Do you have any enemies?"

Her face paled, but she shook her head. "No one I would think capable of this."

Marcus racked his brain. Was there anyone who would follow him all this way for the sake of wreaking havoc on his new life here? Father would be too busy with the Regulators, and not give him a second thought other than to curse his name. And this wasn't his style. He'd barge into the cabin and make his demands known, not skulk in the woods. But who else hated him or Lorinda?

Chapter 6

Four days was much too long to lie around like a worthless log. Lorinda moved slowly and cautiously to the fireplace. Other than a dull ache low in her abdomen, the cramping had gradually faded over the past few days. What excuse was there for remaining abed? Marcus had not had time to start their supper, nor had he cleaned dishes from their last two meals. The cabin sat in complete disarray.

"How worthless he must think me." His wife of almost a week, and she had only prepared him one meal. She hadn't kept the cabin or helped ready the meat for the smokehouse. The garden lay in weeds. Father and Samuel were proven right. Lazy and useless.

The babe lurched within her, and she laid her hand over her stomach. Lazy or not, she still had her child. Because of Marcus. No matter what he thought of her, he had insisted she lay there while he did. . .everything. Was it possible he would stay so gentle?

Lorinda knelt at the fireplace and used the fire poker to seek out the live coals under the ones Marcus had banked that morning. If only she could keep the hope alive that sparked at Marcus's patience with her. But she could not. He was as much a Cowden as the others, and she'd seen the anger sharpen his actions and words after he'd found the cow dead. Only a matter of time before she became the target of his frustration.

"Lorinda!"

She scampered to her feet and twisted to the sharp voice. What had she done?

"What are you doing out of bed?" Marcus set the musket on the table—he always took it with him now—and hastened to her side. His large hand wrapped her arm.

She flinched, ducking her head. "I was about to fix your supper."

He guided her back across the room. "I do not think that a good idea, *wife*."

There was something about the way he said that word—like this was somehow amusing to him. "But I'm useless lying there, *husband*." Why did that not bother him?

Instead of answering, he drew down the covers she had just straightened and helped her into bed. His mouth curved upward, but his eyes remained serious. "You are keeping that babe safe while he grows." He squeezed her shoulder. "That is plenty for you to do. . .wife."

Warmth moved through her as she peered up into those stormy blue eyes that seemed to smile at her. A strand of sun-touched brown lay over his forehead begging to be brushed aside. And his mouth. . .

Lorinda quickly shrugged his hand away. How dare he confuse her like this? Pretending to care. Touching a hope she had so long ago buried—that love was possible between a husband and wife. Romantic love. Kind love. Samuel had done the same, only to crush her foolish dreams.

"What did I do now?" Frustration marked his words with deeper questioning that tugged at her.

She refused to heed it.

"If you are feeling well enough, I suppose you can do a few light things around the cabin. I do not mean to dictate what you can and cannot do. I only want you to take care of yourself first and foremost. Understood?"

She managed a nod and tried not to watch him as he withdrew to stoke the fire and prepare their evening meal. More beef. The skillet clanged against the table, the knife sliced the raw meat in strong but choppy motions. His brow lowered into a scowl.

"What's wrong?" Lorinda almost didn't want to ask in case he was upset at her, but he hadn't shown the same irritation moments ago.

The knife came down hard, probably sinking into the board beneath it. "Nothing you need worry about."

How could she not worry when it affected him so? "Has something else happened?" She had thought all quiet and peaceful since the cow's slaughter.

"Just little things. Missing tools. Footprints leading into the woods."

"But not a clue as to who is doing this?"

Marcus leaned into the table as though this unseen burden was becoming too much for those broad shoulders to bear. " 'Tis as though they watch me and know exactly when to strike." His hands fisted.

"But who?" Even as she said it, the answer presented itself. Abner was the one who wanted this land. Had he been biding his time, hoping she would give it up on her own? That would never happen now that Marcus had come.

"What do you know?" Marcus watched her, eyes narrowing.

"I think. . .I think I know where to look."

Rage rose through Marcus as Lorinda told him of her brother-in-law and his desires for the better land and water. He didn't know Abner well, hadn't seen him in years before his brief appearance at their wedding, but no use putting off a visit.

Marcus slapped his cocked hat back on his head and started for the door.

"Where are you going?" Lorinda sounded panicked.

"To bid my cousin a good day." No crime in that. His hand hesitated over the musket on the table—he'd not left the cabin without a weapon for most of a week.

"Take it with you if you must go."

He shook his head—he couldn't chance using it against his own kin. Not for the life of a cow and other random pranks. He stepped away from the gun and kept walking.

The rustle of blankets slowed him at the door. Lorinda hurried to his side. "I'm coming with you."

"You are not." He took her arm and again guided her toward the bed. "You are going to rest and wait. Bar the door and keep the musket in case you have any trouble in my absence. I shan't be long."

"*Husband.*"

He almost smiled at the stress of the word, pushed through her teeth. "Wife?"

She sighed and dropped onto the edge of the mattress. "Be careful."

Marcus's smile stretched a little broader. Lorinda was actually worried for him.

Her gaze dropped and she fidgeted with the end of the braid draped over her shoulder. "I've not time for another funeral."

Thankfully her lips betrayed a hint of teasing.

"In that case, I shall use utmost care."

With a lantern in hand, and directions from Lorinda, Marcus fetched the saddle and bridle from the barn and went for his horse. If he rode hard, he'd reach Abner's homestead in minutes.

On second thought, Marcus left the tack on the rail fence and instead set out along a woodland trail on foot. He needed time to wear out his anger toward his cousin. Despite pacing himself, he arrived all too soon at a cabin twice the size of the one he shared with Lorinda. He took a breath, knocked, and listened while footsteps shuffled to the door.

A crack of light grew to the glow of a fireplace behind a man. The younger version of his uncle.

"Good evening, Abner."

"Marcus? I–I'm glad you took the time to call. I intended to bring my family to meet you, but there is much to do out here. I am sure you are beginning to understand that well. Not an easy life in this wilderness."

"Do not concern yourself." Marcus spied a woman and children in the background. "May I come in?"

"Come in?" Abner seemed to hesitate. "Of course. Of course, come in." He stepped back and opened the door wide. "Constance, fix my cousin some tea."

The woman hurried to obey, shooing a young boy out of her way.

"Thank you." Marcus moved to the table and sat.

Abner remained standing. Near the door. He glanced out into the night before closing it, but still remained at a distance. New sweat glistened on his forehead. "How are you liking our valley?"

"I can well understand why you settled here." Marcus took the steaming cup Constance offered. "Fine land. Lorinda is right proud of her piece. Though, as you know, I'm better with iron than earth."

Abner's eyes sparked. "Yes, of course you are. A blacksmith. Just what we need in this valley."

"I would like to set up somewhat of a shop in my barn—once I can spare the time."

A muscle twitched in Abner's cheek. "Yes, quite. I mean, that would be good." He scratched at the back of his neck, his expression anxious. "If you are in need of any assistance, you have only to ask. In fact, with you being not much of a farmer, perhaps I can take some of that land off your hands, trade for what you will need for your shop. I have a friend who comes over these mountains regularly. Perhaps we can arrange shipments of supplies for you."

"Though I'm appreciative of your offer, the land was Lorinda's before it was mine. She has worked it on her own for most of the season, if I understand correctly. I will have to discuss this with her first."

Abner's lip curled. His eyes darkened. "That was my brother's land, never Lorinda's. That woman has been nothing but trouble. 'Tis her fault Samuel is dead."

Marcus heated at the words, something in him chafing on Lorinda's behalf. "I thought his horse fell on him."

"Only because she drove him from his own home that night. Believe me when I say that woman will be the death of you too."

Not likely. Marcus had no fear of Lorinda, but Abner on the other hand might very well be behind the dead cow and missing tools. If only there was a way to prove it. Acting on his hunch tonight would do no good. Marcus was too angry and needed the walk home to cool off and sort through what he knew. And what to do about it.

"I'm sorry you had to come out here, wedged in the middle of all this."

Almost sounded like a confession. "Me too." He wasn't sorry to have come to Lorinda's aide—in fact he was becoming quite glad about that—but he was sorry a fight was brewing over something as inconsequential as land. People and lives mattered much more than dirt.

Marcus took his leave before he did something rash. He mulled over the conversation as he strode in the direction of his and Lorinda's cabin, growing more and more certain with each step that Abner was the culprit. But how to stop him without starting a war?

Smoke wafted through the trees. Strange, unless Lorinda had stoked the fire—stranger still, considering the heat of the day. Then Marcus heard the low roar. Flickering light glowed through the trees.

"No!" He sprinted to the clearing.

A wall of flame engulfed the barn with tongues of orange and red. Yet all he could think about as he raced across the yard was Lorinda and keeping her safe. That, and the fact that Abner couldn't have lit this fire.

Chapter 7

Heat scorched Lorinda's face as she challenged the blaze with yet another pail of water. The flames mocked her, lapping up the moisture with hardly more than a flicker. Useless.

"Lorinda!"

She pivoted to Marcus, who ran toward her, the angles of his face sharp in the hot light of the fire. She allowed for a breath, needful as pain enveloped her center. All her efforts to save the barn had been in vain, and she'd again threatened her baby.

"How did the fire start?"

She shook her head, leaning forward to brace against the pain. "I need. . .one moment." To breathe. To pray that she hadn't killed her child in trying to fight the fire. While grateful that she had at least been able to release the animals from the building, the life of a horse could not compensate her for the loss of her baby.

Powerful arms braced her. "You should not be out of bed." Marcus swept her up, holding her securely against his chest as he hurried to the cabin. "Let me worry about the barn."

Gladly, but what of the cabin? If someone wished to hurt them so vehemently, what would keep him from setting fire to their home or shooting Marcus dead while he worked the fields?

Lorinda held tighter. A week ago, she wanted nothing to do with the man, now suddenly she feared for his life? What a fool to learn to care so easily. Only a matter of time before the anger brewing underneath became too much to contain, and then what? He'd be Samuel all over again.

Lorinda allowed him to lower her onto the bed, then rolled onto her side and pulled the blanket over her. Not that she needed the warmth—the night air was heavy with summer heat and the fire consuming a month's worth of sweat and labor. The blanket only served as a barrier. She would keep her heart safe from this man with the all-too-kind eyes. The future would hurt less that way.

"Did you see anything, or hear anything? The horses, are they out?"

His frantic questions spun in her head, making it difficult to sort through her cascading thoughts. "They are. I heard them whinnying and looked to see what had set them off. But I saw nothing else. Did Abner do this too?" She hadn't believed him evilhearted enough to take his mischief to this extent, but she would wait no longer to inform Dougal of his eldest son's sins.

"It could not have been Abner."

"What do you mean it could not have been him? Nothing else makes any—"

"I was with him, Lorinda. I was with him the whole time. There is no way he could have made it here and back past me. 'Twas not him."

She stared past Marcus to the open door and beyond where blackened and shrinking walls gave way to the flames. With a great moan, the back half of the roof collapsed. "Then who?"

"I wish I knew." He followed her focus to the blaze. "Because I would find a way to stop him." The flint in his voice stiffened Lorinda. The same tone Samuel would take when upset. Only, the rage wasn't directed at her. This time.

"Stay here and rest. I need to make sure the flames die out and the sparks don't start any new blazes."

Lorinda nodded her answer and sank deeper into her pillow as he hastened out, his dark form silhouetted by dancing oranges and reds.

"Lord, protect him from harm."

The prayer came without thought, and Lorinda swallowed hard on the taste of ash and smoke. She didn't have time to waste prayers on another man. Her baby needed her now. The pain seemed to be subsiding, but what would the night bring?

Hours passed and finally Lorinda was able to doze. Sometime in the night—or the wee hours of morning—the bed shifted and the frame creaked with the weight of her new husband, reeking of smoke much more than she. He lay face up and did not twitch again until morning.

She woke to mild cramps and Marcus pulling on his boots. "Where are you going?"

He heaved to his feet and dusted at his clothes, still covered in soot. He frowned at the bedcovers. "I should have undressed before coming to bed. I'm sorry."

"You were exhausted." Necessitating no apology. She only wished she was well enough to wash the growing pile of laundry. Did either of them have anything clean left to change into? Dared she risk the labor? She couldn't very well ask it of Marcus... who was already most of the way to the door. "Where are you going?"

He slung the musket over his shoulder. "I need to check on the horses and other animals—secure them and see they have feed."

"What about you? You have not eaten."

"I'm not hungry," he grumbled, then let out a breath. "Besides, with what we lost in the fire, even if all goes well with the harvest, things might be a little lean this winter." Face drawn and jaw tight, he staggered out the door.

The closed door hazed behind a wall of moisture. Her chest ached even more than her abdomen. How could she lay here with everything going so awry? She had gotten a look at the garden yesterday, and already the weeds pushed their heads up past the vegetables—vital to their winter supply. Laundry waited to be washed, and there was not a clean dish to be found. Food required preparation, water sat at the bottom of the well, and Marcus needed help so he could watch out for whoever wreaked so much havoc. Did she have any choice but to risk her child?

The baby squirmed within her, and tears rolled down her cheeks, tickling her ears. For now, her baby was alive and well, but why did her body struggle to keep it that way? A tightening in her throat increased with the pain in her heart.

"What do I do, Lord?" What was there to do, but what was needed?

But what about what her baby needed?

Lorinda rolled onto her side, drawing her knees up and laying her hands over her belly. Every movement she would hold to and pray it would not be the last.

The door swung wide and Marcus stepped in. His chest sank and he shook his head. "I'm sorry." In four long strides, he was at her side, sinking to his knees. His large hand trembled, hesitating inches from her face. He looked at her with such pleading, as though seeking permission to touch her.

Yes. She shouldn't, but she did desire his touch, his comfort.

Slowly his thumb smoothed up her cheek, catching the stray droplets. "I'm sorry," he said, his voice hardly more than air. "I was so distracted by everything else, I wasn't thinking about you, about the baby. What do *you* need of me?"

Words jammed up her throat, making it hurt. More tears—and no way to stop them. "There's too much. You can't do it on your own."

The corner of his mouth turned up with the softening of his eyes. "Is that not what you were doing before I came?"

She'd had no one but herself to worry about—not a bedridden burden. And even then, she hadn't been able to keep up with everything. Taming this wilderness, surviving it, had always been too much for her alone. . .though she hated admitting it even to herself.

Marcus lowered his hand to hers and squeezed. Never had her fingers felt so warm or protected. "Your task is to take care of that baby. Let me worry about the rest."

Lorinda forced a nod. She would give herself another day and pray it was enough, but though she may agree to stay in bed for the sake of the baby, she couldn't promise not to worry about everything else.

Chapter 8

His hands had never been so clean. If only Marcus could say the same for the line of laundry. He was quite certain Lorinda could do better. For the past two weeks, he had taken over every responsibility, making sure Lorinda took the time she needed to rest. Every few days, she insisted she felt well enough to attempt some of the tasks, but the pains soon returned, and he forced her back to bed. Much to her growing frustration.

Marcus wrung out a woman's undergarment and hung it with the other items on the line. The first time he had washed her clothes, he'd had to pause and remind himself that she was his wife and this was necessary. No woman wanted dirty clothes. Or dishes. Or weeds in the garden. He was also getting quite good at biscuits in the Dutch oven. Every other minute of the day he spent in the fields, watching for signs of the intruder whose pranks continued with no rhyme or reason.

After washing one of his shirts, he frowned at the murky water, more likely to dirty clothes than wash them. He hefted the washbasin, water sloshing as he carried it to the garden to empty into the carrot patch—his favorite, so they received much of his attention. Even still, they were hardly the size of his little finger.

Sometimes he had to question if all this effort was worth anything. What good was trying to build a life here if someone was intent on making it impossible? The sheep had been let out of their pen two days after the barn burned, and they had taken most of the day to round up. Since then, broken eggs had left a path away from the farm, a chicken had been hung from the door of the coop—neck wrung, the pail had gone missing from the well, and the meat was stolen from the smokehouse. Most of the meat. One leg of beef remained, cut down and left in the ash on the floor. As though to tell him something.

But what?

Someone was trying to leave a message—a very unpleasant one. He now kept everything of worth, from tools to the single saddle and bridle that hadn't burned, in the cabin, and spent hours watching for whoever was responsible. But never found more than the damage done. Boot prints led away from the farm in every direction, but he could never manage to follow them far. He was a blacksmith, not a tracker. Mayhap he had not been meant for this wilderness.

"Marcus?"

He started at Lorinda's call, but quickly put his frustration away, focusing instead on filling the basin with fresh water from the clear brook and bringing it back to finish the laundry. She had a sixth sense for his anger, and he didn't like how it affected her.

Her movements as slow as an eighty-year-old grandmother, Lorinda walked toward him, her green-brown gaze on the long line of clothes—mostly hers.

"Are you sure you should be out of bed?"

She laid a hand to her stomach. "I'm all right. I needed to stretch my legs and escape that cabin for at least a few minutes."

"I could set a chair in the shade if you like."

"I would like that." A hint of a smile climbed her cheeks, giving fullness to her lips. Hard not to stare at her mouth when with increasing frequency he found himself wondering at its taste. Safer to focus on her hair, now twisted and pinned at the back of her head. But escaped wisps invoked memories of her dark waves free over her pillow, begging to be felt. Were her tresses as silky as they appeared?

Marcus grabbed another item of clothing, thrust it into the water, and scrubbed hard. Perhaps there was an art to washing, but he was far from learning it. The clothes looked better than when they went into the water though so he considered that a success.

A quick intake of breath drew his attention to Lorinda, whose gaze was on his hands and the bit of fabric he wrung. Another of her unmentionables. Heat crept into his face as he hurried to wring it out and hang it on the line.

When he turned back, she was scanning the line and its burden, her complexion rivaling that of a ripe tomato.

"Not clean enough? You look a little. . ." If she was anything like his sisters, she probably didn't want to hear how deep her blush had become.

Lorinda's gaze flickered to him and then away, never settling on one thing in particular. "They are fine. I'm merely a little warm out here in the sun."

"Let me fetch that chair then."

By the time he reached the house, Marcus changed his mind. The straight-backed chairs would be uncomfortable for any duration. Better she be able to lie down. He collected a quilt and pillow before returning to her. Under the extended branches of a wild cherry, the grape-like fruit hanging from its branches, he laid out a makeshift bed.

Seating herself on the blanket, Lorinda leaned back on her elbows, a question in those beautiful eyes.

As curious as he was about what went on behind the swirls of brown and green, he settled for a safer inquiry. "How is that?"

"Very good. Thank you. But what about you? You're working yourself to death while I sit like an idle goat."

"Hardly idle." And much, much more becoming than a goat. "You mended the shirt I tore yesterday."

She shook her head at him. "You should pause long enough to eat. Why not join me for a picnic?" A pat on the blanket beside her provided an open invitation.

Marcus couldn't hold back his smile as he walked to the house to rummage something for their meal. Despite the worry over the baby and needing to take so much on himself, he'd been given a chance to prove himself to her. Day by day, task by task, he saw her let down her resistance, see him with eyes untarnished by anything Samuel had done. For that, he praised the Lord.

Some aged cheese and the biscuits he'd cooked that morning in hand, he hurried back to her. He sat on the edge of the blanket to share the meager offering.

Nibbling one of the biscuits, Lorinda lay down, facing him. "I was considering this morning how very little I know about you, about your life before you came here. Other than you are a Cowden and a blacksmith."

Not much to build a marriage on. "What do you wish to know?"

She stared up at him with open curiosity. "What of your family? Do you have siblings? Did you enjoy the work of a smithy?" She glanced back to the crumbling biscuit in her hand. "I wish to know everything."

Marcus took a knife to the end of the cheese, trying to decide what to share. How much of "everything." "I have one brother and three sisters. I'm the eldest. My mother was a godly woman who. . ." worked herself to death trying to stay his father's anger. Marcus was the eldest. He should have done more to protect her. "Who passed away shortly after my twelfth birthday. My father. . ." *killed her.*

What was he supposed to say about the man responsible for his existence. . .and so much pain?

"Was a Cowden?" Lorinda sighed. "You should probably relax your grip on that knife."

Marcus opened his hand, letting the knife fall. He forced his lungs to expand to their fullest capacity. How easily she grouped the men in his family under one effective, encompassing title. A Cowden. The name he had been born to. He'd not taken it on himself. He didn't desire it any more than he desired the rage always simmering below his surface, waiting for the slightest excuse to give in to the heat and boil over.

No wonder she feared him.

He closed his eyes and dipped his chin to his chest. "I have no wish to be like them. I *refuse* to." He looked to her with one last. . .plea. "I swear I will never hurt you."

"I think—I think you will try not to," she whispered.

He wanted to argue, but couldn't. His own fears remained.

"I see you trying, Marcus, but I also see that anger in you. The same anger

Samuel had. Only more. More than I have ever seen in a man. I'm not blaming you—with all that is wrong right now—with the barn burning, the farm threatened, and me useless. I know you—"

"You're not useless." He hated her saying as much, hated the dullness in her eyes when she spoke of herself in that light. "You—"

She held up her hand, staying his words. "I know you are striving to do what is right. I see how hard you work to contain your temper, to hold it inside and not let it hurt anyone. . .but for how long? How long can you contain it before you are no longer the master?" She poked at the remains of her food, her voice gone but for a whisper. "How long can you swim against the current?"

"As long as I have to." The answer came, but with none of the confidence he sought. Instead he felt weak and vulnerable against a force that sought to destroy him and all he desired. Her trust. Her love.

Her.

Every night she lay there beside him as she lay here now, so close. . .but out of reach. How could he take her in his arms as he ached to, until he earned that right? Yes, he was her husband, but he wished for more than what was his right by law. He wanted her heart. No matter how inviting the concerned pucker of her lips as she stared up at him as she did now. . .

"I need to take a walk."

He pushed the cheese into her hand and started away, putting distance between him and the craving she raised within him. And the doubts. He looked heavenward. *She is correct, Lord.* "I have anger inside. Always." *Twisting me up inside and burning through me.* Anger from watching his mother put to an early grave under heavy-laid hand and word. Anger because he'd been too afraid to come between her and his father. He could have protected her—saved her.

He pushed deeper into the woods. "I'm angry at the fear I had of that man." *That I gave him dominion over me.*

I'm angry at myself for becoming just like him.

Unwanted memory spurred him on. The blood covering his little brother's face and his own knuckles. He'd beat Jon within an inch of his life.

"I shall never forgive myself, Lord. And I cannot expect You to either."

He ducked under a low branch, and then slowed. He could no longer run from his rage or his fear—the fear that Lorinda was right.

The soft forest ground cushioned his knees as he dropped and clasped his hands. A fern tickled his arm. "Please, God, help me let go of this anger."

Chapter 9

Head resting on her elbow, Lorinda watched for any sign of Marcus behind the heavy foliage he'd disappeared through. If only there was a way to help him fight the awful legacy passed to him. . .but to do that she could no longer keep him at arm's length. Not a difficult thing if she were confident he truly was the man he'd portrayed since arriving in this valley—kind, gentle, and so very afraid of losing hold of the temper he'd been cursed with. But deep within remained her doubts.

She rolled onto her back and closed her eyes, hands coming to the increasing roundness of her stomach. She waited long, quiet minutes for the nudge of the child she carried. All was well, thanks to Marcus and the Lord above.

The breeze kissed her skin and the sun flickered through the dancing leaves overhead. A hen clucked, wandering across the yard in search of bugs, and one of the horses whinnied. For a perfect moment, it was easy to forget everything wrong. Especially with her head so filled with thoughts of that man, his dark blue eyes and all the concern they held. . .and recently something more.

She sighed and tried to think of something else, but it was impossible not to consider the strong lines of his face, so set with determination. His broad chest and powerful arms no longer frightened her as they had, but instead provided security as he willingly saw to every needful chore—even the menial ones most men would consider below them. The image of him hunched over the basin and washboard with her clothes in hand warmed her as surely as the July sun overhead. But nothing stirred her like his powerful presence each night at her side, arm brushing hers.

At the sound of hushed footsteps, Lorinda glanced to where Marcus had fled. No sign of him.

She pinched off a piece of biscuit and popped it into her mouth. She was becoming quite fond of the man's attempts at cooking. This was one of the few things he never failed. She would have to ask him where he'd learned. From his mother, who left him at such a tender age, or his sisters? Difficult to imagine any other Cowden male cooking anything more than his own coffee so long as a woman had breath in her.

The crunch of stone against stone pulled her up again. Nothing looked out of the ordinary, and yet a chill scurried up her arms and across her neck. She slowed her breath and searched the shadows. Surely she was imagining things and the breeze or one of the animals was the culprit. Nothing more.

All the same, she needed to bridle her wandering thoughts. Marcus's anger was just as present as Samuel's had been. Not even he could guarantee that neither she nor her child would ever become its target.

She picked up the cheese and reached for the knife.

A shadow shifted.

Lorinda jumped as a large raven flew from the branch she'd been staring at. A gust of breath and a half laugh relieved some of the tension. What a fool she was, spooking at birds. Marcus would surely have himself a good chuckle if he knew. Better never to tell.

"Marcus seems to be doing well for himself."

She twisted to the rumbling voice and the man who'd spoken. Dark hair, glowering eyes, and every bit as tall as Marcus. Only a little slighter across the chest and shoulders, more like Samuel.

"You aren't near so comely as I was led to believe, but how was I to know, with your *husband* keeping you locked away in that cabin." He stepped up to the tree holding the near end of the laundry line. . .and the musket. Marcus had left the gun leaning against the trunk.

The stranger smiled, stretching the scar marring his chin and lower lip. "He really needs to stop leaving things lying around. I swear I spend far too much time cleaning up after him. A musket. A wife."

Lorinda swallowed the fear closing off her windpipe. If this was the man who'd tormented them for the past three weeks, what else was he capable of? "My husband is not far. I will scream if you come near me."

His smile twisted into a smirk as he hefted the musket. "Go ahead."

"What do you want?" And why did he look familiar?

"What do I want?" He stepped closer and leered as though he'd lost all sanity. "I want him to wriggle on the hook a little while longer. Like a helpless worm nose to nose with a trout."

A horse nickered, and they both glanced to where the animals grazed.

"Don't worry. I'm not here for you. Today." He snickered and shouldered the musket. "But I will take this with me to keep things fair."

Fair? How was any of this fair? Lorinda glanced to the knife at her fingertips. Maybe she should taunt him closer, close enough to end this now.

A shudder shook her, and she pulled back. She'd not be able to bring herself to stab a man.

"Let that husband of yours know his time is running out. The day of reckoning

cometh." The stranger strode away as though he did not have a care in the world. Maybe he didn't. Maybe he was actually insane.

A day of reckoning.

Marcus ripped a robust cob of corn from its stalk and dropped it into the satchel hanging from his neck, the first of the crop, though only enough for a meal or two.

A day of reckoning.

The words haunted Marcus wherever he went the past three days since Lorinda told him of their visitor. They dogged his steps and sat heavy in his gut whenever he thought of his wife alone with a man who swore to do more harm. But nothing made him more ill than the thought of who the stranger might be. The dark hair, familiar features, and scarred lip.

It can't be.

And yet it was the only thing that made sense to him after hearing Lorinda's description. Somehow his brother had not only returned, but had followed him over the Blue Ridge Mountains. Jon would have had to travel hard to arrive in time to be responsible for the cow's death, but it was possible. For a man driven by hate.

Marcus had no one to blame but himself.

But what now? Wait and see what Jon did next, or seek him out and confront him?

Marcus's hand froze on another cob of corn. "I cannot fight my brother, Lord." *Not again.* But why else would Jon have come if not for revenge? What would it cost? A broken nose and bloodied face. Or more?

Did Jon wish him dead?

"No." They were brothers. Jon could have easily killed him before now if that had been his desire. He wanted to stretch out Marcus's suffering, make him wonder, make him question, as he slowly lost everything.

He'd made his little brother into a monster.

"Please, Lord, direct me." Marcus would take whatever punishment Jon had to give if it didn't involve Lorinda. But how could it not? She was dependent on him and this farm. And what if Jon decided he wanted to hurt her as well?

Marcus shoved one last cob into his satchel and hurried through the maze of cornstalks that stretched as tall as he. He shouldn't leave her alone for this long. He'd had her bar the door after he left and made sure the pistol was loaded and ready for her use, but uneasiness plagued him.

Arrow waited where he'd tied her at the edge of the field, and he swung into the saddle. The mare whinnied, anticipating their return, and a horse replied, but. . .from deep within the woods. Marcus spurred Arrow forward, down the rise and past the charred remains of the barn to where he could see the empty paddock.

A curse climbed up his throat as he reined his horse to the cabin. A minute later he'd looped the reins around a post and pounded on the door. "Lorinda, 'tis Marcus. Hurry."

The door swung open to her wide eyes and pinched brow. "What has happened?"

"The horse." Marcus grabbed the pistol off the table. "He stole the gelding. If I hurry, I can catch up with them."

"And then what?"

He stopped midstride to the open door and looked at the gun in his hand. *"And then what?"* One question he could not answer.

Frustration spiked through him, tendrils of a deeper, darker emotion wreaking havoc on his ability to think. With a growl, he threw the pistol against the wall. The weapon fell, broken, to the floor.

Just like he'd broken his brother.

Even now he could see it plain as day. Jon's bloodied face. The seething hate in his eyes. It didn't matter that two days earlier Marcus had received a similar beating from Pa because of a lie Jon had told, pinning the blame for something he had done on Marcus instead. It didn't matter that Jon had landed his share of punches as well. All that Marcus needed to remember was the despair. It wasn't just his brother he had broken that day—he'd broken himself. He'd become the man he despised.

As much as Marcus tried to run from it, to hide it away, he was still that man. Otherwise Lorinda—sweet, fragile Lorinda—would not be looking at him with such horror.

Her eyes welled, taking the fight out of him.

"I'm sorry." His own vision swam, and he staggered toward the door. He needed to walk this off and get back to work. Either that or get away from the cabin so he could fall apart without her seeing.

"Marcus." Lorinda beat him to the door and eased it closed. "You don't have to go."

He dragged his hand down his face with a glance to the rafters above. Was God truly somewhere beyond, and if He was, why make him this way—why give him such weakness?

"Marcus?" She sounded as uncertain as he.

"I don't know what to do." He looked at her and more anger drained away, leaving a vulnerability too reminiscent of his childhood. He didn't want to be vulnerable anymore. Better to be strong and protect oneself. Better to fight.

The tips of her fingers slid down his arm and slipped into his hand. "Breathe. That is all any of us can do. Just breathe. God gave us that much."

Marcus filled his lungs, unable to resist the plea in her voice. "You were right. Mayhap keeping your distance is for the best. There is such a battle going on inside of me." He cupped her cheek with his unsteady hand. "I don't want to hurt you. And yet that is all I have done. All of this is my fault. The barn. Everything is because of me."

"No, Marcus."

He nodded. She needed to understand that she was right. He was no different from any other Cowden—a coward too afraid to confront his own weakness. "I'm not a good man."

"I don't believe that anymore."

"And yet you are afraid 'tis true." Her eyes still held that fear. "You will always be afraid of me."

A tear tumbled down her cheek, leaving a moist path. "You don't have to be like them."

"I keep wanting to believe that, but. . ." He couldn't keep running from the anger. Waking or sleeping, it never let him be. "I need to walk." He turned to the door, but she still held his hand.

"Don't go after him. Not like this."

Angry or unarmed? Either way she was right. He would wait one more day.

Lorinda trimmed the lamp's wick before going to bed, but left it lit on the table for when Marcus returned. For he would return. He had to.

Tears, held at bay for hours, squeezed free when she closed her eyes. What was wrong with her? She'd sworn to never need a man again, to never care for one, and yet she couldn't deny the worry making sleep impossible. Or the bittersweet taste of longing rising in her chest at every thought of Marcus.

"Lord, please let him work through whatever is happening to him, whatever he is feeling."

Was it so wrong to hope she had been wrong about him and his ability to keep his temper at bay? Was it wrong to desire the kind and gentle man she was beginning to care for?

The door sighed open with a gust of warm night air.

"Marcus?"

The low lamplight showed little of his expression as he moved across the room toward the table.

"You must be exhausted. Come to bed. Try to sleep."

She sensed his nod as much as she saw it. He left the lamp in place and sat on the edge of the bed to pull off his boots. His shirt came next, drawn over his head and cast aside. As always, the frame groaned under his weight as he settled beside her, flat on his back.

"Are you all right?"

A moment passed before his head moved from one side to the other. At least the anger appeared to have subsided, but she wasn't sure what remained in its place. He probably desired to be left alone, so she followed his example and lay silently on her back, hands on her stomach as the child moved within. A sudden inward jab drew a gasp.

"What happened?" Marcus sounded so concerned, she had to smile.

"Just the baby. She is active tonight."

He released a breath reminiscent of a laugh.

"What?"

"Nothing. I was. . .I was just thinking about my niece and nephew, my sister's children." The sorrow in his voice tugged at her heart. "Sarah was also with child. She's probably already given birth."

The impulse to reach for his hand was too strong to ignore. She'd never heard a man speak of children with such tenderness. "You love them, don't you?"

"Aye."

Heart thudding, Lorinda guided his hand, laying it over her child's movement. Beside her, Marcus's breathing slowed. Then that airy laugh again.

" 'Tis amazing."

" 'Tis."

"He is a feisty fellow."

"*She*," Lorinda corrected.

Marcus turned toward her, placing his other hand on her stomach, his touch gentle. "You are hopeful for a girl?"

Though she could barely make out his features, it would be wrong to tell him how much she feared having anything to do with a Cowden male—even her own offspring. What if the child were a boy, would he be as much a victim to the Cowden temper as Marcus?

What if he were not raised under a heavy hand and implanted fear?

She grabbed hold of that thought, considering it further. What if the Cowden anger was taught? Generation to generation?

Then perhaps Marcus could break the curse after all.

Chapter 10

I think I know where he is." Marcus dusted his hands over his coat and straightened his hat—not that either required the action. "I can delay this no longer." Or Lorinda wouldn't have much of a farm left.

"I want to come." Lorinda followed him out of the cabin. "Perhaps I can help convince him none of this is necessary."

"No." The last thing he needed when confronting his brother was her to worry about. She claimed she felt better and had no pain this week, but that didn't make a ride across the valley a good idea—especially into a hostile situation. Because whether Marcus gave him one or not, Jon was here for a fight.

"But—"

Marcus braced her arms. "Lorinda, this is something I need to do on my own. And I need you safe." He needed it something fierce. The thought of anything happening to her filled him with a kind of dread even Pa had not invoked in him. Especially seeing her near, eyes large and filled with so much concern, sprigs of chestnut framing her face, lips full and slightly parted.

"Marcus. . ." Her tone had softened, and there was something about watching her mouth form his name. He leaned in, closing the inches that had held them apart.

Each of his senses woke. . .to the sound of her breath hitching in her throat, the taste of a summer apple on her lips, and the gentle touch of her mouth against his, moving as though to speak. But not with an argument this time. Though he'd closed his eyes, he could still see her, her face burned into his thoughts with such detail as to take his breath away. For a moment, it didn't matter what his brother did to him—death itself would not be so difficult to bear when feeling so complete and whole. Even the anger that had plagued him since boyhood had no place in this perfect moment.

Though the kiss ended, Marcus could not step away. He held her against his chest and simply breathed. Oh how his heart ached for her. But she could never truly be his unless he confronted his brother. . .and survived. He had to go.

Lorinda remained silent as Marcus started down the trail on foot. Hopefully the miles between here and there would bring the resolve he needed to not give in to the demons that haunted him.

Instead, they rose to the surface with their taunts.

Abner's children played out in the yard, but all came to a halt at the sight of Marcus's approach. One darted into the house and a moment later Abner's blond-haired wife appeared, eyes wide and jaw loose. "What did you do to him? Where is Abner?"

"What do you mean? I'm here for my brother. I know he has been staying with you."

"But they. . .they. . ." Constance's face continued to lose color as she stammered. "They went to your farm hours ago."

A bolt of raw terror shot through Marcus. "What were they planning?"

"I—I don't know. They did not talk much around me or the children. All I over-heard was Jon mumbling something about being done with games."

"No." Marcus had left Lorinda to them. "Do you have a horse?" He crossed to the woman, but she cowered away. "I need a horse!"

Her head wagged. "They took the horses."

His heart dropped to his boots as he spun on his heel and ran.

Enough waiting. Lorinda collected the bridle and headed out to the pasture. How could Marcus expect her to sit here while he faced a madman, unarmed and with no intention of fighting? Would he even defend himself?

Well it didn't matter. While Marcus refused to lift a hand against his brother, Lorinda held no such resolve. Not when it came to Marcus's life. Samuel's pistol was loaded and tucked in the waistline of her skirts.

"Come now, Arrow." Lorinda crooned so the mare wouldn't sense her anxiety. She slipped her hand down the smooth coat and looped the reins around the horse's neck to hold her in place while Lorinda slid the bit into her mouth. "Easy, now."

Once the mare was bridled, Lorinda led her to where the saddle hung over a fence rail. She fortified herself with a breath and eased it up and over. Next came the cinch strap. Lorinda had to pause after all was done, resting her hand over her stomach. All seemed well so far.

Once on the back of the animal, Lorinda took a second to straighten her skirts.

"Going somewhere, Mrs. Cowden?"

She startled at the voice and jerked to where *he* stood—the stranger. Marcus's brother.

Lorinda squared her shoulders, refusing to show her fear. "I planned to pay Abner and his family a visit. You have been staying with them, I believe? But why not? You are family. Though I believe Marcus to be disappointed that you chose not to stay with us. What would be more natural than to visit your own brother?"

Jon laughed, but with no mirth. "I have been visiting. I'm glad he finally figured it out. It will make today all the more rewarding." He moved quickly and caught the bridle.

"Why today?"

"Get down from the horse, and then we can discuss my. . .intentions."

The way he said the last word sent a chill through her. What choice did she have but do as he asked? "Very well."

She slid from the saddle, and he motioned her toward the cabin. "After you."

"What about the horse?"

He nodded to where a second man stood beside the smokehouse. "Abner will take care of it."

"So Marcus was correct. You two have been behind everything."

He again waved her toward the cabin. "He wanted the land, and I wanted my brother. Besides, we are family." He flashed a smile all too similar to his brother's, but bereft of any of Marcus's warmth.

"What about Marcus? You are brothers—you said so yourself. Why are you trying to hurt him?"

Jon gripped her arm, making her wince. "A slip of the tongue. He is not my brother anymore."

"He still sees you as his. He cares about—"

His palm met the side of her face with a flare of heat and pain. "Stop talking!"

She let him drag her the rest of the way to the cabin in silence, while her heart pled with God to intercede on Marcus's behalf, to keep Jon from whatever he planned.

"Marcus is too light-handed with you—has not taught you to keep your mouth shut. It would have been different if he had not stolen you from me. Imagine my surprise when I arrive home and the first thing I learn is that Marcus took off over the mountains after a bride who was intended to be mine. My sister showed me the letter. They asked for *me*, not him."

Bile rose in the back of her throat. This was the man her father-in-law had intended her to marry? Lorinda waited until he released her into a chair before chancing another question. "You are angry at him for coming here?"

"Quiet!" He lingered near the open door, fidgeting. Every once in a while, his hand hovered near the pistol strapped to his thigh. Most of the time, his back was to her. She only needed long enough to get her own pistol untangled from her skirts. She could save Marcus any pain. . .except for the loss of his brother. The other option would be to hold him at gunpoint until Marcus returned and then decided what to do.

She was still waiting for the perfect moment when Abner jogged into the cabin.

"All the horses are tied in the woods where they won't be seen. I will wait with them there." His gaze fell on Lorinda, and he scowled. "What are your plans with her?"

"That will depend on Marcus and how fond of her he is." Jon glowered at the trail. "But he better hurry back or my patience might not hold."

Chapter 11

Marcus swatted the sweat from his brow, trying to staunch the flow stinging his eyes. His chest hurt from its attempts to supply enough air to the rest of him. The heavy humidity didn't help his plight. His clothes were wet and his muscles depleted by the time he reached the cabin. He gripped the door-frame, his gaze going first to Lorinda before worrying about the man in the room.

"Your grudge against me does not involve her," Marcus panted, finally looking at his little brother—now a grown man. "Jon? Why are you doing this?"

Blue eyes as cool as raw steel stared back at him. "You ruined my life, Pa's life. And now I'm going to ruin yours."

"I'm sorry, Jon. I'm sorry for losing my temper—for what I did to you. I have regretted it every day since. But how did I hurt Pa? All I did was choose a different life."

His brother lunged, yanking him forward before slamming him against the edge of the doorframe. Pain bit his back. "You killed him," Jon yelled, his breath hot on Marcus's face. "*You* killed him!"

"He rode off with the Regulators. That was the last I saw of him."

Jon jerked his collar tight. "Because he died at Alamance. I found him there, a hole in his stomach and barely breathing. But he still had a few things to say about you, how you disobeyed him, abandoned him."

The first punch lit sparks in Marcus's vision and he tried to pull away, but Jon followed him out of the cabin, one hand gripping his collar, the other making the assault. Any thoughts of leaving himself at his brother's mercy drowned under the reflex of self-preservation. Marcus raised his arms to block his face. Just as a knee plowed into his stomach, doubling him over.

The taste of blood in his mouth and ribs smarting, Marcus gripped Jon's sleeves, leaning into him for support. "I won't fight you. You are my brother." One he was supposed to watch out for and defend.

"That did not stop you before." Jon again raised his knee into Marcus's middle, forcing him away, and then attacked again, fists meeting their marks with precision.

Marcus blocked a couple of the strikes, but there was only so much he could do without returning the blows. He couldn't do that no matter how badly Jon beat him.

He would not strike his brother.

A hooked blow to the side of the head knocked him to his knees. He dabbed at a trickle of warmth running into the corner of his eye and his hand came away red. Blood, not sweat.

"Fight me," Jon taunted. "I can take you now."

Marcus shook his head, a most regrettable motion, almost tipping him over. "I can't." He managed to regain his feet, and his brother swung, then faltered. Only then did a pistol's discharge register in Marcus's fogged brain.

A string of curses spewed from Jon's mouth as he grabbed at his torn sleeve, blood leaking through his fingers. He twisted to where Lorinda stood with a gun still raised, though completely useless to her now.

"No!" Marcus threw himself after his brother, catching Jon as he knocked the pistol from Lorinda's hands. Marcus bear-hugged him from behind and held on with all his strength. "I can't let you hurt her. You can do what you like with me, but do not touch her."

"Let me go!" Jon roared.

Instead, Marcus locked his grip. "I'm sorry. I'm sorry I hurt you. I'm sorry I wasn't stronger back then." Not that he was much stronger now. His head throbbed and dark blotches faded over his vision. He leaned his head into his brother's back, his own shoulders trembling. "We are brothers." Moisture leaked out the corners of his eyes. "You are my brother."

"No." The venom had gone from Jon's voice, leaving the word broken. "I hate you."

"I hated myself."

Marcus stiffened at a motion to the side—Abner running toward them, musket in hand. He skidded to a halt as Lorinda crouched for her empty pistol.

"Does your father know what you have been doing to us?" She aimed the gun at him.

Abner's expression wavered, whether from the mention of his father or uncertainty of the pistol's threat. He held his hands and musket to the sides. "None of that was me."

"Then why are you here?" Marcus demanded, not releasing his hold on his brother.

Hesitation preceded a reversed step. "Your horses and his are tied in the woods behind the cabin. I want no more to do with this."

Even after Abner's retreat, Jon made no attempt to move, but his sleeve was quickly soaking with scarlet, his wound gaping.

Though not ready to release his brother and chance another tussle, Marcus looked to his wife. "Lorinda, can you find some cloths and water to wash his arm? And bandages?"

She provided a nod and hurried into the cabin with the pistol. He heard its clunk on the table as she passed by.

When she returned outside, Marcus gradually relaxed his arms, braced for a resuming of the attack. He couldn't see his brother's expression or imagine what he thought.

Jon didn't twitch. Just stood in place, breathing heavily.

Marcus took a damp cloth Lorinda had prepared and pressed it into his brother's wound. He was rewarded by a low grunt, but nothing more.

"Mayhap you should sit down," Marcus offered, still not sure what to expect. "We need to cut your sleeve and dress the wound."

Jon shook his head. "I hated you."

"I know." Marcus understood hate well, and yet no longer felt it. Father was gone, dead, and only sorrow accompanied thoughts of him now. Even anger seemed distant at the moment, overcome by an incredible weariness.

"I want to hate you."

"That is your choice, but I'm finished." Marcus took his knife and cut Jon's sleeve so he could better wash the wound and bind it with a clean cloth Lorinda supplied. She stood stalwartly at his side, guessing his every need before he could speak it, but she had already been through enough today. As soon as he finished with Jon, he'd make sure she spent the rest of the day abed.

Marcus tied off the bandage and moved around to face his brother. "I meant what I said. I wish I'd told you back then how sorry I am—how sorry I have always been. The reason I did not ride with Pa was because I refuse to fight anymore. Only to protect my family."

Jon stared back, his expression crumbling. It was enough. Marcus pulled him into an embrace. "You are my family too." His vision swam and he closed his eyes against the burn.

Lorinda backed into the cabin, basin and bloodied rags her only burden. She left them on the table and sank into a chair. She would give Marcus and his brother the time needed for a hopeful reconciliation. Her child prodded her abdomen as though disappointed to have missed out on the excitement. Lorinda only hoped the excitement was at an end. No more barns burning. No more danger lurking. No more fear.

Eyes closed, she listened to the rumble of Marcus's voice, speaking with his brother. His deep tones seeped through her, offering security, safety. Minutes passed, and he stepped into the cabin. Alone.

A bolt of alarm jarred her. "Where is Jon?"

"He went after the horses." Marcus lowered onto the chair beside hers, weariness extended in his outward breath. "He will settle them in the paddock."

"What about his arm?"

"He will be all right. He needs some time alone, time to think."

Lorinda allowed herself to relax a little. "And you?" She leaned to him and touched the ridge of his ear, one of the few parts of his face unbattered. His left eye showed signs of swelling and blood trickled from a gash on his brow and from one nostril. "What do you need? Besides a good wash and perhaps a stitch or two."

His gaze turned studious as he focused it on her. "I need to put my wife abed before she does herself and the baby harm."

"I'm well. I shall lie down once I have seen to your face. And your ribs. Do they need to be wrapped?"

"I am not concerned about me, *wife.*"

Lorinda smiled at the glint in his oh-so-blue eyes. "*Husband.*"

His smile teased the corners of his mouth. He grunted to his feet and scooped her up in his arms to tote her to the bed. He winced with the motion but held back any complaint. "You may patch me back together from right here." He set her down but didn't pull away, arms braced on either side of her, face only inches from her own. "I was raised in fear, but I have never felt it like I did today, knowing you were in danger." He lowered his forehead until it rested against hers.

Lorinda breathed him in, his masculinity, his strength. Never had she felt so cherished. . .so much trust. Watching him take a beating, while never raising a hand against his brother except to protect her, had washed all her fears aside. She could trust Marcus.

She *did* trust Marcus.

And something more. Another feeling settled in her chest—a possessiveness, a yearning, and a joy she'd not experienced before. It drew her hands to the nape of his neck. She guided him lower until she could taste his mouth. . .and tell him exactly how she felt despite not knowing how to put it into words. *Love* came to mind.

Epilogue

November 1771

The familiar pains clenching Lorinda's abdomen brought a wave of panic, but she pushed it aside. This time she had nothing to fear. She had carried her child as long as needful.

"Deep breaths."

Lorinda eyed her husband and fought the urge to slap his hand away from her arm. "When was the last time *you* delivered a baby?" she demanded as the tightening eased with the pain.

"Pain is pain and breathing is never a bad idea." Despite the concern in those clear blue eyes, he looked far too pleased with the situation. There was some merit to his advice, fortunately. The deeper breaths did ease the intensity of the pains.

The next tightening came on with such strength she couldn't contain the moan in the back of her throat. And lying in bed was doing nothing for her. She shifted onto her knees.

"What is wrong?" Marcus followed the motion, jumping out of his chair to support her shoulders as she moaned again. "Are you all right?"

"No, I'm not!"

"Maybe I should send Jon to find my aunt or Constance. They can help you better than I. You have been laboring for hours now."

Lorinda waited until the end of another tightening before shaking her head. Jon had stayed on to help rebuild the barn and bring in the harvest, but relations with Samuel's family remained strained, and she didn't want either of those women with her.

Now that she thought of it, and with the pressure again growing within her, she wasn't so sure she wanted to finish this whole process. If only there was a way to pause and go back.

No. She didn't want to go back. She wanted this baby. This life. No matter how much it hurt.

Over the next hour, the waves of pain continued to deepen, until there was nothing left to do but give her body free rein. Finally, Marcus scooped up the perfect, wriggling infant and placed him in her arms.

Lorinda laughed as she drew her tiny boy to her chest, no longer afraid of bringing another Cowden male into the world. The man who would raise him was most worthy of the title of father. And husband.

Angela K. Couch is an award-winning author for her short stories and has been published in several anthologies. She was also semi-finalist in ACFW's 2015 Genesis Contest with her Colonial romance, *The Scarlet Coat*, Book One of the Hearts at War series that was released by Pelican Book Group in 2017. As a passionate believer in Christ, Angela's faith permeates the stories she tells. Her martial arts training, experience with horses, and appreciation for good romance sneak in there as well. Connect with Angela at www.angelakcouch.com.

Across Three Autumns

by Denise Weimer

Prologue

S he first sensed someone watching as a prickle of awareness on the back of her neck as she and Hester floated, shift-clad, in the creek. Even in the cool waters, the fine ginger hairs from Jenny's nape to her arms stirred, and she froze.

Casting an eye over her shoulder, she saw him: a brown, bare-chested native, his face smeared with black and red war paint. He did not even attempt to conceal himself. After all, the White family may have brought their livestock out from Augusta and built a cabin four years prior. They might have planted their small patches of corn, wheat, and flax alongside the vegetable garden Jenny and her sister had been weeding in the fork of Long and Dry Fork Creeks before yielding to the urge to cool down from the sun's blistering rays. But this had been his land. Whether Hitchiti Creek of the first people in these parts, or Muskogee who came from the West many years ago, he belonged and she did not.

But the brave's alliance with the British made him Jenny's enemy. She was old enough to remember from North Carolina what the British could do. She had given up too much—her little brother's life and her best years to make a good match, for starters—to just hand over this land.

Thank God Gabriel had not taken the Brown Bess hunting today. Jenny spied it propped against the giant oak that marked the ford. With the steady diagonal trajectory of a water bug, she waded toward Hester and the tree.

Hester's head—curly strawberry-blond hair darkened and dripping—broke the surface. She started to let out an exclamation of delight but gave only a gasp when Jenny's firm hand encircled her wrist. Green eyes wide, she allowed herself to be towed toward the shore.

"Hester, run for the house. Make sure Ma and the baby stay inside."

The younger girl's eyes trained on the forest and found the focus of Jenny's concern. "Oh dear Jesus, please save us," she whispered.

"Jesus saves those who save themselves."

Hester had started to shake like a Quaker overcome by the Spirit. And for good reason. Just last summer, she'd watched Thomas Dooly, a seasoned officer, die at this very spot from a wound inflicted by a member of Creek Chief Emistisiguo's war party. Attempted revenge for that death had sent Thomas's brother John, now their new county's representative, to a court martial. And it had led their father to construct a loopholed stockade, rude but surmounted with lookouts at each angle, around his cabin and outbuildings last fall.

But now their father fought in Florida under their neighbor, Lieutenant Colonel Elijah Clark. And John Dooly, still bent on vengeance for his brother's death, again commanded troops as a colonel of Wilkes County militia. With his troops out against other Creek raiders, and even Hester's twin, Gabriel, not yet fourteen, hoeing corn furrows for a neighbor soldier's wife, the fort house offered pitiful protection to the White women. A few burning arrows could reduce it to ashes in a matter of minutes.

In her gut, Jenny knew only a bold and fearless show of strength might save them. But first she had to get Hester out of view.

She shoved her pretty sister from the water. "Run. Bolt the stockade door."

Hester cowered on the bank, covering her dripping shift with her arms. "Not without you!"

"One gun on the lookout could never hold them off. We only stand a chance if I show we do not fear them. Now go." Jenny hoped her voice conveyed bravado she did not feel.

Jenny stood to her full, wiry height of almost six feet, red hair hanging unbound down her back.

"Have you taken leave of your senses?" Hester gasped.

Another Indian moved into view, finally startling Hester to flight.

Jenny heard the fort door close but never took her eyes off her adversaries. Palm up, she extended a hand toward the forest and said in a calm but loud voice, "We have no fight if you leave in peace. But I will defend this land if I must."

The first Indian did not move. The second, crouched behind a hickory, strung an arrow.

Jenny's legs started quivering like a newborn colt's. *Oh God, Father, hold me up. Send us the protection of Thy mighty angels.*

The next moment, what felt like a large insect brushed her thigh. She looked down to see the ragged tear in her shift left by the Indian's arrow. Jenny gritted her teeth, sudden anger unfurling from her middle and rushing up in a bellow of protest. What cowardly man shot a lone woman standing next to naked on a creek bank?

Jenny took one long step and had fourteen pounds of Brown Bess in her hand. She had already rammed powder, ball, and wadding up to the breech. As she crouched behind the oak, the first brave simply watched her, but she heard war whoops among the trees. She pulled back on the dogshead to cock the weapon and gazed down the barrel.

If she killed the brave who tested her now, the others would kill her and overrun the fort. If she did nothing, they would overrun the fort. In a flash, she noticed the long tree branch extending above the man's roached and feathered head. She sighted from breech pin to muzzle like Father had taught her when they bark-chipped squirrels out of trees. Thank God she had always been a better shot than Gabriel, preserving the most meat possible. May God preserve them today.

Jenny fired. The brave did not even duck until the branch almost hit him. She plastered herself against the tree as a din of yells and shots rose.

She did not look, just prayed. And reloaded. Fast. Jenny had two choices: kill as many as possible as they forded the creek in hopes that Gabriel might hear the din and return before they had their way with Mother, Hester, and Libby. . .or raise the muzzle to her own head and spare herself the certain horrors to come.

Suddenly a voice of command rang out. "*Wahatchee.*"

Following another sharp order, silence fell.

Chapter 1

January 1, 1779

Scarcely after midnight, Jenny had just settled into a slumber as decent as the cold loft allowed when a pounding on the cabin door made her sit bolt upright. Beside her, Hester levered to a similar right angle. Beneath them from the one-legged bed, their mother gasped, "Asa, get the gun!"

They heard Gabriel scramble down the ladder and their parents scuffle around below, loading the musket and igniting a stick of fatwood in the banked embers of the hearth. Hester's small-boned, chilly hand slid over to tangle with Jenny's. "Well, it cannot be Indians," the younger girl whispered. "Else they would have already tomahawked the door down."

"No, but perchance someone fleeing them."

They counted their June escape a miracle. Settlers puzzled over the strange markings that appeared on the "fork tree" at White's the morning after the incident, conjecturing that Jenny's bravery had earned the Indians' protection. To her chagrin, she had become something of a local legend. That fall, word came that Creek Indians destroyed two county forts, McNabb's and Nail's. Now people scurried for the safety of Ft. White's walls at the slightest provocation.

"Who goes there?" their father's voice boomed.

The cheer of the reply belied the scolding words. "Yer fellow hatchet man, freezin' his rear off. Will ye not admit me and me friends from this cold?"

"It cannot be!" They heard the soft thump of the musket's stock contacting the floorboards just installed a month ago. They both lunged for the edge of the loft as their father slid up the bolt. In the low light of the burning brand, he offered a back-thumping embrace to a large, tall form, while several other shapes stood silhouetted in the moonlight behind.

"Happy Hogmanay!" the newcomer exclaimed.

"Whist, man, where did you come from? You cannot have been lurking about the wilderness for the sole purpose of crossing my threshold first on your silly Scottish holiday!"

"From Ft. Martin, and the wilds beyond. But I do admit to using the moonlight to my advantage to claim 'first foot.'"

"Do you bring good luck or bad?" Father questioned, but Jenny could hear the grin in his voice.

"A mixture, I warrant. On such a dire mission, I lack the traditional gifts, but I do have a packet of salt on my horse." He drew out a silver flask. "And this, in hopes you will share your hearth."

Jenny's mother shuffled about said aperture, removing the curfew from the coals and spreading them with her poker, while Gabriel lingered in the awkward waiting stance of youth.

"Dire?" Father's voice lowered, dropping the teasing edge. He waved the men in. "Come in, Caylan, and all your friends. Welcome. Tell us your mission and how we can help."

Hester pinched Jenny's arm, demanding her attention. "He called him Caylan. Jenny, I think he be the McIntosh."

"The McIntosh?" In the noise of the travelers divesting themselves of guns and accoutrements and settling onto benches around the smooth-drawn boards Gabriel brought from the wall and laid over the trestles, Jenny started fumbling for her wool over-petticoat. "Even if he is the Caylan McIntosh Father speaks so highly of, he would hardly be '*the* McIntosh.' I durst say that honor would be due to his grandfather or great uncle or one of the other older and more important heads of that clan near Savannah."

"What are you doing?"

"Getting dressed. They are bound to be hungry." She grabbed her apron from its peg and tied the laces.

Hester's exasperated look said Jenny always demanded to be in the middle of any action. Jenny did not wait for her scolding but pushed aside the bearskin that separated her brother's corner of the loft from theirs and wiggled down the ladder. She landed with a thud just as Father introduced their guest to Gabriel, causing the man's head to swivel in her direction. His look of surprise was nothing new to Jenny. She towered over most men, intimidating and alarming them with her bright-red hair and sturdy frame, but not this one. No, this one was over six feet himself, and the look he gave her. . .could it be admiration? At the notion, embarrassment licked its way from her toes to her scalp, making her cheeks heat.

Father gave a sigh. "This is my eldest, Jenny." As the buckskin-clad arrival reached for her hand and gave a slight bow, he added, "Meet Caylan McIntosh, Jenny, the crazy Scots I told you about."

In the firelight that Mother had managed to resurrect, Jenny could see that Caylan's hair, clubbed with twine, glowed like the rich mahogany of a wealthy merchant's sideboard she'd admired once in Augusta. When he spoke, his voice was teasing. "And what, pray, did he tell you of me?"

He still held her hand. She pulled back. "He said that you led the charge at the Battle of Alligator Bridge and broke your horse's leg trying to leap the last ditch separating you from the British regulars."

The light left those amber-tinged brown eyes. "Dinna think that was my choosing, lass. He was a good horse. When I realized the ditch was purposely dug too wide, 'twas too late. I have never wished to make mince-feet of anyone so bad as I did those red-coated macaronis that day."

"And yet Clark called the retreat," her father supplied. Jenny broke her gaze away from the Scotsman.

"He had little choice," Caylan agreed. "They had us hemmed in, and Clark himself was wounded."

"I was never so glad as to get my husband back from that campaign," Mother put in, "and I hope he never has to repair to the tangled swamps of Florida again."

"Well ma'am, 'tis not to Florida I would take him, but Savannah."

"Savannah?" she asked. "Why?"

"The city has fallen."

A feminine gasp from the loft caused Caylan to look upwards. A dark shape moved out of the light, and he continued.

"General Howe, uncertain where the British would land once their ships were sighted, spread out his troops. When a slave led part of the landing party through the swamp to flank him, he lost eighty-three killed and eleven wounded."

"Oh no," Mother murmured. She knew what this meant, that she would lose her husband again, prematurely, before spring even greened the trees.

Distress written on his gently lined features, Father turned to Jenny. "You should go back upstairs to bed."

"I came down to help Mother," Jenny said, moving to her mother's side. Besides, nothing could prevent her from hearing the rest of Caylan's news now. They would have to drag her back up the ladder, and she doubted any of them were strong enough to do so, save Caylan himself. While her father was built sturdy, the three-month stints of militia service over the last few years had left him worn, shadowed.

"Oh ma'am, we's not expectin' victuals at this hour," one of the men protested.

His burlier companion elbowed him. "Speak for yerself. I ain't et since we left Cherokee Corner."

"My Elizabeth will see that all are satisfied," Father said, with pride in his voice.

"We can heat yesterday's cornmeal mush," Mother told Jenny. Under her mobcap and silvering corkscrew curls, her eyes told Jenny both of her gratefulness for her daughter's assistance and her concern over what the family themselves would now have to break their fast.

Jenny nodded, seeking out the butter bowl as Mother placed her short-legged iron spider over the heat.

"Is Clark at Woburn now?" her father asked.

Jenny knew he referred to their neighbor's plantation, now fortified and known as Clark's Station, about eight miles east on Red Lick Creek, another fork of Long Creek. After recovering from his Florida campaign wound at Sunbury, south of Savannah, Clark had returned to the care of his wife, Hannah. But Jenny guessed the lieutenant colonel had already mobilized in the face of this new aggression.

Caylan confirmed it. "Clark's regiment musters across the river at Ft. Charlotte. He sent me and several other scouts into the backcountry to gather new recruits and those on leave. You have met the Morris brothers here from across the Oconee. Philip Dunst of Scull Shoals is stabling the horses. Others will come. I thought to stay until dawn to set out for Clark Station, then on to South Carolina."

"By all means," Father agreed. "And the enemy?"

Jenny listened intently to the men's now low voices as she fried the mush over the fire. Though she knew better than to give any man a second glance, Caylan McIntosh commanded the room. Scout or no, he clearly hailed from warrior stock.

"The Georgia banks of the Savannah River are controlled by a Loyalist force under Col. Daniel McGirth. We expect Campbell in Savannah to be reinforced and make Augusta his next conquest. The lobsters think to find their own recruits in these parts, to turn the war against us."

"So we take the fight to them."

"Aye. Can we count on ye, Asa White?"

"You know I am always there for Clark. And even his Sawny neighbor on the Broad."

Surprised to hear her normally straight-laced parent, since her youth in North Carolina a convert to the New Light Baptist persuasion, use a slang term for a Scotsman, Jenny glanced up to see her father sit back from the table with a half-smirk. Somehow this McIntosh brought out his youthful, mischievous side. The same, however, could not be said of her mother. No one but Jenny saw the grimace that twisted her dainty features at her husband's military commitment. It vanished by the time the stout, short German, Dunst, seated himself at the table and accepted the hostess's offer of cider.

He twisted around to acknowledge her. "Thank you, ma'am. I am plumb chapt."

Mother offered a stiff smile as she reached for the wooden trenchers on the shelf. After slicing a portion of salted fish onto each, she came to kneel by Jenny. "Almost ready, daughter?"

Wrapping the iron spider's handle with a rag, Jenny moved it forward. "Yes."

Mother passed her the plates as Jenny served with a spatula.

Gabriel's voice came, pitched almost as low as his elders'. "Father, I wish to go with you."

Mother's head jerked around.

"Nae, son, you are too young," Father replied.

"How old are ye, boy?" Caylan inquired.

"Fourteen."

"There are some in the regiment of that age."

Mother stood and scowled. "Not my son. Who would protect us at Ft. White?"

Gabriel's gaze turned toward his sister as she rose from the hearth and brushed off her skirts. "Jenny."

At the guffaw that issued from one of the Morris brothers, Jenny felt telltale color infuse her cheeks again. Gabriel did not help by continuing, "You all know she shoots better than I do, can hoe a straighter row, and even knows how to tan hides. She is no stranger to hard work—"

Father's command cut his son's sentence. "Gabriel, that will be enough."

"Mayhap we ought to enlist the sister, Lieutenant," the older, taller Morris observed, leaning a shoulder into Caylan's.

Father continued as if he had not spoken, his gaze on Gabriel. "I could not do my duty knowing I left my womenfolk alone in the wilderness. You will remain and man this fort house."

Her brother hung his head and released a quiet breath of frustration.

"Many civilians are fleeing to safety in the Carolinas," the German told them.

Jenny put her hands on her hips and spoke without hesitation. "We shan't flee."

When her father nodded, she moved toward the loft ladder. But as she passed the table, Caylan's hand shot out and touched her arm. She glanced down in surprise, her heart skittering to her stockinged toes as their gazes tangled. "Something tells me you must be Wahatchee."

"*What?*" Jenny had not forgotten the word the warrior in the forest had bellowed across the creek. She had just never thought to hear it again.

"The carved letters on the trunk of the tree that stands at the river's fork. They spell '*Wahatchee.*' And there is also a sign instructing travelers to pass by the land in peace."

She placed a hand over her galloping heart. "There is?"

Caylan nodded. Jenny felt the others watching. She could not look away from the Scotsman.

"What does *Wahatchee* mean?"

A slow grin creased the corners of his mouth. "War Woman."

Chapter 2

Caylan's words, "others will come," came to fulfillment. All that day, men and boys slipped into the White compound. Gabriel tended the many horses overflowing their humble stable. Some of the men went hunting and returned with a couple of turkeys that kept Jenny and her mother busy dressing and baking. Hester slipped into the role of hostess, drifting among the men with tankards of cider. They treated her with tender respect, like she was a grand English lady. Jenny grit her teeth at the way Caylan's eyes followed Hester's softly rounded girlish form, laced into her best winter petticoat and stays, her golden curls trailing from beneath her cap.

She was used to it. She was. The frontier had just made her forget a little. The frontier flipped things backwards, making a strong, tough girl desirable and a weak, delicate one a liability. The presence of men always put things back in order.

"What are they doing outside?" Hester stopped to ask Caylan as he sat before their fire oiling his fine Kentucky rifle.

He glanced up with a smile. "Building a bonfire to celebrate Hogmanay. Your father approved it."

"Even though we employ prayers to keep evil spirits at bay," Mother put in from the board where she kneaded the supper bread, "and have no need of fire."

"Aye, 'tis just for fun. We even have a fiddler among us for a bit of music and dancing."

Jenny paused in greasing the bread pan. To cover her lapse, she hurried over to restack the homemade wooden blocks her youngest sister, Liberty, almost three, knocked down.

"I hope your men are keen on dancing with each other," Mother retorted. "You know my husband does not hold with such diversion."

"I am aware of his persuasion, which I believe comes from your time at Sandy Creek?"

"That is correct. The first time Mister White heard Reverend Stearns preach, he left his Congregationalist background behind. I have never heard a man speak with such fire."

Jenny still remembered the sermons that had drawn settlers from the Yadkin

River Valley, up to forty miles away, to the Sandy Creek Baptist Church. She had puzzled a long time over the "new birth" the dynamic preacher referred to. Finally, her mother explained it meant giving her life to Christ and allowing the power of the Holy Spirit, the third member of the Godhead, to enable her to put off the "old Jenny" and live as a "new Jenny." She had agreed to that, but over the years, many times "old Jenny" seemed to keep emerging.

"Then, madam, you must not have heard the address of Elijah Clark." With a smile that made Jenny's heart blood pause in its courses, Caylan put away his cleaning rag and fixed the ramrod of his rifle.

"Oh, 'tis different. I speak of religious fervor, although I own what we experienced during the Regulator Rebellion stirred my husband's patriotism."

"I have heard of the rebellion against Governor Tryon's unfair taxation."

"Oh dear. Your mitten needs mending," Hester observed, fingering a pulled thread on the knit half-glove on Caylan's right hand.

Basting the surface of Mother's bread with melted butter, Jenny frowned.

Caylan smiled at Hester and said, "I was just going to see to that. See here, I have my mending kit." He dug in his haversack.

"Never mind, I will get my sewing needle. A soldier must not concern himself with such trivials."

As though knitting and simple work are so very exhausting, Jenny thought, carrying the bread to the grate her mother had placed over the hearth coals. Jenny situated the bread with a long-handled shovel, turning up the corners of her mouth to show appreciation of her mother's sympathetic look.

While her younger daughter went to fetch her sewing kit, Mother began to clean the board. "As we were saying, Lieutenant McIntosh," she resumed, "not only unfair taxation, including using monies intended for public schools to build his palatial mansion, but repression of the worst kind. Much as it is here, the inland settlers resented the coastal aristocrats occupying all the positions of political power. Separate Baptists and Quakers saw alike on that and formed the Regulators."

"Did not the Regulators use violence to make themselves heard?"

Hester returned and drew Caylan's mitten off with gentle fingers and gentle smile. Jenny's stomach felt sour as the brine they sometimes used to pickle meat.

"Some did, although Shubal Stearns did not sanction violence. But when the governor raised troops to form a militia against the Regulators, we all united. Doubtless you have heard of the Battle of Alamance, in '71?"

Caylan sipped his cider. "I have."

"A hundred and fifty wounded, twenty dead. Six Regulators hanged. Tryon sent troops to Sandy Creek to find those in hiding, burned crops and farms, forced oaths to be signed. Most left the area."

"Did Asa join that fight?" Caylan's tone showed this came as a surprise. "He never mentioned it."

Mother shook her head. "In light of the fact that we lived closer to the Yadkin, and he had a young family, my husband only supported the Regulators in principle. But after that, things changed. And when we heard of the new land opening up in this area. . ."

"A fresh start," Caylan agreed.

On the floor under the table, Libby scattered her blocks and started to cry. Jenny bent to lift her.

"Here, you are busy. Set her on my knee for a horsey ride," Caylan offered.

Jenny paused in surprise. Most men wanted nothing to do with babies, especially those not their own. "Have you little siblings too?" she asked, taking a step in his direction but still holding the toddler.

"Sure an' I have, siblings and cousins aplenty. You can trust me. I shan't spill her."

Jenny lowered her sister onto Caylan's muscular thigh.

"What's her name?"

"Liberty, since she was born in '76. We call her Libby."

"Ah, a fittin' moniker, that one. Hello, Libby." Lightening his voice, Caylan leaned over to tweak the babe's button nose.

Jenny hovered a moment to ensure cries of protest did not break forth. Instead, as the lieutenant began to talk to the little girl and waggle her up and down, her face wreathed in smiles. A longing rose in Jenny's heart that she promptly squashed, asking, "Did Father say all your family remains on the coast?"

"Aye. My grandfather came over from Inverness to found New Inverness, what's now known as Darien, in 1736, with Highlanders recruited to hold off the Indians and Spanish from swarming north to Sunbury and Savannah. He was killed at the Battle of Bloody Marsh."

"How remarkable." Hester's needles paused. "Do the Scots still dress in their native way?"

"Yes, my family wears the *feileadh mhor* and *brogs* and carry their broadswords and targes. And of course, Brown Bess muskets." Caylan grinned.

"Why do you not?"

"I find buckskin and leggings much more practical—and subtler—on the frontier." He gave Hester a wink.

She flushed prettily, not like the pulsing red that frequented Jenny's face.

"What made you leave the coast?" Jenny asked.

Caylan tilted his head to look up at her. "You see before you a maverick, Mistress White, one who prefers quiet to clamor and the solitary to the clan. A Scottish anomaly."

His words pierced her. Had she not often felt the same way? Like she stuck out like a sore thumb in this White family? In this English family? She bit her lip and nodded.

Caylan broke her gaze, looking to Hester as he placed a finger on a hammered metal pin at his waist. "I do wear this though. The clan brooch with the cat-a-mountain."

While Hester murmured her admiration and Caylan brushed a stray curl out of her face so that she could see, Jenny turned away.

As dusk fell and the bonfire in the clearing was lit, Caylan joined his men tossing torches and telling stories. Gabriel escorted Jenny to the river to wash trenchers, causing her to eye the singing, laughing, recumbent linsey-woolsey and buckskin forms around the popping orange flames with longing. But when, hands chapped numb, they returned to the cabin, their mother paused her sweeping long enough to fix them both with a piercing eye.

"Put it from your minds," she said.

"I have to feed the livestock and the soldiers' horses, Mother," Gabriel pointed out in a dry tone.

Jenny hastened to add, "There are so many he will need help."

"Fine, but the minute you hear Old Scratch's fiddle, hasten inside. I fear some of those men have been much in their cups."

Jenny could not tell if Caylan McIntosh was one of those. Judging by the volume of the tale she overheard from the livestock pen, it seemed possible.

" 'We sir, are fighting the battle of America and therefore disdain to remain neutral,' my good cousin wrote." Caylan stood to give the words greater effect. She could see his form silhouetted against the bonfire as she forked hay to the horses.

" 'The battle of America,' what brass," someone exclaimed.

"Wait, it gets better!" Caylan pointed a finger at the recruit. "The good lieutenant colonel in charge of Ft. Morris then stated, 'as to surrendering the Fort receive this reply, *Come and take it!*'"

Hoots, laughter, and cries of "come and take it!" reverberated throughout the stockade. You would have thought the Patriot Highlanders and Howe's troops had mowed down the British ranks of Lord Cornwallis himself, Jenny mused. But the fighting spirit of the militia encouraged her. She knew how these men fought: laying ambushes, tracking, and traveling long distances in record time like the Indians. Once they drew the British regulars into the backcountry, the red-heeled fops wouldn't stand a chance.

The unseen fiddler took his cue. The notes anchored themselves inside Jenny's chest, with invisible strings tugging her toward the sound. Caylan and presumably several other Scots started a jig. From his fancy footwork and agile leaps, the lieutenant appeared dead sober. She found herself propping the pitchfork against a wall and drifting closer in the shadows, her mother's previous warning drowned out in the waterfall of lilting notes.

When the musician warbled into "Soldier's Joy," a woman faced off with her husband. As they greeted and turned, two frontiersmen leapt up to join them. Caylan looked around as though searching for a partner and noticed Jenny standing just outside the circle of light. He came toward her, hand outstretched.

"Come, lass, will ye dance with me? Ye know this one."

Indeed she did. She had seen settlers perform the steps on the Yadkin River. Before Jenny had time to think, Caylan whirled her into the circle, and a man dancing a female part grabbed her for a ladies' chain. She caught a brief glimpse of Gabriel's alarmed face as she whizzed past.

Delighted with the actual women who joined them, the men paid courtly attention that caused Jenny's face to flame. But none more than the sensation of Caylan's eyes, warm amber in the firelight, fixed on her every time they met. The roughened strength of his large hand made hers feel small.

When the song changed, Jenny gave an awkward curtsy and tried to back away, but her partner caught her arm. " 'Tis just a Cumberland Reel."

"I know no Cumberland Reel. Remember, we do not dance."

"Oh. I did forget that." But Caylan's smirk hinted otherwise. "Seems to me Wahatchee would not grow lily-livered at a wee promenade. See, 'tis only a skip step, toe to heel?"

Jenny turned her lips down. "Wahatchee has a mother."

Caylan threw his head back and laughed. "What? That slip of a woman has a Highland princess like you all a'cower?"

"I am English, sir." She clasped her hands behind her petticoats.

"Well, pardon me, my lady," he retorted with mock offense, "but yer regal bearing and coloring beg otherwise. I wager some hint of Celtic besmears the White family past...far back in the recesses of time, no doubt."

The "regal coloring" went up in flames. Jenny repeated what she'd heard her mother proudly state many times. "We come from pure English stock."

"Well then, I dare ye to prove a proper English lady has no fear of a Cumberland Reel."

"Those are break-teeth words, McIntosh. If I chose, I could dance until daybreak, and still be dancing long after you collapse." So saying, Jenny stalked to the tail of the reel and waited for the laughing Scotsman to follow her.

Just like firing a gun, riding a horse, dragging brush, and swimming, dancing provided no challenge. Jenny did all physical things well and with endurance. What she had not expected, however, was the way Caylan's obvious approval made her feel. It answered a craving deep inside that she had attempted to discredit for years. Not to mention the brush of his fingertips, the pressure of his hand on her waist, spread the bonfire to her bones.

Jenny stood off to one side as he went to get cider, fighting the urge to flee before he glimpsed admiration on her face. She would be twenty this spring, too old for girlish fantasies. She heard the Morris brothers talking in front of her.

"Think I shall see if I can steal the ginger-pated wench from McIntosh. A hearty girl like that could bear some strong sons."

"No doubt, brother, if you look the other way as you bed her."

Raucous laughter and spilled cider accompanied the remark that punched like a mule's hoof to Jenny's chest. She had already started for the cabin when she noticed her parents pressing into the celebration, worried faces portents of coming ill. Good. She could slip around behind them and climb up into bed. As for Caylan, she could avoid him when the troop departed at dawn.

He might admire her spirit and strength, but when it came to picking the wife he would want to wake to every morning, like the Morris brothers, like all men, he would choose a Hester over a Jenny every time.

Chapter 3

Jenny's back ached. She paused to rub it, standing upright to survey Gabriel tugging a repaired log onto the split rail fence surrounding the potato and corn patch where she spread manure from a homemade barrow. Her eye caught a moving form on the path across the river.

Calling her brother, she nodded toward the gun propped nearby. He had just palmed the musket when the rider came into view. Jenny released her anxiety in a puff of breath. There might just be some delight in that sigh too.

She hurried to Gabriel's side and waved. After Caylan's brown stallion splashed across the creek, Jenny called, "Lieutenant McIntosh! Do you bring us news?" They had seen and heard little since the troop departed in early January, a month and some ten days now.

"Aye, Miss White, and not of the good variety," he replied, swinging down with the ease of long legs but the stiffness of endless hours spent in the saddle. Caylan nodded to her and shook Gabriel's hand, then glanced toward the stockade as the other womenfolk emerged, Libby on Mother's hip.

"Come inside and let us refresh you," Mother urged.

"I must be speedy, Mrs. White, for a small party of Loyalists be on my tail."

She placed a hand on her heart. "What shall we do?"

"I suggest you repair posthaste to Ft. Martin, for the few behind me are of the least concern." Caylan removed his tricorn hat and smoothed the hair come loose from his queue, then met their wide eyes. "We hemmed some British in at Carr's and were about to fire the fort when General Pickens got word a troop of Loyalists passed through Ninety Six, headed for Georgia. They march under James Boyd, an Irishman from South Carolina commissioned to recruit in these parts. We tried to head them off on the Broad. They got across north of us and are now at the ferries there. Our men head for Clark's. Nail's men scouted north of the Broad, but Clark loosed me south of the river to ride ahead of the enemy and report their movements. I had to warn you I expect the entire British force to cross Long Creek before nightfall."

"Merciful heavens," Hester whispered. Caylan's hand shot out to steady her elbow when she swayed.

"West at John Hill's stockade you should be safe. But you must make haste."

"There will be battle," Gabriel observed. "The armies are too close."

"Yes. I fear so."

"Take me with you, Caylan. I can mount up in ten minutes."

"Gabriel," their mother moaned, a cry of fear at the thought of abandonment in the face of danger.

Jenny reached out and took the musket from her brother's hand. She glowered. "You know what Father said. We need your help getting away on time."

"I do not report to you," Gabriel snapped, squaring his still-slender shoulders. "Clark's son returns from North Carolina to fight by his father. With battle brewing mere miles from our land, would Father not have me do likewise?"

Caylan took in the cringing stances of Jenny's mother and sister before he replied. "You should do your duty as your father last outlined, lad. I spoke to him before riding out, and while he asked me to send you to Hill's, he spoke naught of your enlistment."

Gabriel's jaw, untouched as yet by any fair beard, clenched.

"Go prepare the livestock," Jenny told him, returning the musket. He promptly shouldered it and stalked off. Mother hurried after him. Jenny's fingers twined in the reins of Caylan's stallion, and she looked into his brown eyes. "We must show your horse to ford Dry Fork and continue south, but circle back into the creek and hide in the swamp west of here till they have passed."

"Aye." As he took the leather, his fingers briefly encircled hers. "I will be close enough to come to your aid should there be trouble."

She looked away. He meant the touch to be reassuring, nothing more. What did it say that her fear of McIntosh facing a British scouting party alone frightened her more than diverting them herself? She blinked, focusing on the business at hand. "We shall deal with them. You should keep yourself concealed and complete your mission."

Hester cleared her throat. "And pray, what is my task, to pack?"

Caylan's gaze gentled as he looked at her. "Aye, lass. Hurry."

She gave him a longing look before scurrying away. Jenny called after her, "Hester, should these scouts stop in, conceal your preparations and get in bed as though you are ill."

Wide-eyed, over-the-shoulder glance illustrating her alarm, Hester nodded. Her toe slipped on a patch of grass dampened by recent rain, and she almost fell before running into the stockade.

Caylan looked back at Jenny with a glow in his narrowed eyes. "Clever lass. Methinks we can count on you to keep them alive."

Fifteen minutes later, Jenny felt the absence of the Scot's presence like an ache in a molar when she returned to the fork. She hadn't time to trundle the barrow inside before three mounted men appeared on the Indian path. She grabbed the shovel and went back to work, pausing to act surprised as they splashed into the water.

"Ho! Woman!" called the ringleader, a stout, crusty man with greasy raven's hair, as he pulled up next to her. He wore the dress of the backcountry scout rather than a British regular.

Grateful her childhood pranks had included practice of letting one eye roam on its own, Jenny looked up at him with lack of visual focus and her lower lip hanging slightly slack. *"Ja?"*

"Has a man ridden this way recently?"

"I seen no man." She avoided his gaze, smoothing manure beside the hoofprints of Caylan's horse.

A companion edged his mount closer. "Whaddya mean? Them is fresh tracks right there!" He pointed to the ground with his rifle butt, then poked her shoulder with it. "Where you hidin' him?"

Pretending to be startled, Jenny let loose her shovel, scattering cow dung over the man's boot and stirrup.

"You bracket-faced, stupid wench!" He hit her over the collar bone with his weapon.

Jenny's bellow of protest disintegrated into wailing. Hoping her racket warned her mother and siblings, she fell to the ground and covered her head. "I seen no one, I seen no one!" she kept yelling as she thrashed about.

Out of the corner of her eye, she noticed the third man had followed the tracks. He edged his horse between Jenny and her offender. "Leave off, Little. The frau is clearly betwattled. See here, the rebel rode on south."

"Ja, he went thatta way!" Jenny cried and pointed without looking up.

A clod of flying spit deposited on her neck as a calling card, the Loyalists thundered off. Jenny remained a minute with her head covered, heart thudding, thanking the good Lord above for endowing her with ample acting skills. She could take the stage in Charleston, she could. Then, rubbing her collar bone, she sat up and looked around, laughing.

Her sister came flying out of the stockade sans cap, face the pastiest white Jenny had ever seen. "We saw them leave! Are you all right?"

"Yes." Jenny stood and brushed dirt off her petticoat.

"Will they come back?"

"Not until after we are gone." Jenny studied her sister, touching her arm. "Are you that frightened, little dove?"

"No, silly, Mother put flour on my face when you screamed. She said they would search the house, and I must look pox-stricken."

Laughing again, Jenny grabbed Hester's hand and ran. "It would seem you need me less than McIntosh thought." On the cabin porch, she asked, "Are you packed?"

"Yes, but Jenny?" Hester stopped and glanced toward the shed.

"What?" She tried not to sound as impatient as she felt.

"You have to tie the cows on the rope and take off their bells. I fear our brother has gone to the war."

Like most frontier stockades, the walls of Ft. Martin contained several ramshackle, small cabins apart from the family abode. These now sheltered not just the Whites but women and children from several other area families. After bringing her mother and little sisters to relative safety, Jenny lay awake. From her place on the hard floor, she listened to the sounds of breathing and watched the shuttered window for signs of dawn. When faint pink lit the cracks, she slipped from the quilt next to Hester and made her way to the horse pen.

She found Merry's saddle in the barn and called the mare.

"Where are you going?"

About to mount, Jenny whirled to see her sister wrapped in her cloak against the soft drizzle. Behind her, lights flickered in the Hill family cabin, and a wisp of smoke curled from the chimney. "I. . .have a bad feeling. I cannot hide here and wait for news."

"What is the bad feeling?"

Jenny swung into the saddle. "I only aim to ride out a ways and scout. And if I can, to bring our brother back. I will be safe. I know these woods better than any man."

"Yes, but you are *not* a man. What would happen if the wrong rogue came upon you?"

Jenny lifted her chin. "I would like to see him try anything."

Hester shook her golden curls. "Yes, but you have no gun, Jenny."

Jenny patted the bow and quiver strapped to her back. "I should rejoin you here today or tomorrow."

As Hester launched herself forward, Jenny tapped the mare's sides with her heels. She could not stay to listen to her sister's fears, and she could not explain to Hester the intense pull she felt toward the south.

True, she thought as she rode east along Long Creek, at first she had been angry with Gabriel. But she could not blame him for going. They shared the same volatile blood, the same longing for freedom.

When the walls of Ft. White appeared ahead, Jenny paused long enough to enjoy a moment of relief and investigate the stockade with caution. Provisions had been taken, cleavers strewn about on the floor from the torn-open mattress, the three-legged stool broken. Likely only the extreme haste of the invaders had spared their home the torch. Their livestock remained safe at Ft. Martin, and their hiding place under the floor still concealed their medicinal herbs, precious seasonings, tools, and coin. Jenny lifted out the wooden box of herbs she and her mother had dug and dried the previous season, placing it in her haversack.

Jenny set out following the Indian trail the Loyalists had taken the day before. Since the underbrush was cleared off with annual burnings and the canopy of forest above kept the drizzle off, the going was not rough despite the narrow path.

As she rode, she considered her mission. She did hope to bring Gabriel back. She considered him little more than a boy-child, yet something about a brother's presence transferred the invisible mantle of responsibility from her shoulders. With Gabriel gone, she was less "womanfolk" and more protector. Was she not already capable enough?

But there was more. Looking deep within, Jenny knew she feared not for Gabriel, but for Caylan. She doubted not the Highlander could care for himself. But men died in battle. And the thought of him dead felt as if a panther's claws sundered her chest. Was she really so needy that the passing attention of a kind man enlisted her immediate devotion?

Jenny came to what had been a campsite, deciphering that another large host had crossed the same ground more recently. The Patriots.

A distant din lifted on the morning air. She paused, listening. Yes, drums and muskets. Capping her canteen, she spurred Merry on, sick to her stomach. The sound of battle grew louder for a time, but about noon, silence descended, while thick smoke hovered.

With sounds of her approach no longer covered by the noise of the fray near Kettle Creek, Jenny slowed her pace. Of a sudden, she saw cardinal red through the trees. She dismounted and hid herself until she ascertained the wearer of the cloth lay fixed against a tree. Wounded? Dead? Looping Merry's reins around a sapling, she approached Indian-like until it became clear the regular in white and crimson had expired. Thanking God for His marvelous provision, Jenny lay claim to his Brown Bess and necessary accoutrements.

As she led her mare forward, the trail that wound to a cattle pen atop a hill in a bend in the creek became increasingly littered with men: wounded, dead, and prisoners in small groups herded by soldiers in buff and blue. "What has happened here?" she asked the first Continental line officer she saw.

"A great victory for the Patriots, ma'am, and a clear message to King George III he shall not raise troops from Georgia."

Jenny let out a breath in relief. "And our wounded?" She held down Merry's head as the horse snorted, disturbed by the smell of blood. She tried not to study a British officer a stone's throw from them, his face blown away by a musket ball.

"Still scattered on the battlefield."

"Where did Colonel Clark fight?"

"Pickens spearheaded the main battle here, when we caught Boyd's men parching corn and slaughtering cattle. He tried to hold the fencerow but fell in the retreat. In fact, the colonel was just there, tending the rogue's dying requests. Dooly and Clarke flanked the enemy, bursting from the swamp on the other side of the hill just as the scattering lobster backs re-formed across the creek." He pointed.

"Have the colonels and their regiments quit the area?"

"Yes ma'am, marching on toward Savannah."

Then all that was left was to scan the wounded. Thanking the officer with scarce a look at the contingent of sullen and bedraggled prisoners, Jenny hurried away. Heart in her throat, calling out for her father, brother, or Caylan, she visited each fallen man. The wounded begged for aid. She paused only long enough to offer a word of comfort and a sip from her canteen. She thought of the herb box in her possession but could not spare the time to employ its contents. Not until she knew if those she sought lay crumpled in the tangled bog near Kettle Creek.

Jenny noticed a trampled patch of cane where an English soldier lay face down in the mud. His blood splattered the remaining stalks. On the other side of an oak tree, in a man's inert grasp, lay a rare beauty of a Kentucky rifle—one she had last seen gleaming by the firelight of their cabin. With a cry, she rounded the inlet.

"Caylan!" She knelt beside the scout and slid a hand under his neck.

His eyes sprang open, and he fumbled to raise his weapon.

Jenny waved her hands. "No, no, 'tis me, Jenny White!"

"Zounds, woman, I could have killed you! What are ye doing here?"

"Looking for my father and brother. Gabriel followed you, you know."

"I know. I tried to send him back." Caylan struggled to a sitting position but grimaced and paused on his elbows.

Jenny's lips parted as she saw fresh blood ooze onto his legging below his fringed shirt. "That looks bad."

"The ball's still in there."

Reaching into her haversack, Jenny flicked out a long hunting knife.

"Whoa!" Caylan yelled.

She bit back a grin. "The ball will have to wait," she said as she nipped the linen haversack strap at both ends. "But I do have an ointment that should help staunch the bleeding."

She tugged on the damp rip of Caylan's leggings until the fabric parted a bit more, causing him to grunt. As Jenny opened the herb box and removed a small pot, Caylan craned to watch. She raised her skirt to cut off a length of her linen shift, making a thick pad of the material. After dabbing his wound, she paused with a glob of ointment on her finger.

"What's in that?" he asked with some suspicion.

"Yarrow."

"My people make such an ointment, but how did ye come to know of it?"

"Can you raise your leg up a bit?" As he complied, she smeared the medicine onto the pad, then used it to cover the gaping hole in his flesh. Lower lip between her teeth, Jenny secured the material with half of the haversack strap before glancing up. "I have a way with herbs, and I ask everyone I meet of their herb lore."

Caylan hung his head back and closed his eyes. Through stiff lips he muttered, "Your father and Gabriel are fine. With Clark."

"Thank God. So I suppose the sense of urgency I had was for you."

Confusion clouded Caylan's brown eyes. "For me, lass? What do ye mean?"

Jenny gave her head a dismissive shake. "I did not understand it, I just felt I had to come. I thought I was to bring Gabriel home, alive, wounded, or dead, but I think God put it in my head to follow the armies here to aid you. I will bring you back to our place."

"Why would God send you to me?"

"Do you not believe in Him?" Jenny tied the knot and looked into her companion's eyes.

"Yes." The word hissed out between his teeth. "'Tis for His freedom that I fight."

Jenny nodded. "Then 'tis why. Come, lean on your rifle, try to stand. I must get you on my mare."

As she placed an arm under Caylan's shoulders and moved toward Merry, he muttered in her ear, "'Tis possible He did send you, and with a sense of humor."

"What do you mean?"

"Do you know what today is?"

Jenny shook her head.

"St. Valentine's. The first person ye see of the opposite sex on this day is destined to be yer spouse." His breath stirred her hair in a laugh.

But she had the sense he was not laughing *at* her. Her confusion over that caused her tone to be all the more defensive when she retorted, "Well, you are hardly the first man I have seen today, so to the devil with your Scottish fables."

"Yes, but ye are definitely the first woman I have seen. And ever by far the most remarkable."

Jenny was left to ponder those words long after Caylan passed out and she cradled the slumping weight of him on the ride home.

Chapter 4

Dark had fallen by the time they reached Dry Fork Creek. Despite her cloak, Jenny's face stung from the cold mist, her chapped hands stiffened on the reins, and her arms ached from holding Caylan on the horse. No chance was she continuing to Ft. Martin. She rode into the eerie silence of her family's stockade. Halting Merry right in front of the cabin's porch, she dismounted and tugged until the Highlander slid off with a groan. She barely caught him.

"Lieutenant McIntosh." Jenny lightly slapped at the whiskering face. "You must hold yourself up. I may be strong, but I cannot carry a *gilly gaupus* such as yourself."

"Now ye use my own people's words against me. Why should I wish to enter a house with a woman so set on giving me a good chivy?"

"Because if we do not get that lead shot out, you will surely die."

"Huzzah. More torture ahead." But Caylan shuffled over the threshold, leaning heavily on Jenny.

In the dark, she led him by memory. She was barely able to single-handedly toss the ruined mattress on her parents' bedstead before the lieutenant collapsed on it. His feet hung over the end.

"I will return posthaste once I see to the horse."

Having unsaddled, fed, and watered the horse, Jenny fetched water from the creek. She bolted the stockade gate and carried the pack burdens to the cabin. She heard Caylan's labored breathing as she felt in the inky blackness for the tinderbox. Adding kindling to the grate, she reached for the flint. It took a number of tries, but finally welcome orange light illuminated the room. Jenny sat back with a sigh to find Caylan watching her.

Jenny fed the fire, then brought a dipper of water to the bed. She helped him sip and settled his head on Mother's prized goose down pillow. Lowering the dipper from her own drink, she saw with dismay that Caylan's entire leg was slick and dark. She released a shaky breath.

"Slide the oilcloth from my pack under my leg," Caylan said.

Jenny did so, then told him, "I will boil water."

"Use the whiskey in my haversack. Pour it on that knife of yours and on the wound."

Jenny bristled. "I know what to do."

"Well, ye dinna know about the whiskey, now did ye?"

She placed a hand on her hip. "I might have guessed."

The disheveled head raised in protest. "I never drink to get drunk, lass, just to avoid the galloping sickness when clean water's not to be had. Much like yer cider."

She firmed her lips at the mention of galloping sickness and turned to her task.

"Hey, hand me the flask. Under the circumstances, getting a wee bit rammaged is in order."

"Well, in this case, I agree." Jenny put the silver container in Caylan's hand.

She built up the fire, hung a cauldron of water over the flames, and screwed a precious beeswax candle in the holder beside the bed. Minutes later, she perched next to McIntosh with clean rags, tongs, and the knife. Caylan bit his lip as Jenny removed his boots, then he reached under his shirt to untie the woven garter holding up the sodden legging. Gingerly she peeled it off and dropped it on the floor. A trickle of blood ran from under the useless bandage and dripped on the oilcloth. Breathing shallow, she raised her eyes to his.

He nodded. "Ye can do it, lass."

Jenny swallowed hard, removed the pad, and dabbed the wound with a rag.

"The bullet went straight in. I think it lodged against the bone. Lucky it must not have hit a major channel, or I would have bled out by now."

"Dutch comfort." Jenny splashed the round wound with alcohol and reached for the knife. Holding her breath, she leaned around to avoid creating a shadow and inserted the knife to hold the flesh back. She gasped, "I don't see anything."

Body stiff as a poker, Caylan spoke through gritted teeth. "Then ye're gonna have to fish for it, lass."

The next few minutes were the worst of Jenny's life, and she imagined Caylan's too. How he did not pass out or even scream boggled her senses. By the time the small metal ball chinked into the tin cup on the bedside table, the lieutenant lay as limp as a fought-out fish on a bank. She splashed more whiskey on the wound, which roused him with a stifled curse, then applied another yarrow bandage. Breathing hard, Jenny staggered to the porch, where she washed her blood-soaked hands and leaned on the post to steady her stomach and heart. She drank in lungfuls of the cold, woodsmoke-scented February air.

Finally composed, she returned to the cabin to slide more whiskey and water between Caylan's parched lips and gently wash his leg and hands with the boiled water and lye soap. At last, she pulled Mother's quilt from its hiding place under the floorboard and spread it over his recumbent form. Jenny rose to make her way to the loft when a hand snaked out and took hers.

"Stay," Caylan whispered. His eyes glowed molten in the firelight. "Lie beside me. Please."

Jenny's heart shot to her throat and lodged there, making her unable to speak. She shook her head. "'Twould be unseemly."

His lips turned down. "Tell me how I am to take advantage of you in this state."

"Still, 'tis not right."

"Who will know?"

"That is not the point."

"What are you so afraid of?"

Standing silent, she felt sick.

He dropped her hand, turned his face toward the wall. "Go then."

She could never resist a challenge, and challenge this was, for all its camouflage. Jenny toed off her shoes, lifted the quilt, and slid in beside him. The space was so limited she had to face him. She tried to tuck her arms at her sides, but Caylan caught her hand and pulled it up to his chest, clasped in his. She looked up, surprised.

He smiled down at her. "Ye did good, lass." His fingers chafed hers a minute, then he fell asleep, his deepened breathing accompanied by the popping of the fire.

Exhausted as she was, Jenny lay frozen in wonder. She felt his heartbeat beneath her fingertips, not strong, but strong enough. Smelled his scent, sweat, smoke, leather, and spice. She studied the dark-brown hair fanned out on her mother's pillow and the shadows on Scottish cheekbones and nose. The stubble on the square jaw. The softness of lips in repose. She shuddered with longing. She had better soak in this moment, because it wasn't likely to ever come again.

Jenny woke with the dawn, startled and guilty to find her head cradled on Caylan's chest. She stole from the bed to the fireplace to stir up the coals and boil water. The lieutenant's blood-darkened bandage sent her to the creek beds in search of fresh yarrow or plantain leaves. While she was out, she washed as best she could. Her hair felt heavy, greasy. Seeing that her guest still slept upon her return to the cabin, she left an elderberry and yellow dock tea steeping while she allowed herself a quick hair washing.

The warm water on her scalp felt wonderful. By the fire, she dried and combed the long red locks. Her one beauty. Well, that and her name. Did Caylan like her hair?

The Whites did not own a looking glass, and Jenny avoided them in stores and other people's homes. The Loyalist had called her "bracket-faced." While she did not consider herself harsh featured, her bone structure was strong, and a smattering of freckles kissed her nose. But Gabriel said he could always tell when Jenny was up to something by the light of mischief in her doe-brown eyes, and Hester said Jenny's smile stopped the sun. So it must not be all bad. Mostly, she wished for a dainty form like Hester's. Her height and build made her feel like a mannish oaf, devoid of grace. But last night, lying next to Caylan, for the first time she had felt like a sparrow nestled in a crevice of the rock.

What was this sudden preoccupation with her appearance? Jenny drew in her lips, shoving the comb into one of her shift pockets and going to start the morning mush.

She froze when Caylan called her name. It had the sound of a North Carolina mountain brook. Beautiful indeed. So startling she jerked around and frowned at him.

"Who gave you leave to call me that?"

"'Tis yer name, is it not?"

"Not the one you should be using."

Caylan pulled himself up on his elbows. "Well, no need to get uppish, *Miss* White. I just thought having a lass dig a bullet out of a man's leg, then passing the night side by side, might entitle the pair to the use of Christian names. Can ye look at me leg? 'Tis paining me something fierce."

"Of course." Jenny gathered boiled water and fresh linens and hurried over, contrite. What right had she to sass a wounded soldier? Surely his sacrifice granted him an extra measure of grace. "I brought plantain leaves to make a poultice, and prepared a tea."

"And washed yer hair." Caylan's tone softened as he grasped a stand between his thumb and forefinger, letting it trail through his grasp. She froze in the act of untying the old wrapping. His wistful gaze dissolved in a blink. "Sorry. I don't need you venting your spleen again."

Jenny glanced down. "I won't. And you may call me by my given name, at least when we are alone." To distract both of them as she applied the poultice, she asked, "Will you tell me of my father and brother in the battle? Did Gabriel acquit himself well?"

"Aye, lass. We tied our mounts before the battle—"

Her hands stilled in horror. "Did we leave your horse at Kettle Creek?"

He grinned. "No, some other well-bodied Patriot rides him now. I know the man, and he will return him if both survive."

"You think they go straight to another encounter."

"I think it unavoidable."

Jenny shuddered.

"Your brother will be fine. At least, he has as much chance as any of them. I did not see much of him along that cane-choked creek, but I know he shot at least two of the enemy. He is as much frontiersman as any. And a boy of almost fifteen is considered a man, you know."

She sighed, bathing Caylan's now bandaged leg. "I know. I think it is just extra hard because we lost our younger brother shortly after we moved here."

Caylan cocked his head. "You did?"

"Yes. To rattlesnake bite. Increase was only nine."

" 'Tis a hard land. Lachlan McIntosh lost his younger brother Lewis shortly after he came here too. . .to an alligator during a swim in the creek." As Jenny's widened eyes met his while she offered the tin cup, Caylan nodded. He cradled the tea and continued. "All men die, 'tis just a matter of when, and how bravely. Let it be said of me when I go that I went down fighting. Your brother and father are of the same mind, lass, 'tis why we are such friends. At least we have the comfort of knowing where our family members go when that moment comes."

Jenny nodded, figuring this was not the proper moment to engage the wounded man in a debate over Separatist Baptist free will versus Presbyterian predestination.

Caylan dipped his head to take a sip. Jenny was resisting the powerful urge to smooth back his loose hair when he spit and yelled. "For mercy's sake, woman, what did you put in this brew?"

"Elderberry and yellow dock. To strengthen the blood and ward off possible distemper." Jenny laughed. "Now be a brave Highlander and drink it all down. You must rest."

"Agreed, although I feel powerful in need of a good scrubbing myself."

"Later. Raise your head up a minute."

Caylan eyed her with suspicion but did as she requested. Jenny slipped the wooden comb from her pocket, slid the half-entangled twine from Caylan's mahogany locks, and ran the tines through them. She tried to think as if she was doing Libby's hair, efficient and quick, but it was not like that at all. It felt far more personal than she had expected. He looked handsome and vulnerable with his hair about his strong features. When she finished, she helped him ease back onto the pillow.

"Caylan?" She froze. She had just spoken his given name completely without intention.

He made no comment, but his gaze was tender as it lit on her. "Yes, lass?"

"If the armies go to the coast now, do you think it safe for me to fetch my mother and sisters home?"

"I do."

"Will you be comfortable if I go?"

"Dinna worry about me. I shall probably still be sleeping when you return."

Jenny nodded. "Then I shall prop your gun by your bed and ride out posthaste."

His eyelids drifted shut. "Thank ye, Jenny, for taking such good care of me."

Her heart warmed. She rose, but she stood there watching him sleep. She did not want to go get her family, most especially her lovely little sister. She wanted to linger in this cabin alone with Caylan McIntosh, pretending what would never be.

Chapter 5

Jenny clattered the dishes as she cleared the board, then seized the broom. Maybe if she ignored McIntosh's scout friend who'd arrived today from Nail's troop, he would go away. He told them Lieutenant Colonel Prevost had routed the Americans at Brier Creek near Savannah, returning the lower part of the state to British rule. And worse, hundreds of Indians under a Colonel Taitt laid siege to hapless settlers.

Evidence of the native uprising arrived only minutes ago, a sixteen-year-old boy and his grandmother from the tail of Dry Fork, burned out by the Indians. They now occupied a small cabin in the enclosure. The resultant call to arms for all Wilkes Patriots over the age of sixteen meant Caylan would be leaving with this wiry hatchet man, John Dunn. So would the youth, judging from his murmured conversations with the soldiers.

So now not only must she worry over her father and Gabriel, but Caylan as well.

He was not even healed yet, though he had said to her just yesterday, "I need to go back, Jenny. If I can cross-cut your land, I can sit a horse."

The fact that she would worry for him stung like a hornet. It helped not that the man sat over there now oiling his rifle, his splayed leg almost touching Hester's skirt. Jenny was also out of temper with Hester, who dropped in seeds while Jenny made furrows and sat with piecework in her lap while Jenny cleaned up after dinner. Jenny's back hurt so bad from planting in the new ground around trees Father had girdled before he left that she scarce could swing the broom. Meanwhile, Hester hummed a soft tune to accompany the men's military preparations.

"What is that, Miss White? 'Johnny Has Gone for a Soldier'?" Dunn's glittering, dark eyes fixed on her.

" 'Tis indeed."

"You have a nice voice. Would you sing it for us?"

"I fear singing would slow me, Mr. Dunn, and I must finish this last shirt."

" 'Tis good of ye to make more than one shirt each for yer father and brother, lass," Caylan commented, glancing at Hester's quick, fair hands.

"Why, this shirt is not for them, Lieutenant McIntosh, but for you."

Jenny's sweeping ceased.

"For me?" Surprise colored Caylan's voice.

"Yes. I could not help but notice how threadbare yours is. 'Twas not improper given the circumstances, was it, Mother?"

"I think it good-hearted," Mother said, taking a seat next to her daughter. "And I also think it would be kind to oblige Mr. Dunn's request. Then 'tis my fondest hope Lieutenant McIntosh will read to us from my husband's Bible. I fear this may be the last occasion for a while."

" 'Twould be my pleasure, ma'am." Caylan turned to Hester. "And I thank you for your generous gift."

When her sister rendered her tune, Jenny took the ashes out to the hopper, but the sweet notes followed her into the cool March night.

"Here I sit on Buttermilk Hill
Who can blame me, cryin' my fill
And ev'ry tear would turn a mill
Johnny has gone for a soldier"

Jenny clasped her arms around herself as the haunting melody swirled around her, making her want to dissolve into unexpected sobs. What was wrong with her? She must get hold of herself. Noticing a movement from the smaller cabin, Jenny straightened. The boy stood on the porch, watching her.

When Jenny went back in, her mother suggested, "Let us hear from the Psalms tonight."

Jenny lowered herself onto a bench while her mother placed the priceless Bible from England on Caylan's lap. She expected to hear of God keeping one from the arrow by day and the pestilence by night, or Him being a shield and strong tower, but Caylan read from Psalm 139.

" 'Whither shall I go from thy spirit? Or whither shall I flee from thy presence?' "

Hearing the passage in the man's deep, Scottish lilt made Libby fall asleep in her mother's bed, sucking her thumb, and Jenny's heart flip over.

" 'Thou hast covered me in my mother's womb. I will praise thee; for I am fearfully and wonderfully made: marvelous are thy works; and that my soul knoweth right well. My substance was not hid from thee, when I was made in secret, and curiously wrought in the lowest parts of the earth. Thine eyes did see my substance, yet being unperfect; and in thy book all my members were written, which in continuance were fashioned, when as yet there was none of them.' "

Jenny shifted on the bench, taking pressure off her sore thighs. She glared at him. Had he chosen this passage on purpose? To goad her? She was glad when he concluded, " 'See if there be any wicked way in me, and lead me in the way everlasting.' "

"Amen," said her mother.

Even Dunn bowed his head a moment.

"Thank you, Lieutenant," Hester whispered. The look she turned upon him was almost worshipful. Jenny wondered why everyone would insist on wedding vows had Hester spent the night alone with the wounded man, but when Jenny did, all she earned was a look of concern. Now, the younger girl said, "There, I believe the shirt 'tis done. Would you try it on, Lieutenant?"

Jenny got up. "Excuse me. I shall see to the livestock for the night."

After a few minutes of shoveling hay to the horses in the barn, a long shadow fell over her. She whirled to behold Caylan. In his new shirt. She pressed her lips together and continued her task.

"Soon the livestock can be turned out on the greening grass, the peavines, and wild oats," he observed. Limping slightly, he moved around her and took the pitchfork out of her hand. "Rest. Ye have done enough today."

"And you have not?"

"Can ye never accept an offer of help?"

"Thank you, I shall milk the cow." Jenny turned to fetch a bucket, but Caylan dropped the tool and caught her hand.

"Why are ye out of temper with me, lass?"

"I am not."

"Yes, ye are. Is it because I am leaving? Ye know I have to go."

Jenny pulled her hand away. "Of course. I *want* you to go."

"And why is that?"

"To fight for our freedom, naturally."

"And is that all? 'Twouldn't have anything to do with your sister?"

Why did he insist on speaking what should not be spoken, what she thought remained hidden? "Why should she have bearing on aught?"

"Because her differences from ye stick in yer craw, and make ye think yer own attributes lacking."

Jenny's gaze swung to his, hot and accusing. "You *did* read that passage on purpose."

"I wanted ye to hear how the Creator views ye."

" 'Curiously wrought.' Yes, I caught that part."

"Is that what ye think of yerself?"

"I know what I am, and I know what I am not. And I fail to see how it is any of your concern."

"Then I will tell you. Did ye know the Scots women of New Inverness held property? Were trained in the Manual of Arms? Served the cannon of Ft. Darien when the men left to fight the Spanish? 'Twas the heritage of my own grandmother, and a proud one. When I look at ye, Jenny White, I see her. The kind of woman bred to life on a frontier. The kind who not only survives, but thrives. Yes, yer sister is lovely, but she was not the one who stood her ground before savages, or fed her family through the winter. Or got this wounded lout on a horse, fished a bullet out of his leg, and cured him with herbs. *Ye* did that, Jenny White. It's ye who stirs my blood. So yes, I am leaving tomorrow. But rest assured, I will be back."

Throughout this speech, Jenny stood petrified in the stable door. In two long strides, Caylan took her in his arms. Jenny's world spun when Caylan claimed her mouth with his. Her first kiss. It melted her, seared her, like butter in a hot skillet, immersed her, like the sun-drenched creek water on a fine summer's day, cleansed her sore-aching aloneness with a flood of being desired and desire. She grasped his strong shoulder blades through Hester's shirt as his fingers tangled in her hair and drank in the essence of the man she knew in that instant she loved.

"Sweet heavens, lass." Caylan pulled back long enough to stare at her in wonder and run a thumb over her bottom lip. "Did ye think what passed between us after the battle meant nothing? I knew from that night when I held ye in my arms, rammaged as I was, that ye were the only one I ever wanted there again. Do ye believe it now?"

No. She did not believe it. She was living a wild dream that she would soon wake from.

A dove cooed just outside the fort wall. Caylan cocked his head.

"'Tis only a mourning dove," Jenny whispered. She trembled with longing. She wanted to touch him, run her hand over his hair, his jaw, but she daren't.

His expression hardened, filling her with fear. "No. 'Tis not."

Before she could react, he had her by the hand, running to the cabin. He burst in the front door with speed and, for such a large man, amazing stealth. Everyone inside leapt to their feet. "Indians," Caylan hissed. "Arm yourselves."

A night attack. Almost unheard of. An Indian scaled the fort wall and tomahawked the neighbor boy on his porch before the Whites and their guests gathered their weapons. The wails of the grandmother drew the militia men out. Caylan's gun fired, dispatching the native in the yard, while Dunn picked off another just clearing the stockade. The men ran to the loopholes, Jenny and her mother taking the other two. Mother carried Caylan's sawed-off Bess meant to be used from horseback.

The full moon would have provided just enough light for the Creeks to slip into the fort to murder the settlers, but the settlers still struggled to distinguish the Indians from the shadows in the woods. The Indians fired pitch arrows into the enclosure. Hester ran with wet burlap to beat the flames. More and more arrows sailed in with effect while more and more lead shot zinged out without any. Hester's cries grew frantic. Mother, then Jenny, abandoned their posts to assist. Another two natives tossed grappling hook and line up the wall, but Caylan's and John's expert marksmanship dropped the men in the clearing.

For a few more minutes, the women beat out flames and the scouts rammed and fired. When Jenny ran to the wall, Caylan told her, "I think they are gone, but we should watch till dawn."

"I will resume my post." Her eye fell on the elderly woman, weeping in the yard as her grandson took his last breaths. "The tree's carving did not stay them."

"What would have happened had John and I not been here?" Caylan wanted to know. "They will come back. And next time ye shall have no militia to guard yer walls."

"Other settlers will come now, hearing of the attacks."

"Women and children," Caylan spat, turning his head to scan the trees. A smear of black powder darkened his jawline. "Ye must convince yer mother to go. She will if ye suggest it."

"Go where, Caylan? We have no relatives, no town."

"Better a refugee camp than having yer home burnt down around you. I dinna want to return to that, Jenny."

The anger in his voice pushed her away. She sat at her loophole until dawn, and John's investigation confirmed the party of warriors had retreated. Caylan was still cold, distant, as he packed and saddled the dead boy's horse. She brought him yeastless biscuits, jerky, dried fruit, and nuts, little enough for the miles ahead. She did not care that her family watched, she only wanted him to take her in his arms as he had the night before. Kiss away her fears and anguish.

Having secured his pack, he turned to her. "Come with me."

"I cannot."

His jaw worked, and he looked away.

"Please, I cannot bear your anger." Jenny touched his arm. "The protection of the tree may have failed, but God's has not."

"Ye're a foolhardy woman, and I can see ye're going to be the death of me." He reached down to unpin the McIntosh brooch from his shirt. Stepping up to her, he secured it on her bodice. His eyes bored into hers. "Be here when I come back for ye."

Chapter 6

For about a week after Caylan gave Jenny his brooch, Hester withdrew, but then expressed her pleasure that the lieutenant loved Jenny.

"He did not say he loved me," Jenny corrected her. But then, neither had she spoken those words. Their courtship had been too rushed, too unconventional.

"The feeling between you 'tis clear," Hester disagreed. "I envy you. At least you have known love."

Jenny did not doubt what she felt, but neither could she hold Caylan to a pledge he had not made. She would not be one of those pitiful, pining women. She turned her attention to what lay before her: nurturing the wheat, corn, vegetables, and flax, that plant so vital to the production of clothing. She often scouted the land around the fort for signs of intruders. Despite her vigilance, one day while soap making, Liberty noticed an eye at the knothole.

Lightning quick, Jenny flung hot lye from the cauldron at the peeper. The resulting howl of pain confirmed her accuracy, and she hurried to hog-tie a spying Loyalist. His capture gave her an excuse to visit Hannah Harrington Clark at Ft. Clark, where Jenny turned the man over to militia.

She admired the colonel's wife. A large, decisive woman, Hannah regaled her with tales, including how she had made a dozen frilled-bosom shirts for Elijah the winter past, only to have one of her maids reveal their smokehouse hiding spot to a British raider. She also related the amazing release of Stephen Heard, whose slaves, Daddy Jack and Mammy Kate, rode to Augusta to rescue him from jail. Taking in fresh clothing, six-foot Kate carried the small-statured officer out on her head, concealed in the hamper of dirty linens.

Hannah always possessed the latest political news. Colonel Dooly had dealt a measure of peace to Wilkes County that summer and fall of 1779, staying the Creeks at Gunnell's Fort and condemning seven Tories to death. She told of government wranglings in Augusta, the robbery and murder of Captain Robert Carr, and the capture of their neighbor, Patriot leader Stephen Heard.

On the ride back from Ft. Clark, Jenny basked in the red sourwoods, the birdsong, the earthy scent of decaying leaves, and the camaraderie she'd experienced with another strong, courageous woman. A woman who had found deep love. Hope for her future stirred.

Hester ran out of their cabin before Jenny dismounted Merry. "Oh sister, come. Mother is feverish, casting up her accounts, a rash on her face, hands, and feet. Methinks 'tis the pox!"

So quickly, everything could change. Jenny removed her sisters to the small cabin and tended her mother with warm herbal sponge baths, yarrow tea, drinking water exposed to tar, and as much circulating air as possible. But as her mother's body became covered with the fearful bumps, then pustules, Jenny knew the risk remained huge. Since the birth of the twins, her mother had been weak. Now her body seemed not to have the resources to fight off the invader.

Hester left daily food offerings on the porch and stood in the yard to receive updates. At the beginning of the third week, Jenny leaned on the doorframe and said through choking tears, "Pray."

By the end of the week, she found a spot in view of the stockade but well away from water sources to dig her mother's burial plot. After placing the slight burden in the ground, Jenny tossed the dirt back in while Hester and Libby sobbed a few feet away.

Jenny sank down to rest. The earth spun, and sweat sprang out under her shift despite the sharp November air. Her head felt like it was gripped in a vise. Without Father, Gabriel, and now Mother, the burden on her felt impossible to bear. What a blow this would be to Father and Gabriel.

"I shall move us back into the house," Hester said and started to turn, Libby's hand in hers.

Jenny gasped as she attempted to rise and her knees buckled. "I think not. For I believe I have contracted the pox." At Hester's look of horror, she added, "You and Liberty should go to the neighbors'."

Hester held a hand over her heart. "And abandon you? No, I must stay and nurse you, but I shall take Liberty away now."

"Hester, you may well contract the disease."

The slight girl squared her shoulders. "I am not such a selfish weakling I would leave my sister to die. I am in God's hands."

Over the next month, as Jenny instructed Hester in providing the same care she had rendered to their mother, she marveled at Hester's determination. She did all without complaint, taking little sleep or nourishment, sitting late into the night singing the hymns they had learned in the Yadkin Valley. Hester fought the darkness that tried to claim Jenny with equal strength to what Jenny had exhibited for their mother. But Hester won.

When Jenny's shaking fingers traced the contour of pockmarks on her face left by the pustules after the scabs fell off, she realized that facing death would be easier than facing the man she loved with what little beauty she had possessed ravaged by an invader she could not intimidate or outwit.

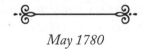

May 1780

"By Old Scratch's britches!" Turning the herb-seasoned trout with a spatula, Jenny jerked the pan off the fire and sat back on her haunches. That unmistakable brogue sounded again. . .and two other dear voices, booming over her sisters' cries of joy.

Jenny leapt to her feet and started to run out into the peach-tinted May twilight, then froze. She stepped away from the fire and waited. A moment later, the door burst open and Hester ran in, followed by three substantial forms in buckskin and linsey-woolsey. "Jenny, look who has come!"

Tears sprang to Jenny's eyes at the sight of her brother, dirty but looking near grown, and her father, holding Liberty with her arms clasped around his neck. She could not look at the Scotsman.

"There's my ginger-hackled Jenny," Father cried, wrapping her in an embrace. He smelled of gunpowder and pine. "But where is my good wife?"

The shock of the men's appearance, relief at being held by her father, and the realization that he knew nothing of his wife's demise launched a triple assault on Jenny's normally firm senses. She started to sob, something she could not recall doing for perhaps ten years.

Her father pulled back in alarm. "What is this?" As he swiped a tear from his daughter's cheek, his thumb encountered an indentation. "You have had the pox." He set Liberty on the floor and looked up toward the loft, then out into the yard. "Elizabeth? Elizabeth!"

Jenny covered her face while Hester caught her father's hand. The middle daughter whispered, "Father, we lost her."

"Lord, help me, no. No!" Like a tree under an ax, their father fell to his knees on the porch. He bent his graying head under his arms and keened.

The sound made Jenny weep harder. Now of equal height, Gabriel embraced her. Jenny noticed Liberty standing by the table with a finger in her mouth, staring with horrified fixation at Hester attempting to comfort their father. "Gabriel, take her up," she said.

Wiping his own face, he did so, while Caylan stepped toward Jenny. "Have ye a hug for me, lass?" he asked gently.

When he held out his arms, Jenny flew into them. She knew he would not want her now, but she did so need his comfort. He smoothed her back with long strokes and buried his face in her hair.

" 'Tis sorry I am to hear about yer ma, Jenny. When did the plague strike?"

"November. I nursed her, then Hester nursed me."

"And ye managed on yer own since then, brave girl, but you are thin as a rail.

Who knew 'twas not the Indians or the Tories I should have fretted about, but the pox."

When Caylan attempted to lift her face, Jenny jerked her chin away. "Pray do not look at me."

" 'Tis hardly noticeable."

He meant she was so bran-faced her freckles almost covered the scars. Jenny stepped away. "So you say in this light."

"Let him look at you and hold you, Jenny," Gabriel snapped, "for he knows he could be like Father right now, unable to do either. He loves you. Your bravery and goodness is all he has talked of for a year. Vanity 'tis not like you."

Surprised by her brother's rebuke, Jenny hung her head. Caylan tipped her chin with his index finger. "Gabriel is right in that ye musn't fear me. I am just so glad ye're alive."

"I apologize, Jenny. 'Tis my grief talking."

Jenny nodded, wiped her face, and turned toward the fireplace. "Hester can take you and Father to Mother's grave. I shall finish supper."

As the others left the cabin, Jenny heard Caylan unload his gear and felt Liberty's arm encircle her skirts. Understandably, the child had been clingy since the fall. Jenny lifted down the plates and utensils and bent to Liberty's level. "Can you set the board, Libby?"

The little girl nodded. With her sister occupied, Jenny stirred the mess of early potatoes and beans and cut the cornbread. "What brings you to these parts?" she asked over her shoulder. "I dare not hope 'tis an end to hostilities."

He settled at the bench. "Not by far. Did ye hear of the attempt to retake Savannah last fall?"

Jenny nodded. "A traveler around Christmas brought news that the French fleet came to our aid, and that one of the Patriot commanders demanded the British surrender the city."

"Aye, but they stalled until reinforcements arrived, so that when the Americans attempted to unseat them, they could not. Our dead and wounded was a thousand to a fraction of that for them. Heard's Fort became the seat of government, while the enemy turned their eye on Charleston. The South Carolinians were weak from the pox themselves, Jenny, and could not hold their city either. It went bad for my relations at both sieges. At Charleston, they faced The Black Watch, fellow Highlanders with the Forty-second Regiment of Foot. It stung like gall for them to surrender. Dooly also surrendered the majority of his men at his fort, only to be killed in his own bed, in front of his family, by six British Regulars."

"Oh no!" Her own struggles forgotten, Jenny turned with her hand at her heart. "So that leaves Colonel Clark in charge of the Georgia militia?"

"Yes. He has furloughed his men for a few weeks to secure their farms, and hopes to rally those who signed the British oath of allegiance under duress."

"That is your job then? To recruit?"

Caylan nodded. "I shall make forays into the backcountry to gather information and men while your father and Gabriel set you on your feet."

Jenny's back, aching from plowing the cornfield and weeding the flax rows, sagged. "I shan't tell a clanker, a bit of assistance 'twould be handy. How long will you remain?"

"With the travel between here and the regiment, about a week. But Jenny?" He stood, frightfully close to her as she poured cider into the tankards.

"Yes?" She felt annoyed her voice sounded so breathless.

He put a hand over the pewter pitcher, forcing it to the table. "I have thought of ye every day, lass. Can ye give me reassurance 'tis been likewise for you. . .that things have not changed?"

She swallowed and focused on the wooden buttons of his vest. "I have thought of you, Caylan McIntosh, but things *have* changed."

Before he could insist on an explanation, steps sounded on the porch.

Caylan had been gone several days, Father and Gabriel prepared a far field, and Jenny stirred their clothes in a pot of boiling lye to rid them of "gentleman's invaders" when she glimpsed through the trees the cardinal red she recalled from Kettle Creek. Hot energy rushed through her veins as she realized they were about to be visited by a British scouting party.

"Sweet Lord, help us," she whispered.

She fished the contents from her pot, deposited them in the half-filled ash hopper, and ran for the cabin. She arrested Hester in her bread making. "British coming! Quick, you must hide all of Father's and Gabriel's things beneath the floorboards."

Jenny darted back to her cauldron and dropped in the bedding. The boil resumed about the time the pounding sounded on the bolted fort door. She doubted hiding or playing simple would pacify this time. She opened to the enemy. Four regulars rode into the stockade, their stallions encircling her.

"Do I address the mistress of this place?" the officer demanded.

"I am Jenny White, daughter of the owner."

"Lieutenant Bradley Adams. Is your father in residence?"

Jenny blinked. "He is not."

"And where might he be?"

Jenny lifted her chin. "Why, away, fighting you British, sir." Hester would have kicked her.

The man's black beetle brows met while florid color stained his neck. "You are the one with the reputation for sass. I warn you, I shall have none of your brazen-faced ways."

Clasping her hands behind her back in a vulnerable gesture, Jenny asked, "How might I be of service today?"

"We seek a recruiting party of Clark's militia, believed to be stopping here."

"You can see they are not."

"I see nothing as yet." With a hand flick, the lieutenant sent his privates to tie their horses and search the buildings. He dismounted and approached, hackles rising when he realized he had to look up at her. "You will prepare victuals and cider for the men."

Jenny glowered. "I will not aid and abet my enemy."

"You will, or suffer this fort burned down around your ears."

Fuming, Jenny considered her options. His was just the sort of arrogance that roused her Patriot ire. With the men gone—thank God!—they were outgunned. She must appear to submit, at least for the moment. She led the oaf into the cabin and introduced her sister. To Hester's credit, she maintained her calm, and the room was free of masculine effects. She had even moved the trestle over the loose floorboard.

While the invaders searched the cabin, tossing the ticks about, rifling through anything closed, and causing Liberty to cry, the women huddled together. Adams returned to the hearth, irritated, just in time to receive the report that nothing outside yielded evidence of militia.

Jenny could not hold her tongue. "I told you as much."

"Shut your bone box!"

"You think yourself so much smarter than us colonists, do you not? Yet I led the last passel of Loyalists to a false track while the man they sought hid in the swamp!"

"Jenny!" Hester hissed.

The lieutenant's rancid breath struck Jenny's face as he demanded, "And just where is this swamp?"

"West of the fort, but you shall find no one there today."

"My men will ascertain that, and in the meantime, you shall cook that turkey caged in your yard."

"I will not!"

"You know what happened to Stephen Heard's wife and daughter."

She certainly did. The two had died in the snow after Tories evicted them. While she knew the fair weather and nearby presence of the men ensured they would not meet a similar fate, neither did she want their home destroyed. Her stupid pride had snared her again. As she stared into the emotional vacancy behind Adams's pale green eyes, an idea formed.

"Sister, is there any corn liquor left over?"

"Why yes, in the hidey-hole. But—"

"Fetch it, please, to ease the lieutenant's temper while we prepare the meal. Then join me in the yard to pluck the fowl."

Hester caught on. "Our apologies for seeming less than hospitable, Lieutenant. I am sure you understand the duress and fear we live under."

The man gave a sanctimonious nod and reached to unstrap his sabre. He lounged before the hearth while everyone did his bidding. When Hester joined Jenny at the bloody chopping block, Jenny whispered, "When the men return empty-handed, we must keep the liquor flowing. Once they are foxed, I shall send you for water. Take Liberty with you. You know where we hid the conch shell at the fork tree. Father and Gabriel should come quick but forewarned."

Hester nodded.

It played out according to plan. Tired and grumpy, the men came in and leaned their muskets near the hearth. Soon the mouth-watering aroma of roasting turkey and vegetables filled the cabin. The strong spirits eased inhibitions, and the men laughed, talked, and flirted with Hester. When one patted Hester's behind, Jenny wanted to run him through with her knife. But with a great effort, she kept her mouth shut as she passed back and forth between the board and fireplace, where Hester had left the chunk of chinking out of the hidey-hole. When the soldiers broke into an off-key rendition of "Barbara Allen," Jenny sent her sisters for the water. She also began to slide the muskets one by one through the hole, out into the yard.

As she raised the third one, one of the privates yelled, "Hey! What're ya doin'?"

Jenny froze. Her heart hammered. She whirled around, the loaded gun trained on the startled company. "I am taking you captive in the name of the independent state of Georgia!" The blast of the conch shell glorified her announcement.

"Get her," the lieutenant shouted.

The three privates lunged. Jenny aimed at the closest man and pulled the trigger. A boom and a puff of smoke filled the cabin. The man dropped to the ground, gut shot, red gushing over his hand as his startled gaze met Jenny's. Astonishment froze everyone for a split second before Jenny grabbed the other musket.

Over the death gurgles of the wounded soldier, she yelled, "I will kill the next man who comes at me!"

"My stars, she shot Martin," one of them exclaimed.

"You dimwits, are you going to let a cribbage-faced Patriot hussy be your undoing? Take her in hand!" ordered the officer.

Jenny considered shooting Adams, but when his minions feinted in her direction, she swiveled the barrel back. Once again, she let her left eye slide to one side, causing the men to bluster in confusion.

"Sit down, all of you, with your hands on the board," she directed.

"Now be reasonable, woman," Adams said. "You cannot expect to hold four men at gunpoint indefinitely."

"No, but I can long enough for my sister to tie you, and my brother and father to come to our aid."

"I will *kill* you!" the lieutenant bellowed.

It took but five or ten minutes of maintaining a granite countenance to cover her boiling fear of a miscalculation, but seemed like an eternity, when not just Hester, Father, and Gabriel, but also Caylan, back, apparently, from Ft. Martin, burst onto the scene.

"We heard shots," Hester gasped. "Are you all right?"

Caylan took one look at Jenny fixing the musket on the British with jaw set, before a grin broke over his rugged features. "Of course she is. She is War Woman."

Chapter 7

September 1780

Flattened onto her belly with her Brown Bess laid across a fallen tree, Jenny tracked the progress of a squirrel storing nuts. Waiting until he perched in the crook of a limb, she prepared to pull the trigger when a rustle sounded behind her. Frowning, she swiveled her head but saw nothing unusual. She looked back. No squirrel. Growling a slang term her mother would have certainly protested, Jenny relaxed her stance. The next moment, someone tackled her from behind.

She spluttered, flipped over, and tried to raise her gun, but the attacker pinned her arms above her head, his weight pressing her struggling body down.

"Dinna scream, 'tis me."

Jenny gasped as she looked into amber eyes alight with mischief. "What are you doing, Caylan McIntosh? I could have shot you!"

"I figured approaching ye from behind safer than the front."

His expression of adoration faded into regret as he perused her face. Jenny wanted to shrink into herself. Her scars would be fully visible up close, in the late-morning sunlight. But she could not get away before he lowered his head, his breath tickling her, making her dizzy, and pressed his lips to hers. Not in passion, but with a soft reverence. Respect. Pity. She could not get up fast enough, brushing dry leaves off her skirt.

"What are you doing here? Are my father and Gabriel here too?"

Caylan came to a sitting position. "Just me, and despite my entrance, my mission is dire. Take me to yer sister so ye both can hear all."

"But I was about to get our supper."

"No time for that." Fetching his accoutrements from a nearby tree, Caylan held out his hand.

Jenny ignored him, taking up her gun and setting out. "We heard of the battle at Musgrove's Mill last month and knew you were nearby."

"Aye, lass, there have been several battles since I saw ye last." Caylan's tone was tinged with sadness. "Elijah and his son were both wounded, Clark almost taken prisoner."

Jenny nodded. As she walked, she untwined her hair, hoping it would hide her imperfections. What must he think of her, skinny and pockmarked? Hester, who met Caylan with a gracious kiss on the cheek, only looked all the more ethereal for her thinness. Hester set out cider and bread for the Highlander before sitting across from him.

"Now tell us your business and why you come alone."

Caylan tore into the bread. "On the fourteenth, we struck Augusta and took it with no trouble, but the British holed up in M'Kay's Trading Post outside town. We drove their Cherokee allies away from the spring they guarded, thinking to deprive them of water. But Brown, whom we shot through both thighs, received word a large host of British were on the way and refused our offer of surrender." He gulped down the cider, wiping his mouth with his sleeve. He looked at them with strangely entreating eyes. "We had to pull back. Clark was wounded again, and we could not take such a force."

Hester touched his hand. "Of course."

He stared at her. "Ye understand this means all the state falls into British hands. We are being called the Georgia Refugees, for all others have taken oaths of loyalty. Everyone is gathering at the Little River for militia escort to the Carolinas."

Jenny scoffed. " 'Everyone' has fled before, but not us."

Caylan turned a blazing gaze on her. " 'Tis different this time. No one will be left to come to yer aid. No men at Clark's Station or Ft. Martin."

She crossed her arms. "We have held off both Indians and Tories before."

He stood, peering down at her. "With *help*, may I remind ye."

"Fine, but what has Father to say?"

Caylan clenched his jaw. "I speak for him. 'Tis the only way, Jenny." That same sadness filled his gaze, making her soften.

"How long do we have?" Hester wanted to know.

"I need ye packed and ready to go in under an hour. I already passed word to Mrs. Clark that her husband was wounded again at Augusta, and she rides ahead to camp. We shall cut across country to the rendezvous."

Jenny did not comply with grace. She banged, stomped, and muttered about the sure demise of their home without their occupancy. It burned her heart to leave the corn standing in the field, the clothes unspun from waiting flax.

They packed oilcloth, quilts, and as much foodstuffs as the packs Caylan prepared on the horses would carry. She could not hide the tears in her eyes as she and Caylan surveyed the stockade.

"I am sorry, Jenny." He held his stallion's reins and glanced at Hester holding Liberty's hand. "Hester should ride with me, and the wee one with Jenny."

Because Jenny was big and heavy. Fine. She huffed into Merry's saddle and took her sister from Caylan's hands, then averted her gaze as he mounted his stallion and helped Hester up. Hester's blushing response to the Highlander's nearness told Jenny her sister was not over Caylan. Jealousy coiled like a serpent in Jenny's belly.

She wanted to ride ahead but knew Caylan must lead the way.

As they rode southeast along an Indian trail, the smell of smoke filled the late September air. "Clark's Station, I reckon," Caylan said.

Approaching the main road to Kettle Creek, they heard a shot fired. Caylan instructed them to wait in the woods while he investigated. Jenny pressed a cloth doll into Liberty's hands and urged her to silence. Minutes later, he whistled.

On the side of the narrow lane, Caylan spoke with a black man and Hannah Clark. Jenny spurred Merry closer. The colonel's wife handed Caylan infant twins from the front of her saddle, then allowed him to help her down. Blood trailed from her snorting mount's wound.

"Mrs. Clark, are you all right?" Jenny cried.

Hannah wiped a tear from her eye. "Take this quilt too, Lieutenant, for we almost died saving it. My Sarah and Betsy sewed it. When the British tried to take it, I got mad all over again thinking of those shirts they stole."

"You challenged British soldiers over a quilt?" Hester gasped.

The woman nodded. "One of them said a woman so brave should not be killed, so they let me go."

The body servant spoke up. "Take my horse, ma'am. I tend yours and catch up wid you at Little River."

Soon Hannah was ready to go and Jenny said, "We pray you find your husband well."

"Yes, and that we will all be together in Watauga."

"Godspeed," said Caylan.

"Watauga?" Jenny turned round eyes on Caylan as their leader's wife sped across the road and continued east on the Indian path, twins clutched in the saddle before her.

Caylan failed to meet her gaze as he remounted behind Hester. "Clark journeys to Fort Caswell at Sycamore Shoals. The settlers there bought land from the Cherokee in '75 outside the realm of any state. They became Washington County, North Carolina, about the time the Cherokee, allied with the British, turned on them. They already repelled that invasion. 'Twill be a place of unquestionable safety."

Jenny fumed. "Yes, but one I never would have agreed to had I been informed! You said 'Carolinas.' I assumed we merely forded the Savannah."

"Well, that was your mistake." Caylan urged his stallion onto the trail opening between the golden trees.

"That journey is impossibly far, slow with those on foot and children, and across a mountain range!"

"Aye. It could take a couple of weeks."

" 'Tis insanity!"

"The Overmountain Men are the toughest bunch of settlers west of the Appalachians. 'Tis a wise choice. Now shut yer clacker, woman. I am trying to save yer life, and all I get for it is complaint!"

Jenny pinched her lips together, horrified to feel tears smart in her eyes. Caylan had never spoken thus to her. His reactions confused her: tenderness, sadness, anger. She had seen all in half a day. Likely he now wished to throw her over but felt constrained by his Scottish chivalry. And why did she feel he hid something from them?

When they paused after fording Fishing Creek for the horses to water, Caylan sidled up to her. "I apologize for snappin' earlier, lass."

She nibbled a piece of jerky and stared at the water. " 'Tis of no account. You have been through much, and now are saddled with two women and a child."

Caylan drew in his lips. "I am not 'saddled.' I love ye, lass. I would ride through hell for ye. But I *am* angry at ye. What is *this*?"

Astonished, Jenny looked down at the clan brooch he shoved toward her.

"When I found this in my pack after I left this spring, I could have wrung yer neck. What kind of coward breaks a pledge in such a fashion? And is that how ye meant it, to break with me?"

"I meant to—to release you."

"*Why?*"

"Because things have changed. *I* have changed."

"Ye mean the pox."

Jenny swallowed. "Another sort of girl would suit you better." The picture of her sister riding in front of Caylan invaded her mind.

"Will ye let *me* decide that?" Noticing Hester's approach, Caylan slid the pin back into his bag and stood. "We must go now, but we are not done with this discussion." He raised his voice. "We should make better time when we reach the other road toward Wrightsboro. When we camp tonight, I must tell you both important news."

Crickets sang and Liberty whimpered by the time they smelled smoke. Dozens of tiny fires licked the russet evening around the millhouse chosen as the gathering point. Jenny could not believe the number of people present, bedraggled and starved settlers fleeing their homeland.

Leading their horses toward one of the first clusters, they were surprised to see one of the Morris brothers and Philip Dunst, who had visited in January '79. Philip's short, round mother, Gertie, and several younger siblings, accompanied him. All bade Caylan and the Whites to partake of their cornbread and fish.

Jenny's stomach rumbled but she said, "Thank you, but we really must find Father and Gabriel." The look of confusion she intercepted from Gertie dissolved into pity as she and Jenny both noticed Liberty had already plunked down next to the Dunst youngest and started scooping fish off a platter with her fingers.

"The wee bairn's famished. Let her eat," Caylan urged. He helped Hester, wobbly from unaccustomed hours in the saddle, to a log. She gave him a grateful smile for the cornpone he placed in her hand.

Jenny lowered herself with unwilling exhaustion onto the ground next to Morris. Mayhap the war and the loss of his brother had softened him, for he glanced at her with a touch of pity. Did she look that bad? She ducked her head and thanked Mrs. Dunst for victuals.

"Has the route been discussed?" Caylan asked Philip.

"We parallel the river up to a crossing below the Tugaloo, as soon as Clark is fit to ride."

Morris said, "No one's survived more wounds than Clark. He shall be back in the saddle by tomorrow, I wager. I don't think he was bad off, leastways not as bad as those we had to leave behind." He cast a regretful glance at the White women.

Vexed with the man's staring, Jenny set down her plate. "What?" she demanded.

"Nothing, I am just sorry for you."

"Have you never seen a pox victim before? When I leave the campfire are you going to call me names again like you did at my home?"

The whiplash curl of her words rendered the gathering silent. The dark-haired man spluttered, "'Twasn't your scars I referred to, and I would never speak ill at such a time."

"What do you mean?" Jenny glanced around, aware of an awkwardness she did not understand. Caylan especially looked pained.

Gertie laid a plump hand on his arm. "Have you not told them, Caylan?"

Hester gasped. "Told us what?" From her expression, Jenny knew her sister's heart pounded like her own, and a damp chill not from the river swirled up to envelop her.

Gertie waddled over to sit next to Hester, placing an arm around her and meeting Jenny's stricken eyes across the fire. "Girls, your father fell at Cedar Spring back in July, and your brother. . ." She paused and sought Caylan's warning gaze. "Your brother was a casualty of the Indians in Augusta."

Chapter 8

Caylan wanted to comfort her, but Jenny's anger would not allow it. How could he have lured them from home by trickery and deceit? She avoided him. It was easy enough to do as the mass of people moved along Indian paths through primeval forests, escorted by the militia. Her anger provided a useful shield against deeper emotions of shock, loss, and terror. What would they do when this exodus ended, having no menfolk or parent to return home with? Who ever heard of three women living alone on the frontier? And who would ever want her, gangly, starved, and scarred, with two younger sisters in tow? Even Caylan could not wish for such a package. Jenny tried to push these thoughts from her mind. She committed herself to seeking provisions and carrying Liberty, but, sensing Jenny's hardness, the child whined for Hester.

Unlike Jenny, Hester allowed her tears to flow unchecked. Not a complaint passed her lips, and receiving comfort from strangers, she started deep friendships. Jenny saw that the new, stronger Hester was the prize Caylan now deserved.

The few provisions brought from home ran out after crossing the Savannah River. The people foraged for berries, nuts, and sour crabapples. They hunted for wildlife, but there was never enough to go around. Jenny figured there must be at least four hundred civilians under the escort of Clark's three hundred. There was no time for dawdling by campfires, for they heard Patrick Ferguson's men pursued under Cornwallis's orders.

One afternoon in the rolling hills of South Carolina, they paused along a stream. Jenny splashed her face with water and looked up to see Hester watching her. Pity lined her smooth features.

"You do not grieve Father and Gabriel," she said. " 'Tis not healthy. You must soon face our loss, sister."

"I feel it. I feel it in *here*." Jenny struck her breast.

"Yes, but you must let it out, or you will explode. Why do you keep Caylan at arm's length?"

"Because he tricked us, Hester. He did not trust us enough to tell us the truth."

"Is that really why?"

Jenny shook her head and stood up, glancing around to where Gertie's children played on the bank. "Liberty?" She saw the child nowhere. Jenny's heart rate picked up. "Liberty!"

"Oh dear, I am sorry. I thought you had her," Gertie cried.

Jenny shot an accusing glance at Hester, then sprang into the woods, calling the girl's name. Around a thick evergreen shrub, she caught a glimpse of striped linen. Cold dread engulfed her when she realized it was a hawthorn bush. When she caught Libby in her arms, the child clutched a handful of the blue-black berries, while a corresponding stain colored her lips.

She thrust her fingers into her sister's mouth. "Spit it out! Did you eat the seeds?" Liberty choked, spit, and started to cry. Several adults rushed up as Jenny demanded, "Did you eat any before those?"

The girl shook her head, letting her handful of tiny fruit fall to the forest floor.

Jenny shook her by the shoulders. "We can eat hawthorn berries, but we must spit out the seeds. I told you to eat *no* berries without asking first!"

"I forgot," Libby sobbed.

"And the thorns are as long as your hand and cut like knives!"

Caylan touched Jenny's shoulder and called her name. "Leave off, ye frighten the lass."

"I mean to frighten her! She could have died!" Jenny pinched her sister's arm, but Hester swooped in and took Liberty up.

" 'Tis fine now, Jenny. She shan't forget again." With a censoring frown, Hester walked back toward the creek.

Embarrassed by the stares and the powerful fear that gripped her more strongly than she had gripped Liberty, Jenny covered her face. "I do not know what is wrong with me."

"I do. Ye're rightfully terrified of losing someone else you love."

"Yes," Jenny admitted as the group around them dispersed in silent understanding. "I am afraid I shall be left with none of the family I came to Georgia with."

"Ye won't. And ye have me."

When he tried to touch her, she pushed him away and fled downstream, fearing the imminent eruption of emotion. She leaned against a massive black oak to gather her wits. Above her shallow breaths, she heard two women talking across the narrow stream.

" 'Tis understandable," one said. "The poor thing's addlepated, and who can blame her? Having lost her father and brother all in one blow, her mother just last fall."

The second agreed. "And to such an awful fate, Gabriel White. Law, for a brave, wounded young man like that to be left to the mercy of the enemy! They say that monster Brown had thirteen of the prisoners hung from the banister where he could see them expire from his sickbed. Then cut down and given to the Indians to be mutilated and thrown into the river."

"The others went straight to the Indians, scalped and roasted."

With a moan of agony, Jenny leaned over and retched up the thin juices of her stomach. Caylan found her doubled over, gasping.

"What is it, Jenny?"

She fixed an intense gaze on him. "Is it true?"

"Is what true?"

"That not only did you deceive us into thinking Father and Gabriel waited for us in camp—"

"I never said that."

"But Gabriel was left with the wounded in Augusta, to be tortured by Indians!"

Caylan's bronzed face paled. "Where did ye hear that?"

Jenny nodded across the creek. "I overheard them just now. So it is true." When he remained silent, she shook her head and tried to walk past him.

His hand snaked out to grip her elbow.

"Do not touch me." When Caylan persisted in trying to pull her into his arms, Jenny fought, slapped, and wriggled.

"Stop it, lass. I can see how ye are hurting. Ye must stop this running."

She pounded his chest with her fists, hard. "How could you not tell me? How could you leave me to hear something like that from prattling strangers?"

"Oh Jenny, I am sorry. I was going to tell ye, just when we reached the mountains. When we had time to. . .deal with it all." Caylan wrapped a fist around her wrists but kept the other arm anchored on her waist. "I knew ye would fight me on leaving if ye thought they were not waiting at the river. And I only held back the details about yer brother because I knew 'twould pain ye so."

Picturing the awful scene described by the women, Jenny choked on horror, her heart rending for her young brother. "Oh Lord, 'tisn't fair!" she wailed.

Caylan released her wrists and ran his fingers through her hair. He breathed against her cheek, "Let it out, lass. We all have a breaking point, even ye."

Alarmed at the wild and tortured sounds coming out of herself, Jenny buried her face in Caylan's frock coat. He wrapped both arms around her and murmured words that must be Gaelic, but they sounded ever so sweet. When her knees crumpled, he held her up. When people started to move down the trail, he stroked her back.

Finally, as her sobs quieted to moans and gasps, he murmured, "Look at me, lass." As she complied with her closed eyes still streaming tears, he added, "Ye have suffered more than any woman ought, and been braver and stronger far longer than ye should have had to be."

He began to kiss the tears away. She shuddered as his tender lips contacted her dimpled flesh. "Do not," Jenny whispered.

"Nae, lass, dinna shrink from me. What kind of blackguard do ye think me, to consider leaving ye alone now?"

"Not a blackguard at all, 'tis why I released you."

"Well, I refuse your release." His mouth skimmed hers, seeking response.

Jenny turned her head. "I am not worthy of you now."

"Does that mean ye forgive me?"

She dropped her arms, stepping back from him, and said in a spent tone, "Yes. I know what you did was for our own good. And you were right, had you told me then what I know now, you would never have gotten me to leave Ft. White."

"Then what is it? Why are ye not worthy?" When she only shook her head, Caylan dug in his haversack. "Is it the way ye look? Because I took this shaving mirror off a dead Brit, expressly to refute yer protests."

"No!"

He shoved it into her hand and held her hand up to her face. "Look, Jenny. See what I see."

Jenny dragged a sleeve across her cheeks and gazed at the first clear reflection she had seen of herself since age thirteen. The woman who stared back lacked the heavy features of adolescence she recalled. Maturity and starvation revealed fine, strong bones, almost noble, framed by a wildness of russet hair, with damp, dark brown lashes. The pox indentations were visible, true, but slight. Her brother had been right. The scattering of freckles across her nose drew attention to her eyes. . .eyes the very color of Caylan's.

Her hand started to shake. Caylan caught the mirror before she dropped it. He drew her against him. "Will ye kiss me now, Jenny, my love? Wahatchee."

Finally, War Woman surrendered.

That night, Jenny lay by the campfire in Caylan's arms, Liberty snuggled between herself and Hester. The oilcloth beneath them rustled against leaves as Caylan nestled closer, brushing her ear with his lips.

"Kiss me again like ye did before," he whispered.

"No, you devil," Jenny hissed. "My sisters! And all these people!"

He growled in frustration and twined his fingers in her hair. Jenny closed her eyes, realizing how long she had coveted such a tender touch. She did not trust herself to turn and face him. It was a testament to the power of her attraction that her exhaustion had not triumphed by culminating in sleep the minute she laid down.

"While I know 'tis no reverend in our company, I am of a mind to find a justice of the peace right this minute," Caylan muttered.

"And what shall you say to him that you have failed to say to me?" Jenny teased.

"By the saints! I plumb forgot to ask." Caylan turned her chin so that she could see him in the firelight. "If ye will forgive this unconventional proposal, Miss White,

I ask ye with all my heart to marry me as soon as we reach Fort Caswell."

"I will, Caylan McIntosh."

"Praise be, and ye willna go back on it?"

She mimicked his brogue. "I willna go back on it."

"That deserves a kiss."

"If I can crane my neck. . ." When she attempted to do so, both dissolved into giggles, earning Hester's shushing. But even her sister's frown could not squelch the joy that bubbled like a fresh spring inside Jenny. She fell asleep listening to Caylan's deep breathing, feeling the rise and fall of his chest at her back, a song in her heart that whispered comfort over her grief.

Clark had sent runners ahead to Watauga with notice of their approach. The next day, one from the river settlement returned, asking to speak to the commander. Jenny watched from a distance as the handsome, dark-haired colonel in his buff and navy uniform consulted with the North Carolinian. Moments later, Caylan strode toward Jenny and Hester.

"The Overmountain Men gathered at Fort Caswell on the twenty-fifth. Hearing of Ferguson's threat to hang their leaders and lay waste to their country with fire and sword, they marched out to meet him. Major Candler and volunteers from our regiment rendezvous with them on the Green River."

"But not you." Jenny's lips felt numb as she spoke. *Please.*

"With such powerful allies, this could end the war in the south."

When Jenny saw the struggle writ on Caylan's face, panic surged. Pride attempted to silence her, but she forced the words out. Caylan drew near, clasping her elbows, as she spoke. "If you leave with them, I think I will not see you again. And I could not bear that, Caylan. I have only just accepted that I do need God, others. . .you."

He looked deep into her eyes. "Ye're outright askin' me to stay, Jenny?"

"Please go with us to Sycamore Shoals."

Did he know what that cost her?

He did. He crushed her to his chest, and she started to sob when he said, "I shan't abandon ye when I just pledged to stay by ye. I can rejoin the fight when Clark returns to Georgia, for return he shall. But. . .will ye marry me now?"

Jenny's eyes opened wide. "Now?"

"Aye. Now. Here." He flung a long arm out toward a magnificent outcropping of rock overlooking a breathtaking mountain vista. "I canna think of a more fitting place to make ye my backcountry bride."

She laughed while the Georgia Refugees, gathered around and watching them with expressions of rapt interest and delight, broke into applause.

"I take that as a 'yes,'" Caylan boomed. "Now where is a justice of the peace?"

Denise Weimer holds a journalism degree with a minor in history from Asbury University. A former magazine writer, Denise authored romantic novella *Redeeming Grace*, as well as The Georgia Gold Series (*Sautee Shadows, The Gray Divide, The Crimson Bloom*, and *Bright as Gold*, winner of the 2015 John Esten Cooke Award for outstanding Southern literature) and The Restoration Trilogy (*White, Widow* and *Witch*) with Canterbury House Publishing. A wife and swim mom of two daughters, Denise always pauses for old houses, coffee and chocolate, and to write any story the Lord lays on her heart. To learn more about Nancy Hart, who inspired this story, visit http://deniseweimerbooks.webs.com.

The Counterfeit Tory

by Shannon McNear

Dedication

For Don Mallicoat—the man I called Daddy, who showed me what
honorable manhood looks like. Thank you for having a
heart to protect the wounded. I still miss you.

And for Mom—who first saw something worth encouraging in my writing.
Though I bitterly miss you too, I'm so glad you and Daddy
are beholding the face of Jesus together.

Acknowledgments

I owe so much to so many people. . .

My dear writing friends and critique partners Lee, Ronie, Beth, Jen,
and Michelle, who listen, empathize, pray, and sometimes
preach. . .and challenge me to be the best writer I can be.

Editor Becky Germany and agent Tamela Hancock Murray
for believing in my stories.

Author and Revolutionary War reenactor Patrick O'Kelley for his painstaking
research on every military action in the Carolinas during the American
Revolution. Without his work, I'd never feel confident tackling this era.

Other friends and extended family who ask every so often, "How is your writing
coming?" with genuine interest, even or maybe especially through the last
dry spell. Your kindness has been the rain that kept hope alive.

My husband Troy, who has always believed in me, even when it meant sending
me to conference year after year with no apparent return, and my darling
children—that includes you, the spouses!—who have been amazingly supportive
and enthusiastic, even when my dedication to writing looked like neglect
on your side. I tell you again, I would not be who I am without you!

And lastly, but most importantly, to our Lord and Savior, Creator of the
universe, the original Storyteller Himself. Any glory here is His.

Prologue

Charlotte Town, North Carolina
Mid-November 1781

D o these people even know they've lost the war?"

"Obviously not."

Tucked in a corner of the tavern where the babble of conversation was not quite louder than his own thoughts, Jedidiah Wheeler dropped the much-folded paper on the tabletop and stared at it with distaste. "And why can't we leave this rascal to Sumter and Marion?"

Harrison leaned on one elbow, dark gaze intent. "We need someone on the inside. Someone he doesn't know yet. Someone he could possibly trust. Doesn't have to be for long."

Jed chewed the inside of his cheek, thinking. "A man would have to have a death wish to accept this appointment."

A smirk twisted the other man's mouth. "I've heard of your exploits over the past five years. One could say that description fits you."

'Twas true he'd little enough to lose. An occupation that became useless with the tide of war sweeping the colonies for the past five years and more. A mother and then a father who succumbed to age and illness during that time.

A sweetheart who spurned him for another, despite her avowed admiration for his service in the militia. And fine by him. He'd always welcomed the adventure that went along with riding first with the local militia and later with the Continental Regulars.

"I'd like to live long enough to return to riding the Great Road up to Philly," he groused.

This time Harrison laughed outright. "Now you're just being sentimental. Deadly dull, that."

Jed lifted his fingers dismissively.

"Besides," Harrison went on, "no one lives forever. And this rapscallion and his band must be stopped. Could you sleep at night if you didn't at least make the attempt?"

"Mm. Next you'll be singing about king and country."

Harrison gave a silent laugh that disappeared under a wave of uncharacteristic sternness. "Outright slaughter, Jed. And after they'd surrendered. For the sake of all that's true and holy."

The weight of it pressed upon his chest. "One could say that about either side." He'd seen enough of the brutality Whigs and Tories meted upon each other these last several years. And gotten his fill of it.

But the fact that loyalists still rampaged across the Carolina countryside, weeks after the surrender of Cornwallis at Yorktown, stuck in his craw as much as it did Harrison's. He'd just not admit it yet.

The severity of the other man's expression did not ease. Jed heaved a great sigh— not entirely manufactured—and slapped a hand across the letter. "Very well."

One might as well die doing something honorable as not.

Chapter 1

L izzy! Where is my good waistcoat?"

Leaning on her broom, Lizzy Cunningham suppressed a huff. "Hanging where you left it, I expect," she called back, then muttered, "Such a shock that you can't find a wife, Dickie."

With firm strokes, she continued sweeping behind the tavern counter. Why would her brothers seek wives when they had a ready servant in their sister?

"Now, don't be like that, Lizzy girl," her father boomed as he rounded the doorjamb, leaning heavily on his cane. "Your brother works hard and deserves a little help."

Schooling her expression, she tucked her head and kept at the task. He couldn't hear her thoughts. Truly.

"A little help don't mean he can't find his own clothing." The words were out before she could stop them.

Papa lumbered toward her, thunder in his face and step, despite the limp. Lizzy gripped the broom and steeled herself—running would only cause him to be harsher later—but he glanced past her and halted, rearranging his face into the false pleasantry she hated.

"Hullo! What can we do for you this fine day?"

"Something hot to drink would be welcome," came a smooth, low voice behind her.

Lizzy returned to her sweeping.

"We've mulled cider, or did you wish something stronger?" Papa shuffled past her with a hard pinch to her upper arm, under the guise of affection.

"Cider is fine. Too early for a toddy."

She couldn't place the voice, but that meant naught. And she wouldn't turn to see, and draw more attention to herself—

"Lizzy, look sharp," Papa said. "Get the man a cider."

With the slightest of curtsies, she scurried to lean the broom against the wall, then fetched an earthenware tankard and went to the hearth to fill it from the kettle hanging there.

She slid it across the counter with practiced swiftness, aiming for the man's open grasp without looking up into his face. Best to keep her head down, not invite any more attention than need be. But when his other hand reached up to remove a dusty cocked hat trimmed in braid and black ribbon—a fancy sort, given the worn hunting shirt and rifleman's gear—her curiosity betrayed her with a flicked glance upward. His face was a broad, honest one, the kind a body would instinctively trust. Blue eyes met hers directly, then crinkled into a smile.

Warmth flooded her. She let go of the tankard and whirled away.

Gracious, but the girl was skittish.

Jed wanted to watch her, see if he could catch her attention again, even for a moment, but his focus was commanded by the man he presumed to be proprietor, leaning on his cane. Who, if Jed did not miss his guess, had been about to strike the girl.

Not his business, he supposed, but—the thought brought a burn to the back of his throat.

The man shifted his bulk closer, his expression wheedling. "Have you business here?"

"I do," Jed said, slowly, deliberately sipping the cider. Not bad. He glanced around the near-empty common room. Clean enough, if shabby. Provisions looked sparse, but the war had been unkind to all, regardless of partisan leanings. "Name's Jed Williams." He offered his hand.

The older man shifted, and after the merest hesitation, shook the outstretched hand. "Charles Cunningham." He twitched a nod toward the girl. "My daughter. My two boys are elsewhere, working."

Jed kept his smile amiable. "A fine establishment you have here." It had nothing on many of the taverns and ordinaries he'd frequented on the Great Road north, but. . .the war had been hard on everyone.

His flattery had its intended effect however. Cunningham drew himself up. "We do well enough."

"Indeed. P'raps you can help me with a delicate matter."

The older man's gaze sharpened with interest.

"I seek a man. Told you are a relative of his—as are others in these parts, but that you are trustworthy."

If he kept this up, he'd need to spend half the night in prayer, repenting of falsehoods.

"Aye?"

"A certain Captain Cunningham—William, I believe?"

"Aye. That's my nephew Billy. A major now, he is. The British gave him a promotion for his service to the Crown."

"Ah, good to hear." Jed let his grin melt into the semblance of a worried frown. "I'd like to speak with this Captain—I mean, Major—Cunningham. Ask if I might join him. Cast out of my own home by these blasted rebels, myself."

The tavern proprietor's brow creased. "Well, now. That might be tricky. A body never knows when Billy might show up. Or where he might be next. But if you were to stick around, like—I might be able to find something out for you. We have a room available for let as well."

Jed clapped a companionable hand on the older man's shoulder. "Many thanks, my good man. I'd be right obliged."

Cunningham's head bobbed. If such a thing were possible, his smile grew more greasy. "Now then, I must go see to matters. I'll return shortly. Might we provide you something to eat?"

"I'd be grateful for that as well."

Jed watched him circle through the common room so he could nudge the girl still busy at her task of sweeping, and mutter something to her. She cast Jed a glance, gave her father a stiff nod, and followed him back to the rear of the tavern.

He released a long sigh and turned to give the place a better look. Again, clean enough, if shabby, but something about it made his skin crawl to think of staying here overnight. *God in heaven, protect me.* Not the first time he'd uttered those words. Wouldn't be the last either, he was sure.

Chapter 2

Lizzy stirred down the stew and reached for a wooden bowl. Just outside the kitchen, Papa had summoned Dickie, who apparently managed to locate his own waistcoat after all. "Take the horse and find your cousin. Let him know there's a man here that wants to speak with him. Appears to be alone, at that."

Her cousin could not be too careful about who joined him, or even professed interest in such, she knew. Not that it mattered one whit to her what kind of trouble he found himself in. The district had been markedly quieter while Billy had stayed in exile in Florida those two years. Billy couldn't resist causing a stir wherever he went.

And this stray fellow wanting to come join Billy's regiment? Must be either a simpleton or fellow mischief-maker.

She slid a roll from a larger, covered bowl on the counter into the stew, hesitated, then grabbed a second. Papa would chide her generosity—possibly—but the bread needed eaten. And she was sick of seeing Papa and her brothers gobble it all down before anyone else got to enjoy it.

Back to the common room then while Papa and Dickie continued whispering together. Still standing at the counter, the stranger turned at her entrance. There went that smile again, meant to be charming, she was sure. They always tried to be charming, at least until they'd had a taste of her scalding tongue. Papa scolded her for it, but if he wished her to be biddable to every clod who walked through that door—

"I expect you'll want to sit down," she said, angling for one of the side tables. "Does this suit you?"

The smile didn't waver. If anything, it brightened, making his unremarkable face something she'd want to stop and study, under other circumstances. The blue eyes twinkled as his head dipped. "Suits fine, thank you."

Simpleton then. She felt a stab of pity for the life that awaited him with her cousin's regiment.

After setting down the bowl and spoon, she sidled away to retrieve her broom.

"So, your cousin," came the man's voice, catching her halfway across the room. "He's a fair man to ride with, by all accounts?"

She plucked the broom from where it stood against the wall and turned to face him. "'Tain't from around here, are you?"

His expression maintained a steady pleasantry as he shoveled in a bite of stew, those eyes still sparkling as if they shared a secret between them. But he didn't reply.

"Well." She applied herself to the last bit of floor she'd already covered. "Some say he's fair enough. Some say he's a right terror."

He nodded thoughtfully, scooped a second bite. "Word has it he first enlisted with the rebel side, when all your family are good royalists."

Lizzy couldn't help her derisive snort. "Wouldn't necessarily call us 'good' royalists. Not all of us." He chewed steadily, still watching her, so she swept with more attention, but the words continued creeping out of her. "He always had a terrible need to make his own way. Have his own opinions. I'm sure 'twas to spite his daddy if nothing else, at least at first. Then when he discovered it meant he'd have to follow orders and go where he didn't always want to. . ."

Why did this man's gaze make her feel so squirmy inside, and yet comfortable talking, at the same time?

"So he was court martialed for insubordination and flogged," he said, then lifted the spoon toward her in salute. "This is right toothsome. You make it?"

She likewise couldn't stop the flush of pleasure that swept over her. She muted her response to a short nod.

She wasn't adding that her father's own loyalties could be wobbly, at best. But Jed couldn't fault her for leaving out that detail, not to someone who purported to be enough of a hotheaded loyalist himself to join Bill Cunningham.

The girl was a contradiction. Quiet industry yet ill at ease. Reluctant to speak even while she spilled bits of information, sweeping that floor as if her life depended on it.

Perhaps it did.

He forced himself to eat slowly, remembering all the times rations were thin while on campaign. And making the stew last longer gave him more time for observation.

The tavern keeper hadn't yet reappeared, which surprised him. His gaze strayed back to the girl. Thin, stoop-shouldered, clad in a petticoat so faded he could barely tell it had once been blue, and a plain brown gown that pinched at the elbows and barely lapped across her front. The tavern keeper couldn't spare a coin to dress his own daughter decently?

But then, the war had been hard on all. . .

She wore no cap either—not that he cared about that. Many girls across the backcountry dispensed with such niceties, but she carried herself with such a proper air, it surprised him. Her hair fell braided, straight down her back, of a shade just darker than the gown.

What color were her eyes?

As if she'd heard his thought, she glanced toward him, affording him a glimpse of her pale, severe face, then twitched away again, head tucked even lower than before.

And what hurts had she suffered to make her so mistrustful? Fire swept his veins at the thought.

"Miss Cunningham—"

Her father chose that moment to lumber through the door. His gaze darted to the girl and back to Jed before a forced smile creased his face again. "'Tis all set. My son will ride to inform my nephew of your presence here, and Lizzy will have your room prepared. The horse out front is yours?"

"Aye. I'll see to her stabling, save you the trouble."

The man seemed to relax a mite. "Shed's out back, with fodder. Just come in the back entrance when you're done."

Jed rose, dipped his head to Miss Cunningham, who hesitated but didn't quite acknowledge him—watching him without looking at him directly—and gathered his hat and rifle.

He found the shed in an arguably better state than the common room, as far as repair and outfitting. Jed smiled grimly as he tied his bay mare into an open stall. Wouldn't be the first time men demanded better accommodations for their horses than for themselves. In fact, if the situation were any less precarious, he'd be tempted to bunk out here with Daisy rather than inside the tavern.

Not that as a tavern, they were as used to hosting overnight guests. The place was supposed to serve as a social center for a town or, in this case, a stopping point for travelers between towns, but the apparent dearth of actual social activity bespoke. . .what? What could he gather from this situation?

After removing the saddle and setting it over the side of the stall, Jed took a bunch of hay and commenced to rubbing Daisy down.

With the recent push by the Continental army under General Greene to clear all loyalists from the backcountry, apparently this tavern keeper, known by many to have loyalist leanings, found it hard to continue doing business among his patriot neighbors. *Rebel,* he reminded himself. If he were to pass himself off as one of these men, he needed to keep the proper wordage firmly in mind. A proper Tory did not think of his Whig neighbors as anything but the sorest of revolutionaries. Even in the face of obvious defeat.

He vented a sigh. Could he even carry this off?

Chapter 3

The common room had been swept and tables wiped down for the night—
not that they'd seen many customers this eve—and the kitchen tidied and
prepared for the morrow. Perhaps she could get to bed now.

She climbed the stairs, weary to her bones, as she so often was at the close of a
day. Down the hall, almost tiptoeing so as not to rouse her father and brothers and
give them a reason to task her with one more thing. Or a dozen.

So intent was she on remaining silent that when the door to the lone guest
room swung open and its occupant stepped out, he was as startled by her presence as she by his. But he recovered quickly and flashed a grin. "Good eve,
Miss—"

She put a finger to her lips, and he fell obligingly silent.

Not a complete simpleton, perhaps.

The grin faded, his gaze sharpening. A scrape sounded inside Robert's room,
and his door creaked open. "Lizzy! I need you to—"

Beside her, their overnight guest straightened and said, "Pardon. I have need of
Miss Cunningham at the moment. Might it wait?"

Her brother's expression went sly. "You do, do you? Well now." His eyes slid
toward her. "I suppose then. . .what I need. . .can wait."

And with great hesitation and obvious reluctance, he withdrew.

Heart pounding but trying not to show it, Lizzy turned back to—"Mr. Williams, is it?"

Something flickered in the man's eyes. "Aye." The smile resurfaced, but with
reserve. "Miss Cunningham. My apologies."

"Mine as well," she said, suddenly breathless under his gaze, and made to dodge
past him.

He caught her by the shoulder, light but firm. "Miss Cunningham—"

"Please," she whispered. "Not here." Meeting his look fully for the first time, she
glanced meaningfully toward her brother's door and back.

He nodded slowly and released her, stepping back. "Where then?" he mouthed.

She shook her head and edged along the wall. His hand came up and stopped.

"I wish you no hurt, Miss Cunningham," he murmured.

She stared at his hand, which turned, palm up. The arm remained outstretched, his face, grave.

Then she did the only thing that made any sense—turned and fled down the hallway and up the narrow set of stairs leading to her attic room. Once inside, she barred the door, as she had every night since she was a young girl, and stood panting against it.

Did such a man exist who wished her no hurt?

Jed stood, still reeling with disbelief. What on earth had this girl suffered, that she'd not even stop to speak with him?

He waited until the sound of her footfalls ended with the close of the door, then crept down the hall in the opposite direction. His contact would wait, but Jed didn't want to delay any more than needed.

Downstairs, out through the tavern's back door, he angled toward the necessary, glancing all around without seeming to, stopping between the necessary and stable to listen. Then he pressed on, into the thickets.

He found the great, multi-trunked maple with little trouble, climbed into the middle, and released a soft whip-poor-will call. A similar call answered, then with a rustle, a shadowy form emerged from along the creek. "Jedidiah Wheeler?"

"Williams now." Jed stepped back into view. "And you are Zacharias Elliot?"

"I am." The man offered his hand, and Jed shook it with good will. "Pleased to make your acquaintance. Even more pleased that you took this task. . .though I do not envy you the carrying of it out."

Jed gave a low laugh. "Nay. 'Tis not to be envied, for sure. I've been lodged for the night and hope to meet the man himself on the morrow or the next day, but the whole place smells of something gone very amiss."

The other man folded his arms across his chest. "You mean, more than them being Tory?" When Jed hesitated, he snorted softly. "Fear not to speak. My own family were staunch loyalists. They turned me out when I turned coat."

"Speaking of being in an unenviable position," Jed said, with respect.

Elliot's head dipped.

"And aye," he went on, slowly, "of something more than that."

'Twas on the tip of his tongue to say something about the girl, but that was not useful intelligence of any sort.

At least not yet. Jed could not shake the niggle that he needed to keep an eye on her.

"I've no idea how often I'll be able to report," he said.

"Understandably. Is there someone at the tavern I might entrust messages to?"

"I'd say avoid the tavern keeper and his boys. But the daughter seems to be a solid enough sort."

Elliot's head came up a little. "Could she be recruited, do you think?"

Jed shrugged. But he couldn't say the thought hadn't occurred to him. "I'll see what I can do."

Chapter 4

When Jed returned to the tavern, a contingent of mounted riders roughly circled the building.

He drew a long breath then emerged from the thicket, straightening his clothing as if returning from nothing more than a leisurely trip to the necessary. Several men swung toward him, weapons raised. About half wore frontier or farmer's garb, the other half regimentals. Green ones, if he didn't misgauge it in the gloom, typical of loyalist troops. "Good evening, gentlemen," he greeted them. "What might I help you with?"

"Are you Williams?" one of the regimentals asked.

"I am."

The plumed hat tipped toward the tavern. "Come with us."

Feeling as though he already had a knife stuck in his gut, Jed went along.

Inside, the common room was lit again by a pair of candelabras, where half a dozen men sat at table and a dozen more lined the walls. The color of the regimentals was a definite green, as he'd guessed. Miss Cunningham scurried along the edges of the group, pitcher in hand, filling tankards as they were lifted. He suppressed a wince at the hunch of her shoulders and gave his attention to the men.

And all their attention was on him. This must be what Daniel felt, being tossed into the lions' den.

He stepped to the middle of the common room and slowly looked around, hands loose at his sides, letting them gauge him as he did them. They were a motley bunch, but no more rough looking than the Continentals and militia he'd ridden with these past months.

The war had been hard on them all. . .

Dismissing the thought, he scanned their faces and met the eyes of each one in the half-light. Ordinary felt hats with pine sprigs shaded lean faces, most clean shaven but some with a few days of whiskers. Several Indians as well, bright bits of color against their shirts and leggings, regarding him impassively.

No one moved. They barely breathed. At last, one man in regimentals rose from his seat nearby, unfolding to his full height, easily a hand or so taller than Jed. "I'm Major William Cunningham. You wished to meet with me?"

A well-formed man he was, and young, no older than Jed himself. Yet commanding. All the other men watched him like trained hounds.

"I did." The trick here would be to strike the right balance of adulation and comradeship. A man like this thrived under having his pride stoked. "Heard you're one of the best to ride with if a man wants to strike back at these blasted rebels."

Cunningham shifted, and his eyes glittered. "And striking back would be your desire, would it?"

"Aye," Jed answered, without hesitation. "Turned out of my home, I was. And with those rascals overrunning the whole of the Carolinas—"

"Where was your home?" Cunningham smoothly interposed.

"North Carolina. Mecklenburg County." Exchanged glances and nods all around at that. "My parents are dead; God rest their souls. No other family willing to have me." He swallowed. That part wasn't strictly true, but he mustn't give it away. Although a little emotion could go a long way toward convincing the others.

"And what mischief were you at, outside?"

"Mischief?" Jed blinked. "Weren't nothing but a trip to the necessary. Except someone were in there, so I—ah—" He slanted a glance at Miss Cunningham.

William Cunningham turned to his female cousin. "Lizzy?"

Jed's heart thudded painfully in his chest. This small thing could be his undoing—

The girl straightened, facing them. Color washed faintly across her cheeks. "Aye, I'd gone out. What of it?"

Air filled his lungs, but Jed barely caught himself from gaping.

Why would she cover for him?

Whatever had possessed her to do that?

Lizzy could see the slight widening of his eyes—the recognition that she knew he was being untruthful there somewhere—but for some reason, maybe the hopeless wish that he truly was as kind as he seemed, she couldn't resist defying her cousin for his sake.

Said cousin released a humorless chuckle as she turned away. "Surely he hasn't been here long enough to secure your affections already, Lizzy?"

"What matter is it to you?" she threw back over her shoulder. "As you all so often remind me, not a man's been made who could bear living with me."

The room exploded with laughter. All except for Mr. Williams, who regarded her with a look of puzzlement and—was that distress? Or merely pity?

She turned her back on him as well. She knew she wasn't well favored. Why heap hurt upon hurt by pretending she ever had the slightest chance to catch his eye?

Not that she wanted to. He was a man, like any other, who only wanted a woman for keeping his house and bearing his children. And she'd not met one yet that she'd willingly shackle herself to, much less risk childbed for.

However, this one was cool as you please. Her cousin was a cruel, bloody man— she did not doubt the accounts that floated back over the past weeks, not when he was wont to come in and brag on his exploits. This stranger had to know that. And yet he answered Billy's questions and cross-questions with no hesitation.

It almost disappointed her to think he'd go riding with Billy without even a show of caution. But—if he was the simpleton she'd first thought him to be, or worse, he'd bear the penalty for it. And rightfully so. No business was it of hers if he brought perdition down on his own head.

Suddenly weary beyond bearing, she returned to the kitchen on the pretext of fetching something, and listened as Billy pronounced the stranger, Jed Williams, fit to join his company.

No business of hers at all.

Chapter 5

Survival was easy the first day.

As a new rider in the company, Jed was expected to do little more than keep up and stand watch. He felt the probing gazes of Cunningham and the others, but as long as he kept quiet, eyes open, laughed along at their jesting, and nodded sagely at their ranting, he invited no undue attention and thus, no trouble.

Such good fortune couldn't last forever.

Around the fire that night—they'd camped that first night at Cunningham's Tavern and taken provisions the next morning before being on their way—he listened to the men's talk, making note of names and where they were from, asking his own questions when he could about why they were there. A common thread of pride bound them all. The overall cause was not so much striking back at a rebellion that had managed to bring the best troops of Mother England to their knees just weeks before, but how that rebellion had hurt them all in personal ways. For one man whose wife had been accidentally shot and killed through the door by her own brother during one of the many skirmishes flaring across the Carolinas over the past couple of years. Both men had grieved hard, but in the end neither could be reconciled to the other's views.

Many told tales similar to Bill Cunningham's, of family members abused by rebel neighbors, crops and livestock ruined or taken, homes burned or confiscated. What had any of them left, besides carrying out as much retribution as possible against those who smugly remained? None wanted to sit in Charles Town and merely wait for transportation elsewhere.

Jed did not doubt the truth of any of their stories. If anything, he'd guess they were more sparing in detail than they could have been. Just weeks ago, he'd left the company of Rutherford, who had exercised such severity against loyalists, regardless of sex or age, that General Greene himself warned him to back off, or he'd authorize the loyalists to retaliate.

One or two of the men here mentioned Rutherford. Jed suppressed a sigh. Sitting here, his face warmed by a fire while the November evening cooled his back, surrounded by anger and sorrow and desperation, he could almost be in sympathy with these men.

Not that he entirely blamed Rutherford either. The man had spent some months in a prison ship in Charles Town harbor.

A very dangerous position he found himself in, but perhaps he could make it serve.

He lifted his head. "So what of the events at Turner's Station?"

They stared at him as if he were an imbecile. He felt rather like one, but it needed to be asked.

"You must understand," one of the men said at last. He cast a glance over his shoulder at another fire several dozen paces away, where Cunningham himself lounged with those Jed had learned already were his most trusted officers, then lowered his voice. "Our wives and children have been thrown out of their homes and forced to the road as refugees—many times with nary a possession but the clothes on their backs. What man of honor does that? And what sort of men would we be if we didn't answer such cruelty on their behalf?"

Jed offered a slow nod.

"See then, the major has determined to hunt down the rascals responsible for these and other despicable acts. Only he knows the full list, or in what order he plans to attack."

"Turner's Station was just one of several," another man said. "Those that died, deserved it. Although"—and Jed could see the man shudder as he looked away—"none of us would argue that the major wasn't a little mad with bloodshed. 'Tis one thing to shoot or hang a man for his crimes, another thing entirely to hew him in pieces."

What a perfect nightmare he'd been dropped into.

Lizzy hated nights like this one. Full already, and then her cousin's men stopped in for refreshment. If only she could hide in her attic room. Or at least the kitchen. But Papa always insisted she be on hand to serve.

Hooting laughter erupted from a dice game in the corner. Suppressing a wince, she deposited the platter of sliced bread and apples on the counter and made to turn away when their overnight guest from several days ago leaned toward her and caught her gaze. "Quite the crowd this evening, Miss Cunningham."

She glanced across the room, taking in not only the games that were yet just short of unruly, and her father holding court near the hearth—it could be called nothing else—and gave a short nod. "Fair enough, it is."

He chuckled, leaning his elbow on the counter. "Come now. A bit more than fair, I'd call it."

With a long, cool look, she straightened and turned, but his hand brushed her sleeve. She yanked away and gave him as scorching a glare as she could summon. His suddenly grave, earnest gaze caught her, however, as his physical touch could not.

"My apologies, Miss Cunningham. Have you been—well?"

"Well enough." Somehow the sharp retort on her lips lost the edge she'd intended.

His eyes searched hers. "What qualifies as 'well enough,' I wonder."

A hot ache bloomed in her chest. "Do not toy with me, Mr. Williams. I am no simpering doxy to be taken in by your sweet words."

Surprise flashed across his expression, then he broke out in another laugh. "Nay. You are most certainly not that."

And as he laughed again—yet not in a way that seemed to be at her expense—the hurt melted and a slight smile tugged at her mouth. She ducked her head lest he see it and misread it as friendliness.

Too late. His hand extended across the counter again. "Please. I only meant to ask—were there any messages for me?"

She slid away. "Nay. No messages."

She scurried back to the kitchen and pressed the heel of her hand to the middle of her chest. What was it about him?

And why was he asking about messages?

Chapter 6

Not much call for a rifle in the work of retribution," Kittery commented. "But that's a right fine pair of dragoon pistols."

Jed hardly glanced at the fine Pennsylvania long rifle hanging from his saddle, tucked snugly under his knee. "It goes where I go," he said mildly. "Where are we headed this misty morning?"

Kittery snickered. "Meet up with Hezekiah Williams, below Ninety-Six. Any relation of yours?"

Jed pretended to think, then shook his head.

He'd joined up, he already knew, at the end of a three-day spree—executions, Cunningham called them—of noted Whig leaders across the South Carolina backcountry.

Cunningham's list wasn't near exhausted yet.

Please, Lord, help me to stay true. Help me to do what's right. Help me put an end to this, and if I share in the bloodguilt in any way. . . Well Lord, I beg your forgiveness.

He thought of Lizzy, serving so faithfully back at her father's tavern. The startled look on her face when he'd asked after her welfare. How in that one moment she'd let him get close enough, he could see flecks of blue and green and gold in her dark eyes—all the colors of a Carolina autumn day.

The shock that had gone through him when she'd actually smiled—just a little, but a definite smile nevertheless, one that had banished the pale severity and transformed her.

Lord, protect her. And let me live to get back and make her smile again. That girl needs more reasons to smile.

But mostly, protect her.

Another morning, another day to get through.

And to make things worse, while she scrubbed the tavern floor, on her knees, the memory of blue eyes and an earnest-sounding inquiry lingering at the edges of her thoughts.

This was why she locked her heart up tight and refused to entertain silly notions, such as the hope that a man could be honorable and good. Such hints either turned out to cover dark motives, or they came from someone who wouldn't stay once they saw the ugliness of her own heart. And in the meantime, she was left longing for something she could never have.

Maybe 'twas time to do as other women did and just take the first offer that came along. At least then she'd be out from under her father's thumb—

Except that with his wounded leg, he'd find some way to claim it her duty to look after him the rest of his life. *Honor your father and mother,* he'd say. She released a little sigh. There was no escape.

Did God really intend life to be so wretched? Papa would argue aye, that mankind was too sinful to expect anything else. Women were certainly too treacherous, and only their evil nature made them desire better.

Of course, her father did plenty of expecting better, himself. And made it her responsibility to see it happen.

Was that truly God's will?

With half the floor yet to do, she rose to her feet and carried the pail of dirty water out through the back door to toss in the yard, then walked to the spring to fetch a fresh one.

She'd just stooped to fill the pail when a man stepped from the thicket. Straightening, she gripped the pail as if it could protect her.

"Easy now," the man said, but did not move closer. A worn hat shaded dark eyes and mostly covered dark hair queued back.

"What do you want?"

"Information. And something to drink if it isn't too early."

"'Tis too early," she blurted. Then, "I have to finish scrubbing the floor. And my father and brothers are still asleep. But if you're quiet, and you're paying—"

He gave a quick nod. "I am indeed."

She filled the pail, still watching him, then allowing him to take it from her, led the way back to the tavern. As he set the pail down at the edge of where she'd left off scrubbing, she drew him a tankard of watered ale. "My thanks," he murmured, and sampled the brew while she withdrew to behind the counter.

He wiped his mouth with his sleeve and nodded his approval. "Very decent, especially in such difficult times."

She bobbed a nod in return.

"Now then. I believe you are acquainted with a certain Mr. Williams?"

The back of her neck prickled. "I am acquainted with several Mr. Williamses. To which do you refer?"

The man laughed softly and shook his head. "I think you know which one I mean. Did he leave any messages behind?"

Lizzy regarded the man in silence for a long moment. "Nay."

He squinted a little and took another sip of his ale. "Miss Cunningham, I am not your enemy."

All the warnings in her head were definitely at full cry now. "Enemy or nay, he did not leave a message."

He measured her in turn. "Very well." After tossing back the rest of the ale, he set the tankard down, put a pair of coins beside it, then pushed away from the counter.

"That's too much," Lizzy said.

The man smiled thinly. "Consider it my thanks for a bit of conversation."

"You should leave now." She lifted her chin. "My father doesn't take kindly to me speaking with men alone."

The smile widened. "I am safely married and no philanderer. Please give Mr. Williams my regards."

Her curiosity got the best of her. "Who should I say was inquiring?"

"Mr. Elliot." He hesitated and lowered his voice further. "Should you be in need of help, Miss Cunningham, you may inquire for me at Dawson's Station, above Orangeburgh."

"Leave," she snapped, but quietly. "This instant."

A laugh was his parting reply. Lizzy snatched the coins off the counter, set the tankard on the shelf below, and whisked herself back to scrubbing before anyone could be the wiser.

A coldness settled deep in her belly and would not go away.

Chapter 7

Jed knew what battle looked like. This was nothing like it.

First order of the day had been for Cunningham to pay a visit to his former commanding officer, where the mischief of a pair of men going on ahead resulted in the old man being shot in his front yard, and Cunningham making a show of tears over it one minute, then in the next ordering the house to be burned, while the man's wife wept over his body.

'Twas all Jed could do not to ride off into the thicket and be sick.

They'd ridden north then to a place called Hayes Station. Galloped across a field in time to see all the men scramble into a blockhouse from where they'd loitered among the shops. Jed held Daisy back as far as he could from the stampede, but still he saw the leading riders chasing a pair of stragglers, one swinging his sword at the last as the blockhouse door closed. Shots answered from inside, and with a shout, Cunningham gave the order to take cover and return fire.

Jed's heart burned. All he could do was watch and deliberately misaim as he fired next to the others. With the whole company taken up by bloodlust, this was not the place to be giving his game away.

Kittery nudged him during a lull. "Time to use that fancy rifle of your'n."

Jed shook his head and started to speak, but the cry went up that the blockhouse had been set on fire. Cunningham was in conversation with its occupants, and Jed could only half hear what was said.

"They'll be coming out, directly." Kittery's eyes glittered. "The major will be picking who he plans to execute. Others will be invited to step up and choose those they want particular vengeance against."

Even in the cold, Jed could feel the sweat breaking out over his body. *Merciful God in heaven! What can I do here?*

Around him, men were leaving their hiding places and creeping closer, drawn by the promise of bloodshed. Jed swallowed and quickly reloaded his pistols, then followed, hanging back, yet an idea tickling the back of his brain.

It was mad. But if he fled, here and now, he'd never have another chance to make a difference.

The men inside the blockhouse trickled out, under a promise of mercy that there was no intention of honoring. Cunningham selected two and hanged them on a pole braced between two trees. The brother of one—barely more than a lad—flew forward, crying out in protest. Cunningham ordered the youth to be hanged as well, but the pole broke. In a fury, Cunningham fell upon them with his sword.

Jed turned away and shoved one of his pistols in his belt. He must remain cool. In the fray, his eyes fell upon the poor wretches stumbling out of the blockhouse, coughing, the building behind them consumed now with flames. Before any could stop him, he seized the shirt of one and hauled the man to his feet. "If you want to live, come with me," he growled, for the man's ears only, holding the other pistol to his temple.

A startled gaze came to his, and gaping, the man let himself be dragged along.

Basket tucked under her arm, shawl wrapped around her shoulders, Lizzy stepped carefully across the muddied road to the butcher's. After nearly a week of twitching at every little sound and having her heart nearly stop any number of times, she'd been told by Papa to expect extra patrons at the tavern tonight. And so they needed extra meat for a stew.

Supplies dwindled all the way around though, and fast. How long they could continue operating, she did not know. Papa didn't seem concerned at all. Either he had sources she knew nothing of—of material goods as well as information, although she knew Dickie rode back and forth between her cousin Billy and the tavern—or he somehow expected their fortunes to change, even with the British having withdrawn to Charles Town.

They might even be forced to declare themselves rebel to keep making a living.

Her gut churned at the very thought. At the reminder of her suspicions, kindled at the visit of Mr. Elliot several days before. Suspicions which had done nothing but fester since.

She stepped through the door, nostrils pinching and stomach threatening to heave at the smell of blood and offal, and slid to the back of the room to wait for the three men already at the counter to finish their conversation. "—twenty-eight dead at Hayes Station," Mr. Foster, the butcher, said. "And before that, Captain Caldwell murdered in his own front yard."

Glancing her way, he fell silent, and as one they all turned to look at her. She swallowed. "If you please, I need—five pounds of beef."

Mr. Foster's chin came up, his eyes narrowing. "All out for today."

She knew better. "My coin's as good as anyone else's."

"Coin don't do you any good if I have no beef to sell."

Desperation choked her. "Look you, I cannot change my family's loyalties. But I've lived here most of my life, and I know each of you—your wives and children as well. I gladly serve all who come through our door, regardless of your own loyalty, and if you came to me in need—"

Richardson and Davis, the men on her side of the counter, seemed to loom over her of a sudden. She fought the urge to shrink back.

"Perhaps it is time you left, and gave the tavern tending over to someone less— oh, loyal," Richardson said.

Davis gave an ugly laugh.

"Very well." Keeping her face calm and her back straight, Lizzy retreated with as much dignity as she could muster.

She stomped all the way back to the tavern. They'd have to live with beans and a bit of salt beef tonight.

Why did her father continue to hang on here, anyway?

By the time she reached the sanctuary of her kitchen, she could hardly breathe, or see. She flung down the basket and her shawl, and gulping back a sob, swiped her apron across her eyes. They'd not reduce her to tears, those rebel bullyboys.

The soup of beans, rice, and salt beef cooked quickly enough, at least, ready to serve by the time darkness fell and her cousin's company came trickling. As the men whooped and jested between themselves, she kept her head down, meeting no one's gaze and seeking no one's attention. Not even—that one particularly troublesome new recruit.

As always, they treated her as invisible, boasting about such deeds the last few days as to turn her stomach completely. She understood their fury—did she not taste of rebel abuse barely an hour or so ago? But was this truly how to go about dealing with it?

Another burst of laughter, and the name she'd tried not to think of caught her ear. "Aye, and Williams here, he lost not one but two prisoners! What do you make of that?"

"I think he needs to wash the crockery this night, to learn him to work more carefully!"

More guffaws, and to her dim horror, Mr. Williams himself scraped his stool back and began gathering dishes. "An honorable enough occupation, I own," he replied with surprising cheer. "Seems I might as well, if I'm fit for nothing else."

She couldn't look away fast enough as he glanced across the crowded room at her and winked.

Familiar panic filled her chest. No refuge this time in the kitchen, for he headed that way, arms loaded with crockery to be washed.

But she couldn't leave him to smash it all either if he proved incapable of the task.

With a ragged sigh, she gathered her own armful and trudged after him.

Chapter 8

He'd hoped against hope that she'd follow him.

Not the slightest hint of softness in her demeanor though as she plunked her stacks of dirtied bowls and plates next to his and wiped her hands on her apron. "Do you truly know what to do with those? Besides break them of course."

The grin stole across his face before he could stop it. "I've washed a tub or two of dishes in my time. I reckon I can keep from breaking them if need be."

Her bearing went beyond severe to openly hostile. He might be safer facing the troops out there in the common room. "Simpleton," she snapped, barely above a breath. "You might also want to have a care who you send asking for messages."

That doused any show of good cheer he might be able to summon.

"Aye. Look at me like you haven't an inkling what I mean. Your Mr. Elliot is like to get himself shot if he shows his face here again."

He still dared not move, dared not breathe. "So he did not get himself shot the first time."

She sustained the glare for a moment longer, then huffed and shook her head. "You men are all alike."

As she went to turn away, he stepped up close, blocking her way. "Nay. Not all."

Her gaze snapped to his, her expression going slack with shock. But she did not move.

That was progress.

"Did he come inside to find you, or. . . ?"

A sharp shake of her head. "He surprised me at the spring. Then came in for a drink."

"Did he leave a message?"

Another shake, softer this time. "Only asked whether you had." She swallowed visibly. "Told me where to find him if—if I encountered trouble."

He nodded, glancing around to make sure no one had witnessed the exchange. Then he eased back, flashing her another smile. "Your dishwater is old. I'll fetch fresh from the spring."

Before she could stop him, he seized two pails from beside the door and ducked out into the night.

If Elliot had been there once, he might be again. Jed would risk it. Too much to tell to trust to the written word, or to—to Miss Cunningham. However much he wanted to.

He reached the spring, filled the pails, then set them down and waited. A slight rustle in the thicket set his pulse racing until Zach Elliot actually stepped into view. "Have a care with who you trust," he said, without preamble.

Jed set his hands on his hips. "I might say the same to you."

"Miss Cunningham is a tart one. I told her nothing of importance, but—watch yourself."

"Trying. 'Tis a bit difficult when she won't hold still long enough to let me even begin inquiring about her loyalties. But she trusts no one, especially not her own family."

They were keeping their voices low, but Elliot listened for a moment before replying. Only the wind in the pines came to Jed's ears.

"Do what you can then," Elliot said. "And what news? I'm hearing some wild tales from the last few days."

Jed gave him a hurried summary of Cunningham's raids since Jed had been with him. The gathering concern on Elliot's face deepened.

"We should pull you if it's too dangerous—"

"I committed to doing this, and do this I will," Jed insisted. "Besides, I cannot go until I know if she can be persuaded to leave her father and brothers."

Elliot tucked his chin, peering at him in the half-dark. "Are you. . .soft on her?"

Half a dozen retorts tangled on his tongue. "I—there are things she's suffered at their hands, that I'd like to see an end to."

"Hmm." Elliot seemed unconvinced, but what did Jed care what the man thought?

Footsteps and a breathless feminine voice floated down the path. "Mr. Williams!"

"Aye, coming!" he called back, and gave a nod to Elliot as the man disappeared once more into the thicket.

He lifted both pails and made it halfway back before Miss Cunningham met him on the path. "Lost, Mr. Williams? There are dishes to be washed and men yet wanting their dinners."

Her chiding lacked much of the edge he was sure she intended.

In fact, if he did not miss his guess, that breathlessness was—fear.

For him, or herself?

"It took longer to fetch water than I expected," he said.

"Indeed."

He made to move past her, but she stayed in the middle of the path. He glanced around, listening, but it seemed they were alone. "Is aught amiss?" he murmured, for her ears alone.

"What are you doing?" she whispered fiercely.

"Naught for you to be concerned about." He tried a smile, but her expression did not change. "Corresponding with someone about family. Back home."

"Your family cast you out." She edged closer. "Or did they?"

Silence was likely his greatest ally in the moment.

"You," she breathed, "are a filthy rebel. Are you not?"

He leaned toward her till a bare handspan lay between their noses. "That's a grave offense to accuse a man of, in this place."

"*Are* you?"

Starlight glimmered in her eyes. Her half-parted lips trembled. The scent of something clean and wholesome washed over him—

A good thing, likely, that both of his hands were busy holding pails of water. He straightened and gave her another smile. "Excuse me, Miss Cunningham. There are dishes to be washed."

And with that, he brushed past her.

How had he done that? So neatly managed to evade answering and then flash that grin as if he could slide by on charm alone, and leave her so completely without words—

Lizzy gritted her teeth as she followed him back to the tavern. Ignored the hoots and jeers at them emerging from the darkness together. What did she care what they thought?

Inside, he was already pouring water into a kettle and hanging it over the kitchen fire, then he tackled the dishes she'd left stacked in the old water.

As she'd thought. Not so used-up, after all. Merely a pretext for him to walk to the spring.

He glanced up and caught her watching him, angled her a half smile and kept washing. With a huff, she found a cloth and took up the task of wiping dry a stack of earthenware bowls.

They worked in silence, settling into a surprisingly comfortable rhythm, even as the common room became more unruly. The call went out for more ale, and her unexpected helper for the evening lifted a staying hand and carried out a pair of pitchers himself, answering the other men's teasing with his own laughter and jests. In the kitchen, Lizzy kept working, listening to his easy way with them all.

If he was a rebel, in truth, he hid it well. She could not reconcile his manner at this moment—nor his kindness to her—with what she'd witnessed earlier at the butcher's.

Of course, there were likely wretches on both sides of the conflict. Honorable men too possibly.

She snorted. Less likely, that.

"Thinking disparaging thoughts about me again, Miss Cunningham?"

She startled at the low voice just behind her—despite the effort not to—and twitched to find him *right there*. Blue eyes sparkling in the lamplight, which traced a warm gold from the strands of his hair falling messily out of its queue. Shoulders impossibly broad in his simple shirt and waistcoat—

"Aye." She shoved her hands back into the dishwater, scrubbing at something she knew was coloration of the earthenware and not a stain. "Always."

His chuckle gusted across her. Drew a sting to her eyes and an ache to her throat. Why, she could not say.

"Likely I deserve it well enough." He lifted the cloth and set to the drying.

She peeked at him from the corner of her eye, found his expression unexpectedly somber. "Why would you say that?"

His smile this time was sad. "Have all men of your acquaintance been so slow to acknowledge their own unworthiness?"

She sniffed again. "Oh, they avow their worth most strenuously, lest I forget."

He did not immediately reply to that. "Miss Cunningham," he began, then hesitated.

"Lizzy," she muttered.

She felt rather than saw his stillness, felt herself growing warm under the weight of his gaze.

"Oh, come now, I know you've heard the others call me by my given name."

"I," he said, quietly but firmly, "am not the others. And I hope most sincerely that you do not feel I am."

He moved away to fetch the now-warmed fresh water and pour some into the washtub, then nudged her aside. "My turn again." Another quick smile. "Lizzy."

Too shocked to resist, she let him take over, numbly reaching for the dampened drying cloth. Where was her tongue?

And how could her name sound so nearly like a caress on his?

As her cheeks flamed, she ducked away under the pretext of arranging clean tankards on a tray.

"I'm Jed," came his low voice, tugging her back around.

"Jed?"

"Short for Jedidiah."

A solid name for a solid man. "It suits you."

Now where had that come from?

His gaze held hers. "And Lizzy is short for—Elizabeth?"

Her face must be positively crimson by now. "Aye," she said faintly.

"Lovely," he said, unmoving. "The name and—the girl who wears it."

Lightning swept through her, head to toe. Her mouth opened, but no sound would come out.

Suddenly he was there, using the cloth in her hands to dry his own, so close she could feel the warmth from his body. His knuckles came up to brush her chin.

Still she could not move.

What in blazes was wrong with her?

A frown knitted his brows. "Has no one ever told you that? Truly?"

She shook her head a little. His eyes held her captive, and his fingers slid across her jaw, toward her ear—

And then—he was kissing her. Everything inside her melted.

Chapter 9

He should not—he really shouldn't. Not without knowing where she stood, if she was willing to defend him once he was able to tell her the truth. But the disbelief in her face, the shattered look in those eyes. . .

Would she believe him now, or would it only seem that he was taking advantage? For half a breath, she stiffened, then almost imperceptibly leaned into him.

It was the sweetest kiss he'd ever taken—or given.

He forced himself to pull back. This time, awe glistened in her eyes. Still touching her cheek, and the other hand holding hers tangled in the drying cloth, he decided to risk all. "Tell me, Lizzy. If you had opportunity to leave here. . . would you?"

Confusion flickered across the features that were, aye, truly lovely.

How had he not seen it before?

"What do you mean? What else is there, besides fleeing to Charles Town like any common refugee?"

He smiled. "I made a very respectable living, before—before the rebellion. I reckon I could do so again. You'd not have to live as a refugee if I had anything to say about it."

Watching the shift of light and feeling in her eyes—suspicion, doubt, hope—*please say aye,* he wanted to beg. And with every beat his heart echoed, *aye, aye, aye. . .*

"Well, this is a pretty sight, to be sure," came a voice, and Jed looked up to see Lizzy's father standing in the doorway.

What a blasted idiot he was for letting himself be caught.

Lizzy wrenched away, her eyes wide, cheeks scarlet, then pale. Jed made up his mind then and there to play the game as far as he could, for her sake if nothing else.

The older man's gaze was narrowed, calculating, as it swept between his daughter and Jed. The corner of his mouth lifted. "I should ask you, Mr. Williams, just what is your intent here with my daughter?"

"We were only washing dishes, Papa," she said, but Jed waved a hand in her direction, hoping she caught the signal to let him speak.

"My intent, Mr. Cunningham," he said, clearing his throat, "is to win your daughter. Honorably."

He sent her a look, hoping, pleading—

The color rose in her cheeks again, though not as sharply as before. "You are daft as well as a simpleton."

He laughed. He couldn't help it. "Perhaps."

"Why would you want Lizzy?" Mr. Cunningham sounded genuinely puzzled. "She ain't much to look at. Suppose she's a decent enough cook and housekeeper—though you must know I won't brook her leaving her aged papa behind." His expression grew sharp again. "A pair of strong hands to run the tavern might be welcome enough."

Jed forced himself to a semblance of proper respect and interest. "I just want Lizzy," he said, then prayed the older man would not feel the veiled threat he found himself putting behind the words.

Halfway across the kitchen, Lizzy put a hand over her mouth.

"I want her safe, and happy," he added.

Head tipped, Mr. Cunningham regarded him as he might an interesting insect. "We will see," he said at last, then nodded toward the common room. "Lizzy, we need more ale."

"We're nearly out," she said, in a small voice.

He halted midturn and shot her a glare. Flicked a glance at Jed. "Ale, or mulled cider, or something then, girl. You know your work. Get to it!"

And with that, he lumbered back to the common room. Jed released a long breath.

Lizzy rounded on him. "Why? Why would you say that?"

He really wanted nothing more than to swoop her into his arms and kiss her again. Longer this time. That impulse must be contained, however, along with the wild grin tugging at his mouth. She needed to know how serious he truly was about all this.

That above all, he was not trifling with her affections.

He took a measured step toward her. "Because. . .I meant it."

She backed away, shaking her head, gaze darting everywhere but at his face. "How—how can you? You heard my father—I'm nothing to look at—"

He gave into the impulse at least in part, and caught her into his arms. "Only because no one has stopped long enough to truly look."

When he tried tipping her chin up, she resisted him. "I'd never be able to escape him," she murmured, her voice mournful. "He'll let you near me only for your help keeping the tavern."

Slipping his hand around the back of her neck, he pressed his lips to her forehead. She felt damp and feverish, all at once. "Your father has your brothers, if it comes to that. Unless you want to stay and keep the tavern?"

Another small head shake, but she was beginning to lose her stiffness in his embrace. "I don't think we'll be able to stay."

He kissed her forehead again. She smelled delightful. "They're determined to chase all loyalists out of the backcountry, aren't they?"

"Aye." She softened against him another fraction, then gave his chest a half-hearted shove. "I need to see what else we have to offer for drink."

Not letting go, he nuzzled her hair. "It can wait another minute."

"You don't know my father."

He huffed. "True. But his kind, I know well enough." Reluctantly he released her. "So, what is this about nearly being out of ale?"

A kettle of warmed cider and half a keg of watered ale later, the common room began to empty and Lizzy retired to the kitchen to tend the last washtub of dishes while Jed swept and tidied elsewhere. Papa finally went upstairs to bed as her cousin's men wandered outside to sleep, but not before a final glare and growl about tending her chores.

Not a word about Jed however. Lizzy winced to think what he'd have to say about that once Jed was away with the other men tomorrow.

Robert drifted into the kitchen and poked around the pantry. "Anything left to eat?"

"Nay," she said, without turning around.

He sniffed. "I'm thinking of riding out with Cousin Billy in the morning."

Good riddance if so. "That would be too much like work for you, wouldn't it?"

Her brother snickered. "What, just because I don't do the washing and sweeping—like your sweetheart out there—you think I couldn't handle it?"

Lizzy slid him a glance. Did everyone know, already?

On the other hand, did she mind?

Robert pulled an apple from the bin at the bottom of the pantry, rubbed it on his shirt, and took a bite. "Is he truly your sweetheart? I didn't figure Williams for being a lackwit, or blind." He grinned at his own humor. "Or are you finally givin' up what you never let anyone else have? What's he promised you, for that?"

"He's kind," she muttered into the dishwater. "Something that never occurred to you, I'm sure."

He sauntered toward her. "You think you're pretty smart, don't you, Lizzy?"

"If I was, you'd let me know."

She tried to keep her voice mild, Lord help her, she did. Would Robert keep his hands to himself while Jed was still in the building? Or—worse—would he bide his time and try to catch her later?

Sniggering again, he edged up close to her. "I could be kind."

She stilled her hands in the dishwater. "Step off, Robbie."

"What, you gonna scream for your sweetheart?" He lifted the apple and took another bite, up close to her ear. So close she could feel his breath and smell his stench. "I wager you won't. Papa would beat you if you caused a ruckus."

Lizzy gritted her teeth. So tempting to fling—

"I'll beat *you* if you cause one," came a low voice behind them.

Robert scrambled away, trying yet to appear cool. Jed stood there, thunder in his face like Lizzy hadn't guessed he was capable of, the broom in his hands held crosswise like a weapon.

"Lizzy, he touch you?" Jed asked, still very quiet.

Heart pounding, she shook her head.

He took a step toward her brother, who'd gone pale, the apple dangling from his fingers. "Let's get one thing straight here. I aim to see your sister cared for, whether that's here or elsewhere. If any of you lays one hand on her, you'll answer to me. Is that understood?"

Robert nodded, then sidled around the edge of the room and scurried away.

Lizzy blew out a breath and turned back to the washtub. Jed set the broom against the wall next to the table. "Are you well, in truth?" he breathed.

Eyes stinging, she couldn't bring herself to look at him. And her heart was still like to climb up in her throat. She managed a quick nod.

"Lizzy?"

From the corner of her eye, she saw his hand, outstretched.

If she let him hold her, 'twould be the end of her composure—

But she wanted it. God forgive her, she did.

She dove into his arms and let his strength wrap her about.

"Shh, it'll be all right," he murmured into her hair.

Hardly knowing where to put her hands, she gripped the back of his shoulders and pressed her face into his chest. "Please—" The word came out strangled, but she had to ask. "Please don't go with my cousin tomorrow."

His breath caught. "Oh Lizzy."

"Please."

One hand smoothed from the crown of her head to the small of her back. "I must," he whispered.

She twitched away, swallowing back the sudden ache at the loss of that warmth, and gave him her best glare. "You—you claim to not be like them. And yet you tell me you must?"

His eyes were shadowed, full of secrets and—a tenderness that would surely break her. "Aye." He reached up to brush the side of her face. "Do you think your cousin's cause true and right?"

"I—" The reply clogged her throat. "I don't know."

Both hands came up to frame her face, and he studied her gravely. "I think you do know. Your asking me not to go is its own judgment against them, whether you realize it or not."

"My asking you not to go"—she gulped back the tears— "is purely selfish." She blinked, looked away, tried to pull back again. "Never you mind. I've borne worse—"

"Lizzy." Jed bent closer, capturing her attention once more. "Do you think your cousin is likely to stop his careening all over the backcountry unless he's forced to?"

Time slowed, then stopped. Her heartbeat became painful.

His eyes held her, like bits of the summer sky, willing her to—what? She could hardly think with him so near.

"Nay," she breathed. "Likely not."

Inexplicably, he smiled. "Then trust me when I say that I must go."

What—*oh!* The implication of his words crashed over her like a storm's flood on the river. "Nay—oh, nay," she whimpered.

His arms gathered her in as she buried her face against his shoulder. The beating of his heart under her cheek echoed the raging of her thoughts.

"You know what he does to anyone who tries to naysay him," she said, trying to keep her voice quiet. "He'll kill you."

"He can try," Jed rumbled. "I've good reason now not to throw my life away." His embrace tightened. "And I promise you, while there's breath left in my body, I'll either send for you, or come myself. Can you trust me with that much?"

The weeping took her, finally. "He won't let you live," was all she could manage.

The heaving breath under her cheek told her he knew the truth of it. "If you can't trust me with it, then at least trust the Almighty."

She rolled her head back and forth. "Why would God listen to me? Why would He not just send me more pain—"

The old anger rose, and with it, a comfortingly familiar strength, however bitter. She wrenched out of his arms and stepped back.

"Lizzy—"

"Nay." She had to distance herself from him. From the hurt.

Which already dug so deep that she couldn't see, couldn't breathe.

"Nay. I'll not stand by and watch you be murdered." He'd told her he cared for her welfare—kissed her—made her believe there might be more to her life than eternal servitude to her father and brothers—and now this?

Knowing he surely would bring perdition down on his head, in the form of her cousin's wrath, no less—her only refuge was in returning to not caring.

If only she'd never cared at all.

Chapter 10

Just that quickly, he'd lost her.

And once again, she'd fled from him, as if he were her enemy.

Which he was, in technical terms, but—having her run to tell someone was not his fear now, oddly enough.

He caught himself still staring at the empty doorway of the kitchen long after the sound of her footsteps had faded, up the stairs, across the hall and up to her own room. Scrubbed both hands across his face, then set to finishing up the washing. 'Twas the least he could do.

Lord—oh Lord—

The prayer faltered against the memory of her wounded fury. All he'd meant to do was tell her to have faith, and she'd flung it back in his face as if he'd asked her to do something vile.

But after seeing firsthand how both father and brother treated her, could he blame her for being too cautious to hope?

Keep protecting her, Lord. Please. And I ask again—if it please You, bring me back to her.

As if in response, a snippet of scripture floated through his thoughts. Elbows on the edge of the washtub, he sank until his forehead rested on his dripping fists.

Please, Lord. I beg you. Do not let this hope disappoint her.

A creak came from the common room, and heavy footsteps after. "Williams? You here?"

Blast it. "Aye. Washing up."

The tall form of Major Cunningham filled the doorway, a sly smile curling his mouth. "Well, well. Our Lizzy has you snared, well and truly?"

Jed snorted and kept at the task. Ignored the prickling at the back of his neck as Cunningham walked closer.

"So, are you with us, or nay?"

"I am with you."

"Are you sure?" Cunningham leaned against the wall.

Jed gave him a long look. "Why would I not be?"

The other man chuckled, affecting a casualness Jed was sure he did not feel. "No particular reason, except my uncle seems to think you bear watching." The teasing grin turned feral. "Our Lizzy is a good girl. She'll do whatever my uncle deems best."

Jed swished the water in search of the last piece of crockery. "I only want what is best for her."

"Hmm. That's admirable enough."

Admirable? Jed lifted his head and met Cunningham's mocking gaze. This man wanted to discuss what was admirable?

"I tell you though," Cunningham went on, "riding with us is likely safer than staying and facing Lizzy's tongue."

"I'm not afraid of Lizzy." Jed hefted the washtub and angled for the back door.

Cunningham's laughter gusted after him. "You should be!"

The next day dawned cold and blustery, but Cunningham insisted they move on before full daylight. Jed was half surprised they hadn't been attacked during the night, but perhaps there hadn't yet been enough time for the intelligence he'd given Elliot to have its effect.

Jed could feel the hostility from the settlement's other inhabitants, though no one dared to speak or do aught against Cunningham's company. He glanced across the sea of green coats mixed with hunting shirts—like his own, and the occasional blanket-swathed form, both Indian and white, some mounted but some waiting beside their horses for the call to move out. Daisy shifted beneath him, and he patted her absently, then sent a glance for the hundredth time to the attic window of the tavern. The shutter lay ajar but no movement could he glimpse behind.

Lizzy had not come downstairs as they'd prepared to leave. They snatched a few bites of cold rations—not that she could have baked anything that would satisfy such a large group, with provisions as they were. The soup she'd prepared the day before had been miraculous, under the circumstances. How they continued to operate the tavern with so little—

He shook his head. Enough gazing up at her window. He had to at least try for a proper farewell.

Dismounting, he handed his reins to Kittery. "Hold her. I'll be back in a moment."

He threaded his way through the other riders, to the tavern's back door, skirting the knot of men that included the Cunninghams, deep in conversation. Inside, he stopped and listened, and when no sound came to his ears, made his way as quietly as possible upstairs and through the hallway to the attic steps.

The narrow door at the top was closed. As it should be. And hopefully barred. He tiptoed upward and listened at the wood. A soft scuffing came from somewhere inside.

He rapped softly. "Lizzy? Lizzy, 'tis me, Jed."

A definite sniffle this time. "Go away."

Of course. "Not until you hear me out. Please."

A rustling came to the door, and stopped, but she did not open it.

He let out a breath and spread his hand against the rough planks. "I'm praying for you, Lizzy. Have been praying, and I won't stop. Not until—until I'm back, and you're in my arms again." The ache that had lodged in his chest since last night began to ease, just a little, at saying the words. "And—I'd be honored if you'd consider that a proposal of marriage. With or without your father's approval."

A sliding sound, and a thump on the other side, but still she did not open.

Not that he expected it.

Maybe he really was a fool.

With a rueful smile, he patted the door. "Be well, Lizzy. And trust the Almighty."

The ache grew again as he retreated down the steps and outside. The Cunninghams had scattered, with both father and son staring when he emerged from the tavern's back door. Jed stared calmly back. Lizzy's father held his gaze, but the brother glanced away.

He made his way back to Kittery and Daisy and swung into the saddle. This time, the attic shutter swung open a little more, a slender hand the only part he could see of the shadow hovering there. Jed waved her a salute and took his place with the column as it moved out.

In the press of horses and riders, Bill Cunningham circled his mount and sidled up to Jed's. His green regimentals were brilliant against the morning gray. "So you've decided to join us after all?"

Jed kept his face impassive, but he gave a determined nod. "I said that I would."

Major Cunningham laughed and clapped him on the shoulder, addressing the company at large. "This one aspires to tame our Lizzy! Think he's worthy of the task?"

Jed's ears and cheeks burned at the guffaws and quips rising in the wake of this pronouncement.

"Tame, or be tamed?" one called out, and another wave of laughter followed. "I'd say the latter, after watching him help her keep tavern last night."

"Aye, well, if he aspires to join himself to our family, he'd best prove himself, hadn't he?"

Chapter 11

I f Lizzy thought a week could be interminable before, it was doubly so now.

The first day of December came and went, and no word was there either from her cousin's company, Jed himself, or Mr. Elliot.

Maybe she'd simply dreamed it all. Because that's surely all it could be, with a man who not only told her she was lovely, but threatened Robbie with bodily harm on her behalf. . .and asked her to be his.

Or else he'd said those things merely to gain her trust, and never intended to make good on them.

"Be well, Lizzy. And trust the Almighty."

She was as well as she could be. But she didn't know how to begin accomplishing the other.

Papa stood out front in the cool sunshine, arguing with Mr. Foster for the fourth time this week. Likely trying to convince their neighbors he meant nothing by hosting her cousin and his company of men. With each passing day, the reports that trickled back to them were more difficult to believe.

She would not let herself think about Jed in the middle of all that. She would not—

And her heart was such a liar.

Peeking out to ensure Papa and the butcher were still deep in conversation, she snatched up her shawl and hurried out the back door of the tavern. Ducking behind the necessary, she cut through the thicket before reemerging on the path.

It wasn't far to the church, and hopefully she'd be back before Papa noticed she was gone.

Thankfully, she met no one on the road, and soon the small log building came into view through the South Carolina forest. No one appeared to be there, but the door was unbarred.

Pushing the door open, she slid inside, then stood still, breathing deeply. The place smelled damply of pine. She'd not been here in, oh, so long she could hardly remember. They'd not had a regular minister in years, and the exchange minister came but once every couple of months or so. But as she recalled, a worn Bible lay on the pulpit.

God in heaven, are You here? And do You see me?

She crept forward. There—aye—the Bible was there, illuminated by a faint pool of light from a small, high window nearby.

Another deep breath, and she walked the rest of the way, between the rows of bench seats and up three steps into the pulpit. Her fingers brushed the dusty leather cover. Where to begin?

Wedging her fingertips somewhere in the middle, she opened the book and smoothed the pages back. *The Song of songs, which is Solomon's,* she read. *"Let him kiss me with the kisses of his mouth: for thy love is better than wine—"*

"Oh, for pity's sake!" She couldn't turn the pages fast enough. Who knew something like that was in the Holy Scriptures? Not helpful in the least.

Psalms. That should be better. *"O LORD God of hosts, how long wilt thou be angry against the prayer of thy people? Thou feedest them with the bread of tears; and givest them tears to drink in great measure. Thou makest us a strife unto our neighbors: and our enemies laugh among themselves. Turn us again, O God of hosts, and cause thy face to shine; and we shall be saved."*

Much better. But still not quite what her heart was longing for.

Perhaps the New Testament.

"The thief cometh not, but for to steal, and to kill, and to destroy: I am come that they might have life, and that they might have it more abundantly. I am the good shepherd: the good shepherd giveth his life for the sheep. . . ."

Further in. *"Let brotherly love continue. Be not forgetful to entertain strangers: for thereby some have entertained angels unawares. . . . Marriage is honourable in all. . . Let your conversation be without covetousness; and be content with such things as ye have: for he hath said, I will never leave thee, nor forsake thee. So that we may boldly say, The LORD is my helper, and I will not fear what man shall do unto me."*

She stopped, considered the words again. *I will never leave thee, nor forsake thee.*

A quick turn of pages backwards. *"Call unto me, and I will answer thee, and show thee great and mighty things, which thou knowest not."*

Call unto me. . . great and mighty things. . .

A few more pages back. *"For I know the thoughts that I think toward you, saith the LORD, thoughts of peace, and not of evil, to give you an expected end. Then shall ye call upon me, and ye shall go and pray unto me, and I will hearken unto you. . . . And I will be found of you, saith the LORD: and I will turn away your captivity. . ."*

. . .thoughts of peace, and not of evil. An expected end.

I will hearken unto you.

She sank to the floor, covering her face with her shawl.

Oh, Lord God, could it be true? You think of me? And You hear me?

She'd not let the tears overcome her since that night Jed had kissed and held her so sweetly—though they'd tried often enough, to be sure—but she could not push them away now. Nor the memories—Jed's lips on hers, surprisingly warm and soft against the slight rasp of his chin—his blue eyes, entreating—the rumble of his voice as he exhorted her to trust God.

If You are there—if You hear me truly—then keep him safe through this madness of my cousin's. And. . .if it is not too presumptuous of me. . .bring him back. . .to me.

The scripture flitted through her thoughts again, *Let him kiss me with the kisses of his mouth. . .*

Heat swept through her, and she sank even lower.

Oh God. . .if my thoughts are unworthy, forgive me. But Your holy scriptures said it. Is it wrong then, to wish for the love of a good man?

Wrapped in his blanket, Jed huddled against the gnarled trunk of a live oak, alternately watching the twinkle of stars in the cold night sky through the branches and the array of campfires a short distance away. In spite of the recent snow, and partly in thanks to the fact that live oaks did not shed their leaves until new ones budded in spring, he'd found a relatively bare, dry spot under its branches and laid claim to it before anyone else could. Most of the other men huddled around the fires, but Jed felt snug and protected here. After nearly a month of pretending he belonged, he had no taste this night for conversation and jesting.

More than a week ago, Major Cunningham and the other commanding officer had divided the company and gone their separate ways to continue finding such mischief as they could. Pursuit by the rebels had become more direct, and some of Cunningham's stragglers had been captured and hung at a crossroads shortly after they'd left Lizzy's tavern. Jed wasn't sure whether to be grateful or not that he'd escaped such a fate simply because Cunningham had kept him close. He'd not had opportunity to slip away and send a message to Elliot either.

The longer he stayed with Cunningham's outfit, the closer he felt himself nudged toward the edge of committing something he'd never be able to justify, regardless of how it might contribute to the bloody major's downfall—and the more despondent he felt.

True to his word, Cunningham had indeed held him under his watchful eye. After splitting from Colonel Williams's troops, Cunningham had further divided his own remaining men into two groups, sending one farther up the backcountry with the intent to hide out among the Cherokee nation. All left were those willing to return to Charles Town, if necessary.

They'd moved often, rarely camping in the same place twice, but mostly around the upper forks of the Edisto River. Once or twice Jed had caught a glimpse of Lizzy's brother—not the one he'd threatened, but the one she'd said often rode back and forth between their tavern and Major Cunningham. Carrying supplies and intelligence both ways, unless Jed missed his guess. Her brother had glanced his direction but not acknowledged him. Just enough for Jed to know he was aware of Jed's presence, but an obvious cut.

The man was gone before Jed could make his way over to him. Not that he cared, but Jed would like to inquire after Lizzy's welfare.

The ache in his chest at the thought of her had grown no less sharp. As always, he tried at least to pour it into prayer for her—in between prayers for his own presence here to have some good purpose.

It didn't help that desperation hung about the camp in a nearly palpable cloud. Cunningham himself had gotten surly. Kittery and the other men whispered that he'd nearly run out of men to cut down. Some feared he'd start in on his own.

Jed guessed that he might just be the first.

He settled himself more comfortably against the oak, and having prayed until he felt fair exhausted, let his eyes slide closed and his thoughts toward his one consolation these days, after prayer itself—the memory of the fiery girl who for a few, sweet moments, actually trusted him enough to let him hold her in his arms.

Chapter 12

L izzy woke from a dream of endless requests for whiskey to shouts and the flicker of torches through her half-shuttered window.

And pounding on the wall at the foot of the attic stairs. "Lizzy! Wake up!"

She bolted out of bed and peered through the shutter. Half the settlement looked to be in their front yard.

"Now, Lizzy! They're going to burn the place!"

Lightning spurted through her veins. With no more thought, she seized various things from around the room and flung them into the middle of her bed, gathered all into a bundle, and wrapped herself in her shawl, then shoved her feet into her shoes.

Robbie was waiting for her at the far end of the hallway, beckoning for her to hurry. "Dickie's already downstairs with Papa."

"What madness is this?"

"Blasted rebels. They've decided to punish us for Cousin Bill's adventures."

He didn't offer to carry her bundle—not that it was much—but at least he'd wakened her and made sure she got out. "Fortunate they've let us come away with our lives," she muttered, as they sped down the stairs.

"So far," Robbie said.

"Not comforting in the least."

The common room was already in flames, and Robbie tugged her out the back door. A pair of men stood by the stable, their faces menacing in the torchlight. Richardson and Davis, from the butcher shop that one day. She hesitated. What if she just slipped away into the thicket, made her way to Dawson's Station, and left her father and brothers to their own fate?

"Get along, missie," Davis said, with a grin and point of his musket. "Stay with the rest of the vermin you call family."

She gritted her teeth. "I'd rather not."

Their sneers deepened. "Rather too late to turn coat now, Lizzy Cunningham. Go on with you now."

With a huff, she turned and followed after Robert. *Oh God, hear my plea. Help me. Preserve me—*

"My Lizzy! Oh, thank the good Lord you're safe."

The false affection in her father's cry turned her stomach, but she let herself be nudged closer to him, on the far edge of the yard. A good heat rose from the blaze of the tavern building at her back.

"You four." Mr. Foster, the butcher, addressed them, the flames glinting off his spectacles. "We've been as forbearing as we could, but your harboring the sorest of Tory scourges ever to plague the backcountry can no longer go unanswered. Consider yourself hereby stripped of all possession in the United States of America."

"Where are we supposed to go?" her father demanded.

"I suggest Charles Town, with the rest of your royalist cronies, to await whatever transportation the Crown deems fit."

Her father chewed his lip for a moment, then spread his hands in a beseeching gesture. "Have pity on us." Lizzy cringed at the whine in his voice. "For years now we've given you all good service—"

"We do have pity." Mr. Foster's gaze went to Lizzy, chilling her through despite the fury behind it. "You're allowed to depart with your lives and whatever you can carry."

She drew a deep breath, and while her father continued to sputter, lifted her head and set out upon the road in the direction of Orangeburgh, and it was to be supposed, Charles Town.

Hours later, near dawn, her father begged for a stop.

A half mile down the road, Lizzy had taken the time to dress more properly, then tied the bundle of what was left across her back with her shawl. Her father and the boys were already trailing her, Dickie complaining that they'd not even let him take his horse, and her father leaning on Robbie's arm. She trudged ahead, acknowledging none of them.

They could follow her, or not. She was determined to find Mr. Elliot and throw herself on his mercy.

"Shouldn't we be going south to the Edisto?" Dickie asked, but Papa shushed him.

Lizzy gritted her teeth. Tempting it was to seek out her cousin and thus hopefully Jed. . .but if she understood Jed's intended purpose aright, they'd best be nowhere near her cousin and his men.

"My feet are freezing," her father complained.

"We're nearly to Dawson's Station," Lizzy said, unclenching her jaw. "You can warm yourself there."

"Insolent chit," he growled.

She walked faster.

Pines and bare-branched sweet gum and oak towered over the road. Through the branches, the sky gradually lightened, helping her forget her own feet and hands, aching with the cold. At least the weather had cleared. If they'd chosen to burn the tavern during that snow a week ago—

Lizzy's eyes stung. Their tavern. The home she remembered best since her childhood. The attic room, her only haven since Mama's death years ago.

God, what do You have for me now? What will I find at the end of this road?

Part of her longed to just lie down, close her eyes, and never open them again.

"Be well, Lizzy."

She let her lids slide closed. Kept putting one foot in front of the other.

He won't let you live, her own heart cried out.

"Trust," came the reply.

I want to, her heart answered. *But if Jed does not survive—*

She could not bear thinking of the alternative.

Please, Lord. Please.

Dawson's Station was a mere fifteen miles from her father's tavern, but it felt like a journey from one lifetime to another.

Perhaps it was.

The sun peeked over the horizon, through the trees, as the cluster of log buildings came into sight—a blockhouse, a trading post, and another tavern much like their own. Lizzy stopped to resettle her burden across her shoulders and rubbed her eyes before trudging on to the tavern, ignoring the racing of her heart.

The shock and necessity of the past hours had worn thoroughly off. She was weary beyond bearing, looked a fright, she was sure, and likely still smelled of smoke. But, this was it. She'd never again return home. Not if she could help it.

She knocked at the tavern door. A shuttered window opened above and a man peered down, hair loose past his shoulders. "What is it at this hour?"

"Please, is a Mr. Elliot here? I need to speak with him."

The man's sleepy glare softened a fraction. "Who might I tell him is inquiring?"

She glanced back. Her father and brothers were just now catching up. "A friend of—Mr. Williams." She tried to keep her voice hushed. "If you please."

With a last severe, searching look, he gave a quick nod and disappeared. Lizzy blew out a breath and after shedding her bundle, collapsed onto the bench beside the door.

Oh God . . . Any prayer she had at this point was inarticulate.

Papa was just limping into the yard, supported by Robbie, when the door was unbarred from within and swung open. Lizzy stood as Mr. Elliot stepped out, his haste evident in his own unbound hair and absence of waistcoat over his shirt and breeches. But he held his rifle at the ready. "Miss Cunningham, this is a surprise."

"Please." She was not above begging if need be, not in this case. "Our Whig neighbors burned the tavern. We've nowhere to go now but Charles Town, but—I'm

381

here to ask your mercy."

He seemed to understand the plea in her words—and in her eyes—for he nodded slowly.

Her father's shuffling footsteps announced his approach. "Lizzy, fool girl, step out of the way and let me have that seat—"

She sidled away, still watching Mr. Elliot as he assessed the three men trailing her. Papa dropped to the bench with a huff and cast his own glare about.

"Does your request include them?" Mr. Elliot asked.

She chewed her lip. Was there any way to say it besides—

Turning to face her father and brothers, she squared her shoulders and lifted her chin. "You may all go on to Charles Town without me. After a suitable rest of course."

Her brothers gaped, with one giving a cry of protest, but Papa surged to his feet once more, leaning on his staff, eyes narrowed and face reddening. "What's the meaning of this, Lizzy?"

She stepped back and folded her hands in front of her. "I'm not going with you, Papa."

Lord help her, she tried to hold herself still, to brace for whatever response he might have, and still his anger took her by surprise. He moved so fast she'd not time to get completely out of the way when he lunged and backhanded her.

She stumbled and fell.

"None of that!" Mr. Elliot roared, and hauled Papa up by the back of his coat. Papa swung his staff but Mr. Elliot caught it and wrenched it away. "Dawson! Lend a hand here."

The other man was already there, and between the two they subdued Papa while Lizzy picked herself up out of the frozen mud.

Papa stood, shaking, alternating between cursing Lizzy and demanding Dickie and Robbie do something. Both edged back, eyes wide, clutching the small bundles they'd managed to carry away with them as well.

Mr. Elliot addressed them tightly. "There's still time to make honorable men of yourselves. But choose—either continue to Charles Town, as your sister suggests, or reconsider your loyalties and apply yourselves to making a new life here. But I warn you, the time is fast approaching that there'll be no room for wavering."

Robert gaped like a fish, opening and closing his mouth. Dickie went completely white, and turned and fled down the road.

"He's bound to go warn my cousin," Lizzy murmured to Mr. Elliot.

Other men were emerging now, in varying states of undress, to see what the ruckus was. With a word from Mr. Elliot, several of them apprehended Dickie, and Robert surrendered without a fight. In short order, all three Cunningham men were dragged away to gaol.

Suddenly finding herself without strength, Lizzy sat down on the bench again. "Are you well?"

She looked up to find Mr. Elliot regarding her with a concerned frown. "I—" Her cheek hurt where Papa had struck her, and a wave of dizziness overcame her. "Well enough." His frown did not waver, so she drew herself up. "My brother has been communicating with my cousin. I heard him mention going to him, south, on the Edisto River. I—I think they must be camped there?"

Mr. Elliot's dark eyes shone. "Thank you. It's a brave thing you've done, coming here."

She had no reply for that.

"Come," he said. "Mistress Dawson will be glad to see to you. Then we can discuss what happens next."

Chapter 13

December deepened until Jed could no longer remember what day it was. He was fairly sure Christmas neared, but how closely was anyone's guess. Even Kittery could not recall.

Cunningham had further divided the company and scattered them in camps all up and down both branches of the Edisto River, in groups of twenty or so. Predictably, he'd kept Jed with him.

At least they'd not been out on any more killing raids, since leaving Lizzy's tavern. But Cunningham grew more restive by the day, as if bloodshed was a kind of craving.

A craving Cunningham would soon find satisfaction for with Jed's own blood, he was sure.

Lord in heaven, have mercy...

'Twas nearly all he could pray anymore.

He lay curled in his blanket in the predawn gray, eyes open even before he was fully awake, listening to early morning on the river—as he did every morning of late. The stamp and muted snorts of horses, the rustle of men just beginning to stir about. The occasional cry of a winter bird, if the weather were quiet.

When the first shots sounded, upriver, he was on his feet without thought, rifle in hand. Others did the same. "It's an attack!" someone shouted.

Jed grabbed his gear, grateful he hadn't unpacked much the night before. He seized his saddle and cinched it down, then swung onto his mount.

At least half of the camp were similarly ready, including Major Cunningham.

"Downriver!" he called. "Let's go!"

This would be the perfect opportunity to slip away in the commotion. Jed edged Daisy away from the river, but the cypress swamp hedged them all in. There'd be no hurrying off in this part of the woods.

"Did you have aught to do with this?" came a snarl, nearly at his elbow, and Jed snapped around to find Cunningham at his flank.

And a familiar bloodlust in his eyes.

"I did not!" he threw back, nudging Daisy on, already plunging as fast as she could through the knee-deep black water.

Cunningham's great red horse matched them, lunge for lunge, and pulled ahead. The big man's attention did not waver. "I've watched you. Heard you avow your desire for retribution, but have you yet killed even one man?"

Jed gritted his teeth and dodged a low-hanging cypress limb. "I swear to you, I am true!"

They gained more solid ground, the horses heaving themselves up the bank, shoulder to shoulder. Cunningham rounded on him, the big horse nearly knocking Daisy back into the swamp. "True to whom, I wonder? And what?"

Jed met his gaze full on, held it despite the curling, reckless grin creasing Cunningham's face, then reined Daisy in amongst the stream of mounted men as they pushed past. "We haven't time for this."

Cunningham's mocking laugh followed him, almost lost in the sound of their flight. 'Twould be too easy to pull out a pistol and simply shoot the man. But the others would be on him in a moment—and he had too much reason now to live.

Oh Lizzy. . .

They broke in on the edges of the next camp downriver, already at a state of alarm and mounting up, and kept going. The cool morning worked to their advantage but 'twas only a matter of time before they needed to halt and rest the horses.

Mercy, oh God. Mercy.

On they forged, through another swamp, another creek. At the next camp after that, they did stop, the horses blowing, their breath clouds of steam in the cold air.

While the camp finished breaking and the men trailing behind caught up, Cunningham swung once more to face Jed. "I still say, something about you don't feel right."

Jed held himself still and as calm as he could be. "You challenge me then because of my attention to Lizzy?"

Cunningham's hand strayed toward the sword at his side, and a raw chuckle rumbled from him.

A few of the other men gathered to watch.

"Not simply that, although it's curious enough." Laughter, though tense, rippled around them.

Jed snorted. "If you cared a whit for her—"

Cunningham nudged his horse closer. "So, this is about love now? When you came to us—why?" He turned to Kittery, hovering near with the others ringing them. "You there—you've ridden close by him these last weeks. What say you about where his loyalties lie?"

Jed's heart pounded. *Please, Lord. . . Please, Lord. . . Please, Lord. . .*

"He's been all right," Kittery said slowly, the shifting of his horse betraying his own sudden nervousness. "Lacking a bit when it comes to keeping his prisoners, but—"

Cunningham's face hardened. "Keeping prisoners?"

THE *Backcountry* BRIDES COLLECTION

"We was all giving him a rough time of it that one night—didn't you hear? He lost two in a day."

Jed felt his face blanch even further than it had, if that were possible. "I shot one, not that you seen it."

Kittery gave a short laugh. "So you claimed."

In truth, Jed had lagged behind the main group with the man he'd dragged away at gunpoint. Once the others were out of sight, he'd told the man to run for his life and then shot deliberately away from him.

A simple way to save a man's life. None could prove he hadn't shot him. . .but neither could he prove he had either.

Was it his imagination, or had the circle of riders tightened about him?

"But you *lost* the other." Cunningham leaned toward him. "My company does not simply lose prisoners. Perhaps you mistake us, but neither do we take prisoners, for that matter."

Another round of hard-edged chuckles.

"I'll not let it happen again," Jed said tightly.

That feral grin lit Cunningham's face once more. "Aye, you'll not."

Jed reached for his pistol at the same time Cunningham drew his sabre, but his shot went wild. He parried the blade's edge with the underside of the pistol, and seizing Cunningham's coat, yanked the man from his horse.

They fell in an untidy heap. Cunningham scrabbled for the sword. Jed kicked it away. Around them, the horses shied, the men yelling and whooping. Cunningham snarled and landed a hard punch to Jed's jaw.

For Lizzy then. For the sake of all that's true and holy.

Jed fought with a strength born of desperation, landing as many blows as he took. He tried to give himself space to draw the other pistol, but Cunningham was relentless.

Lungs burning, he swung and missed. Desperation was not enough when his opponent was taller, heavier, more driven by his need to shed blood.

Not to mention the need to punish those from whom he perceived offense.

Cunningham's elbow cracked Jed's skull. Jed staggered, and a crushing weight took hold of his throat. The morning light seemed to dim, the shouts of the men fading.

God in heaven. . .mercy.

A cry cut across all others. "Pickens! Pickens is coming. You must fly, again!"

With a last burst of determination, Jed scrabbled and came up with the knife at Cunningham's belt. Swung. Stabbed.

A roar, and release from the pressure across his throat.

"No time for this!" a hoarse voice insisted.

He fell, spent. *God. . .mercy. . .*

A gray morning indeed it had been, just three days after the tavern burning, and a gray noon it remained. Lizzy could not find it within herself to be sorrowful, however, despite scrubbing the floor on her knees, in someone else's establishment, in someone else's clothing, at that.

Clothing which fit, though worn. And a proper cap, with her hair pinned up beneath.

For the first time in a very long time, her feelings were, in fact, very near what she might even term *hope*. Despite the gnawing fear for Jed.

As she dipped her brush in the pail and returned to the wet edge of the planking, a man's shadow darkened the front door. Mr. Elliot leaned inside and beckoned to her. "Come, Miss Cunningham. And quickly."

She climbed to her feet and wiped her hands on her apron, then scurried after him.

A horse-drawn wagon stood in the yard, a pair of saddle horses tethered to the side. The driver nodded and touched the brim of his plain felt hat as Lizzy approached in Mr. Elliot's wake.

And then she glimpsed the booted feet sticking out the far end of the wagon.

"I'm sorry to deliver him in this condition," Mr. Elliot said gravely. "But I think—"

With a cry, she flew the last few steps to peer over the edge of the wagon. Blood, mud, and dried leaves matted the fair hair and short beard, and what skin she could see was mottled by cuts and bruises. His filthy, torn hunting shirt lay open, the rest of his clothing in not much better condition. But the waistcoat she thought she recognized—

Swollen eyelids cracked open to reveal blue eyes. "Lizzy?"

"Jed!" She scrambled up the wheel and into the wagon, then knelt beside him in the narrow space, trembling so that she could hardly grasp his hand. "What have they done to you?"

His breathing suddenly labored, he winced. "Nothing—too bad."

Her hand skimmed his face, brushing away the debris, assessing the damage. "Oh Jed—"

"Don't cry, Lizzy. I didn't mean to make you cry. I only—wanted to make it back—to see you smile—"

He grimaced again, shifting and then arching against the hard wood of the wagon bed.

"I'm not crying," she insisted—but she was. Deep, gulping sobs—again. She bent until her forehead rested against his chest, but gently. "Oh Jed, I was so sure he'd kill you."

He hiccupped—was that a chuckle? "He—tried."

She cried harder.

His free hand came up to rest against her shoulder. "Shh. Sweet Elizabeth. . ."

"You're a simpleton and a dolt," she sobbed.

He only smiled, and his eyes drifted closed.

Mopping her face with her apron, she looked over at Mr. Elliot, who was trying unsuccessfully to cover a grin. "How bad is it? Truly?"

His amusement faded. "Bad enough. But he should make a full recovery." His dark gaze held hers for a long moment. "Because of your bravery, we were able to mount a party of men strong enough to hunt your cousin and his band where they were hiding along the Edistoes. And thus we found Jed, left behind as you see him when the rest fled downriver. He hasn't been able to tell me yet how he escaped being cut to pieces—" Mr. Elliot shook his head, and a faint smile returned. "But do I assume rightly that you're willing to at least help nurse him back to health?"

Chapter 14

Waking hurt. So did the sunlight, slanting from the nearby window, searing his eyes.

But the hurt meant he was alive. And alive meant hope that—

He looked around. A real bed, in a tidy room complete with washstand, chest, and beside him a chair, where a girl sat, head bent over a piece of sewing.

A girl he nearly didn't recognize, for the serenity of her face, and the proper cap covering her hair.

"Lizzy?"

She looked up, gave a little gasp, and set aside the stitchery. "Jed! How are you feeling?"

"I—" His voice failed, and she reached for a cup on the bedside table, helped him to drink. That accomplished, he sank back. As good as the cool water tasted, better still was the sight of her.

"Terrible," he admitted.

Leaning near, she examined his face, then met his eyes. A shy smile curved her mouth, chasing some of the shadows from her gaze.

"Ahh, aye. That. That was what I longed to see."

She laughed—outright, ducking her head then lifting it again. "Idiot." White teeth caught her bottom lip and tugged on it.

He laughed too, but silently because it hurt. He reached a hand toward her, palm upward, and after the slightest hesitation, she slid hers across it. Her eyes rounded in wonder.

"How did you survive?" she breathed.

He gave a slow wag of the head. "God's own mercy."

Her lips parted and trembled, but just as she would have spoken, a knock came to the door and it opened to Zach Elliot. A broad grin creased his face. "At last! So good to see you awake."

Jed made to release Lizzy's hand and reach for Elliot's, but the other man laughed and shook his head. "Nay, stay put. You took quite a beating."

"I see that," Jed said drily, and regained Lizzy's grasp.

Some of the gravity returned to Elliot's face. "You seemed to be having trouble extricating yourself, there near the end."

Jed huffed. "I couldn't get away for anything. Cunningham decided, because of Lizzy here, that I best be kept under close watch. And then he became suspicious—whether on her behalf or nay, I don't know—but 'twas near the end of me, I'm sure."

Elliot nodded. "You must know, your girl here walked all the way to Dawson's Station and gave me the intelligence which made it possible for Pickens to find Cunningham's camps."

"Our tavern was burned," she muttered. "Where else could I go?"

"Your—" Jed looked from one to the other, then winced. "Lizzy, what happened?"

"Our neighbors had enough of our Tory ways," she said tartly, then went on more quietly, "They had the good grace at least to let us take what we could carry."

"And your father and brothers?"

"In gaol," Elliot said. His mouth flattened. "They'll be sent on to Charles Town shortly."

Jed considered Lizzy's sober expression, the dip of her lashes. "And you, sweet Elizabeth? What do you wish to do?"

Her eyes came to his, watery pools reflecting as he had observed before, all the colors of a Carolina autumn day. A dozen emotions crossed her face as her lips parted, firmed, and then parted again.

If he could just kiss her again, he was sure all the aches would simply melt away. At least for a moment.

But he had to wait for her to reply.

Or did he?

And Elliot just stood there with a mocking smile. "I told her, your cousin and his wife would likely take her in until she finds a good situation for herself. It's far enough she'd not have fear of anyone finding her. Did you have aught else in mind?"

Jed swallowed. Met Lizzy's eyes again. "I told you that last morning to consider my words a proposal—but you don't have to marry me. Not if you've no wish to. My cousin and his wife would indeed be glad to have you, and—"

She laid her fingers across his lips, cool and soothing. " 'Tis—'tis all right if you've changed your mind."

What? No—he shook his head but the pain lanced through him again, forcing his eyes shut. "Nay, Lizzy, I—haven't."

Her fingers flexed against his palm, and he squeezed back, holding the clasp loosely, in case she was prepared to release him.

"Well," Elliot said briskly. "Now that we have all that settled." Grin still firmly in place, he pulled a packet from his waistcoat and held it out to Jed. "Given your injuries, I've taken the liberty of arranging your furlough from the Continental Army, along with a pass, should you need it, for travel to Virginia whenever you are ready. And there is mention of your wife accompanying you. Whether or not you choose to make that so, in fact, is your business."

Jed accepted the packet with a nod. "I am sorry I did not finish the task I set out to accomplish."

"Oh, on the contrary. Because of your connection with this brave lady, we were able to put Cunningham and his boys to flight, all the way to Charles Town. I'm told he may have sustained injuries of his own. He'll not soon venture back out. And in the meantime, we're determined to guard the enemy lines more closely."

He could hardly think for the wash of relief. "You're saying I succeeded?"

"And well. Even if you did get yourself nearly killed."

"He blamed me for the attack." Jed breathed another weak laugh. "An accusation I am happy now to accept."

Lizzy sat nearly folded in on herself, one hand over her mouth.

"I am," he insisted. "If it means you're finally freed from that particular tyranny—"

Elliot nodded. "Exactly so. And I will take my leave, until later. I'm sure the two of you have plenty to say to each other."

He bowed and left the room.

Lizzy did not move. Jed let his gaze skim the pert oval of her face, the smooth line of her neck and upper shoulder, the blue gown that fit her more neatly than the old brown one. "You're looking very well."

She glanced away, straightened on her chair. Tried to take back her hand, but he tightened his grip. "Mistress Dawson very kindly lent me some clothing." She took an unsteady breath and narrowed her gaze upon him. "So, your intent all along was to use me to get to Billy?"

"What—nay!" Oh, this girl's mind was faster than he could keep pace, at this point. "Never. I promise." He pressed her hand for emphasis. "I meant every word, Lizzy. Every word. Including the proposal."

She sat, hardly moving, but her eyes welled with tears.

"Sweet Elizabeth. You are lovely. You are brave. And I'd be most honored if you'd be my wife. That is—if you can bear being wed to a rebel."

"Your family," she said faintly. "They are rebel as well?"

"They are. But they are good people."

She sniffled. "Mr. Elliot assured me that was so." Her shoulders rose and fell with another deep breath. "And just what was your occupation before the war?"

A grin tugged at his mouth. "I was a wagon master. Hauled goods all up and down the Great Road from Philadelphia to Charlotte Town. May be awhile yet before I can return to that, but—"

Lizzy nodded, then swiped at her eyes and looked out the window for a moment. The tears overflowed, though she dashed them away. "He answered my prayer," she said at last.

His thoughts stuttered. "Your prayer?"

Her head bobbed. Her watery gaze bounced to his and away. "You—told me to trust the Almighty. I—asked Him—to bring you back to me." She swallowed. "And He did."

Something in his own heart warmed and unfurled. He wove his fingers more firmly with hers. "I asked Him the same thing. To bring me safely back to you. So, aye, I would agree—He answered both our prayers."

Her chin tucked, she peered at him again. "I can't remember Him ever doing anything for me before."

"Sweet Elizabeth," he breathed. "I'm sure He must have."

She swayed in her chair. "You'll not break if—I touch you?" she asked.

At last! "Not at all," he murmured gruffly, and tugged her into his arms for that long-awaited kiss.

As he thought, the pain receded far away.

At least for the moment.

She drew away a little and smiled. "I would be honored to accept your proposal, Jedidiah Williams."

He grinned and brushed a strand of hair from her face. " 'Tis Jedidiah Wheeler. If you don't mind, that is. Making you Mistress Wheeler."

She murmured the name. "I like the sound of that." With another smile, she kissed him again.

Epilogue

B rewster's Inn fairly hummed, as it always did on a busy summer's morning when filled to bursting with travelers on their way up and down the Great Road between Philadelphia and Charlotte Town.

Across the table, Sally kneaded and shaped small loaves of bread, while Lizzy rolled piecrust that would become an after-luncheon offering. Behind her, two small boys, one still in skirts and the other newly breeched, sat in the corner and took turns beating on overturned pans with a pair of wooden spoons. Sally spared them hardly a glance, but Lizzy laughed and shook her head in wonder at the commotion.

She was still not quite used to it—but 'twas a joy to belong. To be part of a family that seemed to truly value the contributions others made.

Jacky, the youngest of Sally's twin brothers, ducked under the doorjamb, holding an empty platter. "More sweet breads to the common room!"

"I'll get it," Lizzy said, and headed to replenish the platter from where more of the glazed rolls sat cooling on a side table.

The kitchen became abruptly crowded when Jed shouldered his way past Jacky, followed by his stockier but slightly shorter cousin, Sam. Blue eyes sparkling, Sam angled toward Sally, while Jed made a beeline for Lizzy.

"Hie! I'm trying to work," she protested, but leaned into his warm strength, savoring the contrast of rough and soft in his kiss, and breathing deeply of his scent of sunshine and fresh hay.

Laughing, he pulled back just enough to peer into her eyes. "And doing a fine job of it. How fares my darling wife this morning?"

Behind him, Lizzy caught a glimpse of Sam similarly embracing Sally, his big hands tenderly cradling her very round belly. She smiled and refocused on Jed's roguish grin. "I am very well, thank you."

A softer kiss this time. "And the newest little Wheeler is similarly well?"

She smiled despite the warming of her cheeks. And what a joy to have a man who seemed to hold her as his greatest treasure. "He is, indeed."

Jed chuckled. "Or she. A daughter would not be amiss, you know."

"We'll see," she said pertly, and lifted the platter.

In the buzzing common room, Lizzy made her way to the sideboard and set down her burden, then glanced across the array to see what else needed refilling. A roomful of travelers they had, and hearty appetites all. She and Sally would be cooking for hours yet.

As she turned to go back to the kitchen, a man spoke from the table next to her. "Hey! 'Tis—I can hardly believe it—but is that Lizzy Cunningham?"

Lifting her chin, she regarded him with all the reserve she could muster. An ordinary pair of men, who might be familiar but she could not immediately recall their names.

"What are you doing so far from home, Lizzy?" the other said.

She flashed them both an arch smile. "My apologies, good sirs. You must be mistaken. I am Elizabeth Wheeler, not Lizzy Cunningham. And this is my home."

And with that, she hastened back to the kitchen.

Author's Note

In real history, not all loose ends are neatly tied up, nor do all villains meet a satisfyingly just end. Major William Cunningham, dubbed "Bloody Bill" in later accounts, was an actual historical figure whose atrocities are well documented. I might have taken dramatic license on the timing, but I've rendered the actual events as faithfully as I could. Bloody Bill and his men were indeed never again the terror they had been to the South Carolina backcountry after their retreat on December 20, 1781. When his lands in Saluda County were confiscated by the US government late in 1782, and the British made their final withdrawal from Charleston in December of the same year, Cunningham fled to East Florida, where he lived as an outlaw until he and his men were arrested and tried in Havana for crimes against the Spanish government. Exiled from Florida, he then turned to his cousin Robert Cunningham (not the one mentioned in this story) in the Bahamas, where he died of some tropical malady on January 18, 1787.

There's no mention of him sustaining any injury during the attack by Colonel Pickens and his militia, but where history is silent, we storytellers have room for embellishment. As it is, the facts make it abundantly clear that anyone who tried to infiltrate his regiment would have been fortunate indeed to escape alive. There was record, however, of one follower letting a prisoner go, nearly as I've described, so maybe there was a Jed somewhere among the ranks. We may never know.

Transplanted to North Dakota after more than two decades in Charleston, South Carolina, **Shannon McNear** loves losing herself in local history. She's a military wife, mom of eight, mother-in-law of three, grammy of two, and a member of ACFW and RWA. Her first novella, *Defending Truth* in *A Pioneer Christmas Collection*, was a 2014 RITA® finalist. When she's not sewing, researching, or leaking story from her fingertips, she enjoys being outdoors, basking in the beauty of the northern prairies.

Love's Undoing

by Gabrielle Meyer

Dedication

To my aunties, Vicky Miland, Chrissy Gosiak, Sherry Lemm, Roxie Zettel,
Becky Gosiak, Jackie Gosiak, Shannon Gosiak, Sharon VanRisseghem,
Mary VanRisseghem, Jeanne VanRisseghem, Debbie VanRisseghem,
Nancy VanRisseghem, Connie Massmann, and Colleen VanRisseghem.
My large family is a blessing I don't take for granted!
Thank you for being like second mothers to me.

Acknowledgments

Writing is often called a solitary pursuit, yet I find myself surrounded by
friends and family who cheer me on every day. I'd like to thank my lovely agent,
Wendy Lawton, of Books & Such Literary Management; my editors at Barbour
Publishing; my talented writing friends Erica Vetsch, Alena Tauriainen,
Lindsay Harrel, and Melissa Tagg who have words of encouragement the
moment I need them; my priceless Street Team members; my writing group,
MN N.I.C.E. ACFW; my parents, George and Cathy VanRisseghem;
my husband's parents, Virgil & Carol Meyer; and my church community
that inspires me to write stories that glorify God. A very special thank-you
is always reserved for my husband, David, and our four children, Ellis, Maryn,
Judah, and Asher. Thank you for being my biggest fans and my greatest joy.

Chapter 1

Fort McCrea, Upper Mississippi River
December 4, 1792

Abi McCrea stacked another piece of wood onto the growing pile in her arms, wondering how she'd survive another winter trapped in her father's fur post. A storm the night before had buried the world in more snow; it outlined the pointed stockade walls and the tall evergreen trees beyond. She longed to leave the interior and visit her sister in Montreal—yet her dream was nothing but a fanciful notion. Father would never allow her to go. Not now, not after what her sister had done.

A commotion at the front gate made Abi pause. She squinted against the blinding sun as it reflected off the snow, trying to discover what had caused the *voyageurs* to stop their work. The brawny men had been removing snow, putting it on sleds to haul outside the stockade, but now they stared as a dogsled pulled through the open gate and into the yard. If it was a band of Chippewa Indians, come to trade, it wouldn't cause the men to pause. The natives came and went at all hours of the day.

Abi set the wood down and walked around the building to get a better look. The fort rarely received unexpected visitors, and even less so in the winter months. The last man to arrive was the district manager who had come several weeks ago to share news of the unexpected death of a North West Company partner.

Surprise visits usually brought bad tidings.

The stranger removed himself from the confines of the elaborately painted cariole, pushing aside his buffalo robes, while his Indian guide stood stoically on the back of the sled. The visitor was tall—taller than the half dozen voyageurs staring at him. He had direct blue eyes, which scanned the yard now, missing nothing. He nodded at Jean Claude, the blacksmith, who rested his thick arm on the handle of a shovel.

"Where might I find Mr. McCrea?" the stranger asked in a clear British accent.

"*Excusez-moi? Je ne parle pas anglais.*" Jean Claude lifted his mitted hand and pointed at Abi. "*La jeune fille parle anglais.*"

The stranger turned his intense blue eyes on Abi, a hint of surprise in their depths. Didn't he expect to find a woman at the fort?

"Do you speak English?" he asked.

"I do." She spoke English, French, and her mother's native Chippewa tongue. Her father had insisted his two surviving children learn the three languages since the fur trade brought people from all over Europe, Canada, and America to the upper Mississippi River.

The man stepped toward her, his high leather boots crunching on the hard-packed snow. He winced as he took each step, and she feared his feet had been damaged from the cold. His fancy boots were not meant for such conditions, but she suspected he knew that already. He wore a long gentleman's coat, royal blue with fur at the collar and cloth-covered buttons to match. A beaver top hat sat upon his head and his ears and nose were bright red from the cold. How far had he come dressed in such finery? He must be half-frozen, though the buffalo robes would have protected him from the worst of the elements.

Surely, the Indian guide could have done something to prepare this man for travel.

"I am looking for Mr. McCrea. Could you direct me to him, please?"

She wiped her mittens together, brushing the woodchips from the thick wool. "Follow me."

Father would be in his dwelling room writing in his journal or going over the books. He always spent the morning doing such work. Though he detested it, it was part of the responsibilities of the chief factor.

Abi led the stranger toward the row house, pushing open the door in the center of the long building, and walked over the threshold into her family's dwelling room. Father sat where she knew he would be, at his small desk near the glass window at the back of the room. Mother stood near the blazing fireplace, stirring the stew she had prepared for their midday meal as it hung on a pothook over the flames. The room was filled with the delicious aroma of cooked meat, spices, and wood smoke.

"Father." Abi spoke loudly, as his hearing was no longer what it used to be. "We have a guest."

Mother and Father both looked toward the door at the same moment. Abi wondered what their family must look like to a British gentleman such as this one. Her father was large and burly, with graying hair and beard, his Scottish brogue so thick, some people did not think he spoke English. Her mother was small and dark, her Chippewa ancestry evident, though she tried to hide it beneath her eastern clothing and the culture she had tried to adopt. They had lived as man and wife for nearly thirty-five years, and though Abi knew they were not a common sight for some, they were her parents and she loved them dearly.

Father rose, while Mother seemed to blend into the room.

"Welcome to Fort McCrea." Father's voice boomed and filled the small space as he reached for the man's hand.

Abi closed the door behind the stranger, trying not to stare, wondering what he wanted with her father. Was it good news or bad?

"Thank you, Mr. McCrea. My name is—"

"Warm yerself, laddie." Father's concern for his men was what he was best known for. It extended to all those who entered his fort. "Marie, give this man something to eat and drink. Abi, bring him some warm stones for his feet." Father frowned at the man's attire. "Who let ye come out here in such frippery?"

The man did not move from where he stood. "Your brother."

Abi stopped midstride as the room stilled.

"My brother, you say?" Father's voice lowered and his bushy eyebrows came together in a scowl. "What does my brother want with me?"

Mother dropped her gaze, her face shadowed in the corner of the room. Surely she was thinking the same thing as Abi. Father and his brother, Gregor, had had a falling out when they were younger. Father had come into the interior, while Gregor had stayed in Montreal to become an agent for the North West Company. When Father sent Abi's older sister Isobel to Montreal for school, she had not returned. She had been poisoned by Uncle Gregor's lies, or so Father claimed.

It was the reason he would not let Abi go.

"Your brother has sent a letter." The stranger pulled an envelope from his inner pocket. "As his personal clerk, he asked me to hand deliver it and wait until I receive your reply."

Father hesitated a moment, and Abi feared he would toss this man out into the snow before he had a chance to warm himself.

Instead, Father stepped forward and took the letter. "I dinnae catch yer name."

"He didn't say his name." Abi spoke up—but immediately regretted doing so.

Father cast her a warning look, reminding her that her place was one of silence when a guest was in their home. In moments like this, when his disappointment was so swift, she wished she could blend into the room like her mother. But it was a skill she did not possess.

"My name is Henry Kingsley." There was a sparkle in his eye that Abi could not ignore, as if he smiled often, though he was serious now. "I work for your brother in Montreal."

Father held up the envelope. "Do ye ken what this letter says, Mr. Kingsley?"

"I do not, sir."

"And you risked yer life to bring it to me?" Father squinted, his authority and power as a wintering partner with the North West Company in every ragged line of his weather-worn face.

"I did."

"Why?" The word rolled off Father's tongue and hung thick in the air.

Abi leaned forward. Mr. Kingsley was clearly unprepared for such a journey. Either his devotion to her uncle was admirable—or altogether foolish.

Henry stared at the large man before him. Mr. McCrea waited for an answer, though the truth was hardly worth repeating. Henry risked his life to bring the missive to this backwoodsman because he was dedicated to his employer, yes, but more importantly, because he wanted to prove himself to his employer's daughter, Josephine.

McCrea's daughter—Abi, he believed she had been called—also waited for Henry to reply. Curiosity had shone in her dark-brown eyes since the moment he'd entered the stockade. It had been hard not to notice her standing in the brilliant-red dress with the white capote around her shoulders. She was a beautiful woman, almost exotic in her features, and now he knew why. She was Métis, half Scottish, half Indian.

"Your brother said this business was of the upmost importance," Henry said to Mr. McCrea, pulling his thoughts away from Abi. "He said he would trust no one but me to see it delivered."

"Yer devotion to my brother is unfounded." Mr. McCrea gestured to the table. "Sit and eat my food. Warm yerself by my fire. Sleep under my roof. But in the morning, I will see ye on yer cariole back to Montreal." He started toward the fire, his hand outstretched to toss the envelope into the flames.

"No!" Henry stepped toward the man, but his daughter reached him first.

Abi grasped his arm. "Don't do it, Father."

McCrea's face turned red and the letter shook in his hand. "Dinnae stop me, daughter."

"What if it's news of Isobel?" She beseeched him with her eyes. "What if she needs us?"

"Needs us?" McCrea shook his head, his jaw tight. "She chose my brother's life over mine."

"She is your daughter," Abi said quietly, tenderly.

McCrea swallowed hard and then he glanced at the other woman, who Henry suspected was his wife. Her sorrowful gaze was filled with a longing that made Henry's chest ache.

It must have been enough for McCrea because he sighed and his broad shoulders sank.

Abi's hand fell away from his arm, but she didn't lower her intense gaze from his face.

"Ye read it, lassie." McCrea handed the letter to Abi. "I dinnae have the heart."

Abi slowly took it from him and opened the seal. Removing the paper from the envelope, she scanned the contents, her hand covering her mouth.

McCrea stared into the smoking flames, but he glanced over his shoulder, his eyebrows furrowed. "Well?"

"It's not about Isobel. It's about your brother."

"My brother?" McCrea turned to Henry. "What's wrong with my brother?"

"Not your brother in Montreal," Abi said, lowering the letter. "Your brother in Scotland. He's died without an heir. His title and lands pass to you." She paused and scanned the letter once again. "Gregor has heard of this and sends his clerk to inquire if you will accept the inheritance, or if you will pass it to him. He is willing to return to Scotland, should you decide to relinquish your rights."

Return to Scotland? Henry clenched the back of the chair nearest him. His feet throbbed as the heat began to thaw them, but he hardly noticed. If Gregor McCrea left Montreal, he would take Josephine. Would he ask Henry to follow? Henry had no wish to return to Europe. He rather enjoyed the newness of Montreal and being out from beneath his father's command.

"What will you do?" Abi whispered to her father.

McCrea leaned against the fireplace mantel, his forehead resting on his arm as he stared into the flames. "This news has come out of nowhere. I cannae make the decision without some time and prayer."

"What is there to decide?" Abi clutched the letter like it was a lifeline. "Scotland, Father. We could all go to Scotland."

"*We* could not go to Scotland." He lowered his voice. "If I go, I would go alone."

Silence filled the room once again and Henry suddenly wished he had somewhere to go. He was aware of the situation many wintering partners found themselves in with Indian wives and children. Many abandoned their families when they retired from the fur trade. Some even took white brides when they returned to Montreal or Europe as rich men. Would McCrea do the same?

Abi took a step away from her father as she lowered her gaze to the floor.

Mrs. McCrea left the fireside with a bowl and cup, both steaming into the cool air. She set the offerings upon the table and then stepped through a door into the adjoining room.

McCrea nodded to the table. "Eat and warm yerself, Kingsley. As soon as I make a decision, I'll send ye on yer way." He started toward the door where his wife had disappeared. Before he ducked out of the room, he spoke to his daughter. "Mr. Kingsley might be with us a few days, daughter. Offer him hospitality and make a pallet for him to sleep on there by the fire."

She did not meet his gaze. "Yes, Father."

Without acknowledging Henry again, McCrea left the room, closing the door tightly behind him.

Delicious aromas wafted to Henry's nose and his stomach growled.

"Don't let your food grow cold." Abi crouched beside the fireplace as she placed a few flat stones in the bed of coals.

He wouldn't wait for another invitation. He took a seat at the table, saying grace before he even settled into place. It had been two weeks since he'd left Montreal and had a decent meal. His guide had been a man of few words and fewer cooking skills. They'd lived on tough pemmican and weak tea.

Abi worked quietly as Henry savored the thick stew, nodding his thanks when she gave him a piece of flatbread.

She removed her capote and knit hat, hanging them on a hook near the door. He had never met a woman from the backcountry and was surprised that she wore a gown like Josephine. Maybe not as elaborate, but just as becoming.

Her hair was caught up in a snood. The silken strands shimmered in the light of the fire, just as her eyes did when she looked in his direction.

Without a word, she refilled his bowl and then went back to the fireplace to remove the stones from the coals. Wrapping them in towels, she brought them to the table and knelt before him.

Henry stopped eating.

"May I help you with your boots, Mr. Kingsley?"

"I can manage, thank you." He reached down and began to pull off his boots. The pain made him inhale and grimace.

"Let me." Her eyebrows furrowed. "I hope they are not frostbit."

He clenched his jaw as she removed his boots and then his stockings.

"Only one pair of socks?" Her eyes were filled with compassion and her hands were gentle as she inspected his foot. "You don't need warm stones. You need snow."

She stood and reached for a bucket.

"Snow? Why do I need snow?"

"To rub on your feet."

His eyes grew wide at the thought of putting frozen snow on his painful feet.

"They are frozen, though I don't think they are frostbit." She opened the exterior door and bent to fill the bucket. "If I put heat upon them, they will only get worse. What you need is snow." She came back inside and shoved the door closed.

"You intend to put that snow on my feet?" Alarm rang in his voice.

"It will hurt," she said. "But you must trust me. I've done this many times before."

What choice did he have? He had no experience in the wilderness. He'd been born and raised in an English country home, spent his later school years in London, and traveled to Montreal when he was twenty. He knew nothing of frostbite or its remedies.

She knelt before him, unwrapped one of the stones and set it aside, and then set the towel under his feet. Her movements were purposeful and tender as she scooped up a handful of snow with one hand, while taking his foot in the other.

Very few women had touched his feet before, and part of him wished he had some feeling now to enjoy the ministrations.

But as soon as she placed the snow against his skin and began to rub it vigorously, he wished he was completely numb. The pain was so intense, he clutched the edge of the seat to force himself to stay put.

She winced at his reaction, but didn't stop.

"Are you sure. . .this. . .works?" he asked between gritted teeth.

She nodded, empathy on her pretty face. "I'm afraid it's the only way."

He hoped she was right, but he doubted it very much.

"May I ask you a question?" She picked up more snow and rubbed it between her hands and his bright red skin.

He hated to be rude—he was a gentleman, after all—yet he could hardly think at the moment, let alone answer her question. "Of course," he forced himself to say.

"Will you take me to Montreal?"

For a moment, Henry forgot about the stinging pain in his feet. "Excuse me?"

"Montreal." She stopped rubbing. "I'm desperate to go and see my sister."

"Do you jest?" He sat up straighter. "I cannot take you to Montreal."

"Why not?"

"There are a hundred reasons why not, the least of which is that we haven't even been properly introduced."

She extended her red hand to him. "My name is Abi Marie McCrea, the daughter of John McCrea, chief factor and wintering partner of Fort McCrea."

No proper lady had ever introduced herself to him before, yet he'd never been in the backcountry before either. Maybe this was the way it was done.

"I'm Henry Kingsley, the son of Reginald Kingsley, Earl of Kennewick." He started to rise, to offer a bow, but she put her hand on his arm and forced him to stay seated.

"If you want to use your feet again, you'll need to let me continue." She took another handful of snow and began to rub his ankles, all pleasantries set aside.

He sank back into the chair, relieved that he didn't have to stand anytime soon. "It's a pleasure to meet you," he said a bit lamely.

"Will you consider my request now?"

Of course he'd say no. . .but he couldn't help admiring her tenacity.

Chapter 2

Working with only a candle and the light of the fireplace, Abi set the table for their evening meal, casting furtive glances at her father and Mr. Kingsley who spoke of Montreal and the fur trade. What had her father decided about Scotland? Would he go? And, if he did, what would become of her and Mother? She knew dozens of women who had been discarded by fur traders when they retired. Would she and Mother meet the same fate? She couldn't imagine her father doing such a thing, yet few of the abandoned women she knew had believed it either.

"The rendezvous was successful," Father said to Mr. Kingsley. "The warm spring made travel to Grand Portage easy." Though the men discussed many people, places, and events they had in common, they did not talk as if they were friends. Instead, their conversation had the tone of a business transaction. Abi sensed her father was being cautious, though Mr. Kingsley appeared easygoing and trustworthy.

Mother stood at the table in the corner, slicing the venison roast, her movements so quiet, one would hardly notice she was present in the dim light.

Abi finished setting the table and then brought the roasted vegetables from the fireplace.

Father didn't seem to notice her, but Mr. Kingsley caught her eye a time or two. He'd been patient while she'd attended to his feet. After she'd finished rubbing them with snow, she'd had him draw close to the fire to return the heat to his bones and sinews, while she continued to fill his cup with the steaming mulled wine Mother had made. When Abi was satisfied that his feet were not frostbit, as she'd feared, she had fetched three pairs of wool socks and a pair of moose-skin moccasins, which he wore now.

The whole time she'd worked on his feet, she had waited for him to give her an answer about Montreal, but he'd said nothing more about it. Only smiled at her, as if he found her request amusing.

"Set one more plate, lassie."

Father's words broke into Abi's thoughts.

"One more?"

"Robert will be here shortly."

Abi forced herself not to sigh. Just once, she'd hoped her father's clerk would stay in his own quarters and dine with his own men, leaving her alone with her parents and Mr. Kingsley. But it would not be so. Father hoped Abi would agree to marry Robert one day. He had made his desire about the alliance known over a decade before, when Abi was only seven years old and Robert had been a bright-eyed sixteen-year-old, fresh from Scotland.

A knock at the door was a customary call before Robert entered the room.

"Good evening." Father rose and greeted Robert with a hearty handshake. He'd been grooming the young man to take his place as a chief trader one day, and maybe a chief factor, one of the highest ranks in the fur trade, when he had more experience.

"Good evening, sir." Robert shook Father's hand and then sought Abi's gaze to acknowledge her.

She nodded back as she set a plate, cup, and silverware on the table for him. He was a fine Scottish man, she supposed, but she didn't want to stay in the backcountry and be a fur trader's wife. She longed for things Robert could not give her.

Mother brought the venison to the table and set it next to Father's place. Fresh sourdough bread had been made earlier in the day with her precious store of flour. The ration Father had been given at the last rendezvous was more than the other men received, since he was a chief factor, but it must still be preserved to last until he returned from the next rendezvous in nine months.

"Robert, I'd like ye to meet Henry Kingsley." Father's hand remained on Robert's shoulder. "Mr. Kingsley, this is my clerk, Robert Douglass."

Mr. Kingsley rose and shook Robert's hand. "It's a pleasure to meet you, Mr. Douglass."

Robert was handsome, with light-brown hair and eyes to match, though he wasn't as big and burly as Father, or as tall and well-formed as Mr. Kingsley.

Abi's cheeks warmed and she busied herself pouring milk into her father's pewter mug, wondering what the men would think of her wayward thoughts.

"Is dinner ready?" Father asked Mother.

She gave a quick nod and Father motioned to the table.

"Seat yourself, Robert. Abi has set out the plum preserves ye prefer."

Robert smiled, his white teeth gleaming from behind the beard he wore for the winter months.

Father waited for Abi and Mother to join them, as was his custom.

Bowing his head, he said grace, and then he began to dish up everyone's plates, putting extra plum preserves on Robert's.

They continued to speak of mundane things, but Abi longed to ask Father about his inheritance. He would not tell her until he was ready, so the knowing of it would have to wait.

"It has been more than a decade since I last saw Montreal," Robert said to Mr.

Kingsley. "What can ye tell me about it?"

Abi's hand froze midway to her mouth, the forkful of venison forgotten as she waited for Mr. Kingsley's response. She had seen nothing beyond the rendezvous at Grand Portage, and that was but a summer camp where the wintering voyageurs took their furs to meet with the men who came from Montreal with supplies. The voyageurs exchanged the furs for blankets, cloth, cookware, needles, fishnets, food, and other necessities, and then returned to their posts to trade the supplies with the Indians who brought the furs throughout the winter and spring. It was an endless cycle.

The only thing she knew about Montreal was what her sister told her in the few letters she'd written. Her sister lived with Uncle Gregor in his fine home, and she'd shared details of balls, tea parties, gowns, carriages, restaurants, tall buildings, servants, and all sorts of other things Abi could hardly comprehend. She only hoped she'd be refined enough to live in such a place.

"I've only been in Montreal two years," Mr. Kingsley said. "It's changed since I've been there. It continues to grow at a rapid pace and remains the center of the fur trade."

"And do you attend balls and ride in carriages and eat in restaurants?" Abi asked, breathlessly.

All eyes turned to her, and she could see the displeasure in her father's gaze.

"Yes, of course," Mr. Kingsley said.

"Father—"

"Nae." Father shook his head. "I've made myself clear, daughter. Ye will go to Montreal when ye have a good man to take ye, and not a moment sooner." He nodded at Robert.

A good man to take her. It had been his one condition these past two years since Isobel had decided not to return to the interior. Father feared if Abi went on her own, she would not return. But if she went after she was married to Robert, she'd be forced to come home. Yet, he'd said, *A good man to take ye.* He hadn't specified *which* good man that needed to be. If she could convince Mr. Kingsley, who appeared to be a very good man, Father could not say no.

"I have news to share." Father wiped his mouth and set his cloth napkin aside, apparently changing the subject. "I've come to a decision about Scotland."

Robert didn't appear confused, so Abi suspected that Father had already told him why Mr. Kingsley had come.

No one touched their food as Father crossed his arms over his wide chest. "I will relinquish my inheritance to Gregor. I am a man of the woods now. I could never return to Scotland and resume the life of my youth." He took Mother's hand. "Or leave Marie behind."

Mother lifted her napkin in her free hand and began to weep into the cloth.

So. Nothing would change, after all. Father would stay in the interior, probably retire in two years when Robert would be eligible for a promotion to chief trader. Abi would be expected to marry him and bear children, continuing the drudgery of her existence.

She began to feel the suffocation of panic seize her. She stood, needing to be done with this room and these people who wanted to keep her trapped.

Without excusing herself, she left the dwelling room and stepped into the darkness of the bedroom. A curtain hung between her bed and her parents', with the fireplace in the center of the far wall. Embers flickered, trying to gain new life as she paced in the confines of the small space.

The door creaked open and Father stepped into the room. He closed the door behind him, his green eyes hidden in the shadows of his face, though she knew she would see compassion in their depths. "Why are ye so unhappy, lassie?"

She went to him, as she'd done all her life, and allowed him to wrap her in his big arms. Her father was stern and exacting, but he was kind and good and he loved his family. "I want to be free, Father."

"Ye are free, lassie. We're all made free in Christ."

"No." She shook her head, not wanting to sound ungrateful. She had all that she needed—yet nothing her heart desired. "If I were free, I would be on my way to Montreal."

He sighed, his body sagging. "Not this again, Abi."

"Please, Father. Let me return with Mr. Kingsley. I just want to see Montreal, to know what lies beyond the interior. I want to see it with my own eyes, hear it with my ears, and taste it with my tongue. I won't stay forever."

He stepped away from her and went to the fireplace where he stirred the embers and put new logs onto the flames. "Isobel said nearly the same."

"I'm different than my sister."

"Ye are different, Abi, that's why I dinnae want to lose ye too. I have groomed ye to be the wife of a fur trader. Ye will bring Robert joy, I ken it well. Once ye are married, he will decide if ye go to Montre—"

"No." She crossed her arms and stood her ground. "If I am free, then I will decide."

Anger flared in his eyes and she was afraid she had pushed him too far.

Lowering her arms, she took a tentative step toward him. "Would you rather I choose the life you desire for me—or be forced into it?"

His face betrayed the struggle he fought inside. He wanted to offer her all that her heart longed for, this she knew, yet he was afraid he'd lose her like he lost Isobel.

Finally he nodded, defeat and resignation in his voice. "Aye. I will not force ye to stay."

She touched her fingers to her lips, trying to hold back the smile that would only make this harder for him. "Truly?"

Father put his hands on her shoulders, his face serious. "I have kept ye sheltered here, lassie, to keep ye safe from the realities of this world. Ye will be shocked at Montreal. Ye will see things and learn things that will break yer heart, and I dinnae want that to happen. But I will not force ye to stay any longer if ye cannae stand to be here." He gently touched her chin with his rough fingers. "Just promise me ye will return."

She put her hand over his and nodded, happy tears gathering. "I promise." Wrapping her arms around him, she cried into his chest. "Thank you, Father."

"There's one condition."

"Anything."

"I am sending Robert with ye."

Abi pulled back, her eyes wide. "Robert?"

He frowned at her. "Ye dinnae think I'd send ye alone with Mr. Kingsley and his guide?"

She shook her head, uncertainty crowding in. Would Robert be tasked with keeping an eye on her? Would she have the freedom she longed for, with her father's clerk on her heels?

It didn't truly matter. She'd finally see Montreal and Isobel once again.

"I will send my letter in Robert's care." He smiled down at Abi, though there was sadness in his face. "My letter and my daughter."

Abi hardly heard the rest of his instructions. She began to plan everything she'd finally experience outside the interior, pushing aside the niggling fears that prompted her to stay where it was safe and familiar.

The cold wind nipped at Henry's exposed nose while he shoved the provisions for his return trip to Montreal in the front of his cariole. He's been outfitted by McCrea with everything he'd need, and more. He'd been given fur-lined mittens made of deerskin, which hung on a worsted cord around his neck. A warm capote, made from a two-point trading blanket, was cinched with a red sash around his waist. On his legs, he wore deerskin trousers and cloth leggings. To keep out the worst of the cold, McCrea had given him a shawl to wrap around his neck, and a fur cap with ear pieces, to cover his head. That morning, when he'd donned his new outfit, he'd stood for a moment, feeling like a different man—a sensation that surprised him with how good it felt.

Out here, a man could be anything he wanted to be. He didn't have to bend to the contours and customs of the English aristocracy or Montreal's ever increasing societal expectations. In the backcountry, a man could work his way up the chain of command to one day operate a fur post and make his living off the natural resources of God's creation. Instead of spending his days in a windowless office, working for someone else, he could spend them outside, working for himself.

The idea quickened Henry's heartbeats as he lifted a fifty-pound bag of pemmican out of the snow and shoved it into the cariole. He only wished he had more time to spend at Fort McCrea to see if this life was one he wanted to pursue.

Migizi, the guide who had brought Henry into the interior, quietly walked between the dogs, tightening their harnesses and speaking in low tones. "We will go faster now that you are clothed properly."

Henry readjusted the pemmican, thankful for the moccasins Abi had given him, but unhappy with the turn of events that would force him to take the young lady back to Montreal. Last night, McCrea had promised Henry all the supplies they'd need, as well as a monetary token of appreciation, in exchange for seeing Abi safely to her uncle. Henry had declined the money, only because he imagined it was what Gregor McCrea would want. "I don't see how we'll go faster. The woman will slow us down."

The guide smiled, a rare occurrence, indeed. "*Anishinaabekwe* is wise. She will make trip easier."

"Anishinaabekwe?"

"Indian woman."

The door to the McCrea's dwelling room opened. Abi stepped outside in clothing much like Henry's, though she wore a long gown under her white capote, and a red knitted cap over her dark hair. Her Indian ancestry was evident in her hair and eyes and in her high, sculpted cheekbones, but her Scottish ancestry was present in the fairness of her skin and the shape of her nose and mouth. Now, in the sunlight, he could also see streaks of red highlights in her hair.

Henry forced himself to look away, for fear he might get caught staring. He'd never met a woman whose beauty so intrigued him or captivated his attention. Even Josephine, who was lovely, did not compare with her Métis cousin.

Robert Douglass followed Abi outside, with McCrea and his wife behind him.

McCrea turned to Robert and handed a letter to him. "This is the letter my brother will need for all the legal transactions. See that he gets it."

"I will, sir."

McCrea took his daughter into his arms and kissed her forehead. "Take care, lassie."

Tears glistened in her eyes. "I'll miss you, Father."

"Aye, and we'll miss ye."

Abi hugged her mother as well, and then walked toward the cariole her father had provided for her journey. Her dogs were restless, straining at their harnesses as she walked by. With a few quiet words from her, they stilled and waited for her to put her things inside the sled. Robert would ride behind her, just as Migizi rode behind Henry.

"Kingsley." McCrea approached Henry. "I have a letter of introduction for my daughter." McCrea handed an envelope to Henry, his face and voice stern. "Ye be sure to give this to my brother immediately."

"Yes sir."

McCrea put his hand on Henry's shoulder, squeezing it tight. "I am entrusting ye with my daughter. If any harm befalls her, I'll hold ye accountable."

Though Henry had not been the one to invite Abi along, he still had a responsibility to the woman since he was in charge of the traveling party. "I'll see that she's delivered safely to her uncle."

McCrea offered his hand. "See that ye do." He lowered his voice. "And see that he takes care of her."

Henry knew Gregor McCrea well. He'd always been a generous host. "Of course."

Robert helped Abi into the cariole while the other voyageurs and clerks from Fort McCrea came out to send her off. Among the North West Company men, there were also a handful of Chippewa Indians who had come into the post to trade their furs. They stood with the others, their stoic faces showing little interest in the goings-on of the fort.

After both Henry and Abi were settled, Migizi and Robert spoke and the dogs began to move.

Robert looked confident riding on Abi's cariole, as if he'd spent most of his life on the back of a dogsled, and perhaps he had.

The sides and top of the cariole kept Henry safe from the biting winds as they rode out of the stockade, across a clearing, and into the dense woods.

After a couple hours, they came to a large, frozen lake. It was so wide Henry could not see the opposite shoreline. Snow swirled across the endless expanse of white as Migizi directed the dogs to cross. They kept a steady pace, running without ceasing as they flew over the powdered snow. Migizi had said if they pushed the dogs, they could make it back to Montreal in two weeks, stopping midway at Sault Sainte Marie to refresh their supplies.

Henry prayed for their safety, especially that of Abi. He glanced to his left and saw her eyes and the top of her head over the sides of her cariole. He hated the idea of facing her father if something happened to the young lady.

She turned and caught his gaze, holding it for a moment before Robert called to his dogs and they pulled ahead of Henry and Migizi.

By midday, they had crossed the lake. They came to a halt in a clearing of trees just beyond the shore. Henry was surprised at how warm he had stayed on this leg of the journey and was thankful for the clothing McCrea had provided.

Robert untied the lacings holding Abi's cariole closed and offered a hand to help her out.

While Robert and Migizi saw to the dogs, Abi cleared the snow from the ground with a wooden board.

Henry gathered dry branches from the surrounding area and brought them to Abi.

"Thank you," she said, taking a kit out of her belongings. It contained flint, steel, and tinder, which she used to start the fire.

As she blew the flames to life, Henry couldn't help but stare. He wondered how many women he knew in England or in Montreal who could start a fire in the middle of the woods, and look so confident doing so.

When the fire was going strong, Abi took a tripod from her supplies and set it above the flames. Next, she took a copper kettle, filled it with snow, then hung it from the tripod. While the snow melted, she took pemmican and flour from her stores and added it to the pot with a handful of potatoes and carrots. As it bubbled, it turned into a thick stew-like dish.

"It's called *robbiboo*," Abi said when she caught Henry looking into the kettle. "The pemmican will be much easier to chew once it's boiled down."

Anything would be better than the cold pemmican they'd endured on their trip to Fort McCrea.

In another kettle, which Abi set close to the fire, she melted snow and added tea leaves. After she was done preparing the meal, she took plates, spoons, and cups out of her cariole.

Henry felt a bit helpless as she took care of the meal and Robert and Migizi cared for the dogs. He could have offered to help them, though he didn't know much about dogs, but he would much rather stay with Abi. Her competency surprised him, and again, he found himself comparing her to the other women he knew. He'd assumed she would be a burden on this trip, but so far, she was proving to be more helpful than he was.

"Here." Henry took the cups and dishes from her, hating to see her and the others doing all the work while he watched.

"Thank you," she said again, and this time their gazes met.

Something inside Henry warmed and he couldn't stop himself from smiling. "You're welcome."

They worked side by side until Robert and Migizi joined them at the fire for their midday meal.

"It smells wonderful, Abi." Robert inhaled a deep, appreciative breath as he rubbed his hands together near the flames. "You will make a fine wife."

The expression on Abi's face filled with disquiet as she scooped the robbiboo onto the plates and handed them to the men.

Did Robert mean to make Abi his wife? Was that why McCrea had sent the man with them?

Robert caught Henry watching Abi and his expression changed as well. He had been congenial since they'd met, but now his jaw tightened and the lines of his face deepened as he stared at Henry. Was Robert staking his claim? The man had nothing to worry about from Henry. He intended to marry Josephine one day, if she'd have him. He just hoped that his journey into the interior and back was enough to convince her that he wasn't simply a clerk, but a man who was willing to go to any length to win her hand and affection.

"Are ye married, Mr. Kingsley?" Robert took the steaming plate from Abi and began to eat.

Migizi had already taken his plate of food and crouched near the fire.

Abi handed the next plate to Henry, her curious gaze on his face.

"I am not married," Henry said.

"Engaged, perhaps?" Robert asked.

"No." Henry took a bite of the robbiboo and lifted his eyebrows. The pemmican was actually good, something he couldn't say before he'd tasted Abi's dish. "And you, Mr. Douglass? Are you engaged?"

Robert glanced at Abi, who seemed to avoid eye contact with him as she scooped food onto a plate for herself. "Practically," he said.

"Practically?" Henry smiled, suspecting he would rouse the man's anger by teasing, but he couldn't resist. "Does the young lady know she's 'practically' engaged?"

Again, Robert looked toward Abi, but she bent to stir the robbiboo.

"It's only a matter of time."

"Before what?" Henry asked.

Robert's jaw tightened even more as he lowered his plate of food. "Before she agrees to marry me."

"What is she waiting for?" Henry took another bite of his pemmican, acting as nonchalant as he could, though he was more interested in Robert's answers than he ought to be.

"She is waiting for me to come into my partnership." Robert paused. "At least, I believe that's what she's waiting for."

Abi used the edge of her gown to lift the kettle from the coals and filled four cups with the tea, appearing not to be interested in the conversation.

"I cannae be sure, actually," Robert said. "Since she refuses to discuss the future."

"That cannot be good." For some reason Henry was glad that this discussion was causing both Robert and Abi to be uncomfortable. Perhaps it meant that the marital plans were one-sided, though why it mattered to Henry was a mystery. "Mayhap the lady in question does not want to marry you and she's afraid to hurt your feelings—or her father's."

Abi paused as she set the kettle back into the coals. Henry suspected that he'd discovered the real reason she hadn't agreed to marry Mr. Douglass.

"Mayhap," Robert said in a frosty tone.

"Or mayhap, she's just not ready," Abi said quietly to no one in particular. "Mayhap the young lady wants to see more of the world before she settles down to married life." She handed Robert a cup of tea, finally meeting his gaze. "Or, mayhap she wants something different than you want, Mr. Douglass."

Robert stared at Abi, his jaw tight. "Only time will tell, Miss McCrea."

"But why speculate?" Henry said with a laugh, trying to break the tense moment. "We have a long journey ahead. Maybe we'll unravel this mystery along the way. For now, let's enjoy this delicious robbiboo. Well done, Miss McCrea."

Her cheeks were already pink from the cold, but they grew pinker still as she nodded her thanks.

"Yes," Robert agreed, even louder than Henry. "It's quite delicious, Abi."

Henry took the tea from Abi and drank it down, allowing it to warm his insides.

"We must move on," Migizi said a few minutes later, his plate clean. "I'll get the dogs ready."

They quickly finished their food and broke their temporary camp.

As they worked, Henry couldn't stop whistling.

Chapter 3

On the fourth day of travel, the late afternoon sun hid behind the low-lying clouds as Abi watched Robert and Migizi walk into the dense woods just beyond camp, their laughter trailing behind them. They would spend the last few hours of daylight hunting, and hopefully return with meat for Abi to roast.

Henry had not been invited to join the hunting expedition, and Abi suspected their laughter was at Henry's expense. Only the women, children, and old men stayed in camp during a hunt. No doubt Robert had excluded Henry because of his lack of experience in the woods.

If Henry was insulted, he didn't let on. He had gone to his pack and pulled out a hatchet that Father had given to him to cut pine boughs for their bedding.

Abi set to work clearing the ground for the campfire, while Henry went to the balsam firs at the edge of the woods. They worked silently, catching each other's eye from time to time. At each glance, Abi's heart beat a little harder and her breath came a little faster. Over the past four days, she'd been drawn to Henry more and more. She found herself watching for him, listening for him, waiting for him. When he drew close to her around the fire, or shared a smile with her over a plate of her food, her insides would warm. It was foolishness to feel these things for a man she hardly knew, yet she couldn't stop herself from enjoying these little moments.

Just watching him now, swinging the hatchet, tossing the pine boughs onto a pile, she took pleasure. He didn't move with the same grace as Migizi, or the same raw strength as Robert, though he was taller and broader. He didn't possess the knowledge of the forest like her father, or the confidence that came from a lifetime in the backcountry—but he did seem to enjoy being in the woods and he was eager to learn and pitch in to help.

He pulled a bough lose and tossed it onto his growing pile—and caught her staring.

Without hesitation, he smiled, and his blue eyes sparkled.

Abi's knees grew weak. She forced herself to go back to her work, hitting the steel against the flint. The spark fell onto her tinder, and she leaned forward to blow into it, smoke spiraling up into the frosty air.

The clearing Migizi had chosen was ideal for a camp. Level ground was enclosed on three sides by thick evergreens, so dense she could not see beyond the borders. On the fourth side was a small, frozen river. If the men were not successful in their hunt, she would chop a hole in the ice with her hatchet and drop a fishing line. She'd do practically anything for fresh food.

On her knees, she continued to blow against the flames. The wood crackled and popped in complaint.

"Here." Henry stood above her with her tripod and copper kettle. "Let me."

No man had ever offered to help her make supper. Not here, and not back at the fur post. With some uncertainty, Abi stood and nodded for him to set up the cooking gear.

If Robert was present, he'd find some way to insult Henry's kindness.

Henry fumbled with the tripod for a while. But, instead of looking frustrated or embarrassed, he frowned and studied the apparatus with great curiosity.

"Like this." She stepped next to him and reached for the tripod, her fingers feeling awkward in the large mittens. She adjusted the three legs and connected them at the top with a hook. She set it above the flames and hung a chain with another hook directly down the center.

Henry grinned. "I should have been able to figure that out."

"It's been my job since I was a child," Abi said to reassure him. "I've had years of practice."

"You could do it as a child." His smile grew bigger. "I'm a grown man and still couldn't figure it out."

Warmth filled Abi's cheeks. "I didn't mean—"

"I'm only teasing you," he said with a laugh. "Doesn't anyone ever tease you?"

Robert made harsh comments, meant to make some laugh, but he didn't tease like Henry. Her father was kind and jovial, but he never teased either. "No."

"I can't imagine why not." He didn't take his eyes off her face. "Your cheeks turn the most becoming shade of pink when you're embarrassed."

She lifted her mittened hand to her cheek. The snowflakes clinging to the wool touched her warm skin and melted.

"There they go again," he said with a twinkle in his eye.

Abi couldn't help but smile. It felt good to experience a bit of joy. Her life was so devoid of it, she didn't realize it was missing until she'd met Henry Kingsley. For the past four days, he'd teased her at every turn, and she'd loved it. His comments made her feel like he noticed her and enjoyed her company.

Each morning, she felt more lighthearted than the day before, though she told herself it was because they drew closer to Montreal. Yet, at the end of the day, when she laid down to sleep, it wasn't Montreal that captured her imagination.

Without being asked, Henry took the pemmican out of her cariole and brought it to her with her flour. "Will you show me how to make the robbiboo?"

"You plan to make it once you've reached Montreal?" She tried to hide her smile, but when he grimaced, she couldn't hold it back. She laughed and he joined her as he shook his head.

"I don't believe I will," he said.

"Then you enjoy cooking? Is that why you want to learn?"

Most men she knew didn't enjoy cooking, and only did so if a woman wasn't present. Surely Robert would think him weak for doing woman's work.

"No." Again, he smiled, and his eyes filled with laughter. "But I enjoy helping you."

She wouldn't admit how much she liked hearing his words.

While preparing the tea, she instructed Henry on how to cook the food. When he concentrated, he scrunched up his eyebrows and gave his complete attention to the task. It made her giggle from time to time as he struggled with things she had done all her life.

"Ow." He pulled back his hand and frowned.

"Did you hurt yourself?"

"It's nothing."

She tried to examine his hand, but he turned away and shook his head. "I accidentally touched the side of the kettle. I'll be fine."

Abi removed her mittens and walked to his other side to take his hand into hers. It was large and strong. "It's not nothing," she said quietly. The spot was already red and swollen.

"Truly, it's nothing," he said again.

"I can help ease the pain."

"How?" He chuckled. "By rubbing snow on it?"

"No." She laughed. "Though the snow would take down the swelling." She went to her cariole. "I have a salve that works well on burns."

The tin can was cold as she pried the lid off. Thankfully, the base for the salve was made of lard and would not be frozen. Dipping her finger into the tin, she scraped out enough to cover the small burn.

"Here." She returned to him and took his hand again.

He met her gaze, his beautiful eyes studying her closely. "How do you come by your healing knowledge?"

Abi tenderly rubbed the salve over the red welt, loving the way his skin felt against hers. It wasn't rough and cracked like a man who worked outside—these were the hands of a man who worked hard, though the work he did was different than most of the men she knew.

"My grandmother was a healer," Abi said. "Before she died, I spent hours with her and she taught me all she knew. My mother says I'm a lot like her."

"She must have been a smart woman then."

Abi didn't respond, knowing he was teasing her again.

"And funny," he added, with a smile in his voice.

She continued to massage the salve onto the wound—though it was no longer necessary.

"And very beautiful," he said gently.

Abi stopped applying the salve, yet she still held his hand, unable to move away or meet his gaze. Was he serious, or was he simply teasing? If he was serious, how was she to respond? Father and Mother had always kept her away from the voyageurs and clerks, with the exception of Robert, so she'd never learned to flirt. Was he attracted to her, or was this just his way?

"You'll want to put your mitten back on," she said as she stepped away. "I'll finish the robbiboo."

He was silent as she stirred the pemmican and then added the flour. She forced herself to breathe normally—and to not look his way.

"Thank you," he finally said.

The robbiboo started to thicken as it bubbled. "You're welcome."

When he walked toward the pine boughs and started to clear the snow where they would sleep, she was able to concentrate on her task again—though just barely.

Who was this man and why had he so captured her attention? Was it because he was different from all the other men she knew, and came from a place she'd always dreamed about? Or was it something else?

It didn't matter. In just a couple of weeks, he'd deliver her to her uncle, and then she'd never see him again. She would forget all about Henry Kingsley.

At least, she hoped she would.

Henry didn't know what felt better, sitting near a crackling fireplace in the main room of Pierre Lafond's bustling fur post in Sault Saint Marie, or watching Abi McCrea cradle Lafond's new baby boy, her eyes aglow with wonder. She smiled down at the small bundle, speaking to Lafond's Indian wife in a language he guessed to be Chippewa.

Outside, a storm raged around the snug fur post built on the banks of the St. Mary's River. Migizi had chosen to stay with the dogs in a barn behind the main house, while Abi, Robert, and Henry had been guests of Lafond and his young bride since arriving at the post that afternoon. After enjoying an evening meal of venison and wild rice, they were now being entertained by the baby who was just a few days old.

Mrs. Lafond said something to Abi, who smiled and nodded. She kissed the babe on the cheek and handed him back to his mother.

"Good night," Mrs. Lafond said to Henry and Robert in a thick accent.

Henry stood. "Thank you for your hospitality."

Mrs. Lafond offered a small curtsy and then disappeared through a door on the opposite side of the main room.

"Will these accommodations be adequate?" Mr. Lafond spoke in a heavy French accent as he indicated the room. "I wish we had more space, but many have come in from the cold seeking shelter and this is all we have to offer." Mrs. Lafond had made cots for them on either side of the large fireplace. Henry and Robert would sleep on one side and Abi on the other.

"More than adequate," Abi said kindly, rising to address their host. "We appreciate your generosity."

"We'll be on our way as soon as the storm ends," Robert told Lafond, standing beside Abi. "We'd hoped to only stay a few hours to purchase some supplies. We're eager to reach Montreal."

"Winter travel is not ideal," Lafond agreed. "You are welcome to stay as long as you need."

"Merci." Abi curtsied, dipping with such grace and elegance, she looked as if she were addressing a noble king and not a wintering partner of the North West Company.

"De rien." Lafond bowed, his warm smile an indication that he was taken by Abi's beauty and charm. He started toward the door his wife had just walked through. *"Bonne nuit."* With that, he left the main room.

Henry couldn't take his eyes off Abi. When she turned back to face him and Robert, she caught him watching her—but he didn't try to hide his appreciation. She was beautiful, though he suspected she didn't know it—not like Josephine or the other women he knew back east. Abi's humility and modesty made her even lovelier, if that was possible.

Robert cleared his throat and took a seat near the fireplace, motioning for Abi to join him on the bench.

Abi stood for a moment, her gaze sliding from Robert to Henry.

"I believe Kingsley was about to go to bed." Robert addressed Abi. "So we could be alone, lass."

"Not at all," Henry said with a grin, loving to irritate his traveling companion. He took a seat opposite Robert. "I'm not at all tired. It could be hours until I'm ready to sleep."

Robert clenched his jaw. "I thought after the tiresome week ye've had doing women's work, ye'd be the first one to bed."

Henry wouldn't be baited by this man. "On the contrary, working with Abi has been refreshing."

An awkward silence filled the room as Robert clenched his jaw. "Fine." He stood, his hands fisted. "If ye plan to stay awake, I'm going to bed. I have no wish to hear yer voice any longer than necessary."

"Robert." Abi took a step toward him, reproach in her voice.

"No worries," Henry said, putting his hand up to stop her from reprimanding Robert further. "Mr. Douglass is only exhausted from the long days of travel and his arduous hunting expeditions. It's a shame he couldn't produce more than a small rabbit for all the work he's done."

Robert took a step toward Henry, his eyes narrowed. "Are ye insulting me, sir?"

Henry shook his head, his heart rate escalating, though he tried to keep his face and body relaxed. "I have no need to insult you, simply pointing out—"

Henry paused as he caught sight of Abi. She stood just behind Robert, her hands twisted together and her face filled with dismay.

It wasn't worth her discomfort to finish what he intended to say. Instead, he took a step back and closed his mouth.

The muscles in Robert's cheeks jumped and his fists stayed clenched at his sides.

"Good night, Robert," Abi said quietly.

Robert didn't even bother to answer. He walked to the door and pulled on his coat and hat.

"Where are you going?" she asked.

"Lafond told me there were other forms of entertainment in the fur post." He glared at Abi as he pulled his mittens on. "Ye dinnae think you're the only bonnie lass in the world, did ye? There are others who take pleasure in my company." With that, he opened the door and stepped into the swirling snow, slamming it closed behind him.

Anger, hot and red, flashed inside Henry's gut. He strode toward the door, ready to call the man out.

"No." Abi grasped Henry's arm to stop him. "He's not worth the trouble."

"No gentleman should speak to a lady that way," Henry said. "Or visit the establishment he speaks of."

She removed her hand from his arm and walked to the fireplace where she lifted a poker and readjusted the logs. "I've always suspected as much. My father's fur post is small and people talk about what happens at the rendezvous."

"You're not surprised?"

She didn't answer.

"And you'd still marry him?"

"Is any man perfect?"

"No." He joined her near the fireplace, his admiration for her growing yet again. She was small and delicate, though she'd proven herself to be one of the strongest women he knew. Her resiliency amazed him, and he'd grown to respect her on their week-long journey. With each new day, he'd looked forward to the time spent with her. He hated that their journey was half over.

THE *Backcountry* BRIDES COLLECTION

"No man is perfect," Henry said quietly, staring into the flaming embers, thinking of his own life and his many transgressions. "But there are some who seek Christ in their weakness and do not flaunt their sins to manipulate or hurt others."

They stood so close to one another, Abi's shoulder brushed Henry's coat sleeve and he could smell the scent of wood smoke and pine in her hair. When she turned to him, firelight danced in her brown eyes as she openly studied him in a way he'd come to appreciate. She didn't shy away, or play coquette, like so many other women. Her gaze was direct and purposeful, just like everything else she did.

"What do you want from life, Henry?"

It was the first time she'd said his name. He savored the sound of it on her lips. Why did a simple word sound more elegant when she said it?

"That's a very personal question, Abi." He teased her with a smile.

She studied him with a serious, knowing gaze. "You use humor to hide your insecurities."

His smile faded and he kicked an ember back into the fireplace. "I decided a long time ago that if people were going to laugh at me, I might as well be the first to do so."

A frown creased her smooth brow. "I can't imagine anyone having a reason to laugh at you. The only reason Robert laughs is because of his own insecurities. It makes him feel powerful to belittle others, especially when they are as strong and smart and handsome as you."

Her words, spoken so eloquently and sincerely, humbled Henry like nothing ever had. "You honor me with your wisdom, Abi."

"And you honor me with your friendship." Her cheeks blossomed with color and she smiled. "That is, if I may call you a friend."

A part of him longed to invite her to call him more than friend, but they came from two separate worlds. They wanted such different things, it was impossible to think such a thing. "I am privileged to be your friend."

As the quiet evening hours pressed on, and the morning dawn beckoned, he wished to hold it at bay and spend more time with Abi McCrea.

Once they left Sault Saint Marie, they'd have only a week left on the trail to Montreal. When they arrived, Henry would share the news with Gregor that he was the heir to the McCrea title and wealth. No doubt he would ask Henry to sail with them to Scotland. But whether Henry went or stayed, he would probably never see Abi again.

A prospect that left him feeling far more disheartened than it should.

422

Chapter 4

A week later, Abi stared out of her cariole as the woods opened before her to reveal Montreal. Migizi called out to the dogs, and both sleds came to stop on a ridge overlooking the beautiful city below.

No clouds marred the vast expanse of bright-blue sky. The temperature was mild with no biting wind to numb her exposed skin. She allowed herself to feast on the bustling city below. A river wrapped around the city, frozen now, and covered with snow. Large stone and wood buildings ran up and down the length of each street, smoke spiraling out of more chimneys than Abi could count. Sleighs carried people from one place to another, while children ran and played in the snow, and dogs barked in the distance.

"We're sitting atop Mount Royal," Henry said from the cariole beside her, his blue eyes watching her with joy. "The St. Lawrence River brings the trade ships in from the Atlantic Ocean, making Montreal an ideal spot for the headquarters of the North West Company. Your uncle's home is over there."

He pointed toward the north, but she wouldn't even know where to look for Uncle Gregor's home.

"It's. . ." Abi couldn't form the words swirling inside her heart and mind.

Henry smiled. "I know."

Robert called for the dogs to move. His impatience had grown more pronounced each day. He'd hardly spoken a word to Abi or Henry since their night at Sault Sainte Marie, keeping his thoughts about Henry to himself.

Migizi pulled his cariole ahead of Abi, leading the way down Mount Royal into the heart of the town. Abi caught a glimpse of Henry now and again. Each time their eyes met, she thought back to the evenings around the fire this past week, when Robert and Migizi had bedded down for the night, when neither she nor Henry could sleep. They spent hours together, sometimes in silence, sometimes teasing, but most of the time just talking.

Henry had become a good friend.

They swished through the streets and Abi feasted on every detail. The stone buildings were her favorite, having never seen one before. Standing two or three stories tall, they were perfect rectangles, with pitched roofs and no eaves.

As they passed one of these buildings, Henry waved to get her attention and then pointed toward it. "A restaurant," he said with a wink.

She laughed and nodded, though her heart skipped a beat—but whether it was from seeing this oddity, or the smile on Henry's face, she couldn't be sure.

Finally, they came to a stop before a large, three-story stone house. A matching stone fence wrapped around the property, low and perfectly formed. It was so different than the tall stockade back home, Abi couldn't hide her astonishment. Was this fence meant to keep people out? Or simply a decoration? It seemed a waste of money and materials for it to be decorative—yet it couldn't possibly add protection to the home.

Large windows gleamed in the brilliant sun, and a solid oak door stood in the center of the main floor, with a brass knocker in the middle.

"Welcome to Gregor McCrea's home," Henry said as he climbed out of the cariole.

Abi stared in amazement.

"Do you like it?" he asked.

"It's so. . .big." She began to rise and both Robert and Henry stepped forward to offer their hand. Since Robert was closer, she used his assistance—and didn't miss the look of triumph he sent in Henry's direction. "Do they truly need all this space for just a few people?"

Henry shrugged. "No, they don't. But some people prefer large homes."

"Why?"

"I don't know." Henry shifted his weight from one foot to the other. "I suppose it's meant to impress people and display the owner's wealth. If a person can afford a large house, he usually owns one."

"Do you own a large house?" Abi asked.

"I live in a rented room near your uncle's office, close to the harbor, but I grew up in a much larger home than this in England. It was called Meadowbrook." He offered his arm to escort her toward the house. "The home your father gave up in Scotland is ten times the size of this house."

She took in the house before her, larger than any home she'd ever seen, and suddenly realized the magnitude of what her father had given up for her and her mother.

"Your father must love your mother a great deal," Henry said gently beside her.

"He does."

"I envy him that kind of love."

Abi met Henry's gaze and saw there was no teasing in his eyes. "So do I."

"Shall we go?" Robert asked, impatience in his tone. "I'd like to give Gregor McCrea this missive so I can find suitable accommodations for my time in Montreal."

"Won't you be leaving again soon?" It was the first question Henry had directed at Robert since they'd left Sault Sainte Marie.

"Mr. McCrea asked me to stay in Montreal until Abi is ready to come home." Robert started to walk toward the house. "I won't leave until that time."

"But I don't know when I'll be ready to return," Abi said quickly. "It could be months—a year, even."

"Yer father insisted I stay, in case ye need me."

"Abi will be well taken care of by her uncle." Henry stood straighter. "I'll see that she's properly escorted anywhere in the city."

"I'm sure ye would." Robert's eyes narrowed.

"I'm eager to meet my uncle and see my sister." Abi pulled on Henry's arm. "Shall we go?"

He responded by walking her through the iron gate and up the path toward the large front door. He lifted the brass knocker and let it fall back into place several times.

Within seconds, the door opened and a tall, thin man stood in the opening, his white hair combed perfectly, his black suit impeccably clean. Abi had never seen anything like it, though Henry's had been similar. Was this her uncle? He looked nothing like Father.

"Mr. Henry Kingsley to see Mr. McCrea," Henry said, very formally. "I've brought his niece, Miss Abi McCrea, as well as his brother's clerk, Mr. Douglass, on official business."

The man stood very straight. He didn't bother to tilt his head down as he looked Abi over, disdain in his haughty eyes. "Follow me, please."

Henry escorted Abi through the doorway and into the house. Her eyes grew wide as she inspected the room. It was larger than the main dwelling room at her father's fur post. All it housed was a stairway, which ran up one wall and turned to disappear upstairs. The floors were a polished wood, the walls decorated with painted silver flowers, and the woodwork was thick and coated white.

Henry took off his capote and his fur-lined hat, and handed them to the man, who bowed and nodded at Henry. "You'll wait here in the foyer." He spoke with little expression. "I'll tell Mr. McCrea you've come."

"Wouldn't we be more comfortable in the parlor?" Henry asked.

The man lifted an eyebrow but didn't answer, and then disappeared at the back of the foyer.

"That's peculiar," Henry said to himself.

Three doors stood around the room, but all of them were closed. Abi's curiosity burned as she longed to see what was behind those doors.

"Henry!" A booming voice filled the room even before Abi saw who it belonged to. "Ye've made it back in record time."

A large man walked through the door at the back of the room. He was tall, like Father, but his waist spread wide, and he wore his hair short and his face shaved clean. He spoke with the same brogue her father had, but there were few other similarities. Uncle Gregor wore a black suit like the man at the door, and he was pale, as if he spent little time outdoors. Abi's father was lean, muscular, and tanned. He despised indoor work and only did it when necessary.

"Hello, Mr. McCrea." Henry reached out and shook the hand of his employer. "May I present your niece, Miss Abi McCrea?"

Uncle Gregor's gaze passed over Abi with little interest as he looked beyond her to Robert. "Are you my brother's clerk?"

Robert cleared his throat, stepping forward for the first time since entering the house. "Yes sir."

"And what news do you bring from my brother?" he asked.

Robert pulled the letter from his pocket and handed it to Uncle Gregor.

Henry looked from Uncle Gregor to Abi, uncertainty in his gaze. Surely, he hadn't missed her uncle's cold response to her. "He has given his inheritance to you," Henry said, haltingly. "The land, the title—everything."

Uncle Gregor tore open the envelope and looked it over like a man devouring a large meal after a long fast. "Finally."

"Your brother also sent this letter." Henry pulled the letter out of his pocket that Father had given him. "It's an introduction for his daughter, I believe."

"What?" Uncle Gregor pulled his attention away from the inheritance letter, a frown on his face. Impatiently, he took the letter from Henry and tore it open. He looked it over quickly and then tilted his head toward the back of the room. "My butler will show ye to the housekeeper. She'll take care of ye."

"And my sister?" Abi asked.

He didn't smile, or make her feel welcomed, but neither did he turn her away. "Someone will locate her."

The butler stepped forward, the same disdainful scowl on his face. "This way."

Abi was eager to see her sister, but unsure about leaving Henry and Robert.

Henry smiled and nodded encouragement at her, while Robert hardly gave her a glance. She'd wounded his pride, yet if she said the word, he'd still marry her if it meant an alliance with her father. But all of that could wait.

With a timid smile for Henry, Abi followed the butler out of the foyer and down a long hall toward the back of the house.

"Your sister will be in the kitchen," the butler said.

Abi tried to take in everything as they passed. She was so excited to see Isobel after all these years, she would never remember anything.

They passed through another door and into a kitchen much larger than the dwelling room back home.

At first, Abi didn't recognize her sister. She wore a black dress with a white apron and a white cap on her head. In one hand she held a broom and in the other a coal bucket.

"Abi?" Isobel's eyes grew wide.

Confusion clouded Abi's mind as another lady turned from the stove. "Are you here to work?"

"Work?" Abi frowned.

"Mrs. Beale will be in here shortly," the butler said to Abi. "She'll find suitable clothes for you and give you instructions."

"Instructions?" What did he mean?

"What are you doing here?" Isobel walked across the room, her pretty features scrunched in concern.

Abi finally found her voice. "What are *you* doing here?"

Isobel bit her bottom lip and lowered her eyes. "I work here."

"In our uncle's house?"

"Don't call him that," Isobel said quickly.

"Why not?"

Isobel set down the bucket and finally met Abi's gaze. "You're so innocent." She took Abi's hand in hers, sadness in the depths of her eyes. "Our mother is an Indian, Abi, and he doesn't acknowledge us as kin."

Realization began to dawn. "You're not a guest?"

Isobel shook her head.

Abi felt as if she'd been punched in the gut. "What about the letters? The descriptions of Montreal, the balls, the. . .the. . ." She couldn't continue.

"All of it was true." Isobel dropped her gaze, her cheeks pale. "I simply saw it from my position as a maid."

"Then why didn't you come home?"

Isobel let go of Abi's hand, resignation in her shoulders. "I was too ashamed to face Father. It's easier for him and Mother to believe I am Mr. McCrea's guest than it is to admit I'm his scullery maid."

"But, Father would understand—"

"Yes, but it would devastate him to know how his brother feels about his wife and children."

Another woman entered the room, her hair drawn back in a tight bun. She looked Abi up and down. "I'm Mrs. Beale, the housekeeper. If you'll follow me, I'll show you where you can put your things. You can start work tomorrow."

"My sister hasn't come for a job," Isobel said as she put her arm around Abi's shoulder. "She's my guest."

"We don't allow maids to have guests." Mrs. Beale crossed her arms. "If she's staying, then she needs to work."

Abi was so confused, she had a difficult time focusing on what the others were saying. "I'll be happy to work."

"No." Isobel shook her head. "Go home, Abi."

"I will," Abi promised, tears stinging the back of her eyes. "But not without you."

She'd do whatever it would take to get her sister out of Gregor McCrea's home.

Henry already missed Abi and she'd only been gone a few minutes. When would he see her again? Would it be awkward to attend social gatherings in Gregor's home with Josephine and Abi together? His thoughts were so muddled, he could hardly concentrate on what Gregor was saying.

"When you return to the interior," Gregor said to Robert, "tell my brother I will bring honor to our family name."

"I will, sir." Robert continued to stand in the foyer, his hat in hand.

Gregor nodded toward the door. "You're dismissed."

Robert glanced from Gregor to Henry and back. "Yer brother asked me to keep an eye on his daughters while I'm here."

"That won't be necessary," Gregor said. "I'll see that they have everything they need."

"I'm to escort Miss Abi home when she's ready."

Gregor frowned. "Doesn't she plan to stay long?"

"She's unsure how long she will stay," Henry supplied. "She's only come to see her sister and get a taste of Montreal, then she plans to return home."

"She'll hardly have time to see Montreal." Gregor started toward his office, dismissing Robert with a wave of his hand. "She'll only have half a day off on Sundays."

"Half a day off?" Henry followed close behind his employer. "What does that mean?"

Gregor opened his office door and stepped into the dark interior. "That's all any of the maids are allowed. It's standard, I've heard, but I leave all such things in the hands of my housekeeper."

"I'm confused." Henry stood just inside Gregor's office, his brow furrowed.

"Why are you confused? My brother sent me another illegitimate brat to house and feed, so I expect some work out of her."

Incredulity marked Henry's voice. "She's your niece."

"John never legally married that Indian woman, and even if he had, she's not fit to be part of our family." He waved aside the discussion as if it were a pesky fly. "Now, we must discuss more important matters, like my move to Scotland. It'll be a massive undertaking—"

"Abi is your niece and her father entrusted her to your care."

"Entrusted?" Gregor sighed and lowered his bulk into a chair. "He dumped those Indian girls in my lap and he expects some special favor?"

"He expects nothing beyond what a brother should do for his nieces, especially one he's just gifted with his entire inheritance."

Gregor's stare was hard and unyielding. "I am not forcing them to stay here. They're free to go at any time."

What must Abi be thinking right now? She'd come, expecting a warm welcome, only to discover that her uncle had no regard for her. She must be upset and confused. No wonder Henry had never heard of her sister before. She was a maid. "I must go and speak with her." Henry took a step back. "Help her arrange transportation home."

"You've only just arrived," Gregor said, indicating a chair on the other side of his large desk. "We need to discuss the future—your future, and mine. You've been a trusted employee. I would like to have ye join Josephine and me in Scotland." He grinned. "What do ye think of that?"

"I really must speak with Abi." Henry hated to walk away from Gregor, knew it could cost him his job, but he didn't care. Right now, he could only think of Abi.

"Henry?" Josephine's voice drifted into the office just a moment before she appeared at the door.

She looked lovely in a pink gown flowing freely near her feet and tight around her bodice and sleeves. No matter what social situation she was in, she was always in control. Even now, seeing Henry this way after dismissing him with cold indifference at their last parting, she was completely composed—charming. "How have you been?"

All the muscles in Henry's back and shoulders stiffened as he saw Josephine through new eyes. Was she the type of woman he wanted as a wife and possibly a mother to his children? She was graceful and poised in a ballroom and while serving tea—she would make a perfect mistress of McCrea Manor in Scotland—but what would she be like in private? How would she respond if life was unkind? Would she grow bitter, angry, and impossible to live with? What would happen if she were forced to fend for herself, to live off nature the way Abi had?

"Henry, you've come just in time for my Christmas Eve ball tomorrow." She took his arm and pulled him toward the foyer. "You don't mind if I steal him away, do you, Father? I need his help for just a little while."

"Go ahead." Gregor laughed, seeming to put aside all his other cares while his daughter was in the room. "But I need to speak with him soon."

Josephine blew her father a kiss and wrapped her other hand around Henry's arm, hugging him close to her side. She smelled of rosewater and powder. Her blond hair was styled in a high mess of curls at the top of her head, and her gown accentuated all the right curves. Henry forced himself to look away from her and give himself as much space as she would permit, which was precious little.

"I had so hoped you'd be home in time for my ball," she purred like a kitten. "Everyone loves to dance with you. You're ever so handsome in your evening clothes." She frowned as she looked him over. "Whatever are you wearing?" She laughed. "You look like a voyageur."

The foyer was empty, which meant that Robert had probably left to find accommodations. No doubt he'd return to check on Abi as soon as he could. He'd probably be eager to take her back to her father the moment he learned the truth.

Henry couldn't stand the thought of Abi being alone with Robert. He'd be a gentleman, of that Henry was certain, but he'd also use the opportunity to convince Abi to marry him. That was something Henry couldn't abide. Robert didn't deserve Abi, not if he only wanted her for political or financial gains.

"Josephine." Henry tried to pull loose of her grasp. "I need to speak with someone."

"Can't it wait? I want to show you the new drapes I had made for the ballroom."

Drapes? Was that what occupied her time? It wasn't her fault that she was pampered and spoiled—but he suddenly realized he had no desire to be married to a woman whose main preoccupation was parties and drapery.

At each turn, he saw Josephine for who she truly was. For so many years, he'd longed for her to be the right woman for him, when all along, she never had been—and never would be.

After getting to know Abi, he didn't think he'd ever look at another woman the same way.

Chapter 5

A bi sat alone on the narrow bed where she'd been assigned to sleep with Isobel in the cold basement. Her sister was busy preparing for a ball Josephine would host the following evening. After the cold and confusing welcome she'd received, the thought of a ball held no interest to Abi any longer. She just wanted to go home.

She stood, thankful she was still wearing her capote to keep off the chill, and rested her forearms on the only windowsill in the room. It looked out onto an alley that separated Uncle Gregor's house from the one behind it. The window was eye-level with the road. Dirty snow had piled up so that she could hardly see out. All she could see was the top of the other house and the overcast sky beyond. The day had become dreary, with a few light flurries falling.

A cart rumbled through the alley and stopped right in front of the window, blocking the little view she had. Abi heard the muffled voices, but didn't know what they were saying. Maybe they had come with food or drinks for the ball tomorrow. Maybe it was a baker with fresh tarts, or a dressmaker, come to fit Josephine for her gown.

Whoever it was, Abi would not have the pleasure of watching the preparations unfold.

She sighed and her breath fogged the glass.

Beyond the window, Montreal awaited—but she had no way to see it. She didn't want to go out alone. Even if she did, she wouldn't know where to go or what to see. Besides, her heart no longer cared what this town had to offer. All she knew was that it hadn't been kind to her or her sister.

She turned away from the window, trying to imagine what the rest of the house might look like. Would anyone be angry if she explored? She could do it silently and stay out of everyone's way. Surely they'd understand.

Abi left the room and entered a cool, musty hall. Footsteps echoed above, but all was quiet in the basement.

She walked up the steps and tiptoed down another long, dark hall. This one had several doors, one of which she suspected was her uncle's office.

Walking as quietly as possible, and thankful for her soft moccasins, she left the hall and entered the foyer, peeking around the door to make sure no one was there. Thankfully, it was empty. She proceeded across the room to the double doors that stood open.

"Why must you go?" a feminine voice whined. "I want to show you the new upholstery I chose to match the drapes."

"There's someone I need to speak with immediately."

Henry.

Just hearing him in this strange house made her feel a measure of comfort and peace—but then embarrassment crowded in. What would he think when he learned her sister was not a guest, but a maid? And that Abi would be a maid too—at least for as long as it took to make plans to go home.

Suddenly, Henry appeared at the open door, his moccasins making it hard for her to detect that he'd been coming closer.

A smile lifted his handsome lips. "I was just coming to see you."

"You were?" Why would he come to see her? Didn't he have more important things to do?

He stepped closer and took her hand, his smile fading. "I only just learned about your sister. I'm sorry, Abi. I didn't know."

She wished they were back in the woods, just the two of them. Back where things were familiar and safe, before she knew the truth.

"What will you do?" Concern made his voice deepen and his eyes pool with compassion.

She dropped her gaze. "I—I don't know."

"Would you like me to take you back to your father?"

Abi looked up quickly. "You would do that for me?"

The lines of his face softened and he lifted his free hand, as if he were going to touch her cheek, but lowered it again. "I would do anything for you."

Her heart beat a joyful rhythm and she couldn't find her voice to say thank you.

"Does your sister want to go?"

She shrugged. "I don't know. I haven't had a chance to speak with her about returning. Everyone is busy preparing for the ball."

"And you? What are you doing today?"

The heaviness she felt earlier returned. "Nothing."

"Let me take you into the city," he said. "We'll make plans to leave for Fort McCrea the morning after the ball. Would you like that?"

Hope filled her chest. Abi smiled for the first time since arriving at her uncle's home. "I would."

He returned the smile and squeezed her hand, pulling her toward the front door.

"Henry?" A young lady appeared at the ballroom doors, a frown marring her beautiful features. "What are you doing? Who is she?" She turned up her nose, as if seeing Abi was distasteful.

Instead of dropping Abi's hand, like she thought he would, Henry tightened his grasp. "This is Miss Abi McCrea, your cousin from the backcountry. Abi, this is Miss Josephine McCrea, the mistress of this home."

"How do you do?" Abi asked with a tentative smile. She'd always wondered about this cousin of hers.

Josephine crossed her arms and pointed her gaze at Henry. "Where are you going? Father wanted to speak with you as soon as you and I were done."

Henry looked down at Abi, a sad smile on his face. "I'm sorry for the way your family is treating you, Abi. You should be welcomed like royalty and treated as no less."

A flutter filled her stomach at his words and at the look in his eyes.

"I demand an answer, Henry." Josephine's voice ripped apart the tender moment.

Henry finally addressed Josephine. "I am taking Abi out to see a bit of Montreal before it grows dark. Tell your father I'll return her after supper and we can speak then."

With that, he opened the exterior door and walked a surprised Abi outside.

She took a deep breath the moment the cold hit her face, letting it out on a sigh.

Henry wrapped her arm through his, pulling her tight against him. "Where to first?"

"Wherever you'd like."

"Are you hungry?"

"Famished."

"Then let's find a restaurant."

Abi couldn't contain the grin.

He walked her down the street, the snow falling around them. She marveled at the large homes crowding around her uncle's. They went on and on, one after the other. Just when she thought they would go on this way forever, Henry turned her down another street and the homes gave way to shops with large front windows. Some held meats, others baked goods, and some were filled with hats and boots and other sundries.

"There's one of my favorite restaurants." Henry pointed ahead to a two-story, stone building with a wide blue door. The men and women entering and exiting were dressed in beautiful clothing, with top hats and furs.

Abi paused, causing Henry to stop.

"What's wrong?" he asked.

She lifted the edge of her capote, which was made from a scratchy trade blanket. Though it was warm, and served her well in the woods, it would not be suitable for this restaurant. "I'm not dressed to dine there."

"Nonsense. I know the proprietor well. We'll be served the finest food and drink,

433

no matter what we're wearing."

The same niggle of doubt Abi felt back at the fort before she left on this journey wedged its way into her happiness. She allowed Henry to take her forward, smiling for his benefit.

They entered the restaurant and were greeted with the warm scents of roasting meat, baked bread, and unfamiliar spices. Abi's mouth began to water as she took in the dark paneled walls, the dripping candles, and the white tablecloths. At least a dozen tables filled the room. Many of them were full of patrons.

The conversation came to a halt as everyone in the restaurant turned to look at who had entered. Disapproving stares gave way to shaking heads, which gave way to murmurs of complaint.

Abi pulled back, using Henry as a shield, though he didn't seem to notice her discomfort—or the irritation of the diners.

"A table for two, please." Henry spoke to a man near the door.

The man wore a black suit like the one the butler wore at Uncle Gregor's house. He, like the butler, looked down his nose at Abi. "I don't believe we have a table available, sir."

Henry frowned. "I see one near the window."

The man pinched his lips together. "It isn't available."

Henry stiffened beside Abi. "I've been dining here for two years. There's always been a table available for me. If you'd please get the owner, Mr. Valdez, I'm sure he'll clear up any misunderstanding."

"As you wish." The man turned on his heel and disappeared through a door.

Henry glanced around the room, meeting the glares sent in Abi's direction. Anger and frustration wedged between his eyes.

Abi pulled away from Henry. Her father had warned her that she would learn things in Montreal that would break her heart—and she had, though not like he probably thought. Yes, it hurt to know that she was not welcome in Montreal's polite society, but it hurt far more to know that she and Henry belonged in two different worlds. There was no way to bridge the gap separating them.

"I want to go home, Henry."

"We haven't eaten."

She took a step toward the door. "I don't belong here. All of them know it."

"Don't say such things." His anger faded and grief filled his face. "You are the most refined, elegant, and charming lady in this restaurant."

"It's not just the restaurant. I don't belong here, in Montreal." She took a deep breath, disheartened that she had come all this way to discover the truth. "I belong in a fur post, on the banks of the Mississippi River. Right now, I don't want anything more than I want that."

He studied her for a moment. "I had so hoped to show you this city."

She met all the haughty glares and then offered him a tremulous smile. "You have." She lifted her chin and tilted her head toward the door. "I'm ready to leave."

Henry took her hand in his and nodded. "I'll take you home."

They left the restaurant and walked back to her uncle's house. The whole way Abi was comforted by one thing: she finally knew where her home truly was. The wilderness no longer felt like a prison, but an oasis.

Abi stood behind the cloth screen, holding a pile of dirty plates as she watched the dancers circle around the ballroom through the crack dividing the panels. The room was more brilliant than she would have ever imagined. Hundreds of candles gleamed from chandeliers, wall sconces, and candelabras placed throughout the room. Evergreens and holly decorated the mantels, while an abundance of food filled several tables. Musicians played their beautiful instruments from a raised platform on one end of the room as dozens of couples twirled over the polished floor. Every color of the rainbow was represented in the gowns the women wore. Abi had never seen the like, or imagined women wore such elaborate clothing.

"Be about your work," Mrs. Beale said to Abi when she caught her staring through the crack of the screen. "We need those plates in the kitchen so they can be cleaned and returned."

Abi nodded and turned away from the ballroom, her heart both heavy and light. Heavy because she was wearing a scratchy black gown and squeaky shoes that pinched, but light because she had finally seen a real ball—even if she hadn't been able to dance.

She deposited the stack of dirty dishes in the kitchen and picked up the clean stack to return it to the ballroom.

"Stay out of the way," the cook said over her shoulder. "The help isn't supposed to be noticed. You're no more than a fixture in the room, like a piece of furniture."

Abi had already learned all the rules and expectations earlier from Mrs. Beale, but everyone had taken to reminding her whenever they could. She gave a brief nod and left the kitchen again.

Isobel was refreshing a plate of deviled eggs, her gaze cast down. Abi had spoken to her briefly the night before about returning with her and Henry to Father's fur post, but Isobel had been uncertain. This morning and afternoon, they had been too busy with the ball preparations to find a moment to speak alone. If they did not discuss it soon, Abi and Henry would have to postpone their plans to leave in the morning.

After setting the plates down and gathering up others that had been left sitting about, Abi returned to the screen to watch the dancers once again. She had not caught a glimpse of Henry, though she'd heard his voice coming from Uncle

Gregor's office earlier. The conversation had sounded tense, but Abi wasn't sure why. Was Uncle Gregor angry that Henry would be leaving again so soon? Surely her uncle wanted to make plans to leave for Scotland. Would Henry be expected to help—possibly go with them?

The very thought of Henry going to Scotland, and never seeing him again, made her chest ache with a longing she didn't understand. How could she feel this way about a man she'd only met a few weeks ago?

Henry entered the ballroom just then, with Josephine on his arm. Abi's cousin looked radiant in a green gown, her hair dripping with curls. Jewels sparkled from her earrings and necklace. When she turned to look up at Henry, with such grace and elegance, a pang of jealousy thudded through Abi, surprising her with its intensity.

The dancers moved to the outside of the room, leaving the center open for Josephine and Henry. He bowed and she curtsied, and then they began to waltz in perfect harmony.

Everyone smiled with approval, some twittering behind their fans with knowing glances. Henry looked so dashing in his evening coat, his dark hair combed back, his shoes shining in the candlelight. He was born for this room and this place. What he lacked in the wilderness, he more than made up for in this ballroom. His back was straight, his arms perfectly curved around Josephine, and his feet moved effortlessly over the parquet floor. If Robert had been standing there, he could have found no fault in Henry now.

The plates became heavy in Abi's arms. Truth be told, she'd grown weary of watching Henry and Josephine smiling at each other.

She returned to the kitchen and delivered the dirty dishes once again, taking her time so she wouldn't have to see Josephine in Henry's arms.

"Take that platter of cookies out to the ballroom," the cook finally told Abi. "Be quick about it too."

Trying not to feel melancholy, knowing she was missing the Christmas Eve traditions back home, Abi lifted the tray and started back to deliver the cookies.

"Abi?" Henry stood in the dark hall, his face covered in the flickering shadows of a lone candle to light the way. The music from the ballroom drifted into the hall, wrapping them in a poignant melody.

"Hello, Henry."

He took a step closer, taking in her maid's uniform. "I've wanted to see you all day, but I had much to discuss with your uncle before the ball."

She focused on the large silver platter she held, willing her heart to steady its beating and her breath to come naturally. Up close, he looked even more handsome than he had on the dance floor. "I've been busy as well." She lifted the tray. "I should get these to the ballroom."

She started to move past him, but he put his hand on her arm to stop her.

"Please don't go yet. You and I have much to discuss."

"I need to get these to the—"

"Meet me in the library when you're finished." He tilted his head to the door next to the ballroom. "We can speak privately in there."

There was work to be done—yet she wanted to spend time with Henry. She nodded and walked back to the ballroom, her arm tingling where he'd touched her.

Making sure not to meet anyone's eye, lest they ask her to do something else, she slipped in and out of the ballroom without encountering any of the other staff. She looked both ways to make sure no one was watching, then stepped into the library.

Henry stood with his back to the door, looking out the window on the dark, snowy night.

When Abi closed the door, he turned and met her gaze.

A lamp glowed from a table in the center of the room. Though it didn't offer enough light to fill the space, it was enough for her to see the longing in his eyes— and that alone was all the illumination she needed.

"Why did you ask me here?" she whispered, afraid of what he might say. Though her heart longed for Henry to love her, she knew it was an impossible match. Especially after seeing him here in Montreal. Henry belonged in this world. He thrived here and had made a good home for himself. If Uncle Gregor asked him to go to Scotland, he'd probably do even better.

Henry walked around the table and stopped in front of Abi. He stood close, much closer than he ever had. She half feared, half hoped that he wanted to kiss her.

"You've always dreamed of going to a ball, so may I have this dance?" he asked.

The music was muted, though it was loud enough to hear through the walls of the library. But dance?

"Here?"

"I would prefer to dance with you in the ballroom, or alone in the wilderness." He smiled. "But I'm afraid this will have to do." He extended his hand, hope and expectation in his gaze.

Abi lifted a pleat of the starched black gown she wore. "But I'm hardly dressed for—"

"You've never looked more beautiful."

His sincerity warmed her and she finally nodded.

Taking his hand, she allowed him to pull her into his arms. He wore a spicy cologne she'd never smelled before. It wrapped around her, enveloping her senses and setting her mind to spinning. He was so tall, she had to tilt her head back to look into his dear face.

He took a step, and she followed. Soon they were waltzing around the table in the center of the room. Abi grinned as they kept time to the music. They had a natural rhythm to their movements, as if they'd been dancing together all their lives.

"You're an excellent dancer," Henry said. "Who taught you?"

"My father." She had always loved dancing with her father, but she was never more thankful for the lessons than now.

"Do you miss him terribly?" Henry asked.

"More than I ever thought I would."

"And your sister? Does she miss home?"

"We haven't had time to speak of such things, but I believe she does."

He was quiet for a moment, and then he said, "I'll be ready to take you in the morning, with or without her."

"I won't leave without Isobel."

Neither one spoke for a while as they continued to twirl around the room.

"Is my uncle angry that you're leaving again so soon?" she asked.

"I haven't told him yet."

Abi stopped dancing and stared up at him. "Why not?"

"I didn't want to upset him before the ball. I plan to tell him in the morning."

The lamplight cast shadows across his handsome face, making it hard for her to read the expression in his blue eyes. As he studied her, she found herself holding her breath, wondering what it was he saw. Did he see her father's blood or her mother's? Or, perhaps, could he look past everything else and simply see her?

Henry lifted his hand and touched a strand of hair that had come loose from her bun. A smile played about his lips as he ran it between his fingers.

"It's even softer than I expected." His gaze focused on her face again and the look he'd given her when she entered the room returned. "Abi."

She couldn't move, couldn't speak, couldn't think beyond this moment.

His hand rested on her cheek and she inhaled, closing her eyes briefly to revel in the feel of his touch.

Slowly, and with great care, he placed his other hand on her other cheek and waited for a heartbeat, a question in his eyes.

When she gave a slight nod, he lowered his face to a mere inch from hers. She thought she might die from the anticipation of his kiss.

Then the door swung open with a bang and Abi wrenched herself away from Henry's touch, heat filling her cheeks.

"What is the meaning of this?" Josephine stood in the doorway, her eyes wide and her nostrils flaring. "Explain yourself, maid."

Henry hadn't moved, nor did he look remorseful being caught with Abi this way. "She is not your maid, but your cousin." His gaze fell on Abi. "And I was about to kiss her."

The heat in Abi's cheeks deepened, and she was afraid it might burn her completely.

"Kiss this. . .this. . .creature?" Josephine's anger faded away and she began to laugh. "You can't be serious, Henry."

Henry frowned. "I've never been more serious about anyone in my life."

Abi's lips parted at the declaration.

"And you think she is suitable for you?" Josephine continued to laugh. "Do you really think she'll be accepted into Montreal's polite society?" Her laughter turned cynical. "Or do you plan to go to the backcountry with her and the other savages, to live off the land? You could never survive there." Her eyes grew cold. "You're a fool, Henry, if you think either one of you could be happy."

It was as if Josephine had looked inside Abi's heart to see all the fears written there. What good could come of loving Henry? One of them would have to give up the world they knew, while the other would suffer the unhappy consequences.

When Abi met Henry's gaze, she knew he was having the same troubling thoughts.

Without another word, Abi left the library.

She prayed Henry would not follow.

Chapter 6

The morning was cold and gray as Henry walked across the foyer toward Gregor's office. It was Christmas Day, but Gregor would be at work, at least until the evening meal when Josephine would entertain yet another party, one Henry would miss for the first time in two years.

He should have gone after Abi last night when Josephine had laughed at them, but he had seen the look in Abi's eyes and he knew she wouldn't want him to. She needed time and space to sort through her feelings, and he had too. He'd been dissatisfied with his life in Montreal for a long time, but he didn't know what it was his heart was looking for. Now he did.

Henry knocked on Gregor's door and waited for an invitation to enter. When it came, he stepped over the threshold and into his employer's office.

"Henry." Gregor looked up from a letter on his desk, his eyebrows tilted down. "Why are you dressed that way?"

Henry had put on the clothing Abi's father had given him. "I'm taking Abi back to her father." He had spoken to Migizi about two sleds and dogs, and told him to be ready to go when Henry sent word, but he still didn't know if Abi's sister would be joining them.

Gregor's thoughts were imperceptible. "You're under no obligation to see her home. You have no business in the interior—"

"I do have business. I would like to speak to her father."

"I don't need anything from my brother. We have his letter. My lawyers are already seeing to the transition—"

"I have personal business to see to this time." Henry clutched his fur-lined hat and stood tall. He hadn't slept the night before. Not because he was upset, but because he was excited. His life wasn't back in Europe, following Gregor to the McCrea ancestral home. His path was west, following his heart to the interior where he and Abi could create a new life and a new legacy for the generations who would follow them—if she'd have him. "I will not be returning to Montreal."

Gregor stood slowly, scrutinizing Henry's face. "You're sailing with Josephine and me when we leave for Scotland in the spring."

"I am leaving for the interior this morning. I have no plans to return."

Gregor leaned forward and placed his fists on his desk. "And what of Josephine? What of your future? Your prospects? You'd throw it all away for a backcountry bride?"

"I'm throwing nothing away." Henry shook his head, amazed that he could feel such peace as he walked away from everything he'd been working to build these past couple of years. "If she'll have me, my future and my prospects will look better than ever."

Straightening, Gregor crossed his arms. "Go, and don't bother to return when you discover the wilderness is no place for a civilized man."

Henry had had enough of civilization these past couple of days, watching the world respond to Abi.

"Goodbye." Henry extended his hand, but Gregor didn't accept it. Exhaling a breath, Henry nodded. "Merry Christmas."

He left Gregor's office and walked down the hall, nerves making his muscles tighten. What would Abi say when he declared his heart and intentions? Would she laugh at him? Turn him away? He didn't know how she'd respond, but he couldn't live with himself if he didn't try.

The kitchen was bustling with activity and filled with the fragrance of Christmas. Plum pudding, gingerbread, roast goose, and more. It would be a shame to miss the meal, but Henry would take Abi's robbiboo in the wilderness over anything made in this kitchen.

"May I help you?" An older lady turned from the stove, wiping her hands on her stained apron.

"I'm looking for Miss Abi McCrea." Henry glanced around the room. Disappointment filled his chest, but anticipation for the moment she appeared was so great, it didn't matter.

"She's gone."

Henry blinked several times. "Pardon me?"

"She and her sister left before daybreak this morning." The cook walked to the table, lifted a knife, and began to cut a loaf of bread.

"Left? Where did they go?"

"Home." She continued to slice the bread, apparently done with their conversation.

"But how? Who took them?"

"Couldn't rightly say. . .though Isobel addressed him by name." She shrugged. "But I don't recall what it was."

"Robert?"

She shook her head and placed a few slices of bread on a toasting rack.

"Robert Douglass?"

"That's it." She nodded. "Mr. Douglass. Came in a fancy-looking sled with a team of dogs."

Henry balled his fists. He hated to think of Abi on the trail with Robert for the next two weeks. If she was unhappy and disillusioned by her dreams, she might be liable to marry him, only because she thought it was her last option.

"I must leave immediately." Henry thanked the woman for her help and left the house through the back door.

He prayed Migizi was ready to go because they were already several hours behind.

More importantly, he prayed that Robert hadn't stopped somewhere to marry Abi before they left Montreal.

Abi stood over the campfire and stirred the bubbling robbiboo, adding a few root vegetables the cook had given her before they left Uncle Gregor's house that morning. They had traveled a long way that day, farther than they ever had on the trip to Montreal. It was now growing dark and Robert had not yet returned from hunting. Isobel had talked incessantly most of the day, her excitement about going home filling the small cariole they had shared. But now Isobel was silent as she stared into the flames, allowing Abi to make their evening meal.

"You've hardly spoken all day," Isobel finally said as she used a long stick to adjust the logs under their fire. "Are you not happy to return to Father?"

A wolf howled in the distance and Abi wrapped her arms around herself, thankful for the warm capote. "I'm happy to go home."

"Then what is it?" Isobel frowned, her beautiful brown eyes filled with concern.

Abi hadn't spoken a word about Henry to her sister. She was afraid if she did, Isobel might laugh or tell her how foolish she was to give her heart to a man she didn't deserve. No. It was better to keep her memories of Henry safely tucked away where no one could harm them.

"Is it Robert?" Isobel whispered. "Does he make you unhappy?"

Thoughts of marrying Robert, especially now, after she knew what love felt like, gave her a deep sense of melancholy. "I'd rather never marry than marry a man I do not love."

"But Father?" Isobel left the question hanging.

"Yes, Father desires a match."

"And you don't?"

Abi stirred the robbiboo again and shook her head. "No."

A smile toyed about Isobel's lips. "Perhaps Father would not care who Robert married, as long as he married one of us."

"Do you mean?" Abi gave her sister her full attention. "You?"

Isobel didn't meet Abi's eyes, but toyed with one of the strings hanging from her knit bonnet. "I could be persuaded. He is quite handsome and masculine."

Relief washed over Abi. If Isobel was agreeable to marrying Robert, then her father would be satisfied, and Abi would be free. . .but free to do what?

Thoughts of Henry filled her again and the sadness returned. Where was he now? Dining with Josephine at her fine table? Though Abi didn't care for her cousin, she thought Henry and Josephine made a handsome couple. He'd do well to marry Josephine and go to Scotland with her and Uncle Gregor.

Abi didn't doubt that Henry had feelings for her. She couldn't deny it after their dance last evening and the kiss that had almost been, yet what did it matter? There was no way forward for them.

But knowing he might have feelings for her only deepened her melancholy. If he was indifferent toward her, she might forget these past three weeks. It was the longing in his eyes that had been seared into her soul. She would not easily forget how her heart had responded to see it.

The dogs became restless, some standing to their feet, others lifting their noses in the air, pointing to the east. Was it Robert they were reacting to? He should have been back by now, though he'd gone toward the west and not the east.

"Who could it be?" Isobel stood, coming near the fire with Abi. "It sounds like another dogsled."

The darkness was almost complete now, but the glow of the fire extended to the outskirts of the camp, jumping and dancing against the tall evergreens encircling the space. A team of dogs appeared in the break between trees, pulling a familiar cariole behind them.

"It's Migizi." Abi didn't move as the sled came closer.

"Migizi?" Isobel asked.

"He's the guide that brought Henry—Mr. Kingsley—to Father's fur post." But why had he come? Unless. . ."Henry." Abi whispered his name with disbelief. He sat in the cariole, his head covered in the cap Father had given him, his gaze searching the clearing.

"Henry." Isobel repeated the name, understanding in her voice. "Is he the reason you've been so miserable today?"

Abi didn't have time to answer before the cariole came to a stop a few feet away from the campfire. The dogs stood still, panting from the strain of their long haul.

Migizi remained on the back of the sled while Henry unlaced the strings holding the cariole's opening together. He stood, his gaze not leaving Abi's face.

She shook her head, confusion tilting her brow. Why had he come?

When Henry stepped out of the sled, Migizi drove it away, to the opposite side of the clearing, beyond the reach of light.

Isobel silently stepped away from the fire and went to the stack of pine boughs they'd cut earlier. She began to clear the snow from where they would sleep, her back toward the fire, far enough away for Abi to speak to Henry privately.

He stood before her, watching her, waiting. . .but for what?

"Why have you come?" she whispered, barely able to form the words.

"To take you home, just as I promised."

She shook her head. "Didn't someone tell you?"

"Yes. They said you left with Robert." He took a step closer to her, his voice lowering. "But I didn't like the idea of Robert getting you all to himself, especially when you and I have so much to discuss."

"What do we have to discuss?" she asked quietly. "I thought we'd said all there was to say last night."

He took another step toward her, this time, standing right in front of her, as close as he'd been the night before when he'd almost kissed her. "Even if we live to be a hundred, I don't believe you and I will say everything there is to say to one another." He leaned forward until his forehead was pressed against hers, his warm breath tingling her cold nose and lips. "I love you, Abi McCrea." His voice was strong and passionate. "I want to spend the rest of my life with you by my side."

Delight and dismay warred within Abi's chest. "You can't love me. You must love someone like you—someone who could make you happy."

He tilted his head back and laughed, a sweet, joyful sound.

Abi frowned and crossed her arms.

"You make me happier than anyone I've ever known." He took one of his mittens off and placed his warm hand against her cheek. "And you're nothing like the people I know, which makes me love you all the more."

The touch of his hand broke down her defenses and she lowered her arms to her side. "What about your life in Montreal, or your opportunity to go to Scotland?"

"I have no desire to return to Europe and no wish to stay in Montreal."

"Where will you live then?"

He searched her face, his blue eyes full of love and hope. "Wherever you'd like."

"Here? In the wilderness?"

"If you'll have me."

"Have you?"

Henry put his free hand around her back, pulling her closer to him. "As your husband."

A smile tickled the edges of her lips. "Are you certain you'll be happy here?"

He leaned down and placed his lips against Abi's. The kiss was sweet and gentle, yet it set her heart to pounding in a way that made her feel as if she'd just completed a race. When he pulled away, it left her breathless and dizzy.

"I've never been more certain in my life." Longing returned to his eyes. "I love you, and I can't imagine going anywhere or doing anything without you."

Abi's heart felt as if it would burst. She couldn't hide her feelings any longer. "I love you too."

His eyes softened and he kissed her again. When he was done, he whispered, "Will you marry me?"

She wrapped her arms around Henry, drawing from his warmth, and smiled into the darkness beyond him. "I will."

He tightened his hold on her, and she suspected he wouldn't soon let go.

Love had undone her preconceived ideas about life and the world, and she couldn't be happier. She had followed her heart to Montreal, traveling hundreds of miles to get there, only to discover that she belonged right where she had started. She was going home, with the man she loved by her side, content to know that she had everything her heart truly desired.

Gabrielle Meyer lives in central Minnesota on the banks of the Mississippi River with her husband and four young children. As an employee of the Minnesota Historical Society, she fell in love with the rich history of her state and enjoys writing fictional stories inspired by real people and events. Gabrielle can be found at www.gabriellemeyer.com where she writes about her passion for history, Minnesota, and her faith.

If You Liked This Book, You'll Also Like...

A Bouquet of Brides Romance Collection

Flowers fade, but not these seven young women who were named for flora. Struggling to see her own value, each woman must face the reason God planted her where she is. Will the love of a good man help each woman blossom to her full potential?

Paperback / 978-1-68322-381-8 / $14.99

The Mail-Order Brides Collection

Advertisements for a bride lead nine couples into unique romances as women move west in search of new beginnings within mail-order marriages. Placing their dreams for the future in the hands of a stranger, will each bride be disappointed, or will some find true love?

Paperback / 978-1-68322-444-0 / $14.99